EMPIRE

OF THE

ANTS

BERNARD WERBER

TRANSLATED BY
MARGARET ROCQUES

BANTAM BOOKS

New York Toronto London Sydney Auckland

EMPIRE OF THE ANTS

A Bantam Book / published by arrangement with Bantam Press,
a division of Transworld Publishers Ltd.

PUBLISHING HISTORY

Originally published as *Les Fourmis* by Albin Michel in 1991
Bantam Press edition published 1996
Bantam Books hardcover edition / February 1998
Bantam Books paperback edition / February 1999

BOOK DESIGN BY JAMES SINCLAIR.

Library of Congress Catalog Card Number: 96-76501

ISBN 978-0-553-57352-7

Published simultaneously in the United States and Canada

Bantam Books are published by Bantam Books, a division of
Random House, Inc. Its trademark, consisting of the words
"Bantam Books" and the portrayal of a rooster, is Registered in U.S.
Patent and Trademark Office and in other countries. Marca
Registrada. Bantam Books, 1540 Broadway, New York, New York
10036.

PRINTED IN THE UNITED STATES OF AMERICA

TO MY PARENTS

AND TO ALL MY FRIENDS AND FELLOW
RESEARCHERS WHO HAVE HELPED BUILD
THIS EDIFICE

In the few seconds it will take you to read these four
lines:
    —40 human beings and 700 million ants will have
    been born on Earth.
    —30 human beings and 500 million ants will have
    died on Earth.

HUMAN BEING: A mammal between 1 and 2 meters in
    height, weighing between 30 and 100 kilos.
    Gestation period: 9 months. Mode of nutrition:
    omnivore. Estimated population: over 5 billion
    individuals.
ANT: An insect between 0.01 and 3 centimeters in
    length, weighing between 1 and 150 milligrams. Egg-
    laying capacity limited only by sperm stock. Mode
    of nutrition: omnivore. Likely population: over a
    million trillion individuals.

EDMOND WELLS,
ENCYCLOPEDIA OF RELATIVE AND ABSOLUTE KNOWLEDGE

CONTENTS

THE AWAKENING

"I'm afraid it isn't at all what you expected."

The lawyer explained that the building was listed and that some old Renaissance scholars had lived there, though he couldn't remember who.

They went downstairs and emerged into a dark corridor. The lawyer groped about for a switch, then tried to turn on the light. "Damn, it isn't working."

They plunged into the shadows, feeling their way noisily along the walls. By the time the lawyer had found the door, opened it and turned on the light, he could see that his client was upset.

"Are you all right, Mr. Wells?"

"I've got a thing about the dark. It's nothing, really."

"You mean a phobia?"

"I'm afraid so. I feel better already, though."

They looked the place over. It was a large basement apartment. Jonathan liked it even though the only openings to the outside were a few small windows at ceiling level. The walls were all papered a uniform gray and there was dust everywhere. But he could not afford to be fussy.

His present apartment was about a fifth of the size of this one. Besides, he could no longer afford the rent. The locksmith he worked for had recently seen fit to dispense with his services.

It meant Uncle Edmond's inheritance was a real godsend.

Two days later, he moved into number three, rue des Sybarites, with his wife, Lucie, their son, Nicolas, and their dog, Ouarzazate, a clipped toy poodle.

"I don't mind all these gray walls," announced Lucie, pushing back her thick red hair. "We'll be able to decorate it any way we like. Everything needs doing. It'll be like turning a prison into a hotel."

"Where's my room?" asked Nicolas.

"At the far end on the right."

The dog barked a couple of times and started worrying Lucie's calves, totally disregarding the fact that she was carrying a dinner service that had been a wedding present.

He was promptly shut in the bathroom and the door locked to stop him from opening it by jumping up to the handle.

"Did you know your prodigal uncle well?" went on Lucie.

"Uncle Edmond? The only thing I can really remember about him is that he played airplanes with me when I was very small. I was so frightened once I wet all over him."

They laughed.

"Bit of a hero already, were you?" teased Lucie. Jonathan pretended not to have heard.

"He didn't mind. He just remarked to my mother: 'Well, now we know we'll never make a pilot of him.' Later on, my mother told me he kept track of me but I never saw him again."

"What did he do for a living?"

"He was a scientist. A biologist, I think." Jonathan looked thoughtful. In point of fact, he didn't even know his benefactor.

6 kilometers away:
BEL-O-KAN,

1 meter high.
50 floors below the ground.
50 floors above the ground.
The biggest city in the region.
Estimated population: 18 million inhabitants.

Annual production:
—50 liters of greenfly honeydew.
—10 liters of ladybird honeydew.
—4 kilos of agaric mushrooms.
—Gravel expelled: 1 ton.
Kilometers of practicable corridors: 120.
Surface area at ground level: 2 square meters.

A ray of sunlight passed over. A leg stirred, the first thing to move since the start of hibernation three months earlier. Another leg moved slowly forward, the two claws in which it ended gradually opening. A third leg stretched. Then a thorax. Then a whole individual. Then twelve individuals. They trembled to help their transparent blood circulate through the networks of arteries, thinning as it went from paste to liquor to liquid. Little by little, their hearts started to beat again, pumping the life-giving fluid to their extremities. Their biomechanisms warmed up. The hypercomplex joints pivoted. All around, the ball and socket joints, covered in protective plates, twisted and turned to their full extent.

They stood up. Their bodies started to breathe again, moving in an uncoordinated slow-motion dance. They shook themselves slightly. Their forelegs met in front of their mouths as if in prayer but they were only wetting their claws to polish their antennae.

The twelve who were awake massaged one another, then tried to wake their neighbors. But they scarcely had the strength to move their own bodies and had no energy to offer. They gave up.

Then they moved with difficulty between the statue-like bodies of their sisters, making their way toward the Great Outside. Their cold-blooded organisms needed to absorb calories from the sun.

They went on, harassed, every step painful. They longed to lie down again and rest in peace like all the millions of others. But it was impossible. They were the first to wake. Now they must bring the whole city to life again.

They crossed the fabric of the city. The sunlight blinded them but the touch of pure energy was so comforting.

> Enter our empty bodies, sun,
> Move our aching muscles
> And assemble our divided thoughts.

This old dawn chorus had been sung by the russet ants ever since the hundredth millennium. Even then, there had been a singing in their brains when they first felt the warmth of the sun.

Once outside, they started to wash methodically. They secreted white saliva and smeared it over their jaws and legs.

Their wash and brush-up followed an unchanging ritual. First, the eyes. The one thousand, three hundred little portholes that made up each spherical eye were dusted, moistened and dried. Then the antennae, lower limbs, mid-limbs and upper limbs received the same treatment. Finally, they polished their beautiful russet shells until they sparkled like drops of fire.

. . .

Among the twelve ants who were awake was a reproductive male. He was a little smaller than average for the Belokanian population. He had narrow mandibles and was programmed to live no more than a few months, but he had advantages unshared by others of his kind.

The first privilege of his royal caste was to possess five eyes, two big globular eyes that gave him a 180° field of vision plus three small simple eyes set in a triangle on his forehead. These additional eyes were actually infrared receivers that allowed him to detect any source of heat from a distance, even in pitch darkness.

This was a particularly valuable characteristic since most of the inhabitants of the big cities of the hundred thousandth millennium were completely blind, having spent their whole lives underground.

But this was not the only thing that was different about him. Like the females, he also had wings, which would one day allow him to make love in flight.

His thorax was protected by a special shield plate, the mesonotum.

His antennae were longer and more sensitive than those of the other inhabitants.

This young reproductive male remained on the dome for a long time, gorging himself on the sun. Then, when he was nice and warm again, he went back into the city. He temporarily belonged to the "thermal messenger" caste of ants.

He moved along the corridors of the lower third floor. Everyone there was still sound asleep, their frozen bodies transfixed, their antennae abandoned.

The ants were still dreaming.

The young male stretched out his leg toward a young worker he wanted to wake with his body heat. His warm touch gave her a pleasant electric shock.

. . . .

The patter of feet could be heard after he had rung the doorbell twice. The door opened, with a pause while Grandmother Augusta removed the safety chain.

Since the death of her two children, she had lived alone in the two-room apartment, going over old memories. It could not have been good for her but had in no way diminished her kindness.

"Mind you don't slip now. I've just polished the floor."

Jonathan promised to be careful. She trotted ahead of him and showed him into a living room full of furniture shrouded in dust sheets. Jonathan perched on the edge of the big sofa but it creaked anyway when he sat down.

"I'm so glad you've come. You may not believe it but I've been meaning to call you for the last few days."

"Really?"

"Believe it or not, Edmond gave me something for you. A letter. He said: 'If I die, it's vital you give Jonathan this letter.' "

"A letter?"

"Yes, a letter. Now, where did I put it? Let me see. He gave me the letter, I told him I'd put it away and I put it in a box. It must have been one of the tin boxes in the big cupboard."

She started to go over to the cupboard but stopped after a few steps.

"Really, how silly of me! What a way to welcome you! How would you like a nice cup of herb tea?"

"That'd be lovely."

She disappeared into the kitchen and put the kettle on.

"How're things with you, Jonathan?" she called.

"Not that fantastic. I've lost my job."

Grandmother poked her little white head around the door for a second, then reappeared fully, wrapped in a long blue apron and looking serious.

"Did they fire you?"

"Yes. It's a funny sort of a job, being a locksmith. Our company, SOS Locks, operates twenty-four hours a day all over Paris. Well, ever since one of my colleagues got mugged, I've refused to go into the rough districts, so they sacked me."

"You did the right thing. It's better to be out of work and in one piece than the other way 'round."

"I didn't get along very well with my boss, either."

"How did you get on in those communes of yours? In my day, we called them New Age communes." She turned her head away to hide a smile.

"I gave all that up when the farm in the Pyrenees folded. Lucie had had enough of cooking and washing up for everyone. Some people were only out for a free ride. We fell out. It's just Lucie, Nicolas and me, now. How about you, Gran, how are you?"

"Me? I'm alive. It's a full-time occupation at my age."

"I envy you. You were around for the millennium."

"Oh, that. What's really surprising is that nothing has changed. When I was a girl, we thought something wonderful would happen but nothing's really changed, you know. Old people still live alone, plenty of people are still out of work and cars still give off toxic fumes. We even have the same old ideas. Last year, for example, surrealism was rediscovered, the year before it was rock 'n' roll, and the newspapers have already announced that miniskirts will be in again this summer. If we carry on like this, the old ideas from early last century will be coming back: communism, psychoanalysis and relativity."

Jonathan smiled.

"There has been some progress, though. The average life expectancy has gone up, as well as the number of divorces, the level of air pollution and the length of lines in the subway."

"So what? I thought we'd all have private planes and take off from our own balconies by now. You know, when I was young, people were afraid of atomic war. Terribly afraid. I thought I'd go up in a nuclear holocaust and die with the planet when I was a hundred. That would have been quite something. Instead of which, I'm going to die like a rotten old potato. And no one will care."

"Of course they'll care, Gran."

She wiped her forehead.

"It's getting hotter and hotter, too. In my day, it wasn't this hot. There were real winters and real summers. Now the heat wave starts in March."

She went back into the kitchen and nimbly organized everything she needed to make a nice pot of herb tea. After she had struck a match and the sound of the gas blowing through the ancient pipes of her stove could be heard, she came back looking much more relaxed.

"You must have had a special reason for coming, though. You young people don't visit us oldies without a particular reason these days."

"Don't be so cynical, Gran."

"I'm not being cynical, I'm just being realistic. Now, stop prevaricating and tell me what brings you here."

"I'd like you to tell me about 'him.' He left me his apartment and I didn't even know him."

"Edmond? You mean you don't remember Edmond? He used to like playing airplanes with you when you were little. I remember one time . . ."

"Yes, I remember, too, but apart from that one story, I can't remember anything else."

She settled herself in a big armchair, taking care not to crease the dust cover too badly.

"Edmond is—well, was—quite a character. Even when he was very small, he used to give me plenty to worry about. It wasn't easy being his mother. He used to break all his toys systematically, you know. He liked to take them apart but didn't often put them back together again. And it wasn't just his toys. He used to take everything apart: the clock, the stereo, the electric toothbrush. Once he even took the refrigerator apart."

As if to confirm what she was saying, the old clock in the living room started to chime lugubriously. It had been through the mill with little Edmond, too.

"His other craze was building dens. He used to turn

the house upside down to make hidey-holes. He built one out of blankets and umbrellas in the attic and another out of chairs and fur coats in his bedroom. He just liked to burrow inside them with all his treasures. Once when I looked in one, it was full of cushions and bits and pieces of machinery. It actually looked quite cozy."

"All children do that."

"Maybe, but it got really out of hand with him. He wouldn't sleep in his own bed anymore, only in one of his little nests. He sometimes stayed in them for days at a time without moving. As if he were hibernating. Your mother said he must have been a squirrel in a previous life."

Jonathan smiled to encourage her to go on.

"One day, he wanted to build a hut under the living room table. That was the last straw as far as your grandfather was concerned. He was absolutely livid. He gave him a good hiding, got rid of all his nests and made him sleep in his bed."

She gave a sigh.

"From that day on, we lost him. It was as if we'd cut his umbilical cord. We were no longer part of his world. I think it had to be done, though. He had to find out he couldn't get his own way all the time. It caused problems later on when he was growing up. He couldn't stand school. I know you're going to say 'Like all children' again, but it went much deeper than that with him. Do you know many children who hang themselves with their belts in the bathroom because their teacher has told them off? He hanged himself when he was seven. It was the janitor who took him down."

"Maybe he was too sensitive."

"Sensitive? You must be joking. A year later, he tried to stab one of his teachers with a pair of scissors. He was aiming for the heart. It was lucky he only damaged his wallet."

She raised her eyes to heaven. Scattered memories were falling on her thoughts like snowflakes.

"Things got a bit better later because some of the

teachers managed to capture his interest. He got A's in the subjects he liked and E's in all the others. It was always either A or E."

"Mum said he was a genius."

"Your mother was fascinated by him because he'd told her he was trying to attain 'absolute knowledge.' Your mother had believed in reincarnation since the age of ten and thought he must have been Einstein or Leonardo da Vinci in a previous life."

"As well as a squirrel?"

"Why not? According to Buddha, it takes many lives to make a soul."

"Did he take any IQ tests?"

"Yes. He did very badly in them. He scored eighty-five, which meant he was slightly retarded. The educational psychologist thought he was disturbed and should be sent to a special school. I knew he wasn't, though. He was just 'elsewhere.' I remember once—he couldn't have been more than eleven—he challenged me to try to make four equilateral triangles using only six matches. It isn't easy. Here, have a go and you'll see."

She went into the kitchen, took a quick look at the kettle and came back with six matches. Jonathan hesitated for a moment. It seemed feasible. He tried arranging the six little sticks in various ways but was forced to give up after a few minutes.

"How do you do it?"

Grandmother Augusta concentrated.

"Well, I don't think he ever told me, actually. All I can remember is the clue he gave me: "You have to think about it differently. If you think about it in the usual way, you don't get anywhere." Can you imagine, a kid of eleven coming out with things like that? Ah, I think I can hear the kettle whistling."

She came back carrying two steaming cups of herb tea.

"You know, I'm really pleased to see you taking an interest in your uncle. Nowadays, when someone dies, people forget they ever existed."

Jonathan put the matches aside and took a few sips of herb tea.

"What happened after that?"

"I can't remember. Once he started studying science at the university we didn't hear from him anymore. I heard vaguely from your mother that he got a brilliant doctorate, worked for a food manufacturer, left to go to Africa, then came back and lived in the rue des Sybarites, where nothing more was heard of him until the day he died."

"How did he die?"

"Oh, don't you know? It's quite incredible. It was in all the papers. He was killed by wasps, would you believe it!"

"Wasps? How did it happen?"

"He was walking by himself in the forest. He must have accidentally disturbed a nest. They all rushed to attack him. The pathologist claimed he'd never seen so many stings on one person. He had over 0.3 grams of poison per liter of blood when he died. It was unheard of."

"Where's he buried?"

"He hasn't got a proper grave. He'd asked to be buried under a pine tree in the forest."

"Have you got a photograph of him?"

"Yes, look, over there on the wall above the chest. Your mother, Suzy, is on the right. Have you ever seen such a young-looking picture of her before? And Edmond's on the left."

He had a receding hairline, a small pointed mustache and lobeless ears that extended above his eyebrows. He was smiling mischievously and looked quite a devil.

Beside him, Suzy was resplendent in a white dress. She had married a few years later but had insisted on keeping her maiden name, Wells. As if she wanted her husband to leave no trace of his name on her offspring.

Moving closer, Jonathan saw that Edmond was holding two fingers up above his sister's head.

"He was always playing jokes on people, wasn't he?"

Augusta did not answer. Her eyes had misted over

with sorrow as she looked at her daughter's radiant face. Suzy had died six years earlier. A fifteen-ton truck in the hands of a drunken driver had pushed her car into a ravine. She had taken two days to die. She had asked for Edmond but Edmond had not come. Yet again, he had been elsewhere.

"Do you know anyone else who could tell me about Edmond?"

"Mmm. He used to see a lot of one of his childhood friends. They went to college together. He was called Jason Bragel. I must still have his number."

Augusta quickly consulted her computer and gave Jonathan his address. She looked at her grandson affectionately. He was the last survivor of the Wells family. A good boy.

"Drink up now or your tea'll get cold. I've got some little sponge cakes as well, if you like. I make them myself with quails' eggs."

"No, thank you, I'll have to be going. Come and see us in our new apartment one day. We've finished moving in."

"All right. Wait a minute, though. Don't go without the letter."

She delved frantically among tin boxes in the big cupboard and at last came up with a white envelope bearing the words "For Jonathan Wells" written in a feverish hand. The flap of the envelope had been stuck down with several layers of sticky tape so that it could not be opened by mistake. He tore it open carefully. A crumpled page from an exercise book fell out. He read the only sentence written on it:

ABOVE ALL, NEVER GO DOWN INTO
THE CELLAR!

The ant's antennae were trembling. She was like a car that had been left out in the snow too long and would not start. The male made several tries. He rubbed her and bathed her in warm saliva.

Life flowed back. At last the motor started again. A season had gone by. Everything was beginning anew as if it had never slept the deathlike sleep.

He rubbed her again to generate some calories. She was all right now. He carried on with his efforts, and the blind worker pointed her antennae in his direction. She wanted to know who he was.

She touched the first segment of his head and read his age: a hundred and seventy-three days. On the second, she discovered his caste: reproductive male. On the third, his species and city: a russet ant from the mother city of Bel-o-kan. On the fourth, she discovered the clutch number by which he was known: the 327th male laid since the start of autumn.

She ceased her olfactory decoding at this point. The other segments were not emitters. The fifth acted as a receiver for trail molecules. The sixth was used for simple dialogues. The seventh made more complex sexual dialogues possible. The eighth was intended for dialogues with Mother. The last three, finally, could be used as small clubs.

There, she had examined the eleven segments of the second half of the antenna but it had nothing to tell her. She moved off and went in turn to warm herself on the roof of the city.

He did likewise. He had finished his task as thermal messenger and it was time to get down to repairs.

When he reached the top, the 327th male assessed the damage. The city had been built in the shape of a cone to offer less resistance to the elements, but the winter had been destructive. The wind, snow and hail had torn away the first layer of twigs. Some of the entrances were blocked with bird droppings. He must start work at once. He bore down on a big yellow stain and attacked the hard, foul matter with his mandibles. Through it he could see the outline of an insect digging toward him from the inside.

• • •

The spyhole had gotten darker. Someone was looking at him through the door.

"Who's there?"

"Mr. Gougne. I've come about the binding."

The door opened a crack and Gougne looked down on a fair-haired ten-year-old boy, then noticed even farther down a tiny dog that poked its nose between the boy's legs and started to growl.

"Dad's out."

"Are you sure? Professor Wells was supposed to come and see me and . . ."

"Professor Wells is my great-uncle. He's dead, though."

Nicolas tried to shut the door, but the man stuck his foot inside the door frame and insisted.

"I'm very sorry to hear about the professor's death, but are you sure he didn't leave a big file full of papers? I'm a bookbinder. He paid me in advance to bind his working notes in a leather cover. I think he was hoping to make them into an encyclopedia. He was supposed to call me but I haven't heard from him for a long time."

"He's dead, I tell you."

The man stuck his foot farther into the apartment, pressing his knee against the door as if he were going to push the little boy out of the way. The tiny dog started to yap furiously. He stood still.

"You must understand I'd be very unhappy not to stick to the deal, even posthumously. Please check. There really has to be a big red file somewhere."

"Did you say it was an encyclopedia?"

"Yes, he used to call it the *Encyclopedia of Relative and Absolute Knowledge* when he was talking about it, but I'd be surprised if that's written on the cover."

"We'd already have found it if he'd left it at our house."

"I'm sorry to insist, but—"

The toy poodle began to bark again. The man started back just enough for the boy to slam the door in his face.

• • •

The whole city was awake now. The corridors were full of thermal messenger ants hurrying to warm up the Tribe, but motionless citizens were still to be found at some crossroads. They failed to move even when the messengers shook and pummelled them.

They would never move again. They were dead. Hibernation had proved fatal for them. Having a practically nonexistent heartbeat for three months is a risky business. They had not suffered. They had passed from sleep to death when a sudden draft enveloped the city. Their bodies were taken out and thrown on the rubbish heap. That was how the city disposed of its dead cells each morning, along with any other rubbish.

Once the arteries had been cleansed of their impurities, the insect city started to hum. All around, legs scurried and jaws dug. Everything began again as before, before the anesthetizing winter.

As the 327th male was dragging along a twig a good sixty times his own weight, he was approached by a warrior over five hundred days old. She tapped on his head with her club segments to attract his attention. He raised his head and she put her antennae close to his.

She wanted him to stop repairing the roof and go on a hunting expedition with a group of ants.

He touched her mouth and eyes.

What hunting expedition?

The other ant let him sniff a scrap of dried meat she was hiding in a fold of her thorax joint.

Apparently, someone found it just before the winter in the western region at an angle of 23° to the midday sun.

He tasted it. It was obviously a beetle. A chrysomelid beetle, to be precise. How odd. Beetles were normally still hibernating. As everyone knew, russet ants woke up when the air temperature was 12°C, termites when it was 13°C, flies when it was 14°C and beetles when it was 15°C.

The old warrior was not put out by this argument. She explained that this piece of meat had come from an extraordinary region artificially heated by an underground spring. There was no winter there. It was a microclimate that had developed its own fauna and flora.

The Tribe's city was always very hungry when it woke up. It needed protein quickly to start working again. Heat alone was not enough.

He agreed.

The expedition consisted of twenty-eight ants of the warrior caste. Most were sexless old ladies, like the one who had solicited his help. The 327th male was the only member of the sexual caste. He scrutinized his companions from a distance through the grid of his eyes.

With their many-faceted eyes, ants do not see the same image repeated thousands of times but a single latticed image. They find it hard to make out detail but can perceive the slightest movement.

The explorers of this expedition all seemed accustomed to long journeys. Their heavy bellies were gorged with acid. Their heads were bristling with the most powerful weapons. Their cuirasses bore the scars of mandible bites received in combat.

They had been walking in a straight line for several hours and had passed several Federation cities standing high against the sky or under trees. These were daughter cities of the Ni dynasty: Yodu-lou-baikan (the biggest cereal producer), Giou-li-aikan (the killer legions of which had defeated a coalition of the termite hills of the south two years previously), Zedi-bei-nakan (famous for its chemical laboratories, which produced hyperconcentrated combat acids) and Li-viu-kan (the ladybird alcohol of which had a much-sought-after taste of resin).

For russet ants do not only organize themselves into cities but also into coalitions of cities. There is strength in union. In the Jura, there have been federations of russet ants comprising fifteen thousand anthills, covering an area of eighty hectares and with a total population of over two hundred million individuals.

As yet, Bel-o-kan was nowhere near so large. It was a young federation, the original dynasty of which had been founded five thousand years previously. Local legend had it that a young queen blown astray by a terrible storm had ended up there long ago. Failing to reach her own federation again, she had created Bel-o-kan, and from Bel-o-kan was born the Federation and the hundreds of generations of Ni queens who formed it.

Belo-kiu-kiuni, meaning "lost ant," was the name of that first queen—but also the name taken by all the queens who occupied the central nest.

For the time being, Bel-o-kan consisted only of a large central city and sixty-four federated daughter cities scattered in the neighboring vicinity. But it was already making itself felt as the foremost political force in that part of the Forest of Fontainebleau.

Once they had gone beyond the allied cities, and in particular La-chola-kan, the most easterly Belokanian city, the explorers arrived at some small mounds, the summer nests or "advance posts." They were still empty, but 327th knew that hunting and wars would soon fill them with soldiers.

They carried on in a straight line. The troop made its way through a vast turquoise meadow and down a hill edged with thistles. They left the hunting territories behind. Far away to the north, they could already make out Shi-gae-pou, the city of their enemies. But its occupants would still be asleep at that hour.

They pressed on. Most of the animals around them were still in the grip of their winter sleep. Here and there, a few early risers poked their heads out of their burrows. As soon as they saw the russet armor, they took fright and hid. Ants are not especially well-known for their conviviality, especially when advancing in formation, armed to the antennae.

The explorers had now reached unknown territory. There was no longer a single daughter city or advance post on the horizon or even a path dug by pointed feet, just a trace of an old scent trail to show that Belokanians had passed that way before.

They hesitated. The tall foliage ahead did not appear on any olfactory map. It formed a dark roof no light could penetrate. The plant mass strewn with animal presences seemed to be lying in wait for them.

How could he warn them not to go down into the cellar?

He put down his jacket and kissed his family.

"Have you finished unpacking everything?"

"Yes, Dad."

"Good. By the way, have you noticed that door at the far end of the kitchen?"

"That's just what I wanted to talk to you about," said Lucie. "It must be a cellar. I've tried to open it but it's locked. There's a big crack in it. You can't see much, but it looks as if it goes down a long way. You'll have to break the lock. There must be some point in having a locksmith for a husband."

She smiled and snuggled in his arms. Lucie and Jonathan had been living together for the past thirteen years. They had met in the subway. A hooligan had let off some tear gas in the train one day just for fun. All the passengers had immediately found themselves lying on the ground, crying and coughing their lungs out. Lucie and Jonathan had fallen on top of each other. When they had recovered, Jonathan had offered to see her home. Then he had invited her to join one of his first communes, a squat near the Gare du Nord in Paris. Three months later, they had decided to get married.

"No."

"What do you mean, no?"

"No, we're not going to break the lock and we're not going to use the cellar. We mustn't talk about it anymore or go near it. Most of all, we mustn't open it."

"Are you kidding? What do you mean?"

Jonathan had not had the presence of mind to invent a logical reason for prohibiting access to the cellar and had unwittingly caused the opposite of what he wanted. His wife and son were now intrigued. What could he do? Explain to them that there was a mystery surrounding his benefactor uncle and that he had wanted to warn them that it was dangerous to go down into the cellar?

That was not an explanation. It was at best superstition. Human beings like things to be logical, and there was no way Lucie and Nicolas would ever fall for it.

He mumbled: "The lawyer warned me about it."

"Warned you about what?"

"About the cellar being infested with rats."

"Ugh! Rats? But they're sure to get through the crack," protested the boy.

"Don't worry, we'll seal it off completely."

Jonathan was pleased with the effect this produced. It was lucky he had thought of the rats.

"All right, then. No one will go near the cellar. Okay?"

He made for the bathroom. Lucie immediately joined him there.

"Have you been to see your grandmother?"

"That's right."

"Did it take you all morning?"

"Right again."

"You shouldn't be wasting your time like that. Remember what you told the others on the farm in the Pyrenees: 'Idleness is the root of all evil.' You've got to get another job. Our savings are running out."

"We've just inherited a big apartment in a nice district on the edge of the forest and all you can do is talk about work. Why can't you take it easy?"

He tried to take her in his arms but she took a step backward.

"Yes, I know, but I also know I need to think about the future. I haven't got a job and you're out of work. What'll we live on in a year's time?"

"We've still got some savings left."

"Don't be stupid. We've got enough to get through the next few months, but after that . . ."

She put her hands on her hips and stuck out her chin.

"Listen, Jonathan, you lost your job because you didn't want to go into dangerous districts in the dark. I can understand that, but you must be able to get another one somewhere."

"Of course I'm going to look for a job. Just let me have a break. I promise you after that, in about a month's time, I'll have a look at the ads."

A fair head appeared, quickly followed by a ball of fur. It was Nicolas and Ouarzazate.

"Dad, a man came while you were out. It was something about binding a book."

"A book? What book?"

"I don't know. He said something about a big encyclopedia written by Uncle Edmond."

"Did he, now? Did he come in? Did you find it?"

"No, he didn't seem very nice, and as there isn't a book anyway . . ."

"Good for you, son. You did the right thing."

Jonathan was both perplexed and intrigued by the news. He stood for some time in the kitchen inspecting the cellar door with its big lock and wide crack. What mystery lay behind it?

They had to enter the undergrowth.

One of the oldest explorers suggested they adopt the "big-headed serpent" formation as the best means of advancing in hostile territory. There was immediate consensus. They had all thought of it at the same time.

At the front, five scouts, arranged in an inverted triangle, acted as the troop's eyes. With small, measured steps, they checked the lie of the land, sniffed the air and inspected the moss. If all was well, they sent an olfactory message signifying "All clear ahead," then they moved to the rear of the procession to be replaced by "new" individuals. This system of rotation transformed the group into a sort of long animal whose "nose" always remained hypersensitive.

The "All clear ahead" rang out loud and clear twenty times. The twenty-first was interrupted by a sickening squawk. One of the scouts had just gone too near a carnivorous plant, a Venus's-flytrap. She had been attracted by its heady scent and her legs had got stuck in the glue.

From then on she was done for. Her contact with the plant's hairs had triggered the mechanism that activated the organic hinge. The two broad, jointed leaves closed inexorably, their long fringes acting like teeth. Once crossed, they became solid bars. When its victim had been completely flattened, the predatory plant secreted powerful enzymes capable of digesting even the toughest shells.

The ant was melting away, her whole body turning into effervescent sap. She let out a haze of distress.

But it was too late to help her. It was one of the imponderables common to all long-distance expeditions. It only remained for them to signal "Look out, danger," in the vicinity of the trap.

They put the incident out of their minds and set off again along the scented path with the trail pheromones pointing the way. Once they had crossed the thickets, they carried on westward, always at an angle of 23° to the sun's rays. They stopped to rest only when it got too cold or too hot. They had to act quickly if they were to avoid being caught up in a war on their return.

Explorers had returned to find their city surrounded by enemy troops before, and it was never easy to break through the blockade.

At last they came across the trail pheromone showing the entrance to the cave. Heat was rising from the ground. They plunged into the depths of the rocky earth.

The deeper they went, the more clearly they could discern the trickle of water. It came from a fuming hot-water spring, from which rose a strong smell of sulfur.

The ants quenched their thirst.

At one point, they came across a strange-looking animal: it looked like a ball on legs but was really a dung beetle pushing along a sphere of dung and sand with its eggs safe inside. Like Atlas in the legend, it was carrying its "world" on its back. When the ground sloped down, the ball rolled of its own accord and the beetle followed. When it sloped up, the beetle wore itself out pushing and sliding and often had to go back down to the bottom to retrieve the ball.

The Belokanians let it pass. It did not have a very nice taste and its shell made it too heavy to transport anyway.

To their left, a dark silhouette scurried off to hide in a crevice in the rock. This time, it was something really tasty, an earwig. The oldest explorer was first off the mark. She tipped her abdomen over her head, took up the firing position, balancing on her hind legs, aimed instinctively and fired a drop of 40 percent formic acid from a distance. The corrosive liquid sliced through the air.

A hit!

The earwig was struck down in its tracks. The formic acid was strong stuff! It stings at forty parts per thousand, so at forty per hundred, it really shifts things! The insect collapsed and they all rushed to devour its burned flesh. The past autumn's explorers had left behind good pheromones. There seemed to be plenty of game in the region. It would be a good hunt.

They went down into an artesian well and terrorized all sorts of underground species they had never come across before. A bat tried to cut short their visit but it took flight when they enveloped it in a cloud of formic acid.

As the days went by, they continued to comb the hot cave, piling up the bodies of small white animals and pieces of pale-green fungus. They laid down new trail pheromones with their anal glands so that their sisters would be able to hunt there without mishap.

The mission had been a success. As the hunters were

about to set off on their return journey, heavily laden with food, they planted the chemical flag of the Federation. Its scent flapped in the air: "BEL-O-KAN."

"Sorry, I didn't quite catch that."

"Wells. I'm Edmond Wells's nephew."

The door opened on a man over six feet tall.

"Mr. Bragel? Forgive me for disturbing you but I'd like to have a word with you about my uncle. I never knew him and my grandmother told me you were his best friend."

"Please come in. What do you want to know about Edmond?"

"Everything. I never knew him and wish I had."

"Oh, I see. Edmond was always a bit of a mystery, anyway. He was that kind of man."

"Did you know him well?"

"Can we ever really know anyone well? Let's just say we often found ourselves in each other's company and neither of us minded."

"How did you meet?"

"At college, in the biology department. I was working on plants and he was working on bacteria."

"Two parallel worlds."

"Yes, except that mine's far more savage." To underline his point, Jason Bragel indicated the mass of green plants filling the dining room. "Look at them. They're all in competition with one another, ready to kill for a ray of light or a drop of water. As soon as one of its leaves is in the shade, a plant abandons it and the neighboring leaves develop more. The plant kingdom is really merciless."

"What about Edmond's bacteria?"

"He said himself that he was only studying his ancestors. You could say he was just tracing his family tree a little further back than most."

"But why bacteria? Why not monkeys or fish?"

"He wanted to understand the cell in its most primitive form. For him, man is a mere conglomerate of cells and only a thorough understanding of the 'psychology' of a single cell will allow us to understand the workings of the whole. He took literally the saying, 'A big complex problem is really only a combination of small simple problems.' "

"Did he work only on bacteria?"

"No, no. He was a kind of mystic, a real generalist. He would have liked to know everything. He got ideas into his head . . . like the time he tried to control his own heartbeat."

"But that's impossible."

"Apparently some Indian and Tibetan yogis can do it."

"What's the point?"

"I really couldn't say. He wanted to be able to do it so that he could commit suicide whenever he liked simply by stopping his heartbeat. He thought it would allow him to opt out whenever he chose."

"Why would he have wanted to do that?"

"Perhaps he was afraid of growing old."

"Perhaps. What did he do once he'd finished his doctorate?"

"He went to work for a private company, Sweetmilk Corporation, which produced live bacteria for yogurt. He did well there. He discovered a bacterium which developed aroma as well as taste. He was awarded the prize for the best invention of 1963 for it."

"And after that?"

"After that, he married a Chinese girl, Ling Mi. She was sweet-natured and cheerful. He'd always been grouchy but he changed overnight. He was very much in love with her. I saw less of him after that. It's often the case."

"I heard he went to Africa."

"Yes, but that was after."

"After what?"

"After Ling Mi's fatal illness. It was a tragedy. She developed leukemia and was dead within three months. Poor Edmond. He'd always been so convinced cells were everything and human beings nothing, it was a cruel lesson for him. And he'd been powerless to help her. While this disaster was taking place, he also fell out with his colleagues at Sweetmilk. He left his job and shut himself in his apartment, a shattered man. Ling Mi had restored his faith in humanity and when he lost her, he became even more unsociable."

"Did he go to Africa to forget Ling Mi?"

"Possibly. He wanted to heal the wound by throwing himself heart and soul into his work as a biologist. He must have found a fascinating topic to study. I don't know what it was exactly, but I know it wasn't bacteria. He probably moved to Africa because it was easier to work on it there. He sent me a postcard simply explaining that he was with a team from the National Center for Scientific Research and was working with a Professor Rosenfeld. I don't know him."

"Did you see Edmond again after that?"

"Yes. I met him once by chance in the Champs-Elysées. We had a chat. He'd obviously recovered his zest for living but he was very evasive. He didn't answer when I asked him about his work."

"Apparently he was writing an encyclopedia as well."

"He was doing that before. It was his big idea. He wanted to put everything he knew into one book."

"Have you seen it?"

"No. I don't think he ever showed it to anyone. If I know Edmond, he will have hidden it in the depths of Alaska with a fire-breathing dragon to guard it. He liked to be mysterious."

Jonathan was preparing to leave.

"Oh! One more question. Do you know how to make four equilateral triangles with six matches?"

"Of course I do. That was his favorite intelligence test."

"How do you do it, then?"

Jason burst out laughing.

"I'm not telling you. As Edmond used to say, "Everyone has to find out for himself." You'll see, you'll get far more satisfaction out of it that way."

With all that meat on their backs, the way home seemed longer than the way out. The troop kept up a good pace in order not to be overtaken by the rigors of night.

Ants are capable of working twenty-four hours a day from March to November without rest, but a drop in temperature sends them to sleep. That is why expeditions rarely stay away for more than a day.

The russet ant city had discussed the problem at length. It knew that it was important to extend the hunting territories and find out about distant countries, where there were different plants and animals with different customs.

In the eight hundred and fiftieth millennium, Bi-stinga, a russet ant queen of the Ga dynasty (an eastern dynasty that had vanished a hundred thousand years earlier), had had the mad ambition of discovering the "limits" of the world. She had sent hundreds of expeditions to all four points of the compass. None had ever returned.

The present queen, Belo-kiu-kiuni, was not so greedy. She was content to discover the little golden beetles that looked like precious gems (and were found in the deep south), or to observe the carnivorous plants that were sometimes brought back to her alive with their roots and that she hoped some day to tame.

Belo-kiu-kiuni knew that the best way to find out about new territories was to extend the Federation with more and more long-distance expeditions, more and more daughter cities, more and more advance posts, and death to anyone who tried to stop the advance.

Admittedly, it would take a long time to conquer the edge of the world, but this policy of small stubborn steps was in perfect harmony with the ants' general philosophy of "slowly but surely."

Today, the Federation of Bel-o-kan comprised sixty-four daughter cities; sixty-four cities that shared the same scent; sixty-four cities linked by a network of one hundred and twenty-five kilometers of hollowed-out trails and seven hundred and eighty kilometers of scent trails; sixty-four cities that stuck together in time of war and famine.

The concept of a federation of cities meant that some of them could specialize. Belo-kiu-kiuni even dreamed of the day when one of the cities would deal in cereals, another would supply meat and a third would concern itself only with war.

They still had a long way to go.

In any event, it was a concept that fitted in well with another principle of the ants' overall philosophy, "The future belongs to specialists."

The explorers were still a long way from the advance posts so they decided to increase their pace. When they passed near the carnivorous plant again, a warrior proposed that they dig it up by the roots and take it back to Belo-kiu-kiuni.

They conferred by putting their antennae together and sending and receiving minute volatile scent molecules called pheromones. These were actually hormones that escaped from the ants' bodies. Each molecule could be pictured as a fishbowl, with each fish a word.

By means of pheromones, the ants could express virtually any shade of meaning. If the agitation of their antennae was anything to go by, the debate was becoming heated.

It's too big to carry.

Mother isn't familiar with this kind of plant.

We may suffer losses and there won't be as many of us to carry the booty.

Once we've tamed carnivorous plants, they'll be weapons in their own right and we'll be able to hold a front simply by planting them in a row.

We're tired and it'll soon be dark.

They decided to abandon the idea, skirted the plant and continued on their way. As the group was drawing near a flowery thicket, the 327th male, who was bringing up the rear, spotted a red daisy. He had never seen one like it before and immediately made up his mind to have it.

We didn't get the Venus's-flytrap but we are taking this back.

He let the others get ahead a little and cut the flower off by the stem. *Snip!* Then, holding his discovery tightly, he ran to catch up with his colleagues.

Except that he no longer had any colleagues. The first expedition of the new year was there all right, but what a state it was in! The 327th male's legs began to tremble from shock and stress. All his companions lay dead on the ground.

What could possibly have happened? The attack must have been devastating. They had not even had time to take up combat formation and were all still in the "big-headed serpent" formation.

He inspected the bodies. Not a single jet of acid had been fired. The russet ants had not even had time to let out their alarm pheromones.

He decided to investigate.

He searched one of his sisters' antennae for scent, but no chemical image had been recorded. They had been walking along and then, suddenly, the record was cut off.

He had to find out what had happened. There must be an explanation. He began by cleaning his sensory apparatus. Using the two curved claws of his foreleg, he scraped his frontal scapes to remove the acid froth caused by stress. He folded them back to his mouth and licked them, then wiped them on the little brush spur handily situated above his third elbow.

Once his antennae were clean, he lowered them to eye level and beat them at a gentle three hundred vibrations a second. Nothing. He accelerated to five hundred, then one thousand, two thousand, five thousand, eight thousand vibrations a second, until he had reached two thirds of his maximum reception power.

He instantly picked up the slightest scents floating in

the breeze: vapors of dew, pollen and spores and a faint odor he had already smelled but could not readily identify.

He accelerated still more, reaching maximum power, twelve thousand vibrations a second. As they twirled, his antennae set up a slight draft that sucked all the dust toward him.

Now he could identify the faint scent. It was the smell of the culprits. Yes, it could only have been their pitiless northern neighbors, the dwarf ants of Shi-gae-pou, who had already caused them so much trouble the previous year.

So they, too, were already awake. They must have lain in ambush and used a devastating new weapon.

There was not a second to lose. He must alert the whole Federation.

"They were all killed by a high-powered laser beam, Chief."

"A laser beam?"

"Yes, a new weapon capable of melting our biggest ships from a distance. Chief . . ."

"Do you think it was . . ."

"Yes, Chief, only Venusians could have done such a thing. It's got their name written all over it."

"In that case, our revenge will be terrible. How many combat rockets do we have left in the Belt of Orion?"

"Four, Chief."

"That won't be enough. We'll have to get help from the—"

"Would you like some more soup?"

"No, thank you," said Nicolas, completely hypnotized by the images.

"Pay attention to what you're eating for a minute or I'll turn the television off."

"Oh no, Mom, please don't."

"Haven't you had enough of stories about little green

men and planets with names that sound like washing powder yet?" asked Jonathan.

"No, I think they're great. We're sure to meet extraterrestrials one day."

"We've been going on about them for long enough!"

"There's a probe on its way to the nearest star. It's called *Marco Polo*. We ought to know all about the people who live there soon."

"It'll draw a blank like all the other probes they've sent into space. They just end up polluting it. It's too far, I tell you."

"Maybe, but who's to say extraterrestrials won't come and see us instead? After all, there've been plenty of unexplained UFO sightings."

"I don't see what difference it'd make. We'd only end up fighting them. Don't you think Earthmen cause each other enough trouble as it is?"

"It'd be fantastic. There might be cool new places to go to on vacation."

"And exciting new things to worry about."

He ruffled Nicolas's hair.

"You'll see what I mean when you're bigger, Nick, and probably agree with me then. The only really fascinating animals, the only ones whose intelligence is really different from our own, are . . . women."

Lucie protested for form's sake. They both laughed. Nicolas scowled. It must be the grown-ups' idea of a joke. He felt around under the table for the dog's soothing fur.

There was nothing there.

"Where's Ouarzazate gone?"

He was not in the dining room.

"Ouarzi, Ouarzi."

Nicolas put his fingers in his mouth and whistled. It usually produced immediate results, a bark followed by the sound of paws. He whistled again but nothing happened. He looked in every room of the apartment. His parents joined him, but the dog was no longer there. The door was shut and locked, and he would not have been able to get out unaided.

They automatically made their way to the kitchen and, more precisely, to the cellar door. The crack had still not been sealed and was just wide enough to let an animal Ouarzazate's size through.

"He's in there. I'm sure he's in there," sobbed Nicolas. "We must go and get him."

As if in answer to this plea, they heard a fitful yapping coming from the cellar. It seemed to be a long way away.

They all moved nearer the forbidden door. Jonathan blocked their path.

"I've already told you you're not to go down into the cellar."

"But, darling," said Lucie, "we've got to go and get him. He might be attacked by rats. You said yourself there were rats down there."

His face froze.

"It's tough luck on the dog. We'll go and buy another one tomorrow."

The child was flabbergasted.

"But, Dad, I don't want another one. Ouarzazate's my friend. You can't just leave him to die."

"What's got into you?" added Lucie. "Let me go if you're afraid."

"Are you scared of going, Dad? Are you chicken?"

Jonathan could no longer contain himself. He muttered, "All right, I'll go and have a look," and went to get a torch. He shone it through the crack. It was pitch-dark on the other side.

He shivered, longing to run away, but his wife and son were pushing him toward the abyss. Sour thoughts filled his mind as his fear of the dark gained the upper hand.

Nicolas burst into tears.

"He's dead. I'm sure he's dead. It's all your fault."

"He may be injured," said Lucie soothingly. "We ought to go and see."

Jonathan thought back to Edmond's message. Its tone was imperative, but what could he do? One of them would inevitably crack in the end and have to have a look. He had to take the bull by the horns. It was now or never. He passed a hand over his damp forehead.

No, it wasn't going to be that way. At last he had a chance to brave his fears, take the plunge and face the danger. If the dark wanted to swallow him up, so much the better. He was ready to get to the bottom of things. In any case, he had nothing left to lose.

"I'm going in."

He went to get his tools and broke the lock.

"Whatever happens, don't move from here. Above all, don't try and come after me or call the police. Just wait for me."

"That's a funny way to talk. It's only a cellar, after all, a cellar like any other."

"I'm not so sure about that."

Lit on his way by the orange oval of the setting sun, the 327th male, last survivor of the first spring hunting expedition, ran on alone. Unbearably alone.

He had been splashing through puddles, mud and moldy leaves for some time. The wind had dried all his lips. His body was coated in amber dust. He could no longer feel his muscles. Several of his claws were broken.

But at the end of the olfactory trail along which he was hurtling, he soon made out his objective. Among the mounds forming the Belokanian cities, one shape loomed larger with every stride. The enormous pyramid of Bel-o-kan, the mother city, was like a scent lighthouse attracting him and drawing him in.

He at last reached the foot of the imposing anthill and raised his head. His city had grown even bigger. The construction of the dome's new protective layer had begun. The summit of the mountain of twigs almost reached the moon.

The young male searched around for a moment, found a ground-level entrance that was still open and dived in.

He was just in the nick of time. All the workers and

soldiers working outside had already returned. The guards were about to block up the exits to preserve the inner warmth. He had barely crossed the threshold when the masons set to and the hole closed behind him with a slam.

Nothing more could be seen of the cold, barbarous world outside. The 327th male was once more immersed in civilization and could merge with the soothing Tribe. He was no longer alone; he was manifold.

Sentries approached him. They had not recognized him under his film of dust. He quickly emitted his identification scents and the others recovered their serenity.

A worker noticed his scent of tiredness. She offered him trophallaxis, the ritual gift of her body.

Every ant had a kind of pocket in its abdomen, a second stomach that did not digest food but kept it fresh and intact indefinitely. Food could be stored and regurgitated at a later date and passed into its "normal" stomach for digestion or spat out and offered to another of its kind.

The gestures were always the same. The ant offering trophallaxis accosted the object of its desire by tapping it on the head. If the ant approached in this way accepted, it lowered its antennae. If it raised them, it was a sign of refusal. It was not really hungry.

The 327th male did not hesitate. His energy reserves were so low he was on the verge of catalepsy. They joined mouths and food came back up. The ant offering trophallaxis regurgitated first saliva, then honeydew and a mush of cereals. It tasted good and gave the 327th male a real boost.

Once he had received the gift, the male immediately withdrew. It was all coming back to him now, the deaths, the ambush. There was not a moment to lose. He lifted his antennae and sprayed the information in fine droplets around him.

To arms! We're at war. The dwarves have destroyed our first expedition. They've a terrible new weapon. Clear for action! War has been declared.

The sentry withdrew. The alarm scents were grating on her nerves. A crowd was already gathering around the 327th male.

What's the matter?

What's happening?

He says war's been declared.

Can he prove it?

Ants came running from all directions.

He's talking about a new weapon and an expedition that's been decimated.

It's serious.

Can he prove it?

The male was now at the center of a knot of ants.

To arms, to arms! War has been declared. Clear for action!

Can he prove it?

They all started repeating the scent question.

No, he could not prove it. He had been in such a state of shock that he had not thought of bringing anything back with him. Antennae stirred. Heads moved doubtfully.

Where did it happen?

To the west of La-chola-kan, between the new hunting ground found by our scouts and our cities. It's an area often patrolled by dwarves.

That's impossible. Our spies have returned. They state quite categorically that the dwarves aren't awake yet.

An anonymous antenna had just emitted this pheromone sentence. The crowd dispersed. They believed it; they did not believe him. He sounded as if he were telling the truth but his story was so unlikely. The spring wars never began so early. The dwarves would have been mad to attack before they were even all awake. Everyone went back to work without taking heed of the information emitted by the 327th male.

The sole survivor of the first hunting expedition was dumbfounded. He had not made up all those deaths, damn it! They were bound to notice gaps in a caste's ranks in the end.

His antennae drooped stupidly on his forehead. He felt useless and degraded, as if he no longer lived for others but for himself alone.

He shivered with horror at the thought, then rushed forward, ran about feverishly, roused the workers and summoned them to witness. But they scarcely stopped even when he repeated the time-honored saying:

> I was the exploring leg
> I was the eye on the spot
> Now I'm home, I'm the nerve stimulus.

No one gave a damn. They listened to him without paying attention, then went away again without panicking. If only he'd stop trying to stimulate them.

Jonathan had been down in the cellar for four hours now. His wife and son were sick with worry.

"Shall we call the police, Mom?"

"No, not yet."

She went to the cellar door.

"Is Dad dead, Mom? Did he die like Ouarzi?"

"No, darling, of course not. What a lot of nonsense you talk!"

Lucie was dreadfully worried. She leaned forward to look through the crack. Using the powerful halogen flashlight she had just bought, she thought she could make out a spiral staircase a little way ahead.

She sat down on the floor. Nicolas came and joined her. She kissed him.

"He'll come back. We've just got to be patient. He asked us to wait, so we'll just have to go on waiting."

"What if he never comes back?"

• • • •

The 327th male was tired. He felt as if he were struggling in water. You move but you don't get anywhere.

He decided to go and see Belo-kiu-kiuni in person. Mother was fourteen winters old and possessed of incomparable experience whereas the asexual ants who made up the bulk of the population lived for three years at most. Only she could help him find a way to get the information across.

The young male took the express route leading to the heart of the city. Several thousand egg-laden workers were scurrying along the wide gallery. They were bringing their burdens up from the fortieth floor of the basement to the nurseries in the solarium on the thirty-fifth floor above ground level. The vast flow of white shells carried at leg's length was moving from below to above and from right to left.

He had to go in the opposite direction. It wasn't easy. He bumped into several nurses who called him a vandal. He himself was jostled, trodden on, shoved and scratched. Fortunately, the corridor was not completely jammed. He managed to force a way through the teeming mass.

After that, he made his way along small tunnels. It was a longer way around but the going was easier and he kept up a good pace. He passed from arteries into arterioles and from arterioles into veins and venules. He covered kilometers that way, going over bridges and under arches, through empty and crowded places.

He had no difficulty in finding his way in the dark, thanks to the infrared vision of the three simple eyes on his forehead. As he drew nearer the Forbidden City, the air grew heavier with the sickly sweet scent of Mother, and the number of guards increased.

There were ants there of every warrior subcaste, every size and every shape; small ants with long notched mandibles; powerful ones with wood-hard thoracic plates; stocky ones with short antennae and gunners with tapered abdomens, brimful of convulsive poisons.

Armed with valid passport scents, the 327th male

passed through their screening posts without mishap. The soldiers were calm. You could tell that the big territorial wars had not yet begun.

Very close now to his goal, he presented his ID to the doorkeeper ants, then entered the final corridor leading to the royal chamber.

He stopped on the threshold, overcome by the unique beauty of the place. It was a large circular room built according to very precise architectural and geometrical rules handed down by queen mothers to their daughters, antenna to antenna.

The main vault was twelve heads high by thirty-six in diameter (the head was the federal unit of measurement, a head being equivalent to three normal human millimeters). A few cement pilasters supported this insect temple. With its concave floor, it was designed so that scent molecules emitted by individuals would bounce off the walls for as long as possible before being absorbed. It was a remarkable olfactory amphitheatre.

A fat lady was lying on her stomach in the center, now and then waving a leg at a yellow flower. The flower sometimes snapped shut but not before the leg had been withdrawn.

The lady was Belo-kiu-kiuni.

Belo-kiu-kiuni, the last russet ant queen of the central city.

Belo-kiu-kiuni, the sole egg-layer, who had engendered all the minds and bodies of the Tribe.

Belo-kiu-kiuni, who had already been reigning at the time of the great war against the bees, the conquest of the termite hills of the south, the pacification of the spider-infested territories and the terrible war of attrition forced on them by the oak wasps. Since the previous year, she had also coordinated the cities' efforts to resist the pressure of the dwarf ants on the northern frontiers.

Belo-kiu-kiuni, who had beaten all records for longevity.

Belo-kiu-kiuni, his mother.

This living monument was there beside him as before.

Except that now she was being moistened and caressed by twenty or so servile young workers, when it had once been he, the 327th male, who had cared for her with his clumsy little legs.

The young carnivorous plant snapped its jaws and Mother gave a little scented moan. No one knew why she had such a passion for predatory plants.

He drew nearer. Seen close up, Mother was not very good-looking. Her head was elongated at the front with two enormous globular eyes that seemed to look all ways at once. Her infrared simple eyes were squeezed into the middle of her forehead. Her antennae, on the other hand, were set far too far apart. They were very long and light and vibrated in short, controlled bursts.

Belo-kiu-kiuni had woken a few days earlier from the long sleep and laid ceaselessly ever since. Her abdomen, ten times the normal size, was shaken by continuous spasms. At that very moment, she released eight scrawny eggs. Pale gray and iridescent, they were the latest generation of Belokanians. The round, sticky future escaped from her entrails and rolled into the room, where the nurses immediately took charge of it.

The young male recognized the eggs' scent. They were sterile soldiers and males. It was still cold and the gland for producing "daughters" had not yet been activated. As soon as the weather was right, Mother would lay eggs of every caste according to the city's precise needs. Workers would come and tell her there was a shortage of cereal crushers or gunners and she would supply them to order. It also sometimes happened that Belo-kiu-kiuni left her chamber to go and sniff the corridors. Her antennae were sensitive enough to detect the slightest shortfall in any caste and she immediately made up the strength.

Mother gave birth to five more puny individuals, then turned to face her visitor. She touched him and licked him. The moment of contact with royal saliva is always quite extraordinary. The saliva is not only a universal disinfectant but also a panacea for all wounds except those inside the head.

If Belo-kiu-kiuni was incapable of recognizing a single one of her innumerable offspring personally, she showed by licking him that she had identified his scents. He was hers.

The antenna dialogue could commence.

Welcome to the Tribe's genitals. You left me but you can't help coming back.

It was a mother's ritual greeting to her children. Having communicated it, she sniffed the pheromones of the eleven segments with a composure that impressed the young 327th. She already knew why he had come. The first expedition sent west had been completely wiped out. There had been scents of dwarf ants in the neighborhood of the catastrophe. They had probably discovered a secret weapon.

> *I was the exploring leg*
> *I was the eye on the spot*
> *Now I'm home, I'm the nerve stimulus.*

True enough. The only trouble was, he had not managed to stimulate the Tribe. His scents had convinced no one. He felt that only she, Belo-kiu-kiuni, would know how to get the message across and raise the alarm.

Mother sniffed him more attentively. She picked up the slightest volatile molecules coming from his joints and legs. Yes, there were traces of death and mystery. It might or might not mean war.

She indicated to him that she had no political power anyway. In the Tribe, decisions were made by constant consultation, through the formation of working parties that chose their own projects. If he wasn't capable of generating one of these nerve centers—in short, of forming a group—his experience was useless.

She couldn't even help him.

The 327th male persisted. For once, as he was talking to someone who seemed willing to hear him out, he emitted the most seductive molecules with all his might. According to him, the catastrophe was a matter of priority. Spies should be sent immediately to try to find out about the secret weapon.

Belo-kiu-kiuni replied that the Tribe was collapsing under the weight of "matters of priority." Not only was the spring awakening not yet totally complete but work on the city's skin was still in progress. And as long as the last layer of twigs had not been laid in place, it would be dangerous to go to war. On top of this, the Tribe was short of protein and sugar. Lastly, it was already time to think about preparing for the Festival of Rebirth. All this would take up everyone's energy. Even the spies were overworked, which would explain why his message of anguish couldn't be heard.

There was a pause. Only the sound of the workers' labia licking Mother's shell could be heard. She had started playing with her carnivorous plant again, contorting herself until her abdomen was wedged under her thorax and her two front legs were left dangling. When the plant's jaws clamped shut, she withdrew her leg promptly, demonstrating what a formidable weapon the plant might make.

We could raise a wall of carnivorous plants to protect the whole of the northwest frontier. The only trouble is, the little monsters still can't tell the difference between people from the city and strangers.

The 327th male returned to the subject uppermost in his mind. Belo-kiu-kiuni asked him how many individuals had died in the "accident." Twenty-eight, was the reply. All members of the exploring warrior caste? Yes, he had been the only male in the expedition. She then concentrated and laid twenty-eight pearls in succession.

Twenty-eight ants had died and these twenty-eight liquid sisters would replace them.

ONE DAY INEVITABLY: **One day, inevitably, fingers will turn these pages, eyes will read these words and brains will interpret their meaning.**
I do not wish that moment to come too soon. Its con-

sequences could be terrible. And as I write these sentences, I am still struggling to keep my secret.

However, people will have to know what happened one day. Even the most carefully guarded secrets come out in the end. Time is their worst enemy. Whoever you are, I want firstly to greet you. When you read these words, I shall probably have been dead for ten years or even a hundred. At least, I hope so.

I sometimes regret having acquired this knowledge. But I am a human being, and if I now feel very little solidarity with others of my kind, I recognize all the duties incumbent on me for having been born among you, the inhabitants of the human universe.

I must pass on my story.

All stories resemble one another if you look at them closely. In the beginning, there is a subject in the making who slumbers. He undergoes a crisis that forces him to react and either change or die.

The first story I am going to tell you is about our universe because we live inside it and because all things, large and small, are interdependent and obey the same laws.

When you turn this page, for example, you rub your index finger on the cellulose of the paper. The contact generates an infinitesimal, but very real, quantity of heat. In the context of the infinitely small, this heat causes an electron to jump from its atom and collide with another particle.

But this second particle is in fact so huge in comparison with the electron that the shock of collision changes it completely. Before, it was cold, empty and inert. When you turn the page, it undergoes a crisis. It is shot through with gigantic sparks. The simple gesture sets off a chain of events with unknown consequences. Worlds may be born and there may be people on them. These people may discover metallurgy, Provençal cooking and interstellar voyages. They may even turn out to be more intelligent than us. Yet they would never have existed if you had not held this book in your hands and your finger had not produced heat at that exact spot on the paper. Similarly, our universe also has a place in the corner of the page of a book or on the sole of a shoe or in the froth on a glass of beer of some giant civilization.

Our generation will probably never know for sure. But what we do know is that, a long time ago, our universe, or in any case the particle that contained our universe, was cold, empty, black and still. And then someone or something caused a crisis. Someone turned a page, stepped on a stone or scraped the froth off a glass of beer. Whatever the event, it was traumatic. Our particle woke up. In our case, we know there was a gigantic explosion, which we call the Big Bang.

Every second, in the infinitely big, the infinitely small and the infinitely distant, a universe is perhaps being born, just as ours was born over fifteen billion years ago. We do not know the others. But as far as ours is concerned, we know that it began with the explosion of the "smallest," "simplest" atom, hydrogen.

Imagine vast silent space suddenly woken by a titanic deflagration. Why did someone up there turn the page? Why did they scrape the froth off the beer? It doesn't really matter. The fact remains that hydrogen burnt, exploded and grilled. An immense light flashed through immaculate space. It was a time of crisis. Things that were still began to move. Things that were cold grew hot. Things that were silent hummed.

In the initial furnace, hydrogen was transformed into helium, an atom scarcely more complex. But we can already deduce from this transformation the first great rule of our universe, MORE AND MORE COMPLEX.

This rule seems obvious. But there is nothing to prove that it applies in other universes. Elsewhere, the rule may be HOTTER AND HOTTER, HARDER AND HARDER or FUNNIER AND FUNNIER.

Things get hotter here, too, and harder and funnier, but that is not the initial law, just by the way. Our *basic law, the one around which all others are orga-nized, is* MORE AND MORE COMPLEX.

EDMOND WELLS
ENCYCLOPEDIA OF RELATIVE AND ABSOLUTE KNOWLEDGE

The 327th male was wandering about in the city's south-ern corridors. He had not calmed down. He kept chewing over the famous saying:

> *I was the exploring leg*
> *I was the eye on the spot*
> *Now I'm home, I'm the nerve stimulus.*

Why wouldn't it work? Where was he going wrong? His body was seething with the unprocessed informa-tion. For him, the Tribe had been wounded and had not even noticed. He was the pain stimulus, so it was up to him to make the city react.

Oh, how hard it was to bear a message of suffering and keep it inside oneself, unable to find a single antenna willing to receive it. He would so like to have unbur-dened himself and shared the terrible knowledge with others.

A thermal messenger ant passed close by. Sensing his depression, she thought he was not properly awake and offered him her solar calories. It put a little strength back into him, which he immediately used to try to convince her.

To arms! An expedition has been ambushed and de-stroyed by the dwarves. To arms!

But it no longer even sounded like the truth. The ther-mal messenger went on her way as if nothing were amiss. The 327th male did not give up. He ran along the corridors giving out his alarm message.

Warriors sometimes stopped to listen, and even went as far as to talk to him, but his tale of a devastating weapon was so incredible that no group capable of taking charge of a military mission formed.

He walked on, downcast.

Suddenly, as he was making his way along a deserted tunnel on the fourth floor of the basement, he heard a sound behind him. Someone was following him.

The 327th male turned around. He inspected the corridor with his infrared simple eyes but saw only red and black spots. There was no one there. How strange. He must have been mistaken. But again he heard footsteps behind him. *Scritch . . . tssss, scritch . . . tssss.* It was someone who was limping on two of his six legs and getting nearer.

Just to make sure, he turned off each time he came to a crossroads, then paused. The sound stopped. As soon as he set off again, the *scritch . . . tssss, scritch . . . tssss, scritch . . . tssss,* started again.

There was no doubt about it. Someone was following him.

Someone who hid when he turned around. Such strange behavior was quite unprecedented. Why would one Tribe cell follow another without making itself known? They had nothing to hide from one another.

The "presence" nevertheless persisted, always at a distance, always hidden. *Scritch . . . tssss, scritch . . . tssss.* How should he respond? While he was still a larva, the nurses had taught him he must always face up to danger. He stopped and pretended to wash. The presence was not far away now. He could almost smell it. As he mimed the gestures of washing, he moved his antennae and detected the scent molecules of his pursuer. It was a small, one-year-old warrior. She was giving off a strange scent that masked her usual ID and was not easy to define, like the smell of rock.

The small warrior had stopped hiding. *Scritch . . . tssss, scritch . . . tssss.* He could see her now by infrared. She did indeed have two legs missing, and the smell of rock was getting stronger.

He emitted.

Who's there?

There was no reply.

Why are you following me?

Still no reply.

He tried to put the incident out of his mind and set off again but soon detected a second presence coming the other way. A fat warrior this time. The gallery was narrow and he would not be able to get by.

Should he turn around? That would mean confronting the ant with the limp, who was catching up with him fast.

He was cornered.

He could now sense that both ants were warriors and that both smelled of rock. The fat one opened her long shears.

It was a trap.

It was unthinkable that one ant from the city should wish to kill another. Could the immune system have gone haywire? Had they not recognized his identification scents? Did they take him for a foreign body? It was quite insane, as if his stomach had decided to assassinate his intestines.

The 327th male increased the strength of his emissions.

I'm a Tribe cell like you. We belong to the same organism.

The soldiers were young and must be mistaken. But his chemical message failed to appease them. The small lame ant jumped on his back and held him by the wings, while the fat one squeezed his head between her mandibles. They dragged him off toward the rubbish heap under restraint.

The 327th male struggled to get free. With his sexual dialogue segment, he emitted a whole range of emotions quite unknown to asexual ants, ranging from incomprehension to panic.

To avoid being sullied by these "abstract ideas," the ant with the limp, still clinging to his mesonotum, scraped his antennae with her mandibles. With this gesture, she removed all his pheromones, and in particular his passport scents. They would not be of much use to him where he was going anyway.

The sinister trio made its way breathlessly along little-used corridors, the small lame ant continuing her methodical cleaning as if anxious to leave no trace of information on 327th's head. The male had stopped struggling. He had resigned himself to his fate and was preparing to die by slowing down his heartbeats.

"Why so much violence and hatred, brothers? Why? We are all one, children of the Earth and of God. Let us cease now our vain disputes. The twenty-second century will be a spiritual one, or will not be at all. Let us abandon our old quarrels based on pride and duplicity.

"Individualism is our true enemy. If a brother is in need and you allow him to die of hunger, you are no longer worthy of belonging to the world. If a lost soul asks you for help and you close the door in his face, you are not one of us.

"I know you with your nice, cozy consciences. You think of nothing but your own comfort, you want only individual glory. Happiness, yes, but only your own and that of your nearest and dearest.

"I know you, I tell you. You, you, you and you. You needn't sit there smiling in front of your screens, I'm talking to you about serious matters. I'm talking to you about the future of the human race. Things can't go on like this. Our present way of life is senseless. We are wasting and destroying everything. Forests are being flattened to make disposable handkerchiefs. Everything has become disposable: tableware, pens, clothes, cameras and cars, and without noticing it, you too are becoming disposable. Give up this superficial way of life. Give it up today, before you're forced to tomorrow.

"Come and join the army of the faithful. We're all the soldiers of God, brothers."

A presenter's face appeared on the screen. "The program you have just seen was brought to you by Father

MacDonald of the New Forty-fifth Day Adventist Church and Sweetmilk Frozen Foods. It was broadcast by satellite in globovision. After the break, you can see our science-fiction series, *Extraterrestrial and proud of it*."

Unlike Nicolas, Lucie could not switch off her thoughts by watching television. Jonathan had been down there for eight hours now and there was still no sign of him.

She reached for the telephone. He had told her not to do anything, but what if he had been killed or trapped by falling rocks?

She still could not summon up the courage to go down. She picked up the telephone and dialed 999.

"Hello, Police?"

"I told you not to call them," said a weak, expressionless voice from the kitchen.

"Dad, Dad!"

She slammed down the receiver, cutting off the voice repeating "Hello, are you there? Tell us your address."

"Yes, it really is me. There was no need to worry. I told you to wait patiently."

No need to worry? He must be joking!

Not only was Jonathan clasping Ouarzazate's bloody remains in his arms but he himself was transfigured. He did not seem scared or overcome and even had a kind of smile on his face. No, it wasn't exactly a smile. She couldn't put her finger on it. It was as though he had aged or was ill. His eyes were feverish and his skin livid, he was trembling and he seemed out of breath.

When he saw his dog's tortured body, Nicolas burst into tears. It looked as though the poor poodle had been lacerated by hundreds of little razor cuts.

They laid him on some newspaper.

Nicolas cried his eyes out over his lost companion. It was all over. Never again would he see Ouarzi jump against the wall when someone said the word *cat*. Never again would he see him open door handles with a joyful bound. Never again would he save him from big Alsatians.

Ouarzazate was no more.

"Tomorrow we'll take him to the pets' cemetery," conceded Jonathan. "We'll buy him a 4,500 franc grave. You know, one we can put his photo on."

"Oh, yes! Oh, yes!" said Nicolas between sobs. "That's the least he deserves."

"And then we'll go to the RSPCA and you can choose another dog. Why not have a Maltese this time? They're nice little things, too."

Lucie still could not get over it. She did not know which question to ask first. Why had he taken so long? What had happened to the dog? What had happened to him? Did he want something to eat? Had he thought how worried they must be?

"What's down there?" she finally asked in a flat voice.

"There isn't anything."

"But look at the state you're in. And the dog. He looks as if he's fallen into an electric mincer. What happened to him?"

Jonathan passed a dirty hand over his forehead.

"The lawyer was right. The place is full of rats. Ouarzazate got torn to pieces by angry rats."

"What about you?"

He gave a nervous laugh.

"I'm a bigger animal. I frightened them."

"It's incredible. What were you doing down there for eight hours? What's at the bottom of that damn cellar?" she flared.

"I don't know what's at the bottom. I didn't get there."

"You didn't get to the bottom?"

"No. It's very, very deep."

"You didn't get to the bottom of . . . of our cellar in eight hours?"

"No. I stopped when I saw the dog. There was blood everywhere. Ouarzazate fought tooth and nail. It's incredible such a small dog managed to hold out for so long."

"Where did you stop, then? Halfway down?"

"Who knows? I couldn't go on any longer. I was afraid, too. You know I can't stand the dark and hate violence. Anyone would have stopped in my place. You can't go on into the unknown indefinitely. And then I thought of you two. You don't know what it's like. It's so dark. Dark as the grave."

As he finished speaking, a kind of nervous twitch tugged at the left corner of his mouth. She had never seen him in such a state. She realized she must not overwhelm him with any more questions. She put an arm around him and kissed his cold lips.

"It's all right. It's over now. We'll seal the door and never mention it again."

He started back.

"No, it isn't over. I let myself be stopped by all that blood. Anyone would have stopped. Violence is always frightening even when it's aimed at animals. But I can't give up now when I may be so close to the goal."

"You're not going to tell me you want to go back down there!"

"Yes, I am. Edmond got through and so will I."

"Edmond? Your Uncle Edmond?"

"He did something down there and I want to know what."

Lucie stifled a groan.

"Please, if you love Nicolas and me, don't go down again."

"I haven't any choice."

His mouth twitched some more.

"I've always done things by halves. I've always stopped when common sense told me it was dangerous to go on. And look what I've become. A man who's played safe and ended up a failure. By only ever going halfway, I've never got to the bottom of things. I should have stayed a locksmith and let myself get mugged, never mind the bruises. At least I'd have learned how to handle violence. Instead, I know about as much as a newborn baby."

"You're talking nonsense."

"No, I'm not. I can't wrap myself up in cotton wool forever. This cellar's a chance for me to dive in at the deep end. If I don't, I'll never dare look at myself in the mirror again. I'd only see a coward looking back at me. Anyway, you're the one who made me go down there, remember."

He took off his bloodstained shirt.

"There's no point in going on about it. My mind's made up."

"All right, then, I'm coming with you," she declared, grabbing hold of the torch.

"No, you're staying here."

He had seized her firmly by the wrists.

"Let go of me. What's got into you?"

"I'm sorry, but you must try and understand. The cellar's no one's concern but mine. It's something I have to do. And I don't want anyone interfering, do you hear?"

Behind them, Nicolas was still crying over Ouarzazate's dead body. Jonathan let go of Lucie's wrists and went over to his son.

"Buck up, Nick."

"I'm fed up. Ouarzi's dead and all you can do is argue."

Jonathan thought of a way to distract him. He opened a box of matches, took out six and put them on the table.

"Look, I'll show you a puzzle. It's possible to make four equilateral triangles out of these six matches. Try it. I bet you can do it."

Surprised, the boy sniffed hard and dried his eyes. He immediately started arranging the matches in various ways.

"Here's a piece of advice for you. You have to think differently if you want to find the solution. If you think about it in the usual way, you won't get anywhere."

Nicolas managed to make three triangles. Not four. He looked up at his father, blinking his big, blue eyes.

"Have you found out how to do it, Dad?"

"Not yet, but I don't think it'll take me much longer."

Jonathan had soothed his son for the time being, but

his wife was giving him angry looks. That evening, they had a violent argument. But Jonathan would say nothing about the cellar and its mysteries.

The next day, he got up early and spent the morning fitting a steel door with a heavy padlock at the entrance to the cellar. He hung the only key to the lock around his neck.

Salvation arrived in the unexpected form of an earthquake.

First the walls were shaken by a big lateral tremor. Sand began to cascade down from the ceilings. A second tremor followed almost immediately, then a third and a fourth. Muffled shocks succeeded one another more and more quickly, closer and closer to the strange trio, in an enormous, ceaseless rumbling that made everything vibrate.

Revived by the vibrations, the young male speeded up his heartbeat again, surprised his executioners by lashing out with his mandibles and made off down the collapsed tunnel. He beat his embryonic wings to accelerate his flight and prolong his leaps over rubble.

Each time there was a strong tremor, he had to stop and lie flat on the ground until the avalanches of sand had ceased. Whole sections of tunnels came crashing down into other tunnels. Bridges, arches and crypts collapsed, dragging millions of dazed silhouettes down with them.

Priority alarm scents streamed out and spread. In the first phase, the stimulating pheromones filled the upper galleries like mist. All who breathed in the scent immediately began to tremble and run about in all directions, producing pheromones that were even more arousing and causing the panic to snowball.

The alarm cloud spread like fog, gliding into all the veins of the stricken region and from there into the main arteries. The alien object that had infiltrated the Tribe's body had produced the pain toxins the young male had tried in vain to trigger. As a result, the black blood formed by the crowds of Belokanians began to beat faster. Gangs of workers evacuated the eggs near the disaster area and soldiers formed themselves into combat units.

As the 327th male arrived at a vast crossroads half blocked by sand and crowds, the tremors ceased. There followed an agonizing silence. Everyone stood still, afraid of what would happen next. Raised antennae quivered. They waited.

Suddenly, the knocking that had plagued them earlier was replaced by a kind of muffled growl. They all sensed that the city's fur of twigs had been pierced. Something immense was being inserted into the dome, crushing the walls and sliding between the twigs.

A fine pink tentacle burst in at the heart of the crossroads. It whipped through the air and skimmed the ground at amazing speed, seeking out as many citizens as possible. As the soldiers hurled themselves on it and tried to bite it with their mandibles, a big black cluster formed at the tip. When it was sufficiently coated, the tongue flew up and disappeared, tipped the crowd down an invisible throat and then thrust again, even longer, greedier and more devastating than before.

The second phase of the alert was then triggered. The workers drummed on the ground with the tips of their abdomens to bring out the soldiers on the lower floors, who were still ignorant of the catastrophe.

The whole city resounded with the primal drumbeats. It was as though the city organism were gasping for air: *bang, bang, bang! Bang . . . bang . . . bang*, replied the alien, who had started hammering at the dome again so as to plunge in deeper. They all flattened themselves against the walls to try to escape the raging red serpent lashing the galleries. When one lap produced a poor yield, the tongue stretched farther. A beak, then a gigantic head followed.

It was a woodpecker, the terror of springtime! These greedy birds dug plugs up to sixty centimeters long out of the roofs of ant cities and gorged themselves on their inhabitants.

There was just time to launch phase three of the alert. In a frenzy of unexpressed excitement, some workers began to dance the dance of fear. Their jerky movements involved leaping, mandible-snapping and spitting. Other individuals, by now completely hysterical, ran along the corridors biting everything that moved. Fear had the perverse effect of causing the city to self-destruct when it was unable to destroy its attacker.

The cataclysm was localized on the fifteenth upper-west floor, but since the alert had run all three of its phases, the whole city was now on a war footing. The workers, carrying the eggs down to safety in the deepest basement, passed lines of soldiers with raised mandibles hurrying in the opposite direction.

Over countless generations, the ant city had learned to defend itself against such unpleasantnesses. In the midst of the disorganized movements, the ants of the artillery caste formed commando groups and allocated priority operations.

They encircled the most vulnerable part of the woodpecker, his neck, then turned to take up the close-range firing position. With their abdomens aimed at the bird, they fired, propelling jets of hyperconcentrated formic acid with all the might of their sphincters.

The bird had the sudden, unpleasant feeling that a scarf full of pins was being tightened around his throat. He struggled to get free but was too far in. His wings were imprisoned in the earth and twigs of the dome. He darted his tongue out again to kill as many as possible of his tiny enemies.

A new wave of soldiers took over from the first and fired. The woodpecker started. This time, it felt like spines rather than pins. He rapped his beak nervously. The ants fired again. The bird trembled and began to have difficulty breathing. The acid spurted yet again, eating away at his nerves while he was wedged in tightly.

The firing ceased. Wide-mandibled soldiers rushed up

from all sides and bit into the wounds caused by the formic acid. Another legion went outside onto what remained of the dome, found the animal's tail and started to bore into the most scented part, the anus. The sappers enlarged the entrance to it in no time and disappeared inside the bird's guts.

The first team had managed to break the skin of the neck. When the first red blood began to flow, the pheromone alarm messages ceased. The game was as good as won. The bird's throat was an open wound and whole battalions were hurling themselves into it. The ants still alive in the animal's larynx were saved.

Soldiers then entered the head, looking for the openings to the brain. A worker found a passage, the carotid artery, which led from the heart to the brain. Four soldiers slashed open the duct and flung themselves into the red liquid. Borne on the cardiac current, they were soon propelled into the heart of the cerebral hemispheres. Now they could get down to the job of hacking away at the gray matter.

Crazed with pain, the woodpecker rolled from side to side with no means of countering all the invaders carving him up from the inside. A platoon of ants penetrated his lungs and disgorged acid into them, making him cough horribly.

A whole armed corps plunged into the esophagus to forge a junction in the digestive system with their colleagues coming from the anus. Moving rapidly up the large colon, they wreaked havoc as they worked on all the vital organs within reach of their mandibles. They dug at the living meat in the same way they dug at the earth, and took by assault, one after another, the gizzard, liver, heart, spleen and pancreas.

Blood or lymph sometimes spurted out at the wrong moment, drowning a few individuals. However, it happened only to those who were clumsy and did not know how and where to make clean cuts.

The others progressed methodically in the midst of red and black flesh. They knew how to extricate themselves before being crushed by a spasm and avoided touching areas gorged with bile or digestive acids.

The two armies finally met up in the region of the kidneys. The bird was not yet dead. His slashed heart was still pumping blood into the punctured pipes.

Without waiting for their victim to breathe his last, chains of workers had formed and were passing the pieces of meat, still palpitating, from leg to leg. Nothing escaped the little surgeons. When they started to cut out chunks of the brain, the woodpecker had a final convulsion. The whole city rushed to quarter the monster. The corridors teemed with ants clutching feathers or pieces of down they were keeping as souvenirs.

The teams of masons had already gone into action to rebuild the dome and damaged tunnels.

From a distance, it looked as if the anthill was eating a bird. After swallowing it up, it digested it and distributed its flesh and fat, feathers and hide to all parts of the city where they would be of most use.

GENESIS: How did ant civilization develop? To understand this, it is necessary to go back several hundred million years to the beginning of life on Earth.

Among the first to land were the insects.

They seemed poorly adapted to their world. Small and fragile, they were ideal victims for any predator. To stay alive, some of them, such as the crickets, chose the path of reproduction. They laid so many young that some necessarily survived.

Others, such as the wasps and bees, chose venom, providing themselves, as time went by, with poisonous stings that made them formidable adversaries.

Others, such as the cockroaches, chose to become inedible. A special gland gave their flesh such an unpleasant taste that no one wanted to eat it.

Others, such as the praying mantises and moths, chose camouflage. Resembling grass or bark, they went unnoticed by an inhospitable nature.

However, in this early jungle, plenty of insects had

not discovered the "trick" of survival and seemed con-demned to disappear.

Among those at a disadvantage were, firstly, the ter-mites. When this wood-devouring species appeared on the Earth's surface nearly a hundred and fifty million years ago, it had no chance of surviving. It had too many predators and too few natural defenses.

What would become of the termites?

Many perished, but, with their backs to the wall, the survivors managed to work out an original solution in time: "We won't fight alone anymore, we'll band to-gether. It will be more difficult for our predators to at-tack twenty termites taking a united stand than a single one trying to get away." The termites thus opened up one of the royal roads to complexity: social organization.

They began to live in small units, at first family ones, all grouped around the egg-laying mother. Then the families became villages and the villages grew into towns. Their cities of sand and cement soon rose over the whole surface of the globe.

The termites were the first intelligent masters of our planet and its first society.

EDMOND WELLS,
ENCYCLOPEDIA OF RELATIVE AND ABSOLUTE KNOWLEDGE

The 327th male could no longer see his two rock-scented killers. He really had lost them. With a bit of luck, they had been killed by falling rocks.

He must stop dreaming. It would not get him out of the fix he was in. He had no passport scents left at all. If a single warrior crossed his path now, he was as good as dead. The others would automatically consider him a foreign body and would not even allow him to explain. He would be shot down with acid or bitten by mandi-bles. That was the treatment reserved for anyone who could not emit the passport scents of the Federation.

It was absurd. How had he come to such a pass? It was all the fault of those two damn rock-scented warriors.

What had gotten into them? They must have been out of their minds. Although it was rare, errors in genetic programming sometimes caused psychological accidents of this kind. Rather like the hysterical ants striking out at everyone during the third phase of the alert.

His two assailants had not looked hysterical or defective, though. In fact, they had seemed to know perfectly well what they were doing. It was as if . . . There was only one situation in which cells consciously destroyed other cells belonging to the same organism. The nurses called it cancer. It was as if . . . they were cancer cells.

In that case, the smell of rock was the smell of sickness. He would have to sound the alarm on that account, too. Now the 327th male had two mysteries to solve, the dwarves' secret weapon and the cancer cells of Bel-o-kan. And he could tell no one. He had to think. He might well possess some hidden resource that would solve all his problems.

He set about washing his antennae, moistening them (it gave him a funny feeling to lick antennae without recognizing the characteristic taste of passport pheromones), brushing them, smoothing them with his elbow brush and drying them.

What on earth was he to do?

The first thing was to stay alive.

Only one person could remember his infrared image without needing the confirmation of the ID scents and that was Mother. However, the Forbidden City was packed with soldiers. It could not be helped. After all, was there not an old saying of Belo-kiu-kiuni's that stated: *We are often safest in the midst of danger?*

"Edmond Wells isn't remembered kindly here. No one tried to stop him leaving, either."

The person speaking these words was a pleasant-looking old man, one of Sweetmilk Corporation's assistant managers.

"Didn't he discover a new bacteria for flavoring yogurt?"

"Well, I must admit he had sudden strokes of genius where chemistry was concerned. But they weren't a regular occurrence, they only came in fits and starts."

"Was he a troublemaker?"

"No, not really. He just didn't fit in with the team. He was a loner. His bacteria brought in millions but no one ever really appreciated him."

"What exactly was the problem?"

"Every team has a leader. Edmond couldn't stand leaders or anyone in a position of power. He always despised managers. He used to say they only 'managed for the sake of managing, without producing anything.' When it comes down to it, we all have to do a spot of bootlicking. There's no harm in it. That's how the system works. He had a very high opinion of himself, though. We were his equals, but I think it got on our nerves more than on the bosses'."

"Why did he leave?"

"He had an argument about something with one of our assistant managers. Actually, he was entirely in the right. The assistant manager had gone through his desk and Edmond blew his top. When he saw everyone was on the manager's side, he had no choice but to leave."

"But you've just said he was in the right."

"We thought we'd better side with someone we knew and didn't like rather than stick our necks out for someone we liked but didn't know. Edmond didn't have any friends here. He didn't eat or drink with us. He went around with his head in the clouds."

"Why admit to all that now? You didn't have to tell me."

"Well, I feel bad about it now he's dead. You're his nephew. Telling you helps get it off my chest."

At the end of the dark bottleneck stood a wooden fortress, the Forbidden City.

The building was actually a pine stump around which the dome had been built. It acted as the heart and backbone of Bel-o-kan; the heart because it contained the royal chamber and precious food reserves, and the backbone because it allowed the city to withstand storms and rain.

Seen at close quarters, the wall of the Forbidden City was encrusted with complex patterns like inscriptions in some barbarous script. These were the corridors dug long ago by the first inhabitants of the stump, the termites.

When the founding Belo-kiu-kiuni had landed in the region five thousand years earlier, she had immediately come up against them. The ensuing war had lasted over a thousand years, but the Belokanians had won in the end. They had then been amazed to discover a "hard" city with wooden corridors that never caved in. The pine stump opened up new urban and architectural perspectives.

With the flat, raised table on top and deep roots spreading into the earth below, it was absolutely ideal. However, it soon became too small to shelter the growing population of russet ants. They had then dug outward from the roots to form the basement and piled twigs on top of the decapitated tree to broaden its summit.

These days, the Forbidden City was almost deserted. Except for Mother and her elite guards, everyone lived in the periphery.

The 327th male approached the stump with small, irregular steps. Regular vibrations would have been perceived as someone walking, whereas irregular sounds could pass for small landslides. He just had to hope he didn't stumble on a soldier. He started to crawl until he was less than two hundred heads from the Forbidden City and could make out the dozens of entrances excavated in the stump, or rather the heads of doorkeeper ants blocking the way in.

Their broad heads, shaped by some freak of genetics, were round and flat, like big nails, and fitted the openings they guarded exactly.

These living doors had already proved themselves in the past. At the time of the Strawberry Plant War, seven hundred and eighty years earlier, the city had been invaded by yellow ants. All the surviving Belokanians had taken refuge in the Forbidden City and the doorkeeper ants had entered backward, sealing the entrances hermetically.

It had taken the yellow ants two days to force their way in. The doorkeepers had not only blocked the holes but also bitten them with their long mandibles. The yellow ants had attacked the doorkeepers a hundred to one and had finally broken through by digging into the chitin of their heads. But the living doors had not been sacrificed in vain. The other federal cities had had time to muster reinforcements and the city had been liberated a few hours later.

The 327th male certainly had no intention of facing a doorkeeper alone. He was counting on being able to dive in when one of the doors opened—to let out a nurse laden with some of Mother's eggs, for example.

Just then a head moved and opened to let through a guard. No chance that time. If he had tried, the guard would have come straight back and killed him.

The doorkeeper's head moved again. He crouched down on all six legs, ready to spring. But no, it was a false alarm, she was only shifting her position. It must really give you a cramp to press your neck up against a wooden collar like that.

Suddenly he could wait no longer. He charged at the obstacle. As soon as he was within range of her antennae, the doorkeeper spotted his lack of passport pheromones. She moved back to block the opening better, then let out alarm molecules.

Foreign body in the Forbidden City! Foreign body in the Forbidden City! she repeated like a siren.

She twirled her claws to intimidate the intruder. She longed to advance and fight him but they had received strict orders. Blocking the way took precedence over everything.

He had to act quickly. The male had an advantage: he could see in the dark, while the doorkeeper was blind. He rushed forward, avoided the mandibles striking out blindly and plunged to seize their roots, slicing through them one after another. The transparent blood flowed and the two stumps continued to wave about harmlessly.

However, the 327th male still could not get in with the corpse of his adversary blocking his way and her rigid legs leaning against the wood by reflex. What was he to do? He put his abdomen against the doorkeeper's forehead and pulled. The body jerked and the chitin eaten away by the formic acid started to melt, giving off gray fumes. But the head was thick. It took him four tries before he was able to force his way through the flat skull.

There was just room. On the other side, he discovered an atrophied thorax and abdomen. The ant was nothing but a door.

COMPETITORS: When the first ants appeared, fifty million years later, they had to watch their behavior. The distant descendants of the wild, solitary tiphiid wasp, they had neither big jaws nor stings. They were small and puny, but not stupid, and quickly realized it was in their interests to copy the termites and unite.

They founded villages and built rough cities. The termites soon started to worry about the competition. In their view, there was only room on Earth for one species of social insect.

After that, war was inevitable. All over the world, on islands, trees and mountains, the armies of the termite cities fought the young armies of the ant cities.

Such a thing had never before been seen in the animal world. Millions of mandibles fighting side by side for a nonnutritional objective. A "political" objective.

At first, the more experienced termites won every battle, but the ants adapted. They copied the termites' weapons and invented new ones. Worldwide termite-ant wars set the planet on fire between thirty and fifty million years ago. It was about that time that the ants discovered how to use jets of formic acid as weapons and stole a decisive lead.

Battles are still being fought between the two enemy species today but the termite legions rarely win.

EDMOND WELLS,
ENCYCLOPEDIA OF RELATIVE AND ABSOLUTE KNOWLEDGE

"You met him in Africa, didn't you?"

"Yes," replied the professor. "Edmond was distraught. If I remember rightly, his wife had died. He threw himself into the study of insects."

"Why insects?"

"Why not? Man has always been fascinated by them. Our most distant forebears were afraid of mosquitoes, which gave them fevers; fleas, which made them itch; spiders, which stung them; and weevils, which ate up their food reserves. It's left its mark."

Jonathan was talking to Professor Daniel Rosenfeld in Laboratory 326 of the Entomology Department of the National Center for Scientific Research at Fontainebleau. He was a handsome old man with a ponytail who smiled as he talked.

"Insects are disconcerting. They are smaller and more fragile than us, yet they goad us and menace us. And as maggots feast on our dead bodies, we all end up inside them in the end."

"I've never thought of it like that."

"Insects were long considered evil incarnate. Beelzebub is depicted with the head of a fly, for example. It isn't a coincidence."

"Ants have a better reputation than flies."

"It depends. Every culture views them differently. In the Talmud, they symbolize honesty. For Tibetan Buddhism, they represent the derisory nature of material activity. The Baoulés of the Ivory Coast believe that if a pregnant woman is bitten by an ant, she will give birth to a child with the head of an ant, while some Polynesians hold them to be tiny gods."

"Edmond had previously been working on bacteria. Why did he drop them?"

"He was infinitely less interested in bacteria than in his research on insects, and ants in particular. And when I say 'his research,' I'm talking about total commitment. He was the one who got up the petition against toy ant-hills, those plastic boxes on sale in supermarkets, with a queen and six hundred workers. He also fought to get ants used as an 'insecticide.' He wanted russet ant cities to be introduced systematically into forests to clear them of parasites. It was a good idea. In the past, ants have been used to combat the pine processionary moth in Italy and the fir skipper in Poland, both insects which ravage trees."

"So the idea is to set the insects against one another?"

"Mmm, he called it 'interfering in their diplomacy.' We did so many stupid things with chemical insecticides last century. It's important never to attack insects head-on and even more important never to underestimate them. We can't hope to tame them like mammals. They call for a different way of thinking, a different approach. They can parry all chemical poisons by mithridatizing. If we still can't avert plagues of locusts, it's because the blighters adapt. Zap them with insecticide and ninety-nine percent die—but one percent survive. And the one percent which escape are not only immune but the young locusts they give birth to are 100 percent 'vacci-nated' against the insecticide. Two hundred years ago, we made the mistake of making the chemicals more and more toxic and created hyperresistant strains capable of absorbing the worst poisons without ill effect."

"Do you mean there isn't really any way of combating insects?"

"See for yourself. There are still mosquitoes, locusts, weevils, tsetse flies—and ants. They resist everything. In 1945, we noticed that only ants and scorpions had sur-vived the nuclear holocausts. And they even adapted to that."

• • •

The 327th male had shed the blood of a Tribe cell. He had committed the worst act of violence against his own organism. It had left a bitter taste in his mouth but how else could he, the information hormone, have survived to pursue his mission?

If he had killed, it was because someone had tried to kill him. It was a chain reaction, like cancer. Because the Tribe had behaved abnormally toward him, he was obliged to do likewise. He just had to get used to the idea.

He had killed one sister cell and might perhaps kill others.

"But what did he go to Africa for? You said yourself there are ants everywhere."

"Yes, but not the same ants. I don't think Edmond cared about anything after he lost his wife. With the benefit of hindsight, I even wonder whether he didn't expect the ants to help him commit suicide."

"What?"

"They nearly ate him, for Heaven's sake. The driver ants of Africa . . . Haven't you ever seen the film *When the Marabunta Roars*?"

Jonathan shook his head.

"The Marabunta is the horde of driver ants, or *Annoma nigricans*, that destroys everything in its path as it moves across the plain."

Professor Rosenfeld stood up as if he were about to face an invisible wave.

"First of all you hear a kind of vast rumble made up of all the shouting and screeching, the beating of wings and stamping of feet of the little animals trying to get away. At that stage, you still can't see the driver ants but then a few warriors suddenly appear from behind a mound. After the scouts, the others come up quickly in columns stretching as far as the eye can see. The hill turns black.

It's like a stream of lava that melts everything it touches."

The professor was walking up and down, waving his arms, caught up in his subject.

"They're the poisonous blood of Africa. Living acid. They occur in terrifying numbers. A colony of drivers lays on average five hundred thousand eggs a day. That's whole bucketfuls. Along it flows, then, this stream of black sulfuric acid, up banks and trees, quite unstoppable. Any birds, lizards or insectivorous mammals that have the misfortune to go near it are immediately torn to shreds. It's like something out of the Apocalypse. Driver ants aren't afraid of anything. I once saw an overcurious cat dismembered in a trice. They can even cross streams by making floating bridges out of their own corpses. On the Ivory Coast, in the region round the Lamto research center, where we were studying them, the population still hasn't found a defense against their invasions. When they find out they're going to cross the village, the people run away, taking their most precious belongings with them. They stand the legs of the tables and chairs in buckets of vinegar and pray to their gods. When they return, they find the place cleaned out, as if a typhoon had passed through it. There isn't a scrap of food or any organic substance left anywhere. There aren't any vermin left, either. Drivers are the best way to clean your house from top to bottom."

"How did you go about studying them if they're so ferocious?"

"We waited till midday. Insects can't regulate their body temperatures like us. When it's eighteen degrees outside their bodies, it's eighteen degrees inside, and when there's a heat wave, their blood boils. The drivers find it unbearable. As soon as the sun's rays start to burn, they dig a bivouac nest and wait in it till the weather improves. It's like a mini-hibernation, except that it's the heat that brings them to a standstill, not the cold."

"And then?"

Jonathan did not really know how to carry on a conversation. He thought the purpose of discussion was to pass on information like a communicating vase. There was one person who knew, the full vase, and one who did not know, the empty vase, usually himself. The one who did not know listened intently and kept the speaker going with the occasional "And then?" "Tell me about that" and nods of the head.

If there were any other ways of communicating, he did not know about them. Moreover, from his observations of those around him, it seemed to him that they only engaged in parallel monologues, with each just trying to use the other as a free psychoanalyst. That being so, he preferred his own technique. He might not seem to know anything but at least he never stopped learning. Wasn't there a Chinese proverb that said "Someone who asks a question is stupid for five minutes but someone who doesn't ask is stupid for life"?

"And then? We had a go, damn it. And, believe me, it was quite something. We were hoping to find that blasted queen, the five-hundred-thousand-eggs-a-day lady. We just wanted to see her and photograph her. We put on big sewer workers' boots. Edmond was out of luck. He took size forty-three and there was only a pair of size forties left. He went in desert boots. I remember it as if it were yesterday. At twelve-thirty, we traced out the likely shape of the bivouac nest on the ground and began to dig a trench a meter deep all round it. At one-thirty, we reached the outer chambers. A kind of crackling black liquid started to flow from it. Thousands of overexcited soldiers were snapping their mandibles. In that species, they're as sharp as razors. They planted themselves in our boots but we carried on digging down to the nuptial chamber with spades and pickaxes. At last we found our treasure, the queen. She was ten times the size of our European queens. We photographed her from every angle. She must have been screaming for help the whole time in her scent language. It soon took effect. Warriors converged from all sides and formed mounds at our feet. Some managed to climb up by scaling their sisters who were already stuck in the rubber. From there, they went up under our trousers and then our shirts. We turned into Gullivers, except that our particular Lilliputians wanted to shred us into bite-sized pieces. The main thing was to stop them from getting into any of our natural orifices: the nose, the mouth, the anus, the eardrum. Otherwise, we would have had it; they would have dug away at us from the inside!"

Jonathan kept quiet, clearly moved. The professor seemed to be reliving the scene, acting it out with all the strength of the young man he no longer was.

"I kept slapping at myself to shake them off. I knew that they were guided to us by our breath and our sweat. We had all done yoga exercises to train ourselves to minimize breathing and control fear. I tried not to think, to forget about these little bunches of warriors who wanted to kill us. Meanwhile, I managed to fire off a couple of films, with some flash shots. As soon as we'd finished, we all jumped out of the trench. Except for Edmond. The ants had covered him entirely, up as far as his neck; they were trying to swallow him whole! I grabbed him by the arms and pulled him out, stripped off his clothes and used my machete to scrape off all the mandibles and heads that were embedded in his flesh. We had all suffered, but not to the same extent as him, because he didn't have the right boots. And most of all, because he'd panicked, he'd given off pheromones of fear."

"It's horrible."

"No, it's just good that he got out of there alive. Besides, it didn't turn him off ants. Far from it, he studied them with even more determination."

"And after that?"

"He went back to Paris and we never heard from him again. He didn't even call his old friend Rosenfeld once, the rotter. I finally read about his death in the papers. May he rest in peace."

He pulled the curtain back from the window to look at an old enamelled metal thermometer.

"Hmm, thirty degrees centigrade in the middle of April. It's incredible. It's getting hotter and hotter every year. If it carries on like this, in ten years' time, France is going to turn into a tropical country."

"Is it really that bad?"

"Most people don't notice it because it's happening very gradually. But we entomologists can tell it's happening from a number of details. We keep finding species of insects typical of equatorial regions in the Parisian Basin. Haven't you noticed how gaudy the butterflies are becoming?"

"Yes, I have. I found a fluorescent red and black one on a car only yesterday."

"It was probably a five-spotted zygaena. It's a venomous butterfly only found in Madagascar until now. If it goes on like this . . . Can you imagine driver ants in Paris? There'd be panic. I wouldn't mind seeing it, though."

After cleaning his antennae and eating a few warm hunks of the smashed-in doorkeeper, the odorless male scurried away down the wooden corridors. He could smell that his mother's chamber lay in that direction. Fortunately, it was 25°C-time and there were few people about in the Forbidden City at that temperature. He should be able to slip through easily.

Suddenly, he detected the scent of two warriors coming from the opposite direction. There was a big one and a small one, and the small one had some legs missing.

They smelled each others' scents from a distance.

It's incredible, it's him.

It's incredible, it's them.

The 327th male bolted away in the hope of losing them. He turned this way and that in the three-dimensional labyrinth and left the Forbidden City. The doorkeepers did not slow him down because they were programmed to filter only in-going traffic. There was now loose earth underfoot. He took turn after turn.

But the others were very quick, too, and did not let him outdistance them. Then the male bumped into and knocked over a worker carrying a twig. He had not done it on purpose but it slowed the rock-scented killers down.

Taking advantage of the respite, he quickly hid in a crevice. The ant with the limp was coming closer. He drew back a little farther into his hiding place.

"Where's he got to?"

"He's gone back down."

"What do you mean, gone back down?"

Lucie took Grandmother Augusta's arm and led her over to the cellar door.

"He's been down there since yesterday evening."

"And he's still not back up?"

"No. I don't know what's going on down there, but he strictly forbade me to call the police. He's already been down several times and come back up."

Augusta was dumbfounded.

"But that's crazy. Especially when his uncle had strictly forbidden him to."

"When he goes down now, he takes loads of tools with him, pieces of steel, big slabs of concrete. I haven't a clue what he's up to down there."

Lucie put her head in her hands. She could not take any more and felt she was on the verge of a nervous breakdown.

"And we're not allowed to go down and get him?"

"No. He's put a lock on the door. He locks it from the inside."

Augusta sat down, disconcerted.

"Dear me. If I'd known talking about Edmond would cause so much trouble . . ."

SPECIALIST: In the big, modern ant cities, repeated task-sharing over millions of years has led to genetic mutations.

Some ants are born with huge, shearing mandibles to become soldiers, others have crushing mandibles to produce flour from cereals, and yet others are equipped with overdeveloped salivary glands to moisten and disinfect young larvae.

It's rather as though our soldiers were born with fingers like knives, farmers with claw-feet for climbing trees and picking fruit and wet nurses with a dozen pairs of nipples.

But the most spectacular of all the "professional" mutations is the one for love.

In order for the mass of industrious workers not to be distracted by erotic impulses, they are born asexual. All the city's reproductive energies are concentrated on specialists, the males and females, princes and princesses of this parallel civilization.

They are born and equipped solely for love and benefit from a number of features designed to help them copulate. These range from wings to infrared simple eyes, by way of antennae that emit and receive abstract emotions.

EDMOND WELLS,
ENCYCLOPEDIA OF RELATIVE AND ABSOLUTE KNOWLEDGE

His hiding place was not a dead end but led to a little cave. The 327th male holed up in it. The rock-scented warriors passed by without detecting him. The only trouble was, the cave was not empty. There was someone warm and sweet-smelling in it who emitted a question.

Who are you?

The olfactory message was clear, precise and imperative. Thanks to his infrared simple eyes, he could make out the big animal questioning him. As far as he could tell, it must have weighed at least ninety grains of sand. It was not a soldier, though. It was something he had never seen or smelled until then.

A female.

And what a female! He took the time to look her over.

She had shapely, slender legs decorated with little hairs that were deliciously sticky with sexual hormones. Her thick antennae sparkled with strong scents. The red lights in her eyes made them look like two bilberries. Her massive abdomen was smooth and tapering. Her broad thoracic shield was surmounted by an adorably grainy mesonotum and her wings, lastly, were twice as long as his own.

The female opened her sweet little mandibles and jumped at his throat to decapitate him.

He could not swallow. He was stifling. Given his lack of passports, the female was not about to relax her embrace. He was a foreign body and must be destroyed.

However, the 327th male managed to free himself by taking advantage of his small size. He climbed onto her shoulders and squeezed her head. Now it was her turn to worry. She struggled to get free.

When she had worn herself out, he threw his antennae forward. He did not want to kill her, just get her to listen to him. It was not that simple. He wanted to have AC with her. Yes, absolute communication.

The female (the 56th, according to her clutch number) moved her antennae away to avoid his touch. Then she reared up to rid herself of him, but he remained firmly fixed to her mesonotum and increased the pressure of his mandibles. If he carried on, the female's head would be torn off.

She stopped moving. So did he.

With the 180° vision of her simple eyes, she could see the aggressor perched on her back clearly. He was very small.

A male!

She remembered what the nurses had taught her:

Males are half-beings. Unlike all the city's other cells, they are equipped with only half the chromosomes of the species. They were conceived from unfertilized eggs and are therefore big ova, or rather big sperms, living out in the open.

She had a sperm on her back who was strangling her.

She found the idea almost amusing. Why were some eggs fertilized and others not? Probably because of the temperature. Below 20°C, the sperm store was not activated and Mother laid unfertilized eggs. Males were therefore born of the cold, like death.

It was the first time she had ever seen one in flesh and chitin. Whatever could he be looking for there in the virgins' quarters? It was taboo territory, reserved for female sexual cells only. If any old foreign cell could get into their fragile sanctuary, the door was open to all kinds of infection.

The 327th male again tried to establish antenna communication, but the female would not let him. If he prised her antennae up, she immediately flattened them to her head again. If he touched her second segment, she laid back her antennae.

He increased the pressure of his jaws still more and managed to bring his seventh antenna segment into contact with her seventh segment. The 56th female had never engaged in that kind of communication. She had been taught to avoid all contact and to simply give off and receive scents. But she knew that this ethereal means of communication was deceptive. Mother had emitted a pheromone on the subject one day:

Between two brains, there will always be misunderstandings and lies caused by parasitic smells, drafts and poor-quality reception.

The only way to overcome these difficulties was absolute communication. Direct antenna contact. The unimpeded passage of the neuromediators of one brain to the neuromediators of another brain.

For her, it was something strange and hard, a kind of deflowering of her mind.

But she no longer had any choice. If he went on squeezing her, he would kill her. She laid her frontal scapes on her shoulders in submission.

The AC could now commence. The two pairs of antennae came together unreservedly, with a little electric shock caused by the tension. Slowly at first, then faster and faster, the two insects caressed each other's eleven notched segments. A froth of confused expressions gradually bubbled up, a fatty substance that lubricated their antennae and allowed them to accelerate still more the rhythm of their rubbing. For a while, the two insect heads vibrated uncontrollably before the stalks of their antennae ceased their dance and clung together along their whole length. They were now one being with two heads, two bodies and a single pair of antennae.

The natural miracle was accomplished. Pheromones passed from one body to the other through the thousands of little pores and capillaries of their segments. Their thoughts married. Their ideas were no longer coded and decoded but delivered in all their original simplicity: images, music, emotions and scents.

It was in this immediate language that the 327th male related his entire adventure to the 56th female: the massacre of the expedition, the olfactory traces of the dwarf soldiers, his meeting with Mother, the attempt to eliminate him, his loss of the passports, his struggle with the doorkeeper and the rock-scented killers still pursuing him.

The AC over, she laid back her antennae to show him her good intentions and he got off her back. He was now at her mercy and she could easily have killed him. She came up to him, her mandibles well out of harm's way, and gave him some of her passport pheromones to get him out of trouble temporarily. Then she offered him trophallaxis and he accepted. Finally, she whirred her wings to disperse all trace of their conversation.

At last he'd managed to convince someone. He'd gotten the information across and it had been understood and accepted by another cell.

He had formed his work group.

*TIME: **Human beings and ants perceive the passage of time very differently. For human beings, time is absolute. Whatever happens, seconds always have the same periodicity and duration.***

For ants, on the other hand, time is relative. When it is hot, the seconds are very short. When it is cold, they stretch out indefinitely until consciousness is lost during hibernation.

This elastic time gives them a very different perception of the speed of things from our own. To define a movement, insects use not only space and duration but also a third dimension, temperature.

EDMOND WELLS,
ENCYCLOPEDIA OF RELATIVE AND ABSOLUTE KNOWLEDGE

Now there were two of them who were anxious to convince as many of their sisters as possible of the seriousness of the "Affair of the Secret Weapon." It was not too late, but there were two factors to be taken into account. On the one hand, they would never be able to convert enough workers to their cause before the Festival of Rebirth, which would take up all their energies, and they would therefore need a third accomplice. On the other hand, they would need to find a hideout in case the rock-scented warriors showed up again.

The 56th female proposed her chamber. She had dug a secret passage in it that would allow them to get away in case of a hitch. The 327th male was only partly surprised at this. Digging secret passages was all the rage. It had started a hundred years before during the war against the glue-spitting ants. The queen of a Federation city, Ha-yekte-douni, had fostered security mania and had had a "fortified" Forbidden City built for herself. Its flanks were armed with big stones, themselves soldered together with termite cements.

Unfortunately, there was only one exit. So when her city was surrounded by legions of glue-spitting ants, she was trapped in her own palace. The glue-spitters then captured her with ease and suffocated her in their vile, fast-drying glue. Queen Ha-yekte-douni was later avenged and her city liberated, but her stupid, horrible end left its mark on the minds of the Belokanians.

Since ants have the amazing good fortune to be able to

alter the shape of their dwellings with a bite of their mandibles, they all began to bore secret passages. One ant digging a hole is all very well, but if there are a million doing it, it spells disaster. The "official" tunnels were collapsing because they were being undermined by "private" tunnels. When you went down your secret passage, you came out into a whole labyrinth formed by passages belonging to "the others." Whole districts had started to crumble, compromising Bel-o-kan's very existence.

Mother had put a stop to it. No one was supposed to dig on their own account anymore, but how could a watch be kept on all the chambers?

The 56th female pushed aside a bit of gravel, revealing a dark opening. The 327th male examined the hiding place and pronounced it perfect. A third accomplice remained to be found. They came out and closed the entrance up again carefully. The 56th female emitted:

We'll take the first one who comes. Leave it to me.

They soon met someone, a big asexual soldier dragging along a hunk of butterfly. The female hailed her from a distance with emotive messages telling of a great threat to the Tribe. She handled the language of the emotions with a virtuoso subtlety that took the male's breath away, and the soldier immediately abandoned her prey to come and discuss the matter.

A big threat to the Tribe? Who, how, why, where?

The female explained succinctly the disaster that had befallen the first spring expedition. Her manner of expressing herself gave off a delicious fragrance. She already had the charm and charisma of a queen. The warrior was soon won over.

When do we leave? How many soldiers will we need to attack the dwarves?

She introduced herself. She was the 103,683rd asexual ant of the summer laying. With her big, glossy head, long mandibles, practically nonexistent eyes and short legs, she was a weighty ally. She was also a born enthusiast. The 56th female even had to check her ardor.

She told her there were spies within the Tribe itself, possibly mercenaries in the pay of the dwarves, whose mission was to prevent the Belokanians from solving the mystery of the secret weapon.

You can recognize them by their characteristic smell of rock. You have to act quickly.

You can count on me.

They then divided up the spheres of influence among them. The 327th male would strive to convince the nurses in the solarium, who were generally quite naive.

The 103,683rd asexual ant would try to bring back some soldiers. If she managed to make up a legion, that would be fantastic.

I'll be able to question the scouts, too, and see if anyone else can tell me about the dwarves' secret weapon.

As for the 56th female, she would visit the mushroom beds and greenfly sheds to look for strategic support.

They would report back there at 23°C-time.

Today, in the context of the series on *World Cultures*, the television was showing a report on Japanese costumes:

"The Japanese, an insular people, have been economically self-sufficient for centuries. For them, the world is divided into two: the Japanese and the others, the foreigners with their incomprehensible customs, barbarians they call *Gai jin*. The Japanese have always had a very nice sense of nationality. When a Japanese comes to live in Europe, for example, he is automatically excluded from the group. If he moves back a year later, his parents and family will no longer recognize him as one of them. Living among the *Gai jin* means becoming impregnated with the others' way of thinking and therefore becoming a *Gai jin*. Even his childhood friends will treat him like just another tourist."

Various Shinto temples and holy places filed across the screen. The voice-over resumed:

"Their view of life and death is different from ours.

The death of an individual is not very important here. What is worrying is the disappearance of a productive cell. To tame death, the Japanese like to cultivate the art of wrestling. Children are taught kendo at primary school."

Two combatants appeared in the middle of the screen dressed like the samurai of old. Their chests were covered in articulated black plates and they wore oval helmets on their heads decorated with two long feathers next to their ears. They flung themselves at one another, uttering warlike cries, then started clashing their long kendo swords.

There were more images. A man sitting on his heels was pointing a short sword at his stomach with both hands.

"Ritual suicide, *seppuku*, is another characteristic of Japanese culture. It's certainly difficult for us to understand."

"Not that television again. It's turning us into vegetables. We're all getting our heads stuffed with the same images. They don't know what they're talking about, anyway. Haven't you had enough of it yet?" exclaimed Jonathan, who had been back for a few hours.

"Leave him alone. It does him good. He hasn't been up to much since the dog died," said Lucie mechanically.

She stroked her son's hair.

"What's the matter, darling?"

"Sh, I'm trying to listen."

"Just a minute. That's no way to talk to us."

"No way to talk to *you*. Remember how little time you spend with him. It isn't surprising he's giving you the cold shoulder."

"Hey, Nicolas. Have you managed to make the four triangles with the matches?"

"No. It gets on my nerves. I'm trying to listen."

"Oh, well, if it gets on your nerves . . ."

Looking thoughtful, Jonathan started fiddling with the matches lying on the table.

"What a pity. It's educational."

Nicolas was not listening. His brain was plugged directly into the television. Jonathan went into his room.

"What are you doing?" asked Lucie, following him.

"You can see perfectly well what I'm doing. I'm getting ready to go back down."

"What? Oh no."

"I haven't any choice."

"Jonathan, tell me now, what is there down there you find so fascinating? I'm your wife, after all."

He did not answer. He was avoiding her eyes and he still had that nasty tic. Tired of arguing, she sighed.

"Have you killed the rats?"

"My presence alone is enough. They keep their distance. Otherwise I pull this on them."

He brandished a big kitchen knife that he had honed to a fine edge. Grabbing his halogen flashlight in the other hand, he went into the kitchen and over to the cellar door. On his back was a bag containing a good supply of provisions as well as his emergency locksmith's tools. He barely called out:

"Good-bye, Nicolas. Good-bye, Lucie."

Lucie did not know what to do. She seized Jonathan's arm.

"You can't leave like this. It's too easy. You must talk to me."

"For Heaven's sake."

"How can I get through to you? Since you went down into that damn cellar you haven't been the same. We've no money left and you've spent at least 5,000 francs on equipment and books about ants."

"I'm interested in locks and ants. I've a right to be."

"No, you haven't. Not when you've got a son and a wife to feed. If all the unemployment money goes on books about ants, I'm going to end up . . ."

"Getting a divorce? Is that what you're trying to say?"

She let go of his arm, exhausted.

"No."

He took her by the shoulders. His mouth twitched.

"You must have faith in me. I've got to see it through. I haven't taken leave of my senses."

"Haven't taken leave of your senses? Just look at you. You look like a zombie. Anybody'd think you were permanently running a temperature."

"My body's getting older but my head's getting younger."

"Jonathan, tell me what's going on down there."

"Fascinating things. You have to keep going farther and farther down if you want to be able to come up again one day. It's like a swimming pool. You have to go down to the bottom to be able to push off to come up again."

He broke into crazy laughter. Its sinister sound was still ringing from the spiral staircase thirty seconds later.

On the thirty-fifth floor, the fine covering of twigs produced a stained-glass window effect. The sun's rays sparkled as they passed through it, then fell like a rain of stars on the ground. This was the city's solarium, the "factory" producing Belokanian citizens.

It was baking hot there, 38°C, as was only to be expected. The solarium faced due south to catch the heat of the sun for as long as possible. Sometimes, under the catalytic effect of the twigs, the temperature rose to as high as 50°C.

Hundreds of legs were busying themselves. Nurses, the most numerous caste here, were piling up the eggs Mother laid. Twenty-four piles formed a heap and twelve heaps made a row. The rows stretched away into the distance. When a cloud cast a shadow, the nurses moved the piles of eggs. The youngest had to be kept nice and warm. "Moist heat for eggs, dry heat for cocoons" was an old ant recipe for healthy babies.

On the left, workers responsible for maintaining the temperature were piling up pieces of black wood to accumulate heat and fermented humus to produce it. Thanks to these two "radiators," the solarium remained at a constant temperature of between 25°C and 40°C, even when it was only 15°C outside.

Gunners were patrolling the area. If a woodpecker messed with them, there'd be trouble. . . .

On the right were older eggs, further advanced in the long metamorphosis from egg to adult. With time and the nurses' licking, the little eggs grew bigger and turned yellow. After one to seven weeks, they turned into golden-haired larvae. That, too, depended on the weather.

The nurses were concentrating hard, sparing neither antibiotic saliva nor attention. Not a speck of dirt must be allowed to sully the larvae. They were so fragile. Even conversational pheromones were kept to a strict minimum.

Help me carry them into the corner . . . Look out, your pile's going to fall over. . . .

A nurse was moving a larva twice her length, a gunner for sure. She put the "weapon" down in a corner and licked it.

At the center of this vast incubator were heaps of larvae on whose bodies the ten segments were beginning to show. They were howling to be fed, waving their heads and legs about and stretching their necks until the nurses let them have a little honeydew or insect meat.

After three weeks, when they had "matured" nicely, the larvae stopped eating and moving. They used this lethargic phase to prepare for the coming effort, gathering their energies to secrete the cocoons that would transform them into nymphs.

The nurses then carted the big bundles off to a nearby room filled with dry sand to absorb the moisture from the air. "Moist heat for eggs, dry heat for cocoons" could never be repeated often enough.

Inside this incubator, the cocoons turned from bluish-white to yellow to gray to brown, like the philosopher's stone but in reverse, while a miracle took place inside the shells. Everything changed, the nervous system, respiratory and digestive apparatus, sense organs and shell.

Once inside the incubator, the nymphs swelled within a few days as the eggs cooked and the big moment drew near. When a nymph was on the point of hatching, it was pulled aside, along with others in the same state. Nurses carefully pierced the veil of the cocoon, releasing an antenna or leg, until a kind of white ant was freed to tremble and sway. Its soft, clear chitin turned red after a few days, like that of all the Belokanians.

In the midst of this whirlwind of activity, 327th was unsure whom to address. He threw out a little scent to a nurse who was helping a newborn ant take its first steps.

Something serious is happening. The nurse did not even turn her head in his direction. She gave off a barely perceptible scent sentence:

Hush. Nothing is more serious than birth.

A gunner jostled him, hitting him gently with the clubs at the end of her antennae. *Tap, tap, tap.*

Stop bothering people. Move on.

His energy level was all wrong, the messages he emitted unconvincing. If only he had 56th's gift for communication! He tried again anyway with other nurses, but they ignored him completely. He ended up wondering whether his mission was really as important as he thought. Perhaps Mother had been right. Other tasks had priority. Perpetuating life rather than starting a war, for example.

While he was thinking this strange thought, a jet of formic acid grazed his antennae. A nurse had dropped the cocoon she was carrying and fired at him. Fortunately, she had not aimed properly.

He rushed to catch up with the terrorist but she had already darted off into the first nursery, knocking over a pile of eggs to block his way. The shells broke, letting out a transparent liquid.

She had destroyed some eggs! What had gotten into her? There was panic, with nurses running in all directions, anxious to protect the gestating generation.

Realizing he could not catch up with the fugitive, the 327th male tipped his abdomen under his thorax and took aim, but before he could fire she was struck down by a gunner who had seen her knock over the eggs.

A crowd formed around the charred body. When 327th bent his antennae over it, he was no longer in any doubt. It smelled of rock.

SOCIABILITY: In ants, as in human beings, sociability is predetermined. A newborn ant is too weak on its own to break the cocoon in which it is imprisoned. A human baby cannot even walk or feed itself on its own.

Ants and human beings are species designed to be assisted by those around them and cannot or will not learn on their own.

This dependence on adults is certainly a weakness but it sets in motion another process, the quest for knowledge. If adults can survive while the young cannot, the latter are obliged to ask their elders for knowledge from the start.

EDMOND WELLS,
ENCYCLOPEDIA OF RELATIVE AND ABSOLUTE KNOWLEDGE

On the twentieth floor of the basement the 56th female had not yet gotten as far as discussing the dwarves' secret weapon with the farmers. She was far too interested in what she could see to be able to emit anything whatsoever.

As the caste of females was especially precious, they spent their entire childhood in the princesses' quarters. All they knew of the world was often only a hundred or so corridors, and few of them had ventured below the tenth floor of the basement or above the tenth floor above ground level.

The 56th female had once tried to go and see the Great Outside her nurses had told her so much about, but sentries had turned her back. You could more or less camouflage your scents but not your long wings. The guards had warned her then that there were gigantic monsters outside. They ate little princesses who wanted to go out before the Festival of Rebirth. She had been torn between curiosity and dread ever since.

When she went down to the twentieth floor of the basement, she realized that before moving around in the wild Great Outside she still had lots of wonderful things to discover in her own city. She was now seeing the mushroom beds for the first time.

According to Belokanian mythology, the first mushroom beds were discovered during the Cereal War in the fifty thousandth millennium. An artillery commando had just laid siege to a termite city. They suddenly came to a room of colossal proportions. In the center, an enormous white cake was being endlessly polished by about a hundred termite workers.

They tasted it and found it delicious. It was like an entirely edible village. Prisoners confessed it was made of mushroom. Termites actually live only on cellulose, but they cannot digest it without the help of much rooms.

Ants, on the other hand, can digest cellulose perfectly well and do not need to have recourse to mushrooms. They nevertheless grasped the advantage of growing crops inside their cities: it would allow them to hold out during sieges and famines.

Nowadays, selected mushroom strains were grown in the big rooms on the twentieth floor of the basement of Bel-o-kan. Ants no longer used the same mushrooms as termites, and in Bel-o-kan they mostly grew agarics. A whole new technology based on agricultural activities had developed.

The 56th female circulated between the beds of the white garden. On one side, workers were preparing a bed in which mushrooms would grow. They were cutting leaves into small squares, which were then scraped, ground, kneaded and turned into patties. The leaf patties were arranged on a compost made from ant excrement (which was collected in basins kept for the purpose), then moistened with saliva and left for a time to do the work of germinating the mushrooms.

Patties that had already fermented were surrounded by balls of edible white filaments. Workers then watered them with their disinfectant saliva and cut away any bits that stuck out of the little white cones. If they had let the mushrooms grow, they would soon have split the room apart. From the filaments harvested by flat-mandibled workers, a tasty, nourishing flour was obtained.

Here, too, the workers' concentration was at its height. Not a single weed or parasitic fungus must be allowed to take advantage of the care they were lavishing.

It was in this rather unfavorable context that 56th tried to establish antenna contact with a gardener meticulously cutting up one of the white cones.

A grave danger is threatening the city. We need help. Will you join our work cell?

What kind of danger?

The dwarves have discovered a secret weapon with devastating effects. We must do something as quickly as possible.

The gardener placidly asked her what she thought of her mushroom, a fine agaric. The 56th female complimented her on it, and the gardener offered her a taste. The female bit into the white dough and immediately felt as if her esophagus had been set on fire. The agaric had been impregnated with myrmicacin, a deadly poison usually used in diluted form as a weed killer. The 56th female coughed and spat out the toxic food in time. The gardener let go of the mushroom and leapt at her thorax with her mandibles bared.

They rolled in the compost and dealt each other short, sharp blows on the head with their club antennae, trying to beat each other's brains out. *Crack! Crack! Crack!* Farmers separated them.

What's gotten into the pair of you?

The gardener managed to get away, but 56th opened her wings, gave a tremendous leap and flattened her to the ground. It was then that she identified a faint smell of rock. There was no doubt about it; it was her turn to stumble on a member of the incredible band of assassins.

She pinched her antennae.

Who are you? Why did you try to kill me? What's that smell of rock?

The other remained silent, so she twisted her antennae. The ant writhed in agony but did not answer. The 56th female was not the kind to hurt a sister cell, but she twisted the antennae still more.

The rock-scented ant stopped moving and entered voluntary catalepsy. Her heart had almost stopped beating and she would die before long. The 56th female cut off both her antennae in frustration but she was only wasting her energy on a corpse.

The workers surrounded her once more.

What's happening? What have you done to her?

The 56th female thought now was not the time to justify herself, it was better to get away, which she did by beating her wings. She was right. Something mind-boggling was going on. Some Tribe cells had gone mad.

DEEPER AND DEEPER

On the forty-fifth floor of the basement, the 103,683rd asexual ant made her way into the wrestling halls, low-ceilinged rooms where the soldiers exercised in readiness for the spring wars.

All around, warriors were fighting duels. The opponents first felt each other over to assess build and leg size, then circled, tested each other's flanks, pulled each other's hairs, threw each other scent challenges and provoked each other with the club ends of their antennae.

Finally, they flung themselves together with a clash of their shells. Each of them tried to grab hold of the other's thoracic joints. As soon as one of them managed it, the other tried to bite her knees. Their movements were jerky. They reared up on their hind legs, collapsed in a heap and rolled about furiously.

They usually held their grip, then suddenly struck another limb. They were careful, though. It was only a training exercise. Nothing got broken, no blood was spilled. The fight ended as soon as an ant was turned over and laid back its antennae in submission. The duels were quite realistic all the same. The combatants often stuck their claws in each other's eyes to get a grip and snapped their jaws on empty air.

Some way off, gunners seated on their abdomens were aiming and firing at bits of gravel five hundred heads away. The jets of acid often hit their targets.

An old warrior was teaching a novice that the outcome of the battle was decided before contact was made. The mandible or jet of acid only ratified a situation of dominance already recognized by the two opponents. Before the fray, there was inevitably one who had decided to win and one who consented to be beaten. It was simply a question of assigning the roles. Once they had been allocated, the winner could shoot a jet of acid and hit the bull's-eye without aiming while the loser could go all out with her mandibles without even succeeding in injuring her opponent. Only one piece of advice was worth giving: accept victory. It was all in the mind. Accept victory and nothing could withstand you.

Two duelists jostled the 103,683rd soldier. She shoved them away vigorously and went on her way. She was looking for the mercenaries' quarters, which had been set up below the arena where the fights took place. Soon she caught sight of the passage leading to it.

Their hall was even more vast than that of the legionaries. Admittedly, the mercenaries spent all their time in their exercise area. Their only reason for being there was war. All the peoples of the region, both subject and allied, rubbed shoulders there: yellow ants, red ants, black ants, glue-spitting ants, primitive ants with poisonous stings and even dwarves.

Yet again, it was the termites who had thought up the idea of feeding foreign populations so that they would fight beside them during invasions. The subtleties of diplomacy had led the ant cities to enter into alliances with termites against other ants. This had led the termites to an arresting thought: why not hire ant legions outright to live permanently in the termite hills? It was a revolutionary idea, and the ant armies had been quite surprised when they had to confront sisters of the same species fighting for the termites. The Myrmician civilization, so quick to adapt, had overplayed its hand this time.

The ants would gladly have responded by imitating their enemies and taking termite legions into their pay to fight the termites. But there was one major obstacle to their plan: the termites were absolute royalists. Their loyalty was flawless and they were incapable of fighting their own kind. Only ants, whose political regimes were as varied as their physiology, were capable of coming to terms with all the perverse implications of fighting as mercenaries.

Not that it really mattered. The great russet ant federations had been content to reinforce their armies with a large number of legions of foreign ants, all united under the one Belokanian scent banner.

The 103,683rd soldier approached the dwarf mercenaries and asked them if they had heard of the development of a secret weapon at Shi-gac-pou, a weapon capable of annihilating an entire expedition of twenty-eight russet ants in a flash. They replied that they had never seen or heard of anything so effective.

She questioned other mercenaries. A yellow ant claimed to have witnessed such a wonder. It was not a dwarf attack, however, only a rotten pear that had unexpectedly fallen from a tree. Everyone let out bubbly little pheromones of laughter. It was yellow ant humor.

The 103,683rd asexual ant went back up to a room in which some of her close colleagues were training. She knew them all individually. They listened to her carefully and believed her, and there were soon over thirty determined warriors in the group searching for the dwarves' secret weapon. If only the 327th male could have seen it!

Be careful. An organized band is trying to get rid of anyone who wants to know. They must be russet ant mercenaries working for the dwarves. You can identify them by their smell of rock.

For the sake of security, they decided to hold their first meeting in the very depths of the city in one of the rooms on the fiftieth floor. No one ever went down there. They should be able to organize their offensive without being disturbed.

But 103,683rd's body indicated a sudden acceleration in time. It was 23°C. She took her leave and hurried off to her meeting with 327th and 56th.

AESTHETICS: What could be more beautiful than an ant? Its lines are curved and pure and it is perfectly aerodynamic. Its whole body is designed so that each limb fits perfectly into its intended notch and each joint is a mechanical marvel. The plates fit together as if by computer-assisted design and there is never any creaking or friction. The triangular head slices through the air and the long, flexed legs give the body a low-slung, comfortable suspension. It is like an Italian sports car.

The claws allow it to walk on the ceiling and the eyes have 180° panoramic vision. The antennae pick up thousands of items of information that are invisible to us and their extremities can be used as hammers. The abdomen is full of pockets, sacs and compartments in which the insect can stock chemicals, while the mandibles cut, nip and seize. A formidable network of internal pipes allows it to lay down scent messages.

EDMOND WELLS,
ENCYCLOPEDIA OF RELATIVE AND ABSOLUTE KNOWLEDGE

Nicolas did not want to go to sleep. He was still watching television. The news had just ended with the announcement of the return of the *Marco Polo* probe. The conclusion: there was not the slightest trace of life in the neighboring solar systems. All the planets visited by the probe had offered only images of rocky deserts or liquid ammonia surfaces. There was no sign of moss, amoeba or bacteria.

"Supposing Dad's right?" Nicolas said to himself. "Supposing we're the only intelligent life-form in the whole universe?" It was obviously disappointing but might well be true.

After the news, there was a major report in the *World Cultures* series, this time devoted to the caste problem in India.

"The Hindus belong for life to the caste in which they were born. Each caste operates according to its own set of rules, a rigid code that no one can transgress without being banished from his own caste as well as all the others. To understand such behavior, we have to remember that—"

"It's one o'clock in the morning," butted in Lucie.

Nicolas had had a bellyful of images. Since the trouble with the cellar, he had put in a good four hours of television a day. It was his way of stopping thinking and being himself. His mother's voice brought him back to painful reality.

"Aren't you tired?"

"Where's Dad?"

"He's still in the cellar. You must go to sleep now."

"I can't sleep."

"Would you like me to tell you a story?"

"Oh, yes. A story. A lovely story."

Lucie accompanied him into his room and sat on the edge of the bed loosening her long red hair. She chose an old Hebrew tale.

"Once upon a time, there was a stonecutter who had had enough of wearing himself out digging away at the mountain under the burning rays of the sun. 'I'm fed up with living like this. It's exhausting to be always cutting, cutting the stone and then there's the sun, always the sun. Oh, how I'd love to be in its place. I'd be up there all-powerful and hot, flooding the world with my rays,' said the stonecutter to himself. His call was miraculously heard and the stonecutter was immediately turned into the sun. He was happy to see his wish granted. But, as he was having fun sending his rays everywhere, he noticed they were being stopped by the clouds. 'What's the point in being the sun if mere clouds can stop my rays,' he exclaimed. 'If clouds are stronger than the sun, I'd rather be a cloud.' So he became a cloud. He flew over the world, raced along and scattered rain, but suddenly the wind rose and dispersed the cloud. 'Ah, the wind can disperse clouds so it must be stronger. I want to be the wind,' he decided."

"And so he became the wind?"

"Yes, and he blew all over the world. He made storms, gales and typhoons. But suddenly he noticed a wall in his way. A very high, hard wall. A mountain. 'What's the point in being the wind if a mere mountain can stop me? It must be stronger,' he said to himself."

"And so he became the mountain."

"That's right. And just at that moment, he felt something hitting him. Something stronger than he was, digging away at him from the inside. It was a little stonecutter."

"Aaaah."

"Did you like the story?"

"Oh yes, Mom!"

"Are you sure you haven't seen better ones on television?"

"Oh no, Mom."

She laughed and hugged him.

"Do you think Dad's digging, too, Mom?"

"Maybe, who knows? He seems to think he's going to turn into something different if he goes down there, anyway."

"Doesn't he like it here?"

"No, Nick, he's ashamed of being out of work. He thinks it's better to be the sun. An underground sun."

"Dad thinks he's the king of the ants."

Lucie smiled.

"He'll get over it. He's like a little boy still. And little boys are always interested in anthills. Haven't you ever played with ants?"

"Yes, I have."

Lucie plumped up his pillow and kissed him.

"Time to go to sleep now. Good night, darling."

"Good night, Mom."

Lucie caught sight of the matches on the bedside table. He must have been working on making the four triangles. She went back into the living room and picked up the book on architecture that told the history of the house.

Many scientists had lived in it, most of them Protestants. Michael Servetus, for example, had lived here for a few years.

One passage in particular caught her attention. It said a tunnel had been dug during the Wars of Religion to allow the Protestants to flee from the city; it was an unusually long, deep tunnel.

The three insects made a triangle to take part in absolute communication. That way, they would not need to recount their adventures. They would know everything that had happened to them instantaneously, as if they were a single body that had divided into three in order to investigate better.

They linked antennae. Thoughts began to circulate and merge. It worked. Each brain acted as a transistor, conducting and enriching the electrical message it received. Three ant minds united in this way transcended the simple sum of their talents.

Suddenly the spell was broken; 103,683rd had picked up a parasitic smell. The walls had antennae. To be precise, two antennae, which were sticking out of the opening to 56th's chamber. Someone was listening to them.

Midnight. It was two days since Jonathan had gone back into the cellar and Lucie was walking up and down nervously in the living room. She went to check on Nicolas, who was sound asleep, and the matches suddenly caught her eye. At that moment, she had a sense that the beginning of an answer to the riddle of the cellar might lie in the riddle of the matches. How did you make four equilateral triangles out of six little sticks?

"You have to think about it differently. If you think about it in the usual way, you won't get anywhere," Jonathan had said. Picking up the matches, she went back into the living room, where she played with them for a long time. At last, exhausted with worry, she went to bed.

That night, she had a strange dream. First, she saw Uncle Edmond, or at least someone resembling her husband's description of him. He was standing in a kind of long line in the middle of a desert littered with loose stones. The line was surrounded by Mexican soldiers who were "keeping order." In the distance stood a dozen gallows on which people were being hanged. When they were quite dead, they were taken down and others were strung up. And the line moved forward.

Behind Edmond stood Jonathan, Lucie herself and a fat man wearing very small glasses. All the condemned people were chatting placidly, as if nothing was the matter.

When the noose was finally placed around their necks and the four of them were hanged side by side, they just waited and allowed it to happen. Uncle Edmond was the first to speak. His voice was husky.

"What are we doing here?"

"I don't know. We live. We were born, so we live for as long as possible. But I think it's nearly over now," replied Jonathan.

"Dear Jonathan, what a pessimist you are. Admittedly, we've been hanged and there are Mexican soldiers all around us, but this isn't the end, it's just one of the hazards of life. There has to be a way out of this situation, too. Are your hands tied very tight?"

They struggled with their bonds.

"Mine aren't," said the fat man. "I can undo my ropes."

And he did.

"Right, now set us free."

"How?"

"Swing until you reach my hands."

He twisted about until he turned himself into a living pendulum. When he had undone Edmond's ropes, they could all gradually be freed using the same technique.

Then Uncle Edmond said, "Do as I do!" and bounced from rope to rope, with little jerks of his neck, to the end of the gallows. The others copied him.

"We can't go any farther. There's nothing beyond this beam. They'll spot us."

"Look, there's a little hole in the beam. Let's go inside."

Then Edmond threw himself against the beam, shrank to a minute size and disappeared inside. So did Jonathan and the fat man. Lucie told herself she would never manage it but flung herself against the piece of wood and made her way into the hole.

There was a spiral staircase inside and they took the stairs four at a time. They could already hear the shouts of the soldiers, who had noticed their flight. *Los gringos, los gringos, cuidado!* There was a sound of boots and gunshots as the Mexicans gave chase.

The staircase opened onto a modern hotel room with a view of the sea. It was room eight. They went in and closed the door but it slammed and the vertical eight turned into a horizontal eight, the symbol of infinity. The room was luxurious and they felt safe from the roughneck soldiers there.

Just as everyone was breathing a sigh of relief, Lucie suddenly flew at her husband's throat, shouting, "Where's Nicolas? What about Nicolas?" She knocked him out with an old vase with a painting of Hercules as a child strangling the Serpent. Jonathan fell to the floor and turned into a shelled shrimp that squirmed about, looking quite ridiculous.

Uncle Edmond came forward.

"You're sorry, aren't you?"

"I don't understand."

"You will," he said, smiling. "Follow me."

He showed her to the balcony overlooking the sea and

clicked his fingers. Six lighted matches immediately came down from the sky and hung in a line above his hand.

"Listen carefully," he said. "We always think and perceive the world in the same old way. It's as if we only ever took photographs with a wide-angle lens. It's one view of reality but it's not the only one. YOU . . . HAVE . . . TO . . . THINK . . . DIFFERENTLY. Look."

The matches twirled in the air for an instant, then fell to the ground. They crawled together as if they were alive and made . . .

The next day, Lucie was quite feverish. She went out to buy a blowtorch and finally managed to burn off the lock. Just as she was about to cross the threshold of the cellar, Nicolas appeared in the kitchen, still half asleep.

"Where are you going, Mom?"

"I'm going to find your dad. He thinks he's a cloud and can cross mountains. I want to make sure he doesn't overdo things. I'll tell you all about it when I get back."

"Oh no, Mom, please don't go. I'll be all by myself."

"Don't worry, Nicolas, I'll be back. I won't be long. Wait for me here."

She shone a light into the mouth of the cellar. It was very dark inside.

Who's there?

The two antennae came farther in, revealing a head, a thorax and then an abdomen. It was the small rock-scented ant with the limp.

They were inclined to jump on her but looming behind her were the mandibles of a hundred or so heavily armed soldiers, all smelling of rock.

Let's get away down the secret passage! urged the 56th female.

She moved the bit of gravel aside, revealing her underground passage. Then, beating her wings, she rose to the ceiling and shot acid on the first intruders. Her two associates fled as a brutal suggestion went up from the troop of warriors.

Kill them!

The 56th female in turn dived into the hole, just avoiding the jets of acid. *Quick! After them!* Hundreds of legs raced after her. There were so many of them! Once inside the neck of the tunnel, they made noisy efforts to catch up with the trio.

With flattened antennae, the male, female and soldier went hell for leather down the passage, which was now anything but secret. They left the region of the females' quarters and made their way down to the lower floors. The narrow corridor soon forked. From then on, there were a good many crossroads, but 327th managed to find his way and dragged his companions of misfortune with him.

Suddenly, coming around a bend in the tunnel, they stumbled on a troop of soldiers racing toward them. It was incredible—the lame ant had already met up with them again. The Machiavellian insect certainly knew all the shortcuts.

The three runaways beat a retreat and got away. When they could at last stop to rest for a while, 103,683rd suggested it would be better not to fight on the others' ground as they could find their way around the tangle of corridors a little too easily.

When your enemy seems stronger than you, do something that defies his understanding. It was an old saying of the first Mother's that fitted their situation perfectly. The 56th male came up with the idea of camouflaging themselves inside a wall.

Before the rock-scented warriors could flush them out, they dug like mad at a side wall, attacking the earth and scooping it up with their mandibles. Their eyes and antennae became covered in it. Sometimes they swallowed it by the mouthful to go faster. When the cavity was deep enough, they curled up inside, rebuilt the wall and waited. Their pursuers arrived and went by at the double but they were back again before long, moving much more slowly this time and nosing about just on the other side of the thin wall.

They did not notice anything. It was impossible to stay there, though. The others were sure to detect some of their molecules in the end, so they dug. The 103,683rd soldier had the biggest mandibles and dug at the front. The male and female cleared away the sand by filling in behind them.

The killers had detected the maneuver. They sounded the walls, picked up their trail, and started to dig furiously. The three ants turned downward. It was difficult enough to follow anyone in that black mire anyway. Three corridors were begun and two blocked every second. It would have been impossible to draw a reliable map of the city under those circumstances. The only fixed landmarks were the dome and the stump.

The three ants penetrated slowly deeper into the body of the city. Sometimes they stumbled on a long creeper, one of the ivies planted by the farmer ants to stop the city from collapsing when it rained. Sometimes the earth grew harder and they banged their mandibles on stone. Then they had to make a detour.

When neither of the sexual ants could any longer detect the vibrations of their pursuers, the trio decided to stop. They had chanced on a stray air pocket in the heart of Bel-o-kan; it was a waterproof, odorless capsule no one knew about, a hollow desert island. No one would run them to earth there. They felt as safe as in the dark oval of their mother's abdomen.

The 56th female drummed on her partner's head with the ends of her antennae in an appeal for trophallaxis. The 327th male folded back his antennae in acceptance, then put his mouth to hers. He regurgitated a little of the greenfly honeydew the first guard had given him, and 56th immediately perked up. Then 103,683rd in turn drummed on her head. They cupped their labia together and 56th brought up some of the food she had only just stored away. Then the three of them caressed and massaged one another. Giving was so pleasant for an ant.

They had recovered their strength but knew they could not stay there indefinitely. They would run out of oxygen. No ant could survive forever without food, water, air and heat. Without these vital elements, they would eventually fall into a deathly sleep.

They put their antennae together.

What shall we do now?

The cohort of thirty warriors won over to our cause is waiting for us in a room on the fiftieth floor of the basement.

Let's go.

They started to dig again, finding their way by means of their Johnstonian organs, which were sensitive to the Earth's magnetic fields. Logically speaking, they must be somewhere between the granaries of the eighteenth floor of the basement and the mushroom beds of the twentieth floor. However, the lower they went, the colder it got. Night was falling and frost was penetrating deep into the earth. Their movements were slowing down. They finally stopped moving in a digging position and fell asleep while waiting for the temperature to rise.

"Jonathan, Jonathan, it's me, Lucie."

As she went deeper and deeper into a world of shadows, she felt fear creep up on her. The interminable descent down the spiral staircase had finally sent her into a trance, and she felt as if she were sinking deeper and deeper inside herself. Her throat had suddenly dried up, she felt a knot in the pit of her stomach, followed by heartburn, and now she had a stomachache.

Her knees and feet were still moving automatically. Would they soon stop working properly and start hurting, too? Would that be the end of her descent?

Images of her childhood came back to her: her authoritarian mother, who favored her darling brothers and always made her feel guilty . . . And her father, a broken man who was afraid of his wife and agreed with her whenever possible, giving in to her every whim. He had certainly been no hero.

These painful recollections gave way to a feeling of injustice toward Jonathan. She had reproached him about everything that reminded her of her father, and it was her constant reproaches that had inhibited him, broken him and little by little made him like her father. The cycle had thus begun all over again. Without even realizing it, she had re-created the thing she hated most, the relationship between her father and mother.

She must break the cycle. She was annoyed with herself for all the abuse she had heaped on her husband. She must make amends.

She went on turning and descending, recognizing that her guilt had freed her from the oppressive pain and fear. She was still turning and descending when she almost bumped into a door. It was an ordinary door but it was partly covered with inscriptions she did not stop to read. She turned the handle and the door opened without a sound.

The staircase continued on the other side. The only notable difference lay in the little veins of ferrous rock that appeared in the stone. The iron took on the hues of red ochre where it mixed with water from an underground stream that had infiltrated the walls.

She nevertheless felt that she had embarked on a new stage, and her torch suddenly lit up bloodstains at her feet. It must have been the location of Ouarzazate's death. The plucky little poodle had gotten this far, then. There were splashes of blood everywhere, but it was difficult to distinguish the traces of blood from the rusted iron on the walls.

Suddenly she heard a noise, a patter of feet, as if there were creatures walking toward her. The footsteps were nervous, as if the creatures were timid and dared not come too close. She stopped to search the darkness with her torch. When she saw what was making the noise, she let out an inhuman scream. But there, where she stood, no one was able to hear her.

• • •

Morning came for all Earth's creatures and they began their descent again. When they reached the thirty-sixth floor, 103,683rd thought it would be safe to go out. She knew the area well. The rock-scented warriors could not have followed them that far.

They emerged into low galleries that were completely deserted. Here and there on either side were holes, old granaries abandoned at least ten hibernations earlier. The ground was sticky. That was why the area had been thought insalubrious and had turned into one of the most ill-famed districts of Bel-o-kan.

It stank.

The male and the female did not feel very safe. They could detect hostile presences, antennae spying on them. The area must be full of parasitic insects and squatters.

They made their way through gloomy rooms and tunnels, their mandibles wide open. A shrill, chirping sound suddenly made them jump. *Creak, creak, creak* . . . The sounds did not vary in tone but formed a hypnotic dirge reverberating through the mud caverns.

According to the soldier, it was crickets singing love songs. The male and female were not totally reassured. Things had reached a pretty pass if crickets could flout federal troops in the very heart of the city.

The soldier, for her part, was not surprised. Had not the last Mother said, *It's better to consolidate your strong points than to try to control everything?* This was the result.

There were other noises, as if someone was digging very fast. Had the rock-scented warriors found them? No. Two paws shot out in front of them, their edges forming a kind of rake. They scooped up the earth and drew it back, propelling along an enormous black body.

They only hoped it was not a mole.

All three froze, their mandibles gaping.

It was a mole, a ball of black fur and white claws in a maelstrom of sand.

It seemed to be swimming between the layers of sediment like a frog in a lake. They were slapped and tossed and stuck to cakes of clay, but they escaped unharmed. The digging machine moved on. It had only been looking for worms. What it liked best was to bite their ganglions, paralyze them and store them live in its burrow.

The three ants scraped themselves down and went on their way, after again washing themselves methodically.

When they entered a high, narrow passage, the soldier-guide let out a warning scent and pointed to the ceiling. It was covered in red bugs with black spots. Rove beetles!

The insects were three heads (nine millimeters) long and looked as if they had angry faces drawn on their backs. They usually fed on the clammy flesh of dead insects and occasionally on that of live ones.

One of them immediately dropped on the trio, but before it could reach the ground, 103,683rd tipped her abdomen under her thorax and shot it with a jet of formic acid. By the time it landed, it had turned into hot jam.

They hastily ate it, then crossed the room before another of the monsters could fall on them.

INTELLIGENCE: I started on the experiments proper in January 1958. My first topic was intelligence. Are ants intelligent?

To find out, I confronted an average-sized, asexual russet ant (Formica rufa) with the following problem. I put a lump of hardened honey at the bottom of a hole and blocked the hole with a twig. It was not a very heavy twig but it was very long and it was stuck in firmly. The ant would normally have enlarged the hole to get by but it was made in rigid plastic, which it could not pierce.

Day one: the ant jerked the twig, raised it a little, let it go, then raised it again.

Day two: as before. The ant also tried to slash the base of the twig but without success.

Day three: as before. It seemed to have gone off along the wrong line of reasoning and to have persevered in it because it was incapable of imagining any other. This proved its lack of intelligence.

Day four: as before.

Day five: as before.

Day six: on waking this morning, I found that the twig had been removed from the hole. It must have happened during the night.

EDMOND WELLS,
ENCYCLOPEDIA OF RELATIVE AND ABSOLUTE KNOWLEDGE

The galleries they came to next were partially blocked. The cold, dry earth hung in clumps from the roof, retained by white roots. Occasionally, it broke off and came crashing down. This was known as "indoor hail." The only way to protect yourself from it was to be extra vigilant and jump aside at the least scent of a rockfall.

The three ants moved forward, their abdomens close to the ground, their antennae laid back and their legs wide apart. The soldier seemed to know precisely where she was taking them. The ground grew damp again and there was a sickening smell in the air. It was the smell of something alive, the smell of an animal.

The 327th male stopped. He could not be sure but one of the walls seemed to have moved surreptitiously. He went up to the suspicious part of the wall and it trembled again, as if the outline of a mouth were appearing on it. He moved back. This time, it was too small to be a mole. The mouth changed into a spiral and a protuberance formed at its center, then shot out and threw itself on him.

The male let out an olfactory scream.

An earthworm! He severed it with a bite of his mandibles, but the walls around them began to ooze with the wriggling creatures. Soon there were so many of them it was like being inside a bird's intestines.

One of the earthworms decided to wrap itself around the female's thorax. With a quick snap of her mandibles, she cut it into several sections that snaked off in different directions. Other worms joined in and curled themselves around their legs and heads. They really could not stand it when the worms touched their antennae. The three of them took aim together and fired acid at the harmless creatures. In the end, the ground was littered with bits of ochre flesh hopping about defiantly.

They galloped away.

When they had recovered their wits, 103,683rd showed them a new series of corridors to go down. The farther they went, the worse the smell got and the more used to it they became. You can grow accustomed to anything. The soldier pointed to a wall and explained that that was where they had to dig.

These are the old compost lavatories. The meeting place is just next door. We like to meet here because it's nice and quiet.

They passed through the wall and came out into a big room smelling of excrement on the other side.

The thirty soldiers who had rallied to their cause were indeed waiting for them there, but you would have had to be good at jigsaw puzzles to talk to them. They were in pieces and their heads were often quite a long way from their thoraxes.

They inspected the macabre room, aghast. Who could have killed them there, at the very foot of Bel-o-kan?

It must have been something that came from below, emitted the 327th male.

I don't think so, replied the 56th female, who nevertheless suggested he dig down through the soil.

As he drove in his jaws, it hurt. Beneath them, there was rock.

A huge granite rock, specified 103,683rd a little later. *It's the bottom of the city, its hard floor. It's thick. Very thick. And wide. Very wide. No one has ever got to the end of it.*

It could have been the bottom of the world for all they knew. Then they noticed a strange smell. Something had just come into the room, something they liked very much. No, not a Tribe ant, but a lomechusa beetle.

When she was no more than a larva, 56th had heard Mother speak of this insect:

Once you've tasted lomechusa nectar, there's nothing quite like it. It satisfies every desire and destroys the strongest will.

It really did suspend pain, fear and intelligence, and ants fortunate enough to survive their supplier were irresistibly driven to leave the city to look for further doses. They could not eat or rest and walked until they dropped. If they could not find a lomechusa, they went into withdrawal, attached themselves to a blade of grass and allowed themselves to die.

One day when she was still a child, 56th had asked why they allowed such pests to enter the city, when termites and bees massacred them without pity. Mother had replied that there were two ways of dealing with a problem. You either avoided it or you took it on board. The second way was not necessarily any the worse. In the right doses or mixed with other substances, lomechusa secretions made excellent medicines.

The 327th male was the first to go forward. Captivated by the beauty of the lomechusa's aromas, he licked the hairs of its abdomen, which were oozing hallucinogenic juices. With its two long hairs, the abdomen bore a disturbing resemblance to an ant's head with its two antennae.

The 56th female also rushed forward but did not have time to start her treat. A jet of acid whistled through the air; 103,683rd had aimed and fired. The burned lomechusa writhed in agony.

The soldier made a sober comment on her action:

It isn't normal to find these insects so deep down. Lomechusas can't dig. Someone must have brought it

*here on purpose to stop us from going any farther. We'll
find something here.*

The other two felt sheepish. They could only admire
their friend's perspicacity. The three of them spent a
long time looking. They moved bits of gravel aside and
sniffed every corner of the room. There were few clues to
go on, but they finally detected a familiar musty smell,
the faint rock scent of the assassins. It was barely perceptible, just two or three molecules, but that was enough.
It was coming from under a little rock. They toppled it
over and revealed yet another secret passage.

Only this one had one very important characteristic:
instead of being dug in earth or wood, it was excavated
out of the living granite. No mandible could have made
an impression on anything so hard.

The corridor was quite wide but they made their way
down it cautiously. After going a short way, they came
on a vast room full of food: flour, honey, seeds and meat
of various kinds. There were surprising quantities of it,
enough to feed the city for five hibernations, and it was
all giving off the same smell of rock as the warriors pursuing them.

How could such a well-filled granary have been built
there in secret? And with a lomechusa to block the entrance, too! That little bit of information had never done
the rounds of the Tribe's antennae.

They treated themselves to generous helpings of food,
then put their antennae together to take stock. The mystery was thickening. The secret weapon that had wiped
out the first expedition, the strange-smelling warriors attacking them on all sides, the lomechusa and the food
hidden under the floor of the city could not all be the
work of a group of mercenary spies working for the
dwarves. Unless they were extremely well organized.

The 327th male and his partners did not have time to
pursue their reflections. *Pom pom pompom, pom pom
pompom!* Up above, the workers were drumming on the
ground with the ends of their abdomens. Something serious was happening. It was the second phase of the alert.

They could not ignore the call. Their legs automatically turned them around. Moved by an irresistible force, their bodies were already on their way to join the rest of the Tribe.

The ant with the limp, who had been following them from a distance, breathed a sigh of relief. Phew! They had not discovered anything.

When neither his mother nor his father came back up out of the cellar, Nicolas at last made up his mind to inform the police. It was a starving, red-eyed child who turned up at the police station to explain that his parents had disappeared into the cellar and had probably been eaten by rats or ants. Two dumbfounded policemen followed close on his heels as he made his way back to the basement of number three, rue des Sybarites.

INTELLIGENCE (cont.): I have set up the experiment again, this time using a video camera.

Subject: another ant of the same species and from the same nest.

Day one: she pulls, pushes and bites the twig without success.

Day two: as before.

Day three: she gets the knack, pulls a little, wedges the twig by putting her abdomen in the hole and puffing it out, then lowers her grip and starts again. By fits and starts, she slowly gets the twig out.

So that was how it was done.

EDMOND WELLS,
ENCYCLOPEDIA OF RELATIVE AND ABSOLUTE KNOWLEDGE

The alert had been caused by an extraordinary event. La-chola-kan, the most westerly daughter city, had been attacked by legions of dwarf ants.

So they were at it again.

War was now inevitable.

The survivors who had managed to get through the

blockade set up by the Shigaepouyans had an incredible tale to tell. This is what they said happened:

At 17°C-time, a long acacia branch had come up to the main entrance of La-chola-kan. It had been an abnormally mobile branch and it had suddenly plunged into the opening, wrecking it as it turned.

The sentries had then made a sortie to attack the unidentified digging object but had all been wiped out. After that, they had all stayed safe inside and waited for the branch to cease its ravages, but it had gone on and on.

It had ripped the dome open as if it were a rosebud and poked about in the corridors. Even though the soldiers had bombarded it with everything they had, the acid had not stopped it.

The Lacholakanians had been paralyzed with fear. It had stopped in the end, though, and they had had 2°C-time respite before the dwarf legions arrived at the charge.

The smashed daughter city had found it hard to resist the first attack and had counted its losses in tens of thousands. Those who had escaped had finally taken refuge in their pine stump. They were managing to withstand the siege but would not be able to survive for very long. They were running out of food, and the fighting had already reached the wooden arteries of the Forbidden City.

Since La-chola-kan was a member of the Federation, Bel-o-kan and all the neighboring daughter cities were duty-bound to go to its aid. The end of the first accounts of the tragedy had not even reached their antennae before action stations were declared. There was no more talk of rest and reconstruction now. The first spring war had begun.

As the 327th male, 56th female and 103,683rd soldier hurriedly made their way back up, they were surrounded by bustling ants.

The nurses were taking the eggs, larvae and pupae

down to the forty-third floor of the basement; the green-fly milkmaids were hiding their cattle in the depths of the city; and the farmers were preparing stocks of chopped food to serve as combat rations. In the halls of the military castes, the gunners were filling their abdomens to the brim with formic acid, the shearers were sharpening their mandibles, and the mercenaries were forming up into compact legions. The males and females were withdrawing to their quarters.

They could not attack at once, it was too cold. But tomorrow morning at first light, war would rage.

Up on the dome, the temperature regulation vents were being closed. The city of Bel-o-kan was contracting its pores, pulling in its claws and clenching its teeth, ready to bite.

The fatter of the two policemen put his arm around the boy's shoulders.

"So you really think they're in there, do you?"

The child looked exasperated and pulled away without answering. Inspector Galin leaned over the stairs and shouted a ridiculous "Hello, there," but only the echo answered.

"It seems very deep," he said. "We can't go down like this. We need some equipment."

Superintendent Bilsheim laid a pudgy finger to his lips and looked concerned.

"Of course. Of course."

"I'll go and get the fire brigade," said Inspector Galin.

"All right, and while you're doing that, I'll question the kid."

The superintendent pointed to the melted lock.

"Did your mother do that?"

"Yes."

"You've got a pretty clever mother, then. I don't know many women who could open a reinforced door with a blowtorch . . . and I don't know any who could unblock a sink."

Nicolas was in no mood for jokes.

"She wanted to go and find Dad."

"Yes, of course. I'm sorry. How long have they been down there now?"

"Two days."

Bilsheim scratched his nose.

"And why did your father go down, do you know?"

"In the beginning, it was to go and look for the dog. Afterwards, we don't know. He bought loads of sheets of metal and took them down and then he bought lots of books about ants."

"Ants? Of course, of course."

Somewhat at a loss, Superintendent Bilsheim confined himself to nodding and murmuring "Of course" a few more times. The case was getting off to a bad start. He could not get a feel for it. It was not the first time he had had to deal with a "special" case. You might even have said they handed all the lousy cases over to him systematically, probably because he was good at making lunatics think they had at last found someone who understood them.

It was a gift he had been born with. Even when he was little, his classmates came to him with all their weird ideas. He just shook his head knowingly, gazed at them intently and said, "Of course." It worked every time. Things just got complicated if you tried to make up long, involved sentences for the benefit of others, and Bilsheim had noticed that the simple words "Of course" were quite sufficient. It was one of the mysteries of human communication.

It was odder still that the young Bilsheim, who hardly ever uttered a word, had earned the reputation of being an excellent speaker at school. He was even asked to make end-of-year speeches.

He might have become a psychiatrist but he had a thing about uniforms, and a white coat did not really fit the bill. It was all to do with "keeping up standards," and the police and army were the ones for that.

When he joined the police, his gift was soon spotted by

his superiors. They off-loaded all the "baffling cases" onto him systematically. Most of the time, he did not solve them, but at least he dealt with them and that was something.

"Ah, and then there are the matches."

"What about the matches?"

"You have to make four triangles out of six matches to find the solution."

"What solution?"

"The 'new way of thinking.' The different 'logic' Dad used to talk about."

"Of course."

This time, the boy rebelled.

"There's no 'of course' about it. You have to find the shape that makes four triangles. The ants, Uncle Edmond and the matches are all linked."

"Uncle Edmond? Who's Uncle Edmond?"

Nicolas perked up.

"He's the one who wrote the *Encyclopedia of Relative and Absolute Knowledge*. But he's dead. Maybe it was the rats. It was the rats who killed Ouarzazate."

Superintendent Bilsheim sighed. It was appalling. What was this scrap of a kid going to turn into when he grew up? An alcoholic at the very least. At last Inspector Galin arrived with the fire brigade. Bilsheim looked at him with pride. He was a good partner, Galin. A bit of a pervert, too. He actually got a kick out of cases involving weirdos. The weirder, the better.

The understanding Bilsheim and the enthusiastic Galin together made up the unofficial squad that dealt with the nutty cases no one else wanted. They had already been sent out on the case of the little old lady who got eaten by her cats, the prostitute who stifled her clients with her tongue, and the pork butchers' head shrinker.

"Right then," said Galin. "You stay here, Chief. We'll dive in and bring them back for you on inflatable stretchers."

• • •

In her nuptial chamber, Mother had stopped laying. She raised a single antenna and asked to be left alone. Her servants disappeared.

Belo-kiu-kiuni, the living genitals of the city, was disturbed.

No, she was not afraid of war. She had already won and lost a good fifty of them. It was something else that was worrying her, the affair of the secret weapon. The turning acacia branch that had ripped off the dome. And she had not forgotten, either, the 327th male's eyewitness account of the twenty-eight warriors who had died without even having taken up the firing position. Could she risk not taking that extraordinary information into account?

Not anymore.

But what was she to do?

Belo-kiu-kiuni remembered another occasion when she had had to confront an incomprehensible secret weapon. It had been during the wars against the termites of the south. One fine day they had announced to her that a squadron of a hundred and twenty soldiers had been "immobilized," if not destroyed.

There had been utter panic. They had thought that they would never again be able to vanquish the termites and that their enemies had taken a decisive technological lead.

They had sent out spies and discovered that the termites had come up with a caste of glue-throwing gunners, the nasutitermes, capable of hurling a sticky substance that gummed up the legs and jaws of soldiers two hundred heads away.

The Federation had given it great thought and come up with a means of countering them by advancing under the cover of dead leaves. That led to the famous Battle of Dead Leaves, which the Belokanian troops had won.

This time, however, the adversaries were no longer lumbering termites but dwarves whose vivacity and intelligence had already beaten them on several occasions. Besides, the secret weapon seemed to be particularly destructive.

She fiddled nervously with her antennae.

What exactly did she know about the dwarves?

A great deal and very little.

They had arrived in the region a hundred years before. In the beginning, there had been just a few scouts so small they did not seem to be a cause for concern. Then the caravans of dwarves had arrived, bringing their eggs and food reserves with them. They had spent their first night under the root of the big pine.

In the morning, half of them had been wiped out by a starving hedgehog. The survivors had gone away to the north, where they had set up a bivouac not far from the black ants.

In the Federation, they had told themselves it was between the black ants and them. Some of them had even felt guilty about leaving the puny creatures to act as fodder for the big black ants.

However, the dwarf ants had not been massacred. They could be seen up there daily, carrying twigs and little beetles. What could no longer be seen, on the other hand, were the big black ants.

They still did not know what had happened, but the Belokanian scouts reported that the dwarves now occupied the whole of the black ant nest. The news was received with fatalism and even humor. *It serves those black ants right for being so pretentious*, went the scent in the corridors. And anyway, such trifling little ants were not about to worry the powerful Federation.

However, after the black ants, it was one of the beehives in the dog rose that was occupied by the dwarves. Then the last termite hill of the north and the red stinging ants' nest in turn passed under the dwarves' banner.

The refugees who flooded into Bel-o-kan and swelled the throng of mercenaries related that the dwarves had avant-garde combat strategies. For example, they infected water supply points by pouring poison from rare flowers into them.

They were still not seriously alarmed, though. And it had taken the fall of the city of Niziu-ni-kan the previous year in 2°C-time to make them realize at last that they were dealing with formidable adversaries.

But if the russet ants had underestimated the dwarves, the dwarves had not judged the russet ants at their full worth. Niziu-ni-kan was a very small city but it had links with the entire Federation. The day after the dwarf victory, two hundred and forty legions of one thousand two hundred soldiers each came to wake them up with a fanfare. The outcome of the battle was certain, but that did not prevent the dwarves from fighting fiercely—and it took the federal troops a whole day to enter the liberated city.

They then discovered that the dwarves had installed not one but two hundred queens in Niziu-ni-kan. It came as quite a shock.

ARMY OF AGGRESSION: **Ants are the only social insects to maintain an army of aggression.**

Termites and bees, two less-refined royalist and loyalist species, only use their soldiers to defend the city or protect workers far from the nest. It is relatively rare for a termite hill or beehive to set out on a territorial conquest, but it is not unknown.

EDMOND WELLS,
ENCYCLOPEDIA OF RELATIVE AND ABSOLUTE KNOWLEDGE

The dwarf queens who had been taken prisoner recounted the history and customs of the dwarves. It was an extraordinary tale.

Many years before, according to them, the dwarves lived in another country, billions of heads away.

That country was very different from the Federation forest. Sweet-tasting, brightly colored fruit grew to an enormous size and there was no winter and no hibernation. It was a land of plenty, where the dwarves had built the "old" Shi-gae-pou, a city itself stemming from a very old dynasty. The nest was built at the foot of an oleander bush.

One day, both the oleander and the surrounding sand were torn from the ground and laid in a wooden box. The dwarves tried to escape from the box but it had been placed inside something gigantic and very hard. When they reached the structure's frontiers, they found only water, salt water, stretching as far as the eye could see.

Many dwarves drowned trying to return to the land of their ancestors, but the majority decided they would just have to survive inside the vast, hard structure surrounded by salt water. It went on for days and days.

Thanks to their Johnstonian organs, they could tell that they were moving at great speed over a phenomenal distance.

We crossed about a hundred of the Earth's magnetic barriers. Where was it leading us? Here. We were disembarked along with the oleander. We discovered this world and its exotic flora and fauna.

It turned out to be a disappointing change of scenery. The flowers, fruit and insects were smaller and less colorful. They had left behind a country of reds, yellows and blues for one of greens, blacks and browns. They had exchanged a fluorescent world for a pastel one.

Then there was the winter and the cold, which brought everything to a standstill. Before, they had not even known the cold existed, and the only thing that obliged them to rest was the heat.

First, the dwarves devised various means of combatting the cold. Their two most effective methods were stuffing themselves with sugar and smearing themselves with snails' fatty slime.

For the sugar, they collected the fructose of strawberries, blackberries and cherries, and for the fat, they virtually exterminated the region's snails.

They had really surprising practices in other respects: they had no winged males and females and no nuptial flight. The females made love and laid their eggs at home, under the ground, so that each dwarf city possessed not one but several hundred laying queens. This gave them a real advantage: as well as having a much higher birth rate than the russet ants, they were far less vulnerable. For if killing the queen was sufficient to slay a russet ant city, a dwarf city could be resurrected as long as a single laying female remained.

And that was not all. The dwarves had a different approach to territorial conquest. On their nuptial flights, the russet ants landed as far as possible from their native nests and afterward linked themselves to the dispersed Federation empire by trails. The dwarves, on the other hand, moved forward from their central cities centimeter by centimeter.

Even their small size was an advantage. They needed very few calories to achieve quite a high level of mental and physical activity. It had been possible to measure the speed of their reactions during a heavy rainfall. The russet ants were still having difficulty getting their herds of greenflies and the last of their eggs out of the flooded corridors several hours after the dwarves had finished building a nest in a crevice in the bark of the big pine tree, moving all their treasures into it.

Belo-kiu-kiuni shook herself to dispel her worried thoughts. She laid two eggs, the eggs of warriors. The nurses were not there to collect them, and she felt hungry, so she ate them greedily. They were excellent protein.

She teased her carnivorous plant but her preoccupations were already uppermost in her mind again. The only means of countering the secret weapon would be to invent another even more powerful and terrible. The russet ants had discovered formic acid, the shield leaf and glue traps in succession. They just needed to think of something else. A weapon that would stupefy the dwarves, something even worse than their destructive branch.

She left her chamber, met some soldiers and spoke to them. She suggested setting up think tanks on the topic of finding a secret weapon to combat their secret weapon. The Tribe responded favorably to her stimulus. Small groups of three to five soldiers and workers formed on all sides. By linking their antennae in a triangle or pentagon, they took part in hundreds of absolute communications.

"Watch out, I'm stopping," said Galin, anxious not to get shoved in the back by eight firemen.

"It's so dark in here. Pass me a more powerful flashlight."

He turned around and someone handed him a big flashlight. The firemen looked apprehensive even though they were wearing leather jackets and helmets. If only he had thought of putting on something more suitable for an expedition of this kind than a sports jacket.

The pencil of light from the flashlight swept across an inscription engraved at head height on the arched roof.

> *Examine yourself,*
> *If you have not purified yourself assiduously*
> *The chemical wedding will harm you*
> *Woe betide those who linger there.*
> *Let the light-minded refrain.*
>
> *Ars Magna*

"Have you seen this?" asked a fireman.

"It's just an old inscription," said Inspector Galin soothingly.

"It sounds like witchcraft."

"It seems pretty deep, in any case."

"The meaning of the sentence?"

"No, the staircase. It looks as if it goes down thousands of steps."

They started to go down again. They must have been a hundred and fifty meters below street level and still the staircase was spiraling down. Like a spiral of DNA. It almost made them dizzy. Down they went, deeper and deeper.

"It could go on like this indefinitely," grumbled a fireman. "We didn't come prepared for potholing."

"I thought we just had to get someone out of a cellar," said another, who was carrying the inflatable stretcher. "My wife was expecting me home for dinner at eight. It's after ten now. She must be really pleased."

Galin took his troops in hand.

"Listen, men, we're closer to the bottom than the top now. Just keep going a little longer. We're not going to give up halfway."

In actual fact, they had not gone a tenth of the way.

After several hours of AC at a temperature of nearly 15°C, a group of yellow mercenary ants came up with an idea that was soon recognized as the best by all the other nerve centers.

Bel-o-kan happened to have a large number of mercenaries of a rather special species, the "seed-crushers." They had large heads and long trenchant mandibles, which allowed them to crack open even the hardest seeds, but with their short legs under heavy bodies, they were not very effective in combat.

So what was the point in their dragging themselves with difficulty to the site of a confrontation if they could do little damage there? The russet ants had ended up confining them to household tasks such as cutting up big twigs.

According to the yellow ants, there was a way in which these clumsy, great oafs could be transformed into superlative war machines. They just needed to be carried by six agile little workers.

Guiding their "living legs" by smell, the seed-crushers could sweep down on their adversaries at high speed and cut them to pieces with their long mandibles.

A few soldiers stuffed with sugar carried out tests in the solarium. Six ants lifted up a seed-crusher and ran along, trying to synchronize their steps. It seemed to work very well.

The city of Bel-o-kan had just invented the tank.

They never came back up.

The next day, the newspaper headlines read: FONTAINE-BLEAU—EIGHT FIREMEN AND A POLICE INSPECTOR DISAPPEAR MYSTERIOUSLY IN A CELLAR.

In the purple light of dawn, the dwarf ants surrounding the Forbidden City of La-chola-kan prepared to do battle. The russet ants isolated in the stump were starving and exhausted. They could not hold out much longer.

When the fighting started again, the dwarves captured two more crossroads after long artillery duels with acid. The wood eaten away by the shots spewed forth the bodies of the besieged soldiers.

The last russet survivors were finished. The dwarves advanced through the city, hardly slowed by the sharpshooters hidden in cracks in the ceilings.

The nuptial chamber could not be far away now. Inside it, Queen Lacho-la-kiuni was beginning to slow down her heartbeats. All was lost.

But the dwarf troops who had advanced the farthest suddenly picked up an alarm scent. Something was happening outside. They retraced their steps.

Up on Poppy Hill, overlooking the city, thousands of black dots could be made out amid the red flowers.

The Belokanians had at last made up their minds to attack. That would teach them. The dwarves sent mercenary messenger-gnats to warn the central city.

All the gnats bore the same pheromone:

They're attacking. Send reinforcements from the east to catch them in a pincer movement. Prepare the secret weapon.

• • • •

The warmth of the first ray of sunlight, filtering through a cloud, sparked off the decision to move into the attack. It was three minutes past eight. The Belokanian legions swept down the slope, skirting blades of grass and leaping over bits of gravel. There were millions of soldiers running along with their mandibles wide open. It was quite impressive.

But the dwarves were not afraid. They had foreseen these tactics. On the previous day they had dug holes in the ground in staggered rows and had hidden inside them with only their mandibles poking out, their bodies protected by the sand.

This line of dwarves at once broke the russet ant assault. The Federation troops fenced uselessly with enemies who presented them with nothing but strong points. There was no way of cutting off their legs or ripping out their abdomens.

It was then that the bulk of the infantry of Shi-gae-pou, stationed nearby under cover of a circle of devil's boletuses, launched a counteroffensive that caught the russet ants in a pincer movement.

If there were millions of Belokanians, the Shigae-pouyans could be counted in the tens of millions. There were at least five dwarf soldiers for every russet ant, not to mention the warriors crouched in individual holes who chopped off the heads of all who passed within reach of their mandibles.

The fight quickly turned to the disadvantage of the smaller army. Hammered by the dwarves, who suddenly appeared on all sides, the federal lines broke.

At thirty-six minutes past nine, the russet ants beat a retreat. The dwarves were already raising victory scents. Their stratagem had worked perfectly. They had not even needed to use the secret weapon. They pursued the runaway army and considered the siege of La-chola-kan as good as over.

But with their short legs, the dwarves had to take ten steps for every one a russet ant took. They got out of breath climbing Poppy Hill. It was exactly what the Federation strategists had counted on. The sole purpose of the first charge had been to bring the dwarf troops out of their basin to confront them on the slope.

The russet ants reached the crest of the hill with the dwarf legions in disorderly pursuit. At the top, a forest of thorns suddenly reared up. It was the seed-crushers' giant claws. They brandished them so that they glittered in the sunlight, then lowered them level with the ground and swooped down on the dwarves. Seed-crushers, dwarf-crushers!

They took the dwarves completely by surprise. The stupefied Shigaepouyans, their antennae stiff with fright, were mown down. Taking advantage of the slope, the seed-crushers rushed at the enemy lines and broke them. The six workers under each of them really put their hearts into it. They were the war machines' Caterpillar tracks. Thanks to the perfectly synchronized antenna communication between the turrets and wheels, the thirty-six-legged animals with two giant mandibles moved with ease among their hordes of enemies.

The dwarves scarcely had time to glimpse the juggernauts before they fell on them by the hundred; smashing, flattening and crushing them. Their hypertrophied mandibles plunged into the crowd, browsed and rose again full of bloody legs and heads, which they snapped like straw.

There was total panic. The terrified dwarves bumped into, trampled and sometimes even killed one another.

Having raked through the dwarf ranks, the Belokanian tanks were carried beyond them by their momentum. They eventually came to a halt and immediately started back up the slope for a fresh sweep, still perfectly in line. The survivors would have liked to preempt them, but a second front of tanks appeared above them and started to descend on them.

The two parallel columns met and corpses piled up in front of each tank. It was a massacre.

The Lacholakanians, watching the battle from a distance, came out to encourage their sisters. Their initial surprise gave way to enthusiasm and they sent up pheromones of joy. It was a victory of technology and intelligence. The spirit of the Federation had never been so clearly expressed.

However, Shi-gae-pou had not played out its hand yet. It still had its secret weapon. Normally speaking, this had been designed to dislodge recalcitrant siege defenders, but faced with the nasty turn taken by the fighting, the dwarves decided to go for broke.

The secret weapon took the form of russet ant heads shot through with a brown plant.

A few days earlier, the dwarf ants had discovered the body of a Federation explorer. Her body had burst from the pressure of a parasitic fungus, alternaria. The dwarf researchers had analyzed what had happened and found that the parasitic fungus produced volatile spores. These stuck to the ant's cuirass, ate into it and invaded it, then grew until it exploded.

What a weapon!

And guaranteed safe to use, for although the spores stuck to the russet ants' chitin, they could not get a hold on the shells of the dwarves. Quite simply, this was because the dwarves felt the cold and were in the habit of smearing themselves with snail's slime, and that gave them protection from alternaria.

The Belokanians might have invented the tank, but the Shigaepouyans had discovered bacteriological warfare.

An infantry battalion moved off carrying three hundred infected russet heads collected after the first battle of La-chola-kan.

They threw them into the thick of their enemies. The seed-crushers and their bearers sneezed from the deadly dust. When they saw that their cuirasses were coated with it, they lost their heads. The bearers dropped their burdens and the seed-crushers, once more helpless, panicked and violently took it out on other seed-crushers. It was a rout.

At about ten o'clock, a sudden cold spell separated the combatants. It was impossible to fight in an icy wind. The dwarf troops took advantage of the lull in the fighting to make good their escape, and the russet ant tanks climbed up the slope again with some difficulty.

Both sides counted the wounded and dead. The provisional toll showed heavy losses, and each army longed to tip the battle in its favor.

The Belokanians had recognized the alternaria spores and decided to put all the soldiers hit by the fungus out of their misery.

At that point, spies came running and told them they could protect themselves from the bacteriological weapon by smearing themselves with snail's slime. No sooner said than done. They decided to sacrifice three snails (which were becoming more and more difficult to find), and everyone protected themselves from the scourge.

They made antenna contact, and the russet ant strategists decided they could no longer attack with tanks alone. In the new plan of attack, the tanks would occupy the center but a hundred and twenty legions of regular infantry and sixty legions of foreign infantry would be deployed on the wings.

Morale rose again.

ARGENTINE ANT: **The Argentine Ants** (Iridomyrmex humilis) *arrived in France in 1920. In all likelihood, they were transported in tubs of oleanders destined to brighten up the roads of the Côte d'Azur.*

They were first reported in 1866 in Buenos Aires (hence the name by which they are commonly known). In 1891, they were found in the United States, in New Orleans.

Hidden in the litter of exported Argentine horses, they next arrived in South Africa in 1908, in Chile in 1910, in Australia in 1917 and in France in 1920.

The species is distinguished not only by its minute size, which makes it a pygmy compared with other ants, but also by the intelligence and warlike aggressiveness that are in fact its main characteristics.

No sooner were the Argentine ants established in the south of France than they waged war on all the indigenous species and defeated them.

In 1960, they crossed the Pyrenees and made their way as far south as Barcelona. In 1967, they spanned the Alps and poured down as far as Rome. Then, in the 1970s, the Iridomyrmex *began to move north again. They are thought to have bridged the Loire one hot summer in the late 1990s. The invaders, whose combat strategies equalled those of Caesar or Napoleon, then found themselves up against two rather tougher species: the federative russets (in the south and east of the Parisian region) and the pharaoh ants (to the north and east of Paris).*

EDMOND WELLS,
ENCYCLOPEDIA OF RELATIVE AND ABSOLUTE KNOWLEDGE

The Battle of Poppy Hill was not yet won. At ten-thirteen, Shi-gae-pou decided to send reinforcements. Two hundred and forty legions of reservists joined the survivors of the first charge. When told about the tanks, they put their antennae together for an AC. There must be some way to outwit the terrible machines.

At about ten-thirty, a worker made a suggestion:

The seed-crusher ants owe their mobility to the six ants who carry them. All we have to do is cut off their "living legs."

Someone came up with another idea:

The weak point of their machines is their inability to turn around quickly. We can make use of this handicap. All we have to do is form up into compact squares. When the machines charge, we just move aside to let them pass without resisting. Then, while they are still being carried forward by their momentum, we strike them from the rear. They won't have time to turn around.

And a third:

The movement of the legs is synchronized by antenna contact, as we've seen. All we have to do is jump up and cut off the seed-crushers' antennae so they can no longer direct their bearers.

All the ideas met with approval, and the dwarves began to work out their new battle plan.

SUFFERING: **Are ants capable of suffering? A priori, no. Their nervous system is not designed for it. Where there is no nerve, there can be no pain message. This may explain why parts of ants sometimes go on "living" independently of the rest of their bodies for a very long time.**

The absence of pain leads to a whole new world of science fiction. Without pain, there can be no fear, perhaps no consciousness of "self" even. Entomologists have long been inclined to the theory that ants are incapable of suffering and that this is the basis of their society's cohesion. Which explains everything and nothing. The idea has the added advantage of removing any scruples we might have about killing them.

I, personally, should be very scared of an animal that could not feel pain.

But the whole concept is wrong. A decapitated ant emits a particular smell, the smell of fear. Something therefore happens. The ant does not have a nerve impulse but it does have a chemical impulse. It knows one of its parts is missing and it suffers. It suffers in its own way, which is no doubt very different from ours, but it does suffer.

EDMOND WELLS,
ENCYCLOPEDIA OF RELATIVE AND ABSOLUTE KNOWLEDGE

The battle resumed at eleven-forty-seven. A long, compact line of dwarf soldiers slowly climbed to the assault of Poppy Hill.

The tanks appeared between the flowers. At a given signal, they hurtled down the slope. The legions of russets and their mercenaries paraded on the flanks, ready to finish the juggernauts' work.

Soon the two armies were only a hundred heads apart . . . then fifty . . . twenty . . . ten. The first seed-crusher had barely made contact when something quite unexpected happened. Gaps suddenly opened up in the dense line of Shigaepouyans as they formed squares.

Each tank saw the enemy evaporate and found itself facing an empty corridor. None reacted by zigzagging to engage the dwarves. Instead, their mandibles snapped on empty air and their thirty-six legs raced on uselessly.

A bitter smell spread:

Cut their legs off!

Dwarves immediately dived under the tanks and killed the bearers, then withdrew again on the double in order not to be crushed by the weight of the seed-crushers as they collapsed.

Others boldly threw themselves between the double rows of three bearers and punctured the proffered bellies with a single mandible. Liquid flowed from them, and the seed-crushers' reservoir of life poured out on the ground.

Yet others scaled the juggernauts, cut off their antennae and jumped from them while they were still moving.

The tanks collapsed one after another. The seed-crushers without bearers dragged themselves along like bedridden invalids and were finished off without difficulty.

It was a terrifying sight. The bodies of seed-crushers with their bellies split open were being carried along by their six workers, still unaware of what had happened. Seed-crushers deprived of antennae found their "wheels" going off in different directions and tearing them apart.

Such a debacle sounded the knell of tank technology, no doubt one of many great inventions that disappeared from ant history because the means of countering it had been found too soon.

The russet legions and their mercenaries who were flanking the tank front were left without cover. They had been placed there to pick up the pieces and found themselves obliged to charge desperately, but the massacre of the seed-crushers had been managed so efficiently that the dwarf squares had already closed again. The Belokanians had scarcely made contact with a side before they were drawn in and hacked to pieces by thousands of greedy mandibles.

The russets and their roughnecks could only beat a retreat. Having regrouped on the crest of the hill, they watched the dwarves slowly climbing back up to the assault, still in compact squares. It was a frightening sight.

To gain time, the biggest soldiers fetched bits of gravel and rolled them from the top, but the avalanche barely slowed the dwarf advance. They were vigilant and moved out of the way as the blocks went by, then immediately resumed their places. Few were crushed.

The Belokanian legions desperately tried to find a way out. Some warriors suggested a return to the old combat techniques. Why not simply let fly with the artillery? For though acid killed as many friends as foes in the fray and little use had been made of it since the outbreak of hostilities, it should give very good results against the dense squares of dwarves.

The gunners quickly took up position, wedged firmly on their four hind legs with their abdomens thrust forward. They could thus pivot from left to right and up and down for the best aim.

The dwarves, now just below them, saw the tips of thousands of abdomens jutting over the crest of the hill but did not immediately realize the implications. They increased their pace, gathering speed to cross the last few centimeters of bank.

Attack! Close ranks!

A single order rang out in the opposing camp:

Fire!

The trained abdomens sprayed their burning venom on the dwarf squares. *Whoosh, whoosh, whoosh.* The yellow jets whistled through the air and lashed the first line of assailants full in the face.

Their antennae melted first and trickled down on their heads. Then the poison spread to their cuirasses, liquefying them as if they were made of plastic.

The tormented bodies sank to the ground and formed a slight barrier over which the dwarves behind them stumbled. They rallied furiously and threw themselves all the more fiercely into the assault on the crest.

At the top, a second line of russet gunners had taken over from the first.

Fire!

The squares broke up, but the dwarves continued to advance, trampling the limp, dead bodies underfoot.

A third line of gunners appeared, joined by the glue-spitters.

Fire!

This time, the dwarf squares came apart completely. Whole groups struggled in the pools of glue. The dwarves tried to counterattack by lining up a row of gunners themselves. They advanced backward toward the summit and fired without aiming as they were unable to wedge themselves against the slope.

Fire! emitted the dwarves in turn.

But their short abdomens fired only droplets of acid. Even when they reached their objectives, their jets only irritated the enemy's shells without piercing them.

Fire!

The drops of acid from the two camps crossed in the air, occasionally cancelling one another. In view of the poor results they had obtained, the Shigaepouyans gave up using their artillery, believing they could win by sticking to the tactic of compact infantry squares.

Close ranks!

Fire! replied the russets, whose artillery was still achieving marvels, and the acid and glue spurted yet again.

Despite the effectiveness of the firing, the dwarves

reached the top of Poppy Hill, where their silhouettes formed a black frieze thirsty for revenge.

Rush. Rage. Ravage.

There were no more fancy maneuvers now. The russet gunners could no longer squirt acid, the dwarf squares could no longer remain compact.

Swarm. Storm. Stampede.

Everyone got mixed up, milled about, got into line, ran, turned, fled, charged, dispersed, came together again, instigated small attacks, pushed, dragged, dashed, collapsed, reassured, spat, supported and screamed blue murder. Death was on everyone's mind. They took one another's measure, struggled and clashed mandibles. They ran over live bodies and motionless ones. Each russet ant had at least three furious dwarves on top of her, but the russet ants were three times bigger, so the duels were fought with roughly equal weapons.

Hand to hand, amid scent cries and mists of bitter pheromones.

Millions of mandibles locked together, whether pointed, notched or serrated, in the shape of sabers or flat claws, single-edged or double-edged, smeared with poisonous saliva, glue or blood. The ground trembled.

Hand to hand.

Antennae weighted with little arrows whipped the air to keep the enemy at a distance. Claws struck like little irritating reeds. Catch. Confuse. Confound.

You caught the other by the mandibles, antennae, head, thorax, abdomen, legs, knees, elbows, joint brushes, a breach in the shell, a notch in the chitin or an eye.

Then the bodies toppled over and rolled in the damp earth. Some dwarves scaled an idle poppy and let themselves fall with outstretched claws on top of a well-built russet ant. They pierced her back and stabbed her through the heart.

Hand to hand.

Mandibles scratched smooth armor.

A skillful russet ant used her antennae like javelins, propelling them simultaneously. She transfixed the heads of a dozen enemies without even stopping to wipe her blood-smeared stalks.

Hand to hand. To the death.

There were soon so many severed antennae and legs on the ground that it was like walking on a carpet of pine needles.

The survivors of La-chola-kan came running up and plunged into the fray as if there were not enough dead already.

Overcome by the sheer numbers of her minute assailants, a russet ant panicked, curved her abdomen up, sprayed herself with formic acid and killed her enemies and herself at the same time. They all melted like wax.

Some way off, another warrior pulled off her enemy's head with a sharp tug at the very moment that her own was torn off.

The 103,683rd soldier had seen the first lines of dwarves sweeping down on her. With a few dozen colleagues from her subcaste, she had managed to form a triangle that had spread terror among the knots of dwarves. The triangle had finally broken and she now stood alone facing five Shigaepouyans already steeped in the blood of her beloved sisters.

They bit her all over and she did her best to bite back, automatically remembering the advice thrown at her in the practice arena by the old warrior:

The outcome of the fight is decided before the first blow is struck. The mandible or jet of acid only confirms what both combatants already know. It's all in the mind. If you accept victory, nothing can withstand you.

It might work with one enemy. But what were you to do when there were five of them? At present, she could tell that there were at least two of them who wanted to win at all costs, the dwarf who was methodically cutting through the joint of her thorax and the one who was tearing off her left hind leg. She felt a burst of energy surge through her and struggled to stick her antenna under one of their necks like a stiletto, making the other let go by stunning it with a blow from the flat of her mandible.

Meanwhile, some dwarves had returned to throw dozens of alternaria-infected heads into the thick of the battle. But they were all protected by snails' slime, so the spores fluttered about and slid over their cuirasses before falling sluggishly to the ground. It really was an unlucky day for new weapons. They had all found a response.

At three o'clock in the afternoon, the fighting was at its height. Gusts of oleic acid, the characteristic smell given off by drying ant corpses, filled the air. At half past four, the russet and dwarf ants who still had at least two legs to stand on were still crossing swords beneath the poppies. The fighting finally stopped at five o'clock, when a clap of thunder announced imminent rain. It was as if the heavens had had enough of so much violence. Unless, of course, it was just the April showers arriving late.

The survivors and wounded withdrew. The final toll was five million dead, including four million dwarves. La-chola-kan was liberated.

As far as the eye could see, the ground was littered with contorted corpses, holed cuirasses and sinister parts that sometimes stirred with a last breath of life. Everything was covered in a film of transparent blood and there were puddles of yellow acid everywhere.

A few dwarves stuck in a pool of glue were struggling to return to their city, but some birds arrived to peck them up quickly before the rain came down.

Lightning lit up the dark gray clouds and sparkled off a few tank carcasses with their mandibles still raised to pierce the distant sky. When the actors had left the scene, the rain washed it clean.

• • •

She was speaking with her mouth full.

"Bilsheim?"

"Hello?"

"Grumf, grumf. What kind of fool do you take me for, Bilsheim? Have you seen the papers? Is this Inspector Galin one of yours? He's that irritating little prick who tried to get familiar with me in the first few days, isn't he?"

It was Solange Doumeng, director of the Criminal Investigation Department, who was speaking.

"Er, yes, I think so."

"I told you to boot him out, and now I discover he's a posthumous star. You must be completely out of your mind. Whatever possessed you to send anyone so inexperienced on such a serious case?"

"Galin isn't inexperienced, he's an excellent cop. But I think we underestimated the seriousness of the case."

"Good cops solve cases, bad ones find excuses."

"There are cases which even the best of us—"

"There are cases which even the worst of you have a duty to solve. Fishing a couple out of a cellar falls into that category."

"I'm sorry, but—"

"You know where you can stick your excuses, don't you? Kindly do me the honor of going back down into the cellar and getting everyone out. Your hero Galin deserves a Christian burial. And I want an article praising our department by the end of the month."

"What about?"

"The whole business. And I want you to keep your mouth shut. You're not to make hay with the press until the case is sewn up. You can take six policemen and the latest equipment, if you like. That's all."

"And if . . ."

"If you foul up, you can count on me to spoil your retirement."

She hung up.

Superintendent Bilsheim could handle every other lu-

natic but her. He therefore resigned himself to working
out a plan of descent.

WHEN A MAN: **When a man is frightened, happy or en-
raged, his endocrine glands produce hormones that influence his body alone. They work in isolation. His
heart beats faster, he sweats, makes faces, shouts or
cries. No one else is affected. Others look at him without sympathizing, or sympathize because their intellect
tells them to.**

    **When an ant is frightened, happy or enraged, its hor-
mones circulate inside its body, leave it and enter the
bodies of others. Thanks to the pherohormones, or
pheromones, millions of individuals shout or cry at the
same time. It must be an incredible feeling to live the
experiences of others and make them feel everything
one feels oneself.**

EDMOND WELLS,
ENCYCLOPEDIA OF RELATIVE AND ABSOLUTE KNOWLEDGE

There was jubilation in every city in the Federation. An
abundance of sweet trophallaxis was offered to the exhausted combatants. However, there were no heroes. Everyone had done his or her job, whether well or badly
was of little importance. Everything began again from
zero at the end of missions.

They licked their wounds. A few naive youngsters
held in their mandibles one, two or three of their legs,
which had been torn off in combat and which they had
miraculously recovered. They had to be told they could
not be stuck back on.

In the big wrestling hall on the forty-fifth floor of the
basement, soldiers reenacted the successive episodes of
the Battle of Poppy Hill for the benefit of those who had
not been there. One half played the part of the dwarves,
the other the russet ants.

They mimed the attack of the Forbidden City of La-
chola-kan, the russet charge, the struggle with the infected heads, the false flight, the entry of the tanks, their

rout by the dwarf squares, the assault on the hill, the lines of gunners, and the final fray.

There were many workers there. They commented on each scene of the reenactment. One point in particular held their attention, probably because their caste had played a part in it. They felt the tank technique should not be abandoned but used more intelligently and not just in frontal charges.

The 103,683rd soldier had got off lightly compared with the other survivors of the battle. She had only lost a leg, a trifle when you have six of them at your disposal. It was hardly worth mentioning. The 56th female and the 327th male, who had been unable to take part in the war, drew her aside and made antenna contact.

Has there been any trouble here?

No, the rock-scented warriors all took part in the fighting. We stayed inside the Forbidden City in case the dwarves got this far. How about out there? Did you see the secret weapon?

No.

What do you mean, no? There's been talk of a mobile acacia branch.

The 103,683rd soldier explained that the only new weapon they had been confronted with was the dreadful alternaria but that they had found a means of protecting themselves against it.

It can't be that that killed the first expedition, remarked the male. Alternaria takes a long time to kill. Besides, he was certain none of the bodies he had examined bore the least trace of the deadly spores. *What now?*

Disconcerted, they decided to prolong their AC. They really needed to think things through. Ideas and opinions bubbled up again.

Why had the dwarves not resorted to the weapon that had wiped out the twenty-eight explorers? After all, they had done everything in their power to win. If they had possessed such a weapon, they would not have hesitated to use it. But what if they did not possess it? It might be pure chance that they always arrived before or after the secret weapon had struck.

This hypothesis seemed to square fairly well with the attack on La-chola-kan. As for the first expedition, traces of dwarf passport scents might very well have been left to lead the Tribe down the wrong trail. In whose interest would it have been to do that? If the dwarves were not responsible for all the trouble, then who was? It must be the other implacable adversary, the hereditary enemy, the termites.

There was nothing fantastic about the suspicion. For some time, isolated soldiers from the big termite hill in the east had been crossing the river and stepping up their incursions into federal hunting grounds. Yes, it was surely the termites. They had managed to set the dwarf ants and the russet ants at one another's throats. That way, they got rid of both without striking a blow. With their enemies much weakened, all they had to do was grab the anthills.

And the rock-scented warriors? Mere mercenary spies in the service of the termites.

The more their common thought circulated among their three brains, the more subtle it became and the more convinced they were that it was the termites of the east who possessed the mysterious secret weapon.

But they were disturbed and torn from their conference by the Tribe's general scents. The city had decided to turn the interwar period to good account by bringing forward the Festival of Rebirth. It would take place the next day.

All castes to their places! Males and females, to the gourd rooms to fill up with sugar! Gunners, reload your abdomens in the organic chemistry rooms!

Before leaving her companions, the 103,683rd soldier let out a pheromone:

Enjoy your copulation! Don't worry, I'll carry on with the investigation. When you're in the sky, I'll set out for the big termite hill of the east.

They had hardly separated before the two killers appeared, the big brute and the little one with the limp. They scraped the walls and recovered the volatile pheromones of the conversation.

After the tragic failure of Inspector Galin and the firemen, Nicolas had been put in an orphanage only a few hundred meters from the rue des Sybarites.

Besides actual orphans, children who had been rejected or abused by their parents were also packed in there, the human race being one of the few species capable of abandoning or mistreating its offspring. Young human beings spent testing years there, being kicked around for their own good. As they grew up they grew tough, and most of them ended up joining the regular army.

The first day, Nicolas stayed on the balcony, looking dejectedly at the forest. The next day, though, he went back to his safe television routine. The set was installed in the dining room and the supervisors were glad to get rid of the troublemakers by letting them watch it mindlessly for hours. In the evening, Jean and Philippe, two other orphans, questioned him in the dormitory.

"What's up with you?"

"Nothing."

"Come on, tell. No one comes here just like that at your age. How old are you, anyway?"

"I know why he's here. His parents are supposed to have been eaten by ants."

"Bullshit. Who told you that?"

"Someone, so there. We'll tell you who if you tell us what happened to your parents."

"Get lost."

Jean, the bigger of the two, grabbed Nicolas by the shoulders while Philippe twisted his arm behind his back.

Nicolas lashed out and pulled himself free, then chopped Jean over the back of the neck (as he had seen done on television in a Chinese film). Jean started to cough, and Philippe returned to the attack by trying to strangle Nicolas, who elbowed him in the stomach. He doubled up on his knees while Nicolas, freed of his aggressor, once more confronted Jean by spitting in his face. Jean dived and bit Nicolas's calf until it bled. Then the three young human beings rolled under the beds, fighting like fishwives until Nicolas was finally bested.

"Tell us what happened to your parents or we'll make you eat ants."

Jean had thought that up in the heat of the moment and was quite pleased with himself. He kept the new boy pinned to the ground while Philippe ran to look for a few ants, which were quite plentiful thereabouts, and came back and waved them in his face.

"Look, here are some nice fat ones."

(As if ants, whose bodies are enclosed in a rigid shell, could have layers of fat.)

Then he pinched Nicolas's nose to make him open his mouth and disgustedly threw in three young workers who really had better things to do. Nicolas had the surprise of his life. They were delicious.

The others were surprised not to see him spit out the disgusting food and decided to taste it in their turn.

The honeydew gourd room was one of Bel-o-kan's most recent innovations. The "gourd" technology had been borrowed from the ants of the south, who, since the weather had turned hot, were moving farther and farther north.

The Federation had discovered their gourd room in the course of a victorious war against them. War was not only the best source of inventions but also the best means of circulating them throughout the insect world.

At the time, the Belokanian legionaries were horrified to see workers condemned to spend their entire lives hanging upside down from the ceiling with abdomens so swollen they were twice the size of a queen's. The southerners explained that the ants who had been sacrificed in this way were living honey pots capable of keeping incredible quantities of nectar, dew or honeydew fresh.

In short, they only had to take the idea of the "social crop" to the extreme to end up with that of tanker ants or living refrigerators. When the tips of their abdomens were stimulated, they delivered their precious juice drop by drop or in streams.

By this means, the southerners survived the great droughts that struck the tropical regions. When they migrated, they took their gourds with them and never suffered from dehydration on the journey. To judge from what they said, the honey pots were as precious as eggs.

The Belokanians, therefore, pirated the gourd technique but saw it mainly as a hygienic way of stocking and conserving large quantities of food.

All the males and females in the city made their way to the gourd room to fill up on sugar and water. Stretching in front of each living honey pot was a long line of winged supplicants. The 327th male and the 56th female quenched their thirst together, then went their separate ways.

When all the males and females and all the gunners had passed by, the tanker ants were empty. An army of workers hurried to restock them with nectar, dew and honeydew until the sagging abdomens were once more like little shining balls.

Nicolas, Philippe and Jean were caught by one of the orphanage supervisors and punished together. They naturally became the best of friends.

More often than not, they were to be found glued to the dining room television. The only thing worth watching was an episode of the never-ending series *Extraterrestrial and Proud of It*.

They squealed and nudged one another when they saw it was about astronauts landing on a planet inhabited by giant ants.

"Hello, we are Earthmen."

"Hello, we are giant ants from the planet Zgu."

It was a fairly typical story. The giant ants were telepathic and sent messages to the Earthmen ordering them to kill each other, but the last survivor realized what had happened and set fire to the enemy city.

The children were satisfied with this ending and decided to go and eat some sweet ants but, oddly enough, the ones they caught no longer tasted like sweets. They were smaller and tasted sour, like concentrated lemon. *Ugh!*

It would all take place at midday at the highest point of the city.

At the first dawn warmth the gunners had settled themselves in the protective recesses that formed a kind of crown around the summit. With their anuses aimed at the sky, they were ready to put up an antiaircraft barrage against the birds who would be sure to show up before long. Some of them wedged their abdomens between twigs to cushion the recoil so that they could fire two or three salvos in the same direction without losing their aim.

The 56th female was in her chamber. She was being tended by asexual ants, who were smearing her wings with protective saliva. *Have you ever been to the Great Outside?* The workers did not answer. Of course they had already been outside, but what was the point of telling her. "It's full of trees and grass outside?" In a few minutes, the potential queen would be able to see for herself. It was just like a female to want to find out what the world was like by antenna contact.

The workers nevertheless titivated her. They pulled her legs to limber them up. They made her contort her body to crack her thoracic and abdominal joints. They checked that her social crop was stuffed full of honeydew by pressing it to make her disgorge a drop. The syrup should enable her to keep up several hours' continuous flight.

There. She was ready. It was time to move on to the next.

Perfumed and bedecked in all her finery, the princess left the females' quarters. The 327th male had not been mistaken. She really was a great beauty.

She could hardly lift her wings. They had grown amazingly fast in the last few days. They were now so long and heavy that they trailed on the ground like a bridal veil.

Other females emerged from other corridors. In the company of hundreds of these virgins, 56th made her way through the small branches of the dome. Some snagged themselves on twigs in their elation and their four wings got scratched, pierced or torn off completely. These unfortunates did not go any higher. They would not be able to take off anyway. They went back down to the fifth floor in frustration. Like the dwarf princesses, they would never know the flight of love but were condemned to reproduce in an enclosed room on the ground.

The 56th female herself was still intact. She skipped from twig to twig, taking care not to fall or damage her delicate wings.

One of her sisters walking by her side solicited antenna contact. She was wondering what the reproductive males they had heard so much about could be like. Drones or flies, perhaps?

The 56th female did not answer. She was thinking about 327th again and about the mysterious secret weapon. It was all over. No more work group. Not for the two of them, anyway. The whole affair was henceforth in the claws of 103,683rd.

She recalled with nostalgia all the events that had taken place.

The fugitive male who had landed in her chamber without any passports.

Their first absolute communication.

Their meeting with 103,683rd.

The rock-scented killers.

The race through the depths of the city.

The hiding place full of bodies that could have been those of their "legion."

The lomechusa beetle.

The secret passage in the granite.

As she walked along, she went over her memories and called herself fortunate. None of her sisters had had such adventures before even leaving the city.

Madness could not be the explanation when so many individuals were involved. Could they be mercenaries spying on behalf of the termites? No, that could not be right. There were too many of them and they were too well organized.

And anyway, one thing still did not fit: why were there food reserves under the floor of the city? To feed the spies? No, there was enough there to feed millions, and though there were a lot of them, there were not millions.

And that surprising lomechusa beetle. It was a surface animal. It could not possibly have gone down to the fiftieth floor of the basement on its own and had therefore been taken there. But as soon as you got near the insect, you were captivated by its scent. Quite a large group would have been needed to wrap the monster in supple leaves and take it below discreetly.

The more she thought about it, the more she realized that that suggested considerable means. In fact, when you looked closely, it was just as if part of the Tribe had a secret it was guarding fiercely from the rest.

Her head was spinning with strange ideas. She stopped, and the other ants thought she was faint with emotion before the nuptial flight. It sometimes happened; females were so sensitive. She put her antennae to her mouth and repeated quickly: the wiping out of the first expedition, the secret weapon, the killing of the thirty legionaries, the lomechusa beetle, the secret passage in the granite and the food reserves.

Suddenly everything fell into place. That was it! She rushed back against the stream. If only it were not too late!

EDUCATION: The education of ants includes the following stages:

—From the first to the tenth day, most young ants tend the laying queen. They look after her, lick her and caress her. She in return bathes them in her nourishing, disinfectant saliva.

—From the eleventh to the twentieth day, workers are allowed to look after the cocoons.

—From the twenty-first to the thirtieth day, they guard and feed their younger sisters.

—From the thirty-first to the fortieth day, they devote themselves to domestic duties and highway maintenance while continuing to tend the queen mother and nymphs.

—The fortieth day is an important date. The workers are considered experienced enough to leave the city.

—From the fortieth to the fiftieth day, they act as greenfly keepers and milkers.

—From the fiftieth to the last day of their lives, they may engage in the most exciting occupation for a city ant: hunting and exploring unknown territory.

N.B. From the eleventh day onward, males and females are not obliged to work. More often than not, they remain idly consigned to their quarters until the day of the nuptial flight.

EDMOND WELLS,
ENCYCLOPEDIA OF RELATIVE AND ABSOLUTE KNOWLEDGE

The 327th male was also preparing himself. Within the field of his antennae, the other males were talking of nothing but females. Very few of them had ever seen one or caught more than fleeting glimpses of them in the corridors of the Forbidden City. Many were fantasizing and imagining their heady, erotic perfumes.

One of the princes claimed to have taken part in trophallaxis with a female. Her honeydew tasted of birch sap and her sexual hormones smelled like cut daffodils.

The others silently envied him.

The 327th, who really had tasted the honeydew of a female (and what a female!), knew that it was no different from that of workers or honey pots. However, he did not join in the conversation.

A risqué idea had occurred to him. He very much wanted to supply the 56th female with the sperms she needed to build her future city. If only he could find her. What a pity they had not sorted out a pheromone of recognition so that they could meet up in the crowd.

When the 56th female reached the males' room, there was surprise all around. It was quite against the Tribe's rules for her to go there. Males and females were not supposed to see one another until the time of the nuptial flight. They did not copulate in the corridors like dwarves.

The princes, who had so badly wanted to know what females were like, now knew. As a body, they gave out hostile scents signifying that she should not stay in the room.

She nevertheless carried on through the tumultuous preparations, jostling everyone and dispersing her pheromones for all she was worth.

327th. 327th. Where are you, 327th?

The princes made no bones about telling her that that was no way to go about choosing her partner. She must be patient and trust to chance. She must show a little more modesty.

The 56th female found her companion in the end, though. He was dead. His head had been bitten off by mandibles.

TOTALITARIANISM: People are interested in ants because they think they have managed to create a successful totalitarian system. Certainly, the impression we get from the outside is that everyone in the anthill works, everyone is obedient, everyone is ready to sacrifice and everyone is the same. And for the time being, all human totalitarian systems have failed.

That is why we thought of copying social insects (like Napoleon, whose emblem was the bee). The pheromones that flood the anthill with global information have an equivalent in the planetary television of today. There is a widespread belief that if the best is made available to all, one day we will end up with a perfect human race.

That is not the way of things.

Nature, with all due respect to Mr. Darwin, does not evolve in the direction of the supremacy of the best (according to which criteria, anyway?). Nature draws its strength from diversity. It needs all kinds of people— good, bad, mad, desperate, sporty, bed-ridden, hunchbacked, hare-lipped, happy, sad, intelligent, stupid, selfish, generous, small, tall, black, yellow, red and white. It needs all religions, philosophies, fanaticisms and wisdom. The only danger is that any one species may be eliminated by another.

In the past, fields of maize artificially designed by men and made up of clones of the best heads (the ones that need least water, are most frost-resistant or produce the best grains) have suddenly succumbed to trivial infections while fields of wild maize made up of several different strains, each with its own peculiar strengths and weaknesses, have always managed to survive epidemics.

Nature hates uniformity and loves diversity. It is in this perhaps that its essential genius lies.

EDMOND WELLS,
ENCYCLOPEDIA OF RELATIVE AND ABSOLUTE KNOWLEDGE

Slowly and despondently, she made her way back to the dome. In a corridor near the females' quarters, her infrared simple eyes made out two silhouettes. It was the rock-scented assassins, the big one and the little one with the limp!

As they came straight for her, 56th whirred her wings

and leaped at the neck of the lame one. They soon immobilized her, but instead of executing her, they subjected her to antenna contact.

The female was furious. She asked them why they had killed the 327th male, since he would have died anyway during the flight. Why had they assassinated him?

The two killers tried to reason with her. According to them, some things could not wait, whatever the cost. It was sometimes necessary to do things that were frowned upon if you wanted the Tribe to go on working normally. She must not be naive. The unity of Bel-o-kan had to be earned and, if necessary, taken care of.

So they weren't spies, then?

No, they weren't spies. They even claimed to be the chief guardians of the Tribe's safety and welfare.

The princess screamed pheromones of rage. They had killed 327th because he was a threat to the Tribe's safety? Yes, replied the two killers. She was too young now, but one day she would understand.

Understand? Understand what? That there were highly organized assassins in the very heart of the city and that they were claiming to save her by eliminating males who had "seen things that were crucial for the Tribe's survival"?

The ant with the limp condescended to explain. From what she said, it transpired that the rock-scented warriors were "anti–bad stress soldiers." There was good stress, which caused the Tribe to progress and fight. And there was bad stress, which caused the Tribe to self-destruct.

There were some things it was better not to know. They caused "metaphysical" anguish, for which there was as yet no remedy. When it was worried, the Tribe was inhibited and unable to act.

It was very bad for everyone. The Tribe started to produce toxins that poisoned it. Its long-term survival was more important than short-term knowledge of the truth. If an eye had seen something that the brain knew was dangerous for the rest of the organism, it was better for the brain to put out that eye.

The big ant joined the lame one in summing up these wise words as follows:

> *We have put out the eye,*
> *We have cut off the nerve stimulus,*
> *We have ended the anguish.*

The antennae insisted that all organisms possess precisely such a safety mechanism. Those that do not die of fright or commit suicide in order to avoid facing reality, that is.

The 56th female was quite surprised but did not falter. Fine pheromones, indeed! If they were hoping to conceal the existence of the secret weapon, they were too late anyway. In the first place, everyone knew La-chola-kan had been a victim of it, even if it was still a complete mystery from the technological point of view.

The two soldiers remained impassive and did not relax their grip. Everyone had forgotten about La-chola-kan. Victory had stilled their curiosity. Anyway, you only had to sniff the corridors: there was not the slightest whiff of toxin. The whole Tribe was quietly awaiting the next day's Festival of Rebirth.

What did they want from her, then? Why were they holding her head so tightly?

While racing through the lower floors during the chase, the lame ant had detected a third ant. A soldier. What was her identification number?

So that was why they had not killed her outright. In reply, the female poked the ends of both her antennae deep into the big ant's eyes. The fact that she had been blind from birth did not make it any the less painful. The lame ant was astounded and slackened her grip.

The female ran and flew in order to get away more quickly. Her wings raised a cloud of dust that put her pursuers off her track. She had to get back to the dome quickly.

She had just had a brush with death. Now she was going to begin another life.

The following is an extract from Edmond Wells's address to the Parliamentary commission of inquiry in support of his petition against toy anthills:

In the shops yesterday, I saw the new toys that are being given to children as Christmas presents. They're transparent plastic boxes filled with earth containing six hundred ants and a queen whose fertility is guaranteed.

You can see them working, digging and running about.

It's fascinating for a child. It's as if he were being given a city. Except that the inhabitants are minute. Like hundreds of small, autonomous dolls moving about.

To tell the truth, I have anthills like them myself, simply because my work as a biologist involves studying them. I've set them up in vivariums covered with perforated cardboard.

However, I get a strange feeling each time I stand in front of my anthill, as if I were omnipotent in their world, as if I were their God.

If I feel like depriving them of food, my ants will all die. If I take it into my head to make it rain, I merely have to pour a little water over their city from a watering can. If I decide to increase the temperature in the anthill, I just have to put them on the radiator. If I want to kidnap one to examine it under a microscope, I only have to plunge my tweezers into the vivarium, and if I feel like killing some, I won't meet with any resistance. They won't even understand what's happening to them.

I tell you, gentlemen, we have inordinate power over these tiny creatures simply by virtue of their size.

I don't abuse that power myself, but just imagine what a child might do to them.

Sometimes I have crazy ideas. When I see a sand city, I say to myself: What if it were ours? What if we, too, have been set up in a prison vivarium and another giant species is watching us?

What if Adam and Eve were guinea pigs in an experiment to see what would happen if they were placed in an artificial setting?

What if their banishment from Paradise were just a change of prison vivarium?

What if the Flood were, after all, just a glass of water tipped over us by a careless or curious God?

Impossible, do I hear you say? Who knows. Maybe the only difference is that my ants are shut in by glass walls and we are held in by a physical force: the Earth's attraction.

My ants always manage to slash through the cardboard, however, and several have already escaped. And we manage to launch rockets that escape the Earth's gravity.

Coming back to the vivarium cities. I am, as I mentioned just now, a magnanimous, merciful and even slightly superstitious god, so I never make my subjects suffer. I don't do anything to them I wouldn't like to have done to me.

But the thousands of anthills sold at Christmas are going to turn children into little gods. Will they all be as magnanimous and merciful as I?

Most of them will surely understand that they are responsible for a city and that that gives them rights but also divine duties: to feed them, keep them at the right temperature and not kill them for fun.

However, when things go wrong for them, when their parents are fighting or they do badly at school or have fights with their friends, children, especially very young children, who are not yet responsible for their actions, may very well forget their duties as "young gods." I dread to think what they might do to their "citizens" in a fit of rage.

I am not asking you to pass this law prohibiting toy

*anthills out of pity for ants or in the name of animal
rights. Animals have no rights: we hatch them in bat-
teries and sacrifice them for our consumption. I am asking you to pass it because you would not want the
Earth to be given to an irresponsible young god one day
as a Christmas present.*

The sun was high in the sky.

Latecomers, both male and female, were hurrying
along the arteries just below the city's skin. Workers
were pushing them along, licking and encouraging them.

The 56th female vanished in time into the jubilant
crowd, where all passport scents merged. No one there
would be able to identify hers. She allowed herself to be
carried along by the flow of her sisters and climbed
higher and higher, passing through hitherto unknown
districts.

Suddenly, at the end of a corridor, she encountered
something she had never seen before. The light of day.
At first, it was only a halo on the walls but soon it became a blinding light. Here at last was the mysterious
force the nurses had described to her. The warm, gentle,
beautiful light. The promise of a fabulous new world.

The raw photons she absorbed through her eyes made
her feel drunk, as if she had indulged in too much of the
fermented honeydew on the thirty-second floor.

The 56th princess continued to move forward. There
were splashes of hard white light on the ground, and she
floundered in the hot photons. For someone who had
grown up underground, this was in violent contrast with
the dark she had always known.

As she turned another bend, a pencil of pure light shot
through her before widening into a dazzling circle, then a
silver veil. She was forced back, bombarded by the light.
She could feel its grains entering her eyes, burning the
optical nerves and eating into her three brains. The three
brains were an ancient inheritance from her worm ancestors, who had a nerve ganglion for each segment and a
nervous system for each part of the body.

She carried on into the wind of photons. In the distance, she could make out the silhouettes of her sisters, who were being swallowed up by the sun. They looked like ghosts.

Still she moved forward, her chitin growing warm. People had tried to describe this light to her thousands of times but words could not describe it, it had to be experienced. She spared a thought for all the workers of the doorkeeper subcaste who spent their whole lives shut up in the city and would never know what the outside world and its sun were like.

She entered the wall of light and was flung to the other side, outside the city. Her many-faceted eyes gradually focused as she felt the sting of the wild air, a cold, moving, scented air quite unlike the tame atmosphere of the world in which she had lived.

Her antennae twirled. She had difficulty in pointing them in the direction she wanted. A faster gust flattened them to her face. Her wings flapped.

Up on the high point of the dome, workers received her. They grabbed her by her legs, pulled her up and pushed her forward into a crowd of winged ants, hundreds of swarming males and females crammed onto a narrow surface. The 56th princess understood that she was on the runway ready for takeoff on the nuptial flight but that they must wait for the weather to improve.

However, while the wind was still playing havoc with their plans, a dozen sparrows had spotted the winged ants. Excited by the windfall, they fluttered closer and closer. When they got too near, the gunners crowning the summit rewarded them with jets of acid.

Just then, one of the birds tried his luck. He dived into the crowd, seized three females and flew off. Before he could regain height, he was shot down by the gunners. He rolled in the grass pitifully, his beak still full, in an attempt to wipe the poison off his wings.

It was an example to all the sparrows and they drew back a little. No one was taken in, though. They would soon be back to put the antiaircraft defenses to the test again.

PREDATOR: **What would our human civilization be like if it had not got rid of its major predators, such as wolves, lions, bears and hyenas?**

Certainly an anxious civilization, perpetually at risk.

To give themselves a fright in the midst of their libations, the Romans used to have a corpse brought in. That was their way of reminding themselves that nothing is permanent and that death can occur at any time.

But nowadays, man has crushed, eliminated and relegated to the museum every species capable of eating him, leaving only germs, and possibly ants, to worry about.

The Myrmician civilization, on the other hand, has developed without managing to eliminate its major predators. As a result of this, the insect is perpetually at risk. It knows it has only gone halfway, since even the most stupid animal can destroy the fruit of thousands of years of considered experience with a blow of the paw.

EDMOND WELLS,
ENCYCLOPEDIA OF RELATIVE AND ABSOLUTE KNOWLEDGE

The wind had dropped, there were fewer gusts and the temperature was rising again. At 22°C-time, the city decided to let go of its children.

The females whirred their four wings. They were ready and more than ready. The smell of all the mature males had raised their sexual appetite to a peak.

The first virgins took off gracefully. They rose to a height of about a hundred heads and were cut down by the sparrows. None got through.

There was dismay down below, but a second wave took off, undeterred. Four females out of a hundred managed to get through the barrage of beaks and feathers. The males pursued them in close formation. They were too puny to interest the sparrows and were allowed through.

A third wave of females launched their attack on the clouds. There were more than fifty birds in its path. It was carnage and there were no survivors. More and more birds gathered, as if word had got around. There were sparrows, blackbirds, robins, chaffinches and pigeons all squawking away up there now. They were having a festival, too.

A fourth wave took off. Not a single female got through this time, either. The birds fought among themselves for the best morsels.

The gunners were getting rattled. They were shooting straight up in the air with all the might of their formic acid glands, but the predators were too high. The drops of acid fell back on the city in a deadly rain, causing a great deal of injury and damage.

Some females gave up in terror. They decided that it was impossible to get through and that they had better go back down and copulate indoors along with other princesses who had been involved in accidents.

The fifth wave rose up, ready to make the supreme sacrifice. They had to get through the wall of beaks at all costs. Seventeen females got through, with forty-three males close on their tails.

Of the sixth wave, twelve females got through.

Of the seventh, thirty-four made it.

The 56th princess fluttered her wings. She dared not go yet. The head of one of her sisters had just landed at her feet, softly followed by some ominous down. She had wanted to know what the Great Outside was like. Well, now she knew.

Would she take off with the eighth wave? No, and she was right not to, for it was completely wiped out.

The princess was feeling nervous. She whirred her four wings and rose slightly off the ground. Well, at least that worked, no problem there, it was just that . . . Suddenly, she was filled with fear. She must keep a clear head. She knew she had very little chance of succeeding.

She stopped beating her wings; seventy-three females in the ninth wave had just gotten through. The workers let out pheromones of encouragement. Hope sprang anew. Would she leave with the tenth wave?

As she hesitated, she suddenly spotted the small lame ant and the big killer with lifeless eyes a little way ahead of her. She needed no further persuading. All at once, she took flight and the mandibles of the other two closed on empty air. They had only just missed her.

She hovered a moment halfway between the city and the horde of birds. Then she was enveloped in the flight of the tenth wave and took advantage of it to fly straight up into the void above. Her two neighbors were snapped up, while she passed unexpectedly between the enormous talons of a tit.

It was just a question of luck.

There, fourteen of them had come out of the tenth wave unharmed. But 56th had few illusions. She had overcome only the first ordeal. The hardest was yet to come. She knew the figures. In general, out of fifteen hundred princesses who took flight, only a dozen touched down without mishap. Four queens at best would manage to build a city.

SOMETIMES, WHEN: Sometimes, when I go for a walk in the summer, I notice I have almost stepped on a kind of fly. I look at it more closely and see that it is a queen ant. If there is one, there are a thousand. They writhe about on the ground and get crushed underfoot or crash into car windshields. When they are exhausted, they lose all control of their flight. How many cities have been annihilated by windshield wipers on a summer road?

EDMOND WELLS,
ENCYCLOPEDIA OF RELATIVE AND ABSOLUTE KNOWLEDGE

As the 56th female beat her four long stained-glass wings faster, she saw the wall of feathers behind her close on the eleventh and twelfth waves. Poor things. Another five waves of females and the city would have spat out all its hopes.

She had already stopped thinking about them, sucked up by the infinite blue. It was all so blue. How wonderful it was to cleave the air for an ant who had known only life underground. It seemed to her that she was moving in a different world. She had left her narrow galleries for a dizzy space where everything exploded in three dimensions.

She discovered intuitively all the possibilities of flight. By leaning on one wing, she could turn right. She could ascend by altering the pitch of her wing beats. Or descend. Or accelerate. She noticed that to make a perfect turn she had to place her wing tips along an imaginary axis and not hesitate to position her body at an angle of over 45°.

The 56th female discovered that the sky was not empty. Far from it. It was full of currents. Some of them, the thermals, made her go up. Air pockets, on the other hand, made her lose altitude. You could spot them only by watching the insects ahead of you and preparing yourself according to their movements.

She felt cold. It was cold at this altitude. Sometimes there were whirlwinds, gusts of warm or freezing air, that spun her like a top.

A group of males had rushed in pursuit of her. The 56th female went faster so that only the fastest and most stubborn would catch up with her. It was the first genetic selection.

She felt a touch. A male was securing himself to her abdomen, climbing up her, scaling her. He was quite small, but because he had stopped beating his wings, he felt heavy.

She lost a little altitude. Above, the male was twisting about to avoid being hampered by her wing beats. Completely off balance, he curved his abdomen under to reach the female's sex organs with his sting.

She waited curiously to see what it would feel like. She began to feel a delicious tingling sensation. That gave her an idea. Without warning, she tipped forward and went into a nosedive. It was marvelous, total ecstasy! Her first great cocktail of pleasure was made up of speed and sex.

An image of the 327th male appeared furtively in her brain. The wind whistled between the hairs of her eyes. A spicy sap made her antennae tremble. Her thoughts became a stormy sea. Strange liquids ran from her glands and mingled to form an effervescent soup that poured into her encephalon.

When she reached the top of the grass, she gathered her strength and started beating her wings again. Then she flew straight up, and by the time she had leveled out, the male was no longer feeling well. His legs were trembling and his mandibles kept opening and shutting for no apparent reason. He had a cardiac arrest and went into free fall.

The males of most insect species are programmed to die the first time they make love. They get only one chance. When the sperms leave their bodies, they take with them the lives of their owners.

In the case of ants, ejaculation kills the male. In other species, it is the female who subsequently massacres her partner for the simple reason that she has worked up an appetite.

You have to bow to the inevitable: the world of insects is largely a world of females—or, to be precise, widows. Males have only a fleeting place in it.

But a second sire was already clinging to her. One had no sooner gone than another took his place. A third came along, then many more. The 56th female lost count of them. At least seventeen or eighteen of them relayed with one another to fill her sperm store with fresh gametes.

She could feel the living liquid seething in her abdomen. It was the store of inhabitants of her future city, millions of male sexual cells that would allow her to lay every day for fifteen years.

All around her, her winged sisters were experiencing

the same emotions. The sky was full of flying females mounted by one or more males copulating with the same females; caravans of love suspended in the clouds. The ladies were drunk with fatigue and happiness. They were no longer princesses, they were queens. They were almost stunned with repeated pleasure and could hardly control their flight paths.

Four majestic swallows chose that moment to fly up suddenly from a flowering cherry tree. With chilling impassiveness, they slid rather than flew between the layers of sky and swooped down on the winged ants with wide-open beaks, swallowing them one after another. The 56th was pursued in her turn.

The 103,683rd soldier was in the explorers' room. She had been counting on continuing the investigation alone by infiltrating the termite hill in the east but someone had suggested she join a group of explorers to go "dragon hunting." A lizard had been spotted on the grazing lands of Zoubi-zoubi-kan. With nine million beasts to milk, it was the city with the largest herd of greenflies in the entire Federation. One lizard could hamper pastoral activities considerably.

As luck would have it, Zoubi-zoubi-kan was on the edge of the Federation, just halfway between the termite city and Bel-o-kan. The 103,683rd soldier had therefore agreed to leave with this expedition so that her departure would go unnoticed.

Around her, the other explorers made careful preparations. They filled their social crops to the brim with sweet energy reserves and their pockets with formic acid. Then they smeared themselves with snails' slime to protect themselves from the cold and also (they now knew) from alternaria spores.

They talked about the lizard hunt. Some of them compared the lizard to salamanders or frogs, but the majority of the thirty-two explorers agreed it was more difficult to hunt.

One old ant maintained that lizards' tails grew again when they were cut off, but the others made fun of her. Another claimed to have seen one of the monsters stay as still as a stone for 10°C. Others recalled tales of the first Belokanians confronting the monsters with their bare mandibles—formic acid had not been so widely used at the time.

The 103,683rd soldier could not restrain a shudder. Until now, she had never seen a lizard, and the prospect of attacking one with her bare mandibles or even a jet of acid was not reassuring. She told herself she would get away at the first opportunity. After all, her investigation into the termites' secret weapon was more vital to the survival of the city than some sporting hunt.

The explorers were ready. They made their way up through the corridors of the outer belt before emerging into the light through exit seven, known as the "eastern exit."

First they had to leave the suburbs of the city, which was no easy matter. The whole area around Bel-o-kan was congested with a crowd of workers and soldiers, all of them in a hurry.

The crowd was flowing in several directions. Some ants were loaded with leaves, fruit, seeds, flowers or mushrooms. Others were carrying twigs or stones that would be used as building materials. Yet others were carting game. There was a babble of smells.

The huntresses forced their way through the jams. Then the traffic began to move more freely. The avenue narrowed down into a road only three heads (nine millimeters) wide, then two, then one. They could no longer pick up the city's collective messages and must be a long way from it already. The group had cut its olfactory umbilical cord and formed an autonomous unit. They adopted the "strolling" formation, with the ants lined up two by two.

Soon they met another group of explorers, who looked as if they had had a tough time. Their meager troop no longer amounted to a single unscathed ant. They had all been mutilated. Some had only one leg left and were dragging themselves miserably along. Those who had no antennae or abdomen left were no better off.

The 103,683rd had never seen soldiers so badly smashed up since the Poppy War. They must have come up against something terrifying. The secret weapon, perhaps?

She tried talking to a big warrior with long, broken mandibles. Where had they been? What had happened? Was it the termites?

The other ant slowed down and turned to face her without answering. She was appalled to see empty sockets and a head split from mouth to neck joint.

She watched her move away. A little farther on, she fell and did not get up again. She just managed to find the strength to crawl off the trail so that her body would not be in the way.

The 56th female tried going into a steep dive to get away from the swallow, but the bird was ten times faster. A big beak was already casting its shadow over the tips of her antennae. It covered her abdomen, her thorax and her head, then overtook her. The touch of the palate was unbearable. Then the beak closed again and it was all over.

SACRIFICE: **When you observe ants, they appear to be motivated only by ambitions external to their own existence. A severed head will still try to make itself useful by biting enemy legs or cutting off a seed. A thorax will drag itself along to block up an entrance and stop enemies from entering.**

Is this self-abnegation, fanaticism about the city or the stupefaction of collectivism?

No, ants can live alone as well. They do not need the Tribe and can even revolt.

Why, then, do they sacrifice themselves?

At the present stage in my work, I should say: out of

modesty. It seems that, for them, their own deaths are not sufficiently important events to distract them from the tasks they were performing immediately beforehand.

EDMOND WELLS,
ENCYCLOPEDIA OF RELATIVE AND ABSOLUTE KNOWLEDGE

Skirting around trees, mounds of earth and thorny bushes, the explorers continued to thread their way eastward into danger.

The road had narrowed but they still passed highway maintenance teams along the way. The access roads leading from one city to another were never neglected. Road menders pulled up the moss, moved aside twigs blocking the way and laid down scent signals with their Dufour glands.

There were now few workers going in the opposite direction. Sometimes they found signpost pheromones on the ground: "At junction twenty-nine, make a detour through the hawthorns," which might be the last trace of an ambush by enemy insects.

As she walked along, 103,683rd had one surprise after another. She had never visited this region before. There were devil's boletuses eighty heads high there, yet the species was characteristic of the western regions.

She also recognized pearly puffballs and stinkhorns, which attracted flies with their fetid smell. She scaled a chanterelle and happily trampled the soft flesh.

She discovered all kinds of strange plants: wild hemp, with its dew-retaining flowers, gorgeous troubling lady's slippers and long-stemmed cat's foot.

She went up to a Busy Lizzie with beelike flowers and incautiously touched it. The ripe fruits immediately burst in her face, covering her with sticky, yellow seeds. It was a good thing it was not alternaria.

Undeterred, she climbed up a lesser celandine to take a look at the sky. High above, she could see bees describing figures of eight to show their sisters where there were flowers containing pollen.

The countryside was getting wilder and wilder. There were mysterious smells in the air. Hundreds of unidentifiable little creatures were fleeing in all directions. You could tell they were there only from the rustle of dry leaves.

She rejoined the troop, her head still tingling all over. In this way, they reached the outskirts of the federal city of Zoubi-zoubi-kan at a gentle pace. From a distance, it appeared to be a grove like any other. If it had not been for the smell and the path traced out, no one would have thought of looking for a city there. Zoubi-zoubi-kan was in fact a classic russet city, with a stump, a dome of twigs and rubbish heaps, but it was all hidden under the bushes.

The entrances to the city were high up, almost level with the top of the dome. You reached them via a cluster of ferns and wild roses, through which the explorers made their way.

Inside, it was teeming with life. You could hardly make out the greenflies, which were the same color as the leaves. However, the informed antenna and eye could easily detect the thousands of small green warts slowly growing as they "grazed" on the sap.

Long ago, the ants and greenflies had reached an agreement. The greenflies would feed the ants, who would in turn protect them. What actually happened was that some cities cut the greenflies' wings off and gave them their own passport scents. It made it easier to look after the herds.

Zoubi-zoubi-kan was one of the cities to have adopted this dubious practice. To make up for it, or perhaps just out of modernity, it had built imposing greenfly sheds fitted with every creature comfort to ensure the greenflies' well-being. Ant nurses tended the eggs of their aphids as carefully as if they were ant eggs. This had no doubt led to the unusual size and healthy appearance of the local livestock.

The 103,683rd soldier and her companions went up to a herd busy sucking sap from a rose branch. They asked two or three questions but the greenflies kept their trunks buried in the plant's flesh and paid them no attention whatsoever. Possibly they did not know the ants' scent language anyway. The explorers searched for the shepherdess with their antennae but could not find her.

Then something terrifying happened. Three ladybirds dropped into the middle of the herd, spreading panic among the poor greenflies, who could not escape because of their clipped wings.

Fortunately, the wolves brought out the shepherdesses. Two Zoubizoubikanian ants leaped out from behind a leaf. They had been lying in wait to take the black-spotted red predators by surprise. They took aim and struck them down with precise shots of acid.

Then they went to calm the herds of frightened greenflies. They milked them, drummed on their abdomens and caressed their antennae. The greenflies then produced big bubbles of transparent sugar, the precious honeydew. As they were drinking their fill of this nectar, the Zoubizoubikanian shepherdesses caught sight of the Belokanian explorers.

They greeted them and made antenna contact.

We've come to hunt the lizard, emitted one of the newcomers.

In that case, you have to continue east. One of the monsters has been spotted over in the direction of the post of Guayei-Tyolot.

Instead of offering them trophallaxis as was customary, the shepherdesses suggested they feed directly from the beasts. The explorers did not wait to be asked twice. Each of them chose a greenfly and started to stimulate its abdomen to milk the delicious honeydew.

Inside the bird's gullet, it was dark and stank of oil. The 56th female slid down her predator's throat, covered in saliva. He had not chewed her since he had no teeth, and she was still intact. It was out of the question for her to resign herself to her fate—a whole city would disappear with her.

She made a supreme effort and sank her mandibles into the smooth flesh of the esophagus. This reflex saved her. The swallow retched and coughed out the food irritating his throat. Blinded, the 56th female tried to fly, but her sticky wings were far too heavy. She fell into the middle of a river.

Dying males were falling all around her. High above, she detected the arrhythmical flight of twenty or so of her sisters who had survived the swallows' passage. They were exhausted and losing altitude.

One of them landed on a water lily, where two salamanders immediately gave chase, caught her and tore her to pieces. The other queens had lost their lives to a succession of pigeons, toads, moles, snakes, bats, hedgehogs, chickens and chicks. In the end, out of the fifteen hundred females who had taken off, only six had survived.

The 56th was one of them, saved by a miracle. She had to live. She had to establish her own city and solve the mystery of the secret weapon. She knew she would need help and that she would be able to count on the friendly crowd already populating her stomach. All she had to do was bring them forth.

But first of all, she had to get out of there.

By calculating the angle of the sun's rays, she found that she had fallen into the eastern river. It was not the ideal place to be since ants cannot swim (we still do not know how they have managed to reach every island in the world).

A leaf passed within reach, and she clung to it with her mandibles. She thrashed about with her hind legs but scarcely moved forward. She had been trailing along on the surface of the water like that for some time when she saw an enormous shadow. Was it a tadpole? No, it was a thousand times larger than a tadpole. The 56th female could make out a streamlined shape and smooth, striped skin. It was something new to her, a trout.

Small crustaceans, cyclops and daphnia, were fleeing in front of the monster. It dived, then came up again near the queen, who clung to her leaf, terrified.

The trout propelled itself forward with all the power in its fins and broke the surface. As a great wave buffeted the ant, the trout seemed to hang suspended in the air. It opened a mouth armed with fine teeth and swallowed a gnat hovering nearby. Then it twisted its tail around and fell back into its crystalline world, causing a tidal wave that submerged the ant.

Some frogs hastily dived in to fight over the queen and her caviar. She managed to surface again but was sucked back down into the inhospitable depths by an eddy. The frogs pursued her until she became rigid with cold and lost consciousness.

Nicolas was watching television in the dining room with his two new friends, Jean and Philippe. Around them, other pink-faced orphans were allowing themselves to be lulled by the unbroken succession of images.

Through their eyes and ears, the film's story was entering the memories in their brains at a speed of 500 kilometers an hour. A human brain can stock up to sixty billion items of information, but when its memory cells are saturated, they are automatically cleared and the information considered least interesting is forgotten. Only traumatic memories and nostalgia for past happiness remain.

Immediately after the serial that day, there was a televised discussion about insects. Most of the young human beings dispersed. They were not interested in scientific waffle.

"Professor Leduc, you and Professor Rosenfeld are considered the greatest European specialists on ants. What led you to study them?"

"When I opened my kitchen cupboard one day, I came face-to-face with a colony of them. I watched them working for hours. It was a lesson in life and humility. I wanted to find out more about them. It's as simple as that."

He laughed.

"How do your views differ from those of that other eminent scientist, Professor Rosenfeld?"

"Oh, Professor Rosenfeld. Hasn't he retired yet?" He laughed again. "No, seriously, we don't belong to the same school. There are several ways of 'understanding' ants, you know. We used to think all the social species— termites, bees and ants—were royalists. It was simple but wrong. Then we noticed that the only power the ant queens had was that of giving birth. Ant governments can actually take many forms: monarchy, oligarchy, a triumvirate of warriors, democracy, anarchy, et cetera. When the citizens are not satisfied with their governments, they may even revolt, and then there are civil wars right inside the cities."

"How fantastic."

"For me, and for the so-called German school to which I belong, the organization of the ant world is primarily based on a hierarchy of castes and on the domination of alpha individuals who are more gifted than the rest and who direct groups of workers. For Rosenfeld, who belongs to the so-called Italian school, ants are all anarchists to the core and there are no alphas, no individuals more gifted than the rest. Ant leaders sometimes emerge spontaneously in order to solve practical problems. But they are only temporary."

"I don't quite understand."

"We could say that the Italian school thinks any ant can be in charge as long as she has an original idea which is of interest to the rest, whereas the German school thinks it is always ants with 'leadership qualities' who take charge of missions."

"Are the two schools so very different?"

"Since you ask, they've already ended up fighting at big international congresses."

"Is it still the same old rivalry between the Saxon and Latin turns of mind?"

"No. It's more like the battle between the partisans of the 'innate' and the 'acquired.' Are people born idiots or do they become idiots? It's one of the questions we're trying to answer by studying ant societies."

"But why not do these experiments on rabbits or mice?"

"Ants offer us a fantastic opportunity to see a society in action, one made up of several million individuals. It's like observing a world. To my knowledge, no towns of several million rabbits or mice exist."

Someone nudged him.

"Hear that, Nicolas?"

But Nicolas was not listening. He had seen that face, those yellow eyes, before, but where and when? He searched his memory. Yes, he remembered now. It was the man who had come about the bookbinding. He had said his name was Gougne but he was one and the same person as this Leduc who was showing off on television.

Nicolas's discovery plunged him into deep thought. If the professor had lied, it was to try to get possession of the encyclopedia. Its contents must be vital for the study of ants. It must be down in the cellar. And that was what they had all been after—Dad, Mom and this Leduc. If he went and got that damn encyclopedia, it would all become clear.

He got up.

"Where are you going?"

He made no answer.

"I thought you were interested in ants?"

He walked as far as the door, then ran back to his room. He would not need many of his things, just his beloved leather jacket, his penknife and his thick, crepe-soled shoes.

The supervisors took no notice of him when he crossed the big hall.

He ran away from the orphanage.

•   •   •

From a distance, all that could be seen of Guayei-Tyolot was a sort of rounded crater like a molehill. The "advanced post" was a mini-anthill occupied by about a hundred individuals. It was operative only from April to October and remained empty throughout the remainder of autumn and winter.

Its citizens, like primitive ants, had no queen, no workers and no soldiers. They performed all the different roles at once and they made no bones about criticizing the feverishness of the giant cities. They made fun of the jams, the collapsing corridors, the secret tunnels that turned towns into rotten apples, the highly specialized workers who could no longer hunt and the blind door-keepers who were walled up for life. The 103,683rd soldier inspected the post. Guayei-Tyolot consisted of a granary and a vast main hall. Two rays of sunlight shining through an opening in the ceiling revealed dozens of hunting trophies, empty cuticles hanging from the walls with drafts whistling through them.

She went to take a closer look at the multicolored bodies. A native of the region came and caressed her antennae. She pointed out magnificent specimens killed by every kind of ant ruse. The animals were covered in formic acid, which could also be used as a preservative.

Lined up carefully were all sorts of butterflies and large insects of every shape and color. Yet one well-known animal, the termite queen, was missing from the collection.

The 103,683rd soldier asked whether their termite neighbors ever gave them any trouble. The local ant raised her antennae in surprise. She stopped mumbling between her mandibles and there was a heavy scent silence.

Termites?

Her antennae fell. She had nothing more to communicate. In any case, she had work to do. She was in the middle of cutting something up and had wasted enough time already. She said good-bye and turned around, ready to make off. The 103,683rd soldier repeated her question.

The other ant now seemed to panic, and her antennae began to tremble. The word *termite* visibly conjured up something terrible for her. It seemed quite beyond her strength to engage in conversation on the subject. She rushed off to join a group of workers in the middle of a drinking session.

They had filled their social crops with flower-honey alcohol and were drinking from each other's abdomens in a long, closed chain.

Five huntresses assigned to the advanced post then made rather a noisy entrance, pushing a caterpillar in front of them.

Look what we've found. The amazing thing is, it produces honey!

The one who gave out this news tapped the captive with the tips of her antennae. Then she put a leaf down in front of it and, as soon as the caterpillar started to eat, jumped on its back. The caterpillar reared up in vain. The ant stuck her claws into its flanks and got a good grip, then turned around and licked its last segment until a nectar ran from it.

Everyone congratulated her, and the hitherto unknown honeydew was passed from mandible to mandible. It had a different flavor from greenfly honeydew and was smoother, with a more pronounced aftertaste of sap. As 103,683rd was tasting this exotic liquid, an antennae brushed her head.

It seems you've been asking about the termites.

The ant who had just sent out this pheromone seemed very, very old. Her whole shell was covered in scars from mandible bites. The 103,683rd soldier laid back her antennae in acquiescence.

Follow me!

She was known as the 4,000th warrior. Her head was as flat as a leaf and her eyes were tiny. The quavering scents she emitted were very low in alcohol. That was possibly why she had wanted to talk in a tiny, almost enclosed cavity.

Don't worry, we can talk here. This hole is my chamber.

The 103,683rd soldier asked her what she knew about the termite hill of the east. The other spread her antennae.

Why are you interested in it? You only came here for the lizard hunt, didn't you?

The Belokanian soldier decided to come clean with the old asexual ant. She told her that a baffling secret weapon had been used against the soldiers of La-chola-kan. At first, they had thought it was a dwarf trick, but it wasn't. Their suspicions had naturally then fallen on the termites of the east, their other great enemies.

The old lady folded back her antennae in surprise. She had never heard of the affair. She examined 103,683rd and asked:

Was it the secret weapon that took off your fifth leg?

The young soldier answered no, she had lost it in the Battle of Poppy Hill, during the liberation of La-chola-kan. The 4,000th warrior immediately became enthusiastic. She had been there.

Which legion were you in?

The 15th. How about you?

The 3rd.

During the first charge, one had fought on the left flank and the other on the right. They exchanged recollections. There were always plenty of lessons to be learned from a battlefield. For example, 4,000th had noticed right at the start of the fighting that mercenary messenger-gnats were being used. According to her, they were far superior to the traditional "runners" as a means of long-distance communication.

The Belokanian soldier, who had not noticed them, willingly agreed, then hastily returned to the subject.

Why won't anyone talk to me about the termites?

The old warrior came closer until their heads brushed.

Some very strange things have been happening here, too.

The scents she was giving off were redolent of mystery. *Very strange, very strange.* The phrase bounced off the walls in a scent echo.

Then 4,000th explained that for some time now not a single termite from the eastern city had been seen even though they had previously used the Satei river crossing to send spies to the west. The ants of Satei had known about it and monitored them after a fashion. Now, there were no longer even spies. There was nothing.

An enemy who attacks is worrying, but an enemy who disappears is even more worrying. Because there were no longer any skirmishes with the termite scouts, the ants of the post of Guayei-Tyolot decided to spy in their turn.

A first band of explorers had set out but nothing more was heard of them. A second group followed and disappeared likewise. They thought it might be the lizard or a greedy hedgehog, but when a predator attacked there was always at least one survivor, even if she was wounded. In this case, the soldiers had vanished as if by magic.

That reminds me of something . . . , began 103,683rd.

But the old lady was not to be distracted from her tale. She went on.

After the failure of the first two expeditions, the warriors of Guayei-Tyolot decided to risk their all and dispatched a mini-legion of five hundred heavily armed soldiers. This time, there was one survivor. She dragged herself along for thousands of heads and died in agony just as she reached the nest.

They examined her body but found no trace of a wound. There was no apparent reason for her death.

Now do you understand why no one wants to talk to you about the termite hill of the east?

The 103,683rd soldier understood. What was more, she was satisfied that she was on the right track. If there was a solution to the mystery of the secret weapon, it was to be found in the termite hill of the east.

HOLOGRAM: The human brain and the anthill have something in common, which can be symbolized by a hologram.

What is a hologram? It is a set of printed lines which, when superimposed and lit from a particular angle, produce a three-dimensional image.

The image exists everywhere and nowhere. The combination of printed lines engenders a third dimension and therefore a three-dimensional illusion.

Each neuron in our brains and each individual in the anthill holds all the information, but only their collective activity gives rise to consciousness or "three-dimensional thought."

EDMOND WELLS,
ENCYCLOPEDIA OF RELATIVE AND ABSOLUTE KNOWLEDGE

When the 56th female, recently turned queen, recovered consciousness, she found that she had been washed up on a huge gravel beach. She had probably escaped the frogs thanks only to a rapid current. She would have liked to take off, but her wings were still wet. All she could do was wait.

She cleaned her antennae methodically, then sniffed the surrounding air. Where was she? She only hoped she had not ended up on the wrong side of the river.

She vibrated her antennae at 8,000 strokes a second and caught a few whiffs of familiar smells. By luck, she was on the west bank of the river. However, there were no trail pheromones whatsoever. She would need to move a little nearer the central city if she wanted to link her future city to the Federation.

She flew off westward at last. She would not be able to go far for the time being. Her wing muscles were tired and she hedgehopped.

They returned to the main hall of Guayei-Tyolot. Since 103,683rd had tried to inquire about the termites of the east, the ants there had avoided her as if she were infected with alternaria. She was completely absorbed in her mission and did not falter.

Around her, the Belokanians were taking part in trophallaxis with the Guayeityolotians, getting them to taste the new agaric harvest and savoring honeydew extracted from wild caterpillars in return.

After ranging far and wide, the conversation turned to the lizard hunt. The Guayeityolotians told them that three lizards had recently been spotted terrorizing the greenfly herds of Zoubi-zoubi-kan. They had destroyed two herds of a thousand beasts each and all the accompanying shepherdesses.

There had been panic for a time. The shepherdesses had moved their cattle about only in the protected passages dug into the flesh of branches. But thanks to the acid artillery, they had managed to repulse the three dragons. Two had gone a long way away. The third had been wounded and had settled on a stone fifty thousand heads away. The Zoubizoubikanian legions had already cut off its tail. They had to seize the opportunity and finish it off before it recovered its strength.

Is it true that lizards' tails grow again? asked one explorer.

They replied that it was.

The tail that grows again isn't the same, though. As Mother says, you never get back exactly what you've lost. There are no vertebrae in the second tail, so it's much softer.

A Guayeityolotian supplied more information. Lizards were very sensitive to changes in the weather, far more so than ants. If they had stored up a lot of solar energy, they had incredibly quick reactions. When they were cold, on the other hand, all their movements slowed down. They would need to plan the next day's offensive on the basis of this. Ideally, they should charge the lizard at dawn. It would have cooled down during the night and would be lethargic.

But we'll have cooled down, too! remarked one Belokanian pertinently.

Not if we use the dwarves' techniques for resisting the cold, retorted a huntress. *We'll stuff ourselves with sugar and alcohol for energy and paint our shells with slime to stop the calories from escaping too quickly from our bodies.*

The 103,683rd soldier listened to these words with a distracted antenna. She was thinking about the mystery of the termite hill and the unexplained disappearances related to her by the old warrior.

The first Guayeityolotian, the one who had shown her the trophies but refused to talk about the termites, came up to her again.

Have you talked to 4,000th?

She said that she had.

Don't take any notice of what she said, then. You might just as well have been talking to a corpse. She got stung by an ichneumon wasp a few days ago.

An ichneumon wasp! She shuddered in horror. The ichneumon wasp had a long proboscis with which it made holes in ants' nests in the night. When it came across a warm body, it pierced it and laid its eggs inside.

It was the ant larvae's worst nightmare: a syringe shot out of the ceiling and felt about for soft flesh into which to empty its young. These then grew quietly inside the host organism before changing into voracious larvae that gnawed away at the living animal from the inside.

That night, 103,683rd inevitably dreamed about a terrible trunk that pursued her to inject its carnivorous children into her.

The entry code had not changed. Nicolas still had his keys and only had to break the seals that the police had put on the door to get inside the apartment. Nothing had been touched since the firemen's disappearance. Even the cellar door was still wide open.

He did not have a flashlight, so he calmly got down to

the job of making a torch. He managed to break off a table leg, fixed a tightly packed crown of crumpled paper to it and set fire to it. The wood quickly caught and burned with a small, even flame that would last and withstand drafts.

He immediately vanished down the spiral staircase with the torch in one hand and his penknife in the other. Resolute, his jaws clenched, he felt he was the stuff of heroes.

Down and around he went, endlessly down and around. It seemed to have been going on for hours and he was hungry and thirsty but the will to succeed drove him on.

He got worked up and went even faster, then started to yell out loud, sometimes calling his father and mother and sometimes letting out spirited war cries. His tread had become extraordinarily sure, and he flew from step to step without any conscious control.

Suddenly, he came to a door. He pushed it open. Two tribes of rats were fighting, but they fled from the apparition of the screaming child with his halo of flames.

The oldest rats were worried. For some time now, the "big ones'" visits had become more frequent. What did it mean? They only hoped this one would not go and set fire to the dens of the pregnant females.

Nicolas continued his descent. He had been going so fast he hadn't seen the rats. There were more stairs and more strange inscriptions, which he certainly would not read this time. Suddenly he heard a flapping noise and felt a touch. A bat was clinging to his hair. He was terrified and tried to get away from it, but it seemed to have soldered itself to his head. He tried to repel it with his torch but succeeded only in singeing his own hair. He screamed and broke into a run again, but the bat stayed perched on his head like a hat and flew away only after sucking a little of his blood.

Nicolas no longer felt tired. Breathing noisily, and with his heart and temples beating fit to burst, he suddenly bumped into a wall. He fell down but picked himself up again immediately with his torch intact. He moved the flame about in front of him.

It really was a wall. Better still, he recognized the plates of concrete and steel his father had carted down. And the cement pointing was still fresh.

"Mom, Dad, answer if you're there!"

But only the echo answered. Yet he must be close to his goal. The wall must pivot, because that was what happened in films when there was no door.

What was behind the wall, then? Nicolas at last found an inscription, which read:

> *How do you make four equilateral triangles*
> *out of six matches?*

And just below it there was a small keypad with letters rather than figures, twenty-six letters you had to use to type the answer to the question.

"You have to think differently," he said out loud. He was amazed because the sentence had come to him of its own accord. He thought for a long time without daring to touch the keypad. Then he was filled with a strange silence, a vast silence that emptied him of all thought but that inexplicably guided him to type a succession of seven letters.

He heard the soft hum of a mechanism and the wall swung open. Nicolas went forward, excited and ready for anything, but soon after he had passed through, the wall moved back into place, causing a draft that blew out the remaining stump of torch.

Plunged into total darkness, his mind confused, Nicolas retraced his footsteps. There were no coded keys on this side of the wall, though. It was impossible to go back. He tore at the concrete and steel plates, but his father had made a good job of it. He wasn't a locksmith for nothing.

CLEANLINESS: **What could be cleaner than a fly? It is forever washing itself, not out of duty but out of necessity.**

If its antennae and eye facets are not all impeccably clean, it will never be able to detect food from a distance or see the hand about to squash it. For insects, cleanliness is a major factor in survival.

EDMOND WELLS,
ENCYCLOPEDIA OF RELATIVE AND ABSOLUTE KNOWLEDGE

The next day, the front-page headlines of the popular press read: THE DREADED CELLAR OF FONTAINEBLEAU STRIKES AGAIN. LATEST DISAPPEARANCE: THE ONLY SON OF THE WELLS FAMILY. WHAT ARE THE POLICE DOING?

The spider glanced down from the top of his fern. It was very high. He exuded a drop of liquid silk, stuck it to the leaf, went to the end of the branch and jumped into space. He took some time to fall. The line stretched and stretched, then dried, hardened and broke his fall just before he touched down. He had nearly been squashed like a ripe berry. Many of his sisters had already been smashed to pieces because a sudden cold spell had made the silk harden more slowly.

The spider wriggled his eight legs until he swung like a pendulum, then stretched out and made fast to a leaf. This would be the second mooring point of his web, and he stuck the end of his line to it. You cannot get far with a taut rope, though. He spotted a trunk to the left and ran over to it. A few more branches, a few more leaps, and his support lines were in place. They would take the strain of the winds and the weight of prey. The whole thing formed an octagon.

Spiders' silk is made of a fibrous protein, fibroin, which is strong and waterproof. When certain spiders have had enough to eat, they can produce seven hundred meters of silk two microns in diameter, which is proportionally as strong as nylon and three times as elastic.

To cap it all, they have seven glands, each producing a different kind of thread: a silk for the web support lines; a silk for the safety rope; a silk for the lines at the heart of the web; a sticky-coated silk for a quick grip; a silk to protect the eggs; a silk to build shelters; and a silk to wrap up prey.

The silk is actually the fibrous extension of spider hormones just as pheromones are the volatile extensions of ant hormones.

The spider manufactured a safety rope and made fast to it. He would now be able to drop down at the first sign of danger and escape without wasting any effort. This had already saved his life many times.

He then intertwined four lines at the center of his octagon. His gestures had not changed in a hundred million years. His construction was beginning to look like something. Today, he had decided to make a web out of dry silk. The sticky-coated silks were far more effective but they were too fragile. All the dust and bits of dead leaves got caught in them. Dry silk had less snaring power but at least it would last until nightfall.

Once the spider had got the ridge beams in place, he added a dozen spokes and put the finishing touches to his work with the central spiral. That was the part he liked best. He fastened his dry thread to a branch and jumped from spoke to spoke, always in the direction of the Earth's rotation, taking as long as possible to get to the heart of the web.

He did it in his own special way. Just as no two human beings have the same fingerprints, no two spiders' webs on Earth are alike.

It was important to keep the mesh taut. Once he had reached the center, he looked over his scaffolding of threads to gauge its strength. Then he paced up and down each spoke and shook it with his eight legs. It held.

Most of the spiders in the region built webs on the plan 75/12. Seventy-five turns of the filling-in spiral to twelve spokes. He preferred the fine lace of 95/10.

It might be more conspicuous, but it was stronger. And because he used dry silk, he could not afford to skimp on the quantity. Otherwise insects would only pay passing visits.

However, the long, exacting task had drained him of energy and he needed food urgently. It was a vicious circle. He was starving because he had built a web but it was the web that would enable him to eat.

He hid under a leaf and waited with his twenty-four claws resting on the main beams. Without even using one of his eight eyes, he could sense the surrounding space and feel in his legs the slightest movements of air thanks to the web, which reacted with the sensitivity of a microphone membrane.

The minute vibration he could feel was a bee two hundred heads away. It was describing figures of eight to show the bees in its hive the way to a field of flowers.

That other faint quivering must be a dragonfly. They were delicious. But this one was not flying in the right direction to become his lunch.

He felt something heavy land in his web. It was a spider hoping to lay claim to someone else's work. He quickly chased the thief away before any prey turned up.

Speaking of which, he felt a fly arriving from the east in his left hind leg. She did not seem to be flying very quickly. If she did not change course, it looked as if she would fall right into his trap.

Splat! A hit.

It was a winged ant.

The spider—who had no name, for solitary creatures do not need to recognize others of their kind—waited calmly. When he was younger, he used to get carried away with enthusiasm and lost quite a few of his prey that way. He thought that any insect caught in his web was condemned. In reality, only 50 percent died on contact. The time factor was crucial.

You just had to wait and the terrified game would enmesh itself without any assistance. Such was the first precept of spider philosophy: *There is no better combat technique than to wait for your enemy to destroy himself.*

After a few minutes, he went to take a closer look at

his catch. It was a queen, a russet queen from the western empire, Bel-o-kan.

He had already heard of the ultrasophisticated empire. Its millions of inhabitants had apparently become so interdependent that they could no longer feed themselves unaided. It was a sorry state of affairs and hardly constituted progress!

One of their queens . . . He was holding in his claws a piece of the invaders' future. He had seen his own mother chased by a horde of red weaver ants and he did not like them.

He eyed his prey, who was still struggling. The stupid insects, would they never understand that panic was their worst enemy? The more the winged ant tried to escape, the more entangled it became in the silk, damaging the web and annoying the spider into the bargain.

The 56th female's anger gave way to despondency. She could now hardly move. With her body already swathed in silk, every movement added a layer to her straitjacket. She had never dreamed that she would come to such a stupid end after overcoming so many difficulties.

She was born in a white cocoon and she would die in one, too.

The spider came even nearer, checking the damaged lines on the way, and 56th had a close-up view of a magnificent orange-and-black animal with a head crowned with eight green eyes. She had already eaten ones like it. Now it was her turn to be lunch, and the spider was spitting silk at her.

You can never bundle them up too much, said the spider to himself before displaying two alarming poison hooks. But spiders do not actually kill, not right away. They like their meat warm, so rather than finishing off their prey, they stun it with sedative venom and wake it only to take a little nibble. That way, they have nice fresh meat to eat whenever they like, safe in its silk wrapping. Sometimes it lasts them a week.

The 56th female had heard of the custom. She shivered. It was a fate worse than death. To have all her limbs amputated one by one . . . Every time you woke up, something got ripped off and then you were put to sleep again. There was a little less of you each time, until your vital organs were finally removed and you were at last liberated by the gift of sleep.

It was better to die by her own hand. Trying not to see the horrible hooks so close to her, she set about slowing down her heartbeats.

At that very moment, a mayfly struck the web with such force that he was immediately bound up tight in the silk. He had been born only a few minutes earlier and would die of old age in a few hours' time. The mayfly's life was a short one. He had to act quickly. There was not a fraction of a second to lose. How would you spend your life if you knew that you were born in the morning and would die in the evening?

He had no sooner emerged from his two years' larval life than he set out to look for a female with reproduction on his mind. It was a vain search for immortality through his offspring. He would spend his only day on the quest, with no thought of eating or resting or being particular.

His main predator was time, and every second was an adversary. Compared with time itself, the terrible spider was only a delaying factor, not a full-blown enemy.

He could feel old age coming on apace. In a few hours' time, he would be senile. He was done for and had been born for nothing. It was a bitter blow.

He struggled to get free. The trouble with spiders' webs was that if you moved you had had it, but if you did not move you were done for anyway.

The spider came up to him and gave a few extra turns of the cord. These two fine kills would supply him with all the protein he needed to make a second web the next day. But just as he was about to put his victim to sleep again, he detected a different vibration, this time an intelligent one. *Tap tap taptaptap tap tap taptap.* It was a female. She came toward him along a thread on which she tapped out a signal:

I'm yours. I haven't come to steal your food.

Her way of vibrating was the most erotic thing the male had ever felt. *Tap tap taptaptap.* Ah, he could no longer resist her charms and ran to his beloved (a mere slip of a thing only four moults old, whereas he was already twelve). She was three times as big as he, but then he liked his females big. He pointed to the two prey from which they would later draw fresh strength.

Then they took up the copulating position, no simple matter where spiders are concerned. The male had no penis but a kind of double genital cannon. He hurriedly built a target, a small-scale web, which he showered with gametes, then moistened one of his legs in it and stuffed it into the female's receptacle. He was very excited and did it several times over. For her part, the young beauty was so close to swooning that she suddenly could not stop herself from grabbing hold of the male's head and biting it off.

After that, it would have been stupid not to eat him. Once she had finished she was still hungry. She threw herself on the mayfly and shortened his life still more. Then she turned toward the ant queen, who, seeing that it was injection time again, panicked and squirmed.

It really was 56th's lucky day, for a new character now burst noisily onto the scene from the depths of the horizon and changed the situation. It was another of the creepy crawlies from the south who had recently moved up north. This time it was a very big one, a rhinoceros beetle. It struck the heart of the web, stretched it like glue and broke it (95/10 webs are strong, but only up to a point). The fine silk doily was torn to shreds, and tattered remnants of it floated in the air.

The female spider had already jumped, clinging to her safety rope. Freed from her white straitjacket, the ant queen dragged herself along on the ground discreetly, unable to take off.

But the spider's thoughts were elsewhere. She climbed up a branch to build a silken nursery in which to lay her eggs. When her dozens of offspring hatched, their first thought would be to eat their mother. Spiders were like that. They did not know how to say thank you.

"Bilsheim!"

He hastily held the receiver away from his ear as if it had bitten him. It was his boss, Solange Doumeng.

"Hello?"

"Why haven't you carried out my orders? What are you playing at? Are you waiting for the whole city to disappear into this cellar? I know you, Bilsheim. The only thing you ever want to do is take it easy. I won't have it. I insist you settle this affair within forty-eight hours."

"But . . ."

"There's no but about it. Your guys have been given my instructions. All you have to do now is go down with them tomorrow morning. The equipment will be there. Get off your backside, for God's sake!"

His hands began to tremble. He was not a free man. He had to obey if he wanted to keep his job and avoid becoming a social outcast. At that point in time, the only way he could conceive of gaining freedom was to become a tramp, and he was not quite ready for that. An ulcer formed on the battlefield of his stomach. In the end, his respect for order overcame his taste for freedom and he complied.

The troop of huntresses were watching the lizard from behind a rock. He was a good sixty heads (eighteen centimeters) long. His tough, greenish-yellow armor with black markings was both frightening and disgusting. The

103,683rd soldier had the impression that the markings were splashes of its victims' blood.

As expected, the animal was sluggish with cold. He was walking in slow motion and seemed to hesitate before putting his foot down anywhere.

Just as the sun was about to disappear, a pheromone went out.

Kill the beast!

The lizard saw an army of aggressive little black creatures sweeping down on him. He reared up slowly, opened a pink mouth, lashed the nearest ants with a quick tongue and swallowed them down. Then he gave a little burp and made off in a flash.

Breathless and dumbfounded, the huntresses were left about thirty fewer in number. For someone anesthetized by the cold, the lizard was not exactly defenseless.

The 103,683rd, although she could never be suspected of cowardice, was one of the first to say it was suicide to attack such an animal. He was an impregnable stronghold. His skin was impervious to mandibles and acid, and his size and speed, even at a low temperature, gave him an unassailable superiority.

However, the ants did not give up. Like a pack of tiny wolves, they threw themselves on the trail of the monster. They galloped under the ferns, throwing off menacing pheromones that smelled of death. For the time being, this frightened only the slugs, but it helped the ants to feel terrible and invulnerable. They caught up with the lizard a few thousand heads farther on. He was clinging to the bark of a spruce and digesting his breakfast.

They had to act fast. The longer they waited, the more energy he would have accumulated. If he was quick when it was cold, he would be invincible when stuffed full of solar calories. They put their antennae together to confer and decided on the tactics for their attack.

Some warriors dropped onto the animal's head from a branch. They tried to blind him by nibbling his eyelids and started to bore into his nostrils. But this first commando group failed. The irritated lizard brushed his face with his leg and swallowed the stragglers.

A second wave of assailants came running up. When they were almost within range of his tongue, they made a wide detour before swooping brutally onto the stump of his tail. As Mother said: *Each enemy has his weak point. Find it and concentrate your attacks on it.*

They reopened the scar by burning it with acid and dived inside the lizard, invading his bowels. He rolled on his back, pedaling his hind legs in the air and striking his stomach with his forelegs. A thousand ulcers were gnawing at him.

Then another group at last got a foothold in his nostrils, which were immediately enlarged and hollowed out with jets of boiling acid.

Farther up his face, they were attacking his eyes. They burst the soft marbles, but the eye sockets turned out to be blind alleys. The holes in the optic nerves were too narrow for the ants to use to reach the brain, so they joined forces with the teams already deep inside the nostrils.

The lizard writhed and stuck its leg in its mouth to try to squash the ants piercing its throat, but it was too late.

In a corner of its lungs, 4,000th met up with her young colleague, 103,683rd. It was pitch-black and they could see nothing because asexual ants have no infrared simple eyes. They joined the ends of their antennae together.

Our sisters are busy. Let's take advantage of it to leave for the termite hill of the east. They'll think we've been killed in combat.

They left the same way they had come in, through the caudal stump, which was now bleeding profusely.

The next day, the lizard would be cut up into thousands of edible strips. Some would be covered in sand and carted off to Zoubi-zoubi-kan. Others would reach even Bel-o-kan, and a whole new epic tale would be made up to describe the hunt. The ant civilization needed to take comfort from its strength. Conquering lizards was something it found particularly reassuring.

HYBRIDIZATION: It would be wrong to suppose that the nests are impenetrable to foreigners. Each insect admittedly bears the scent flag of its city, but that does not mean that it is "xenophobic" in the human sense of the word.

If, for example, you mix a hundred Formica rufa ants and a hundred Lasius niger ants, including a fertile queen of each species, in a vivarium full of earth, you notice that after a few nonfatal skirmishes and lengthy antenna discussions, the two species start to build the anthill together. Some corridors are adapted to the size of the russet ants, others to the size of the black ants, but they intersect and mingle, proving that neither species is dominant, and neither tries to shut the other up in a closed quarter, forming a ghetto within the city.

EDMOND WELLS,
ENCYCLOPEDIA OF RELATIVE AND ABSOLUTE KNOWLEDGE

The path leading to the eastern territories had not yet been cleared. The wars against the termites had prevented all pacification of the region.

The 4,000th warrior and the 103,683rd soldier trotted along a trail that had been the scene of a good many skirmishes. There were magnificent, poisonous butterflies flying overhead, which they could not help but find disturbing.

Farther on, 103,683rd felt something crawling under her right leg. She eventually discovered that it was mites, tiny creatures equipped with points and antennae, hairs and hooks, that migrate in herds in search of nice dusty nooks. The 103,683rd was amused at the sight. To think there were beings as small as mites and as big as ants on the same planet.

The 4,000th stopped in front of a flower. The pain was suddenly too much. Within her old body, which had been through a lot that day, the young ichneumon wasp larvae had at last woken up. They were probably having lunch, gaily tucking in to the poor ant's internal organs.

To help her, 103,683rd brought up a few molecules of

lomechusa honeydew from the bottom of her social crop. After the fight in the underground passages of Bel-o-kan, she had stored a minute amount of it in case she needed an analgesic. She had handled it very carefully and had not been contaminated by the delicious poison.

The 4,000th's pain was relieved as soon as she ingested the liqueur, but she wanted more. The 103,683rd soldier tried to reason with her, but 4,000th was not to be deterred. She was ready to fight her friend for the precious drug and was about to leap to the attack when she slid into a kind of sandy crater. A lion ant trap!

Lion ants—or, to be more precise, their larvae—have shovel-shaped heads with which they dig their notorious craters. All they have to do then is bury themselves and wait for passersby.

The 4,000th warrior realized a little too late what was happening to her. Generally speaking, ants are light enough to get out of such a spot, but before she could even begin her climb, two long mandibles bristling with spikes suddenly appeared from the bottom of the bowl and sprayed her with sand.

Help!

She forgot the suffering caused by her uninvited guests and her craving for the lomechusa liqueur. She was afraid and did not want to die that way.

She struggled with all her might, but like spiders' webs, lion ant traps are designed to work on their victims' panic. The more 4,000th flailed about in an effort to climb out of the crater, the more its sides collapsed and dragged her down to the bottom, where the lion ant was still spraying her with fine sand.

The 103,683rd soldier had quickly grasped that if she leaned over to hold out a helping leg, she would be in danger of falling in as well. She went away to look for a blade of grass that would be sufficiently long and strong.

The old ant grew tired of waiting and let out a scent cry. She pedaled harder than ever in the almost liquid sand and went down even faster. She was now no more than five heads from the shears. Seen close-up, they were absolutely terrifying. Each mandible was notched with hundreds of sharp little teeth, themselves separated by long, curved pikes. The tip resembled an awl that could pierce any ant shell without too much difficulty.

The 103,683rd soldier at last reappeared at the edge of the bowl and held out a daisy to her companion. The old ant quickly reached up to grasp the stem, but the lion ant had no intention of relinquishing his prey. He frantically showered the two ants with sand so that they could no longer see or hear anything. Then he began to throw pebbles, which made an ugly sound as they bounced off their chitin. Half buried, 4,000th continued to slide.

The 103,683rd gripped the stem in her mandibles and braced herself for a jolt that did not come. Just as she was about to give up, a leg shot out of the sand. The 4,000th warrior was safe. At last she jumped out of the death trap.

Down below, the greedy claws snapped with rage and disappointment. The lion ant needed protein for his metamorphosis into an adult. How long would he have to wait before another prey slid down to him?

The 4,000th warrior and the 103,683rd soldier washed and indulged over and over again in trophallaxis. This time, lomechusa honeydew was not on the menu.

"Good morning, Bilsheim."

She held out a limp hand.

"Yes, I know you're surprised to see me here, but this case is dragging on too long. It's become too serious now. The chief's already taking a personal interest in it. I've decided to lend a hand before the minister steps in as well. Cheer up, Bilsheim, I'm only kidding. Where's your sense of humor?"

The old policeman was at a loss for words. This had been going on for fifteen years. Saying "Of course" to Solange Doumeng had never worked, and she had soured considerably with age. He glared at her, but her eyes were hidden under a lock of the hair she dyed a fashionable red. It did not make her any less unattractive.

"Why did you come? Do you want to go down into the cellar?" asked the policeman.

"You must be joking! No, you're going down, I'm staying here. I've got everything I need, a flask of tea and my walkie-talkie."

"What if something happens to me?"

"Why imagine the worst? Haven't you got any guts? I told you, we're linked by radio. At the first sign of danger, let me know and I'll do whatever's necessary. We're really looking after you, you know. You're going down with all the latest equipment. Look, you'll have a mountaineering rope and guns, not to mention six strong men."

She indicated the policemen standing at attention. Bilsheim muttered, "Galin went down with eight firemen. It didn't do him much good."

"But they didn't have any weapons or radio contact. Don't look like that, Bilsheim."

He did not feel like arguing. It only exasperated him. If you argued with Solange Doumeng, you became like her. She was like a weed. He had to try to grow without being contaminated.

The disenchanted inspector put on a spelunking outfit, tied the mountaineering rope around his waist and slung his walkie-talkie across his shoulder.

"If I don't come back up, I'd like all my belongings to go to the police orphanage."

"Stop bullshitting, Bilsheim. You'll come back up and we'll all go to a restaurant together and celebrate."

"Just in case I don't come back up, there's something I'd like you to know."

She frowned.

"Stop being childish, Bilsheim!"

"I'd like you to know we all have to pay for what we do in the end."

"Now he's gone all mystical on us. No, Bilsheim, you're wrong. We don't have to pay for what we do.

Maybe there is a God, as you say, but if there is, he couldn't care less about us. And if you don't enjoy yourself while you're alive, you certainly won't get a chance to when you're dead!"

She sniggered briefly, then went up to her subordinate until she was close enough to touch him. He held his breath. There'd be enough unpleasant smells in the cellar.

"But you're not going to die. You're going to solve this case. It wouldn't help much if you died."

The inspector was growing childish with vexation. He was like a little boy who had had something taken away from him and was resorting to insults because he knew he was never going to get it back.

"Of course, my death would mean the failure of your 'personal' investigation. They'd see what happens when you 'lend a hand,' as you say."

She came still closer, as if she meant to kiss him on the lips. Instead, she spat deliberately.

"You don't like me, do you, Bilsheim? Nobody likes me and I couldn't care less. I don't like you, either. I don't need to be liked. There's something you should know, though. If you die down there, I won't be in the least put out. I'll just send in a third team. If you really want to harm me, come back alive and successful and I'll be in your debt."

He did not answer. He had caught sight of the white roots in her fashionable hairdo and felt better already.

"We're ready," said one of the policemen, picking up his gun.

They had roped themselves together.

"Okay, let's go."

They nodded to the three policemen who would stay in touch with them on the surface, then disappeared into the cellar.

Solange Doumeng sat down at a desk on which she had set up her two-way radio.

"Good luck. Come back soon."

THREE JOURNEYS

The 56th female had at last found the ideal place to build her city. It was a round hill. When she climbed to the top, she could see the easternmost cities, Zoubi-zoubi-kan and Gloubi-diu-kan. If all went well, it should not be too difficult to link up with the rest of the Federation.

She examined her surroundings. The ground was quite hard and gray in color. The new queen looked for a soft spot, but the ground was hard all over. When she stuck her mandible in to try to dig her first nuptial chamber, she felt a strange little tremor, reminiscent of an earth-quake but far too localized to be one. She stabbed the ground once more and the trembling began again, except that this time it was worse. The whole hill rose up and slid to the left.

In living memory the ants had seen a great many things—but never a hill that was alive. This one was now moving along at a good pace, cleaving through the tall grass and crushing the undergrowth.

The 56th female had still not gotten over her surprise when she saw a second hill approaching as if by magic.

She did not have time to get off and was carried away into a parade of amorous hills. It was bad enough when they pawed each other shamelessly, but her hill was female and another hill climbed slowly on top of her. A stony head gradually emerged and this dreadful gargoyle opened its mouth.

It was too much for the young queen and she gave up the idea of founding her city in the area. Rolling to the bottom of the headland, she realized the full extent of the peril she had escaped. The hills not only had heads but also four clawed feet and small triangular tails.

It was her first sight of tortoises.

THE TIME OF CONSPIRATORS: The most widespread system of organization among human beings is a complex hierarchy of "administrators," powerful men and women who supervise, or rather manage, smaller "creative" groups whose work is then appropriated by "commercial" personnel in the name of distribution. The administrative, creative and commercial personnel make up the three castes that nowadays correspond to ant workers, soldiers and reproductive forms.

The struggle between Stalin and Trotsky, two early-twentieth-century Russian leaders, is a marvelous illustration of the change from a system favoring the "creative" group to a system favoring the administrators. Trotsky, the mathematician and inventor of the Red Army, was ousted by Stalin, the conspirator. A page had been turned.

It is quicker and easier to get ahead in society by exercising charm, uniting assassins and putting out disinformation than by producing new ideas and things.

EDMOND WELLS,
ENCYCLOPEDIA OF RELATIVE AND ABSOLUTE KNOWLEDGE

The 4,000th warrior and the 103,683rd soldier had set off again on the scent trail leading to the termite hill of the east. On the way, they met beetles pushing along balls of humus and explorer ants of a species so small they were hard to see and others so big the two soldiers could hardly make themselves seen.

There are over twelve thousand species of ants, each with its own morphology. The smallest measure only a few hundred microns and the largest can reach up to seven centimeters in length. Russet ants are medium-sized.

The 4,000th at last seemed to get her bearings. They still had to cross the patch of green moss, climb up the acacia bush and pass under the daffodils, and it should be behind the dead tree trunk.

And once they had crossed the stump, the eastern river and port of Satei did indeed appear in front of them through the sea grass and buckthorns.

"Hello, hello, Bilsheim, are you receiving me?"

"Loud and clear."

"Is everything all right?"

"Yes, fine."

"The length of rope unrolled shows you've gone four hundred and eighty meters."

"Great."

"Have you seen anything?"

"Nothing worth mentioning. Just a few inscriptions engraved on the stone."

"What sort of inscriptions?"

"Esoteric formulae. Would you like me to read you one?"

"No. I'll take your word for it."

The 56th female's belly was seething. Inside, the inhabitants of her future city were pushing and pulling and waving their legs about with impatience.

She therefore stopped being fussy, chose a bowl of ochre and black earth and decided to found her city there.

The place was not too badly situated. She couldn't detect any smell of dwarves, termites or wasps there-abouts, and she even noticed a few trail pheromones indicating that the Belokanians had already passed this way.

She tasted the earth. The soil was rich in trace elements and was moist without being wet. There was even a little overhanging shrub.

She cleared a circular area three hundred heads in diameter, which was the best shape for her city.

She felt exhausted and swallowed to bring up the food in her social crop, but it had been empty for some time. She had no energy reserves left. She therefore tore off her wings with a sharp tug and greedily ate the muscles in their roots.

With this intake of calories, she should be able to hold out for a few more days.

She then buried herself up to her antennae. No one must be able to spot her while she was easy prey.

She waited. The town hidden in her body was slowly waking. What would she call it?

First she had to think of a queen's name. For ants, having a name meant existing as an independent entity. Workers, soldiers and virgin males and females were designated only by the number of their birth. Fertilized females, on the other hand, could take a name.

Hmm. When she left, she was being pursued by the rock-scented warriors, so she could simply call herself "the pursued queen." But, no, she was being pursued because she had tried to solve the mystery of the secret weapon. She must not forget that. So she became "the mystery-born queen."

And she decided to name her city "city of the mystery-born queen," which, in the scent language of ants, smells like this: Chli-pou-kan.

Two hours later, he got another call.

"How's it going, Bilsheim?"

"We're in front of a door, an ordinary door. There's a big inscription on it in ancient-looking script."

"What does it say?"

"Shall I read it to you this time?"

"Yes, please."

The inspector shone his flashlight on the inscription and started to read in a slow, solemn voice because he was deciphering the text as he went along:

"At the moment of death, the soul's impressions are similar to those of initiates in the ways of the Great Mysteries.

"First they rush along blindly, twisting and turning, on an endless, anxious journey through the shadows.

"Then, just before the end, their fear reaches its height. Bathed in cold sweat, they shiver and tremble, utterly terrified.

"This phase is almost immediately followed by a return to the light, a sudden illumination.

"They are surrounded by a marvelous glow and move through pure places and meadows ringing with voices and dancing.

"Sacred words inspire religious respect. The perfect initiate is free to celebrate the Mysteries."

A policeman shivered.

"And what's behind the door?" asked the walkie-talkie.

"Hold on, I'll open it. You men follow me."

There was a long pause.

"Hello, Bilsheim. Hello, Bilsheim. Answer me, damn you! What can you see?"

She heard a shot, then once more silence.

"Say something, Bilsheim!"

"Bilsheim speaking."

"Go ahead, tell us what's happening."

"There are rats. Thousands of them. They attacked us but we managed to drive them away."

"Was that the shot I heard?"

"Yes. They're lying low now."

"Tell me what you can see."

"There's red everywhere you look, traces of ferrous rocks on the walls and blood on the ground. We're going on."

"Maintain radio contact. Why are you switching off?"

"I'd rather do things my way than have you tell me what to do from a distance, if you don't mind."

"But Bilsheim—"

Click. He had switched off his radio.

Satei was not exactly a port and it was not an advance post either, but it was certainly the Belokanian expeditions' favorite place for crossing the river.

In ancient times, when the first ants of the Ni dynasty came to this stretch of water, they realized it would not be easy to cross. But an ant never gives up. If necessary, it will bang its head against an obstacle fifteen thousand times in fifteen thousand different ways until either it dies or the obstacle gives way.

This might not seem a very logical way of proceeding, and it has certainly cost the Myrmician civilization a good deal of time and lives, but it has paid off. In the end, at the cost of enormous effort, ants have always succeeded in overcoming their difficulties.

At Satei, the explorers had initially attempted to get across on foot. The skin on the water was strong enough to support their weight but they could not get a grip on it with their claws. They skated about on the edge of the water as if it were an ice rink and could take only two steps forward and three steps sideways before being eaten by frogs.

After a hundred fruitless attempts and the loss of several thousand explorers, the ants decided to try something else. Workers formed a chain, holding each other by the legs and antennae until they reached the other side. That experiment might have worked if the river had not been so rough and wide. It left two hundred and forty thousand dead, but the ants did not give up. At the instigation of their then-queen, Biu-pa-ni, they tried to build a bridge of leaves, then a bridge of twigs, then a bridge of cockchafers, then a bridge of pebbles. Those four experiments cost the lives of nearly six hundred and seventy thousand workers. Biu-pa-ni had already killed more of her subjects to build the bridge of her dreams than all the territorial battles fought during her reign had.

Nevertheless, she did not give up. They had to cross over into the eastern territories. After the bridges, she had the idea of bypassing the river by following it north to its source. None of those expeditions ever came back and they left eight thousand dead. Then she said to herself that the ants should learn how to swim. Fifteen thousand dead. Then she told herself the ants should try to tame the frogs. Sixty-eight thousand dead. Or glide across on leaves from the big tree. Fifty-two dead. Or walk under the water by weighting their legs with hardened honey. Twenty-seven dead. Legend had it that, when told that there were only a dozen unscathed workers left in the city and that they had to abandon the project for the time being, she had declared:

Pity. I still had plenty of ideas left.

The Federation ants came up with a satisfactory solution in the end, though. Three hundred thousand years later, Queen Lifougryuni suggested to her daughters that they dig a tunnel under the river. It was so simple no one had ever thought of it before.

And that is why they could move about with ease under the river at Satei.

The 103,683rd soldier and the 4,000th warrior had been making their way along the famous tunnel for several degrees. It was damp inside but not actually running with water. The termite city was built on the other bank, and the termites used the same underground passage for their incursions into federal territory. Until now, there had been a tacit agreement. There was no fighting in the passage and everyone, termite or ant, passed freely. But it was clear that if one of the two parties ever attempted to get the upper hand, the other would immediately try to block up or flood the passage.

As they walked endlessly down the long gallery, their only problem was the cold. The mass of liquid above them was freezing and it was even colder underground. It was making them sluggish, and every step was more difficult than the last. They knew that if they fell asleep down there, they would hibernate forever. They crawled toward the exit, drawing their last reserves of protein and sugar from their social crops. With their muscles about to seize up, they at last caught sight of the exit. When they came out into the open, 103,683rd and 4,000th were so cold they fell asleep in the middle of the path.

Moving forward in single file like that along the narrow passageway made his mind go blank. There was nothing to think about there, you just had to keep on going until you got to the end. Always supposing there was an end.

The six policemen had fallen silent behind him. Bilsheim could hear their harsh breathing and told himself he was the victim of an injustice.

By now, he should have been a chief inspector on a decent salary. He was good at his job, put in long hours and had already solved a dozen or more cases. Only that Doumeng woman always blocked his promotion.

Suddenly he could not stand it any longer.

"Shit!"

They all stopped.

"Are you all right, Inspector?"

"Yes, I'm fine. Keep moving."

Worst of all, he had even started talking to himself. He bit his lip and tried to pull himself together but he was brooding again not five minutes later.

He had nothing against women but he had something against incompetence. The old bitch can barely read and write, she's never conducted an investigation and she gets promoted to the top of the entire department of a hundred and eighty policemen. And she earns four times as much as me! Join the police, they said! She was appointed by her predecessor, probably screwed her way up. She never gives us any peace, either. She's a busybody and a troublemaker and she sabotages her own department by trying to be indispensable.

As he was turning these thoughts over in his mind, Bilsheim remembered a documentary he had seen about toads. They get so excited during the mating season that they jump on anything that moves: females, males and even stones. They squeeze the eggs they want to fertilize out of their partners' bellies. Those that squeeze females get rewarded for their pains. Those that squeeze males get nothing and change partners. Those that squeeze stones get sore arms and give up.

But there are some that squeeze lumps of earth. The lump of earth is as soft as a female toad's belly so they do not stop squeezing. Their behavior is sterile but they can carry on with it for days on end, thinking they are doing the right thing.

The inspector smiled. Perhaps he should try explaining to old Solange that there were far more effective ways of going about things than being obstructive and causing stress. He did not really think it would do any good, though. After all, he told himself, he was probably the one who was out of place in the lousy department.

The others behind him were also thinking dark thoughts. The silent descent was getting on all their nerves. They had been walking for five hours now without a break. Most of them were working out how much extra pay they would ask for when they got back. Others were thinking about their wives and children, their cars or a pack of beer.

NOTHING: What greater pleasure is there than to stop thinking? To halt at last the flow of more or less useful or more or less important ideas. To stop thinking. To be as though dead yet still be able to come to life again. To be emptiness itself. To return to one's very origins. To stop even being someone thinking about nothing. To be nothing. That is a worthwhile ambition.

EDMOND WELLS,
ENCYCLOPEDIA OF RELATIVE AND ABSOLUTE KNOWLEDGE

After lying inert on the muddy bank all night, the bodies of the two soldiers were revived by the first rays of the sun.

One by one, the facets of 103,683rd's eyes were reactivated, illuminating her brain with the new scene in front of her. It consisted entirely of an enormous eye suspended above her, staring attentively.

The young asexual ant let out a pheromone cry of horror that burned her antennae. The eye also took fright and withdrew hastily along with the long horn bearing it. Both hid beneath a kind of round pebble. A snail!

There were others nearby, five in all, concealed beneath their shells. The two ants went up to one and walked around it. They tried hard to bite it but could not get a grip. It was an impenetrable fortress.

One of Mother's sayings came back to her: *Security is my worst enemy. It dulls my reflexes and robs me of my initiative.*

She told herself that these creatures, safe inside their shells, had always had an easy life grazing on grass that stayed put. They had never had to fight, lure, hunt or flee. They had never had to face up to life and had therefore never evolved.

She suddenly took it into her head to force them to leave their shells and prove to them that they were not invulnerable. Just then, two of the five snails decided that the danger was past and eased their bodies out of their shelters to relieve their nervous tension.

They met and fastened together, belly to belly, slime to slime, soldered in a sticky embrace running the length of their bodies. Their sex organs touched.

Something was happening between them, very slowly. The snail on the right had plunged its calcareous-tipped penis into the egg-filled vagina of the left-hand snail, which had in turn thrust an erect penis into its partner.

Both knew the pleasure of penetrating and being penetrated at the same time. Having both a vagina and a penis, they could experience the sensations of both sexes simultaneously.

The right-hand snail was the first to experience a male orgasm. Its writhing altered and its body went tense, shot through with electricity. The hermaphrodites' four eye horns joined together. The slime turned into foam and then bubbles. They were dancing close together, the sensuality of their movements heightened by the slow rhythm of the dance.

The left-hand snail pricked up its horns as it in turn experienced a male orgasm. But it had hardly finished ejaculating when a second wave of pleasure, this time vaginal, swept over its body. The right-hand snail, too, experienced a female climax.

Their horns then fell back down, their penises were retracted and their vaginas closed up. Once they had completed the act, the lovers repelled one another like magnets with the same polarity. It was the age-old story. The two machines for giving and receiving pleasure moved slowly apart, their eggs fertilized by their partner's sperms.

While 103,683rd was still dazed by the beauty of the sight, 4,000th leaped to attack the larger of the snails, hoping to take advantage of its postcoital fatigue to disembowel it. But it was too late; they were safe inside their shells again.

The old explorer did not give up, knowing they would come out again in the end, and patiently laid siege to them. Finally, a timid eye, followed by a whole horn, inched its way out of the shell. The snail wanted to see what was going on in the world outside.

When the second horn appeared, 4,000th darted forward and bit the eye with all the strength of her mandibles. She tried to sever it but the snail curled up, dragging the explorer inside its shell.

Gloop!

The 103,683rd soldier thought hard. How could she save her companion? Then an idea sprang from one of her three brains. She seized a pebble in her mandibles and started to hit the shell with all her might. She had invented the hammer, but the snail's shell was not made of balsa wood and the knocking only made music. She had to think of something else.

It was surely her lucky day, for she now discovered the lever. She grabbed a strong twig and a bit of gravel to use as an axis, then leaned all her weight on it to overturn the heavy creature. She had to try several times but the shell at last wobbled to and fro before toppling over with the entrance uppermost. She had done it!

She climbed up the coils, leaned over the well formed by the hollow shell and dropped onto the snail. After a long slide, her fall was broken by a gelatinous brown substance. Sickened by the greasy slime in which she was floundering, she began to tear at the soft tissue. She could not use acid for fear of dissolving in it herself.

Soon another liquid mingled with the slime: the snail's transparent blood. The panic-stricken animal uncoiled in a spasm that flung the two ants out of its shell.

They were unharmed but spent some time caressing each other's antennae.

The dying snail tried to get away but lost its entrails en route. The two ants caught up with it and finished it off easily, terrifying the other four snails, who had put out their eye horns to see what was happening. They curled up deep inside their shells and did not stir from them again for the rest of the day.

That morning, 103,683rd and 4,000th gorged themselves on snail. They cut it up into slices and ate it as warm steak in slime. They even found the vaginal pouch full of eggs. Snail caviar was one of the russet ants' favorite dishes and a valuable source of vitamins, fat, sugar and protein.

With their social crops full to the brim and stuffed with energy from the sun, they set off again at a good pace on the road leading southeast.

PHEROMONE ANALYSIS: (Experiment thirty-four). I have succeeded in identifying a few ant communication molecules using chromatography and a mass spectrometer. I have thus been able to undertake the chemical analysis of a communication between a male and a worker intercepted at 10 P.M. The male had discovered a bread crumb. This is what he emitted:
"*6-methyl.*"
"*4-methyl 3-hexanone [2 emissions].*"
"*Ketone.*"
"*3-octanone.*"
Then again:
"*Ketone.*"
"*3-octanone [2 emissions].*"

EDMUND WELLS,
ENCYCLOPEDIA OF RELATIVE AND ABSOLUTE KNOWLEDGE

On the way, they met other snails. All of them hid as if word had gotten around that the ants were dangerous. There was one, however, who did not hide and whose body lay there for all to see.

Intrigued, the two ants went up to it. The animal had been crushed to pieces by something massive. Its body had burst and was spread over a wide area.

The 103,683rd soldier immediately thought of the termites' secret weapon and realized they must be close to the enemy city. They examined the body more closely. It had been a sudden, extremely powerful blow. It was not surprising they had managed to smash the post of La-chola-kan with such a weapon.

She made up her mind. They must enter the termite city and study their weapon or, better still, steal it. The whole Federation might otherwise be annihilated.

Suddenly a strong wind blew up and they were sucked into the sky before their claws had had time to cling to the ground. The two ant soldiers did not have wings, but they flew just the same.

A few hours later, when the team on the surface had dozed off, the walkie-talkie crackled into life again.

"Hello, Madame Doumeng? That's it, we've reached the bottom."

"Well? What can you see?"

"It's a blind alley. There's a concrete-and-steel wall that was built very recently. It seems to be the end. No, wait, there's another inscription."

"What does it say?"

" 'How do you make four equilateral triangles out of six matches?' "

"Is that all?"

"No, there are some keys with letters on them, probably to key in the reply."

"Isn't there a corridor at the side?"

"No, there isn't anything."

"Can't you see the others' bodies either?"

"No, nothing, but there are some footprints, as if lots of feet had been stamped just in front of the wall."

"What shall we do?" murmured a policeman. "Shall we go back up?"

Bilsheim examined the obstacle carefully. All the symbols and steel and concrete plates were hiding some kind of mechanism. Besides, where had the others disappeared to?

Behind him, the policemen were sitting down on the stairs. He concentrated on the keys. You must have to type the letters in a particular order. Jonathan Wells was a locksmith and had probably copied the security systems of the entrances to blocks of apartments. He had to find the code word.

He turned to his men.

"Anyone got any matches?"

The walkie-talkie lost patience.

"Hello, Inspector Bilsheim. What are you doing?"

"If you really want to help, try and make four triangles out of six matches. Call me back as soon as you find the solution."

"Do you take me for a fool, Bilsheim?"

The storm at last abated. In the space of a few seconds, the wind slowed its dance. Leaves, dust and insects were once more subject to the laws of gravity and fell according to their respective weights.

The 103,683rd soldier and the 4,000th warrior had been dropped on the ground a few dozen heads apart. They were reunited without injury and looked about them. They were in a stony region quite unlike the landscape they had left behind. There was not a single tree to be seen, only a few wild grasses scattered by the winds. They did not know where they were.

While they were gathering their strength to leave this sinister place, the heavens decided to display their might again. The clouds grew heavy and turned black. A flash of lightning split the air, discharging the static electricity that had accumulated in it.

All the animals understood this message from nature. Frogs dived, flies hid under pebbles and birds flew low.

Rain began to fall, and the two ants needed to find shelter urgently. Every drop could be fatal. They hurriedly made their way toward the distant outline of a tree or rock.

Little by little, through the heavy drops and creeping mists, the shape grew clearer. It was neither a rock nor a shrub but a veritable cathedral made of earth with the tops of its many towers lost in the clouds. They realized with a shock what they were seeing.

It was a termite hill! The termite hill of the east!

They were caught in a trap between the terrible rainstorm and the enemy city. They had intended to visit it but in very different circumstances. Millions of years of hatred and rivalry were holding them back.

But not for long. After all, they had come this far to

spy on the termite hill. Therefore they went on, trembling, toward a dark entrance at the foot of the edifice. With their antennae raised, mandibles wide open and legs slightly bent, they were ready to sell their lives dearly. However, against all expectation, there were no soldiers at the entrance to the termite hill.

It was very strange. What was going on?

The two asexual ants worked their way inside the vast city, their curiosity already getting the better of the most elementary caution. It was nothing like an anthill. The walls were made of something much less crumbly than earth, a mortar as hard as wood. The corridors were very damp. There was not the slightest draft and the atmosphere was abnormally rich in carbon dioxide.

They advanced inside it for 3°C-time without encountering a single sentry. It was most unusual. The two ants stopped and their antennae met in consultation. It did not take them very long to come to a decision: they would go on.

But by now they were completely disoriented. This foreign city was a maze even more tortuous than the city of their birth. Even the marker scents of their Dufour glands did not cling to the walls and they no longer knew whether they were above or below ground level.

They tried to retrace their steps, which did little to help the problem as they discovered more and more odd-shaped corridors. They were well and truly lost.

The 103,683rd soldier then picked up an extraordinary pheromone, a light. The two soldiers could not get over it. This glimmer of light at the heart of a deserted termite city made no sense whatsoever. They made their way toward the source of the rays.

It was an orangey-yellow light, which sometimes turned green or blue. After an extrabright flash, the light source went out. Then it came on again and started to flash, reflected by the ants' shiny chitin.

They made for the subterranean lighthouse as though hypnotized.

• • •

Bilsheim was hopping with excitement: he'd done it! He showed the policemen how to arrange the matches to make four triangles. At first they were stunned, then they let out cries of enthusiasm.

Solange Doumeng, who had got caught up in the game, belched:

"You've done it? You've done it? Tell me how!"

But he did not obey. She heard an uproar of voices mingled with mechanical noises, then once more silence.

"What's happening, Bilsheim? Tell me!"

The walkie-talkie began to crackle furiously.

"Hello! Hello!"

"Yes [*crackling*], we've opened up the passage. There's a corridor [*crackling*] behind the door. It goes off to the [*crackling*] right. We're going in."

"Wait! How did you make the four triangles?"

But Bilsheim and his men could no longer hear messages from the surface. Their radio loudspeaker wasn't working and had probably short-circuited. They could no longer receive anything but could still transmit.

"It's quite incredible. The farther we go, the more building's taken place. There's a vault overhead, and a light in the distance. We're going on."

"Wait, did you say a light, down there?" Solange Doumeng was shouting herself hoarse in vain.

"They're here!"

"Who's there, damn it? The bodies? Answer me."

"Look out."

She heard shots and cries, then the line was cut off.

The rope no longer unrolled but remained taut. The policemen on the surface gripped it and pulled, thinking it was caught on something. Three of them pulled, then five. Suddenly it gave.

They pulled on the rope and rolled it up—in the dining room rather than the kitchen because of the gigantic coil it formed. At last they got to the broken end. It was ragged enough to have been gnawed by teeth.

"What shall we do, ma'am?" murmured one of the policemen.

"Nothing. Nothing at all. Don't say a word about this to the press or anyone else and wall this cellar up as quickly as possible. The investigation is over. I'm closing the file and I never want to hear about this damn cellar again. Go and buy some bricks and mortar and be quick about it. And you can sort things out with the policemen's widows."

Early that afternoon, as the policemen were about to put the last bricks in place, they heard a muffled noise. Someone was coming back up! They cleared a passage. A head emerged from the shadows, followed by the survivor's whole body. It was a policeman. At last they were going to find out what was happening down there. Fear was written all over his face. Some of his facial muscles were paralyzed as if he had suffered a stroke and the end of his nose had been torn off and was bleeding profusely. He was trembling and his eyes were turned up. He looked like a zombie.

"Gebegeeeege," he uttered.

There was dribble running from the corner of his mouth and he ran a hand covered in cuts over his face. To the experienced eyes of his colleagues, they looked like knife wounds.

"What happened? Did you get attacked?"

"Heebeegeeebegebegee!"

"Is anyone else alive down there?"

"Beegeegeebebebeggbee!"

He was incapable of saying anything else so they dressed his wounds, shut him up in a psychiatric hospital and walled up the cellar door.

The slightest scratching of their legs on the ground caused the light to vary in intensity. It trembled as if it were alive and could hear them coming.

The ants stood still to make sure. The glimmer of light soon grew brighter until it lit up the tiniest crevices in the corridors. The two spies hid hastily to avoid being lit up by the strange projector. Then they took advantage of a drop in the light's intensity to make a dash for the source of the rays.

It turned out to be a phosphorescent beetle, a rutting glowworm. As soon as he spotted the intruders he went out completely. When nothing happened, he slowly glowed pale-green again, a cautious pilot light.

The 103,683rd soldier gave out the scent of nonaggression. Although all beetles understand this language, the glowworm did not reply. His green light faded and turned yellow before gradually taking on a reddish tinge. The ants supposed that this new color expressed a question.

We're lost in this termite hill, emitted the old explorer.

At first, the glowworm did not answer. After a few degrees he started to flash, expressing either joy or irritation. Since they did not know which, they waited. Suddenly he went off down a side corridor, flashing faster and faster. He seemed to want to show them something, so they followed him.

They found themselves in an even colder, damper part of the termite hill. They could hear a mournful whining but could not tell where it was coming from. It was like cries of distress in the form of scents and sounds.

The two explorers wondered what to do. The light-emitting insect could not speak but he could hear perfectly. As if in reply to their question, he lit up and went out in long bursts, as if to say: *Don't be afraid. Follow me.*

All three of them went deeper and deeper into the foreign basement until they reached a very cold sector where the corridors were much wider.

The whining started up again, louder than ever.

Look out! emitted 4,000th suddenly.

The 103,683rd soldier turned around. The glowworm

was lighting up a kind of monster that was coming toward them. It had the wrinkled face of an old man and its body was wrapped in a transparent white shroud. The soldier screamed a powerful scent of terror that suffocated his two companions. The mummy continued to approach them and seemed to be leaning forward to speak to them, but it toppled over and fell full-length on the ground, hitting it hard. The shell opened and the monstrous old man turned into a newborn termite nymph.

The disemboweled mummy had to prop herself up in a corner, where she continued her sad whining and writhing. So that was where the cries had been coming from.

There were mummies all around them, for the three insects were in a nursery. Hundreds of termite nymphs were lined up vertically against the walls. The 4,000th warrior inspected them and noticed that some of them had died of neglect. The survivors were sending out distress scents to call the nurses. They had not been licked for at least 2°C and they were all dying of hunger.

It was all wrong. A social insect would never abandon its brood, even for 1°C-time. Unless . . . The same idea occurred to both ants. Unless all the workers were dead and only the nymphs were left.

The glowworm flashed again as a signal for them to follow him down more corridors. There was a strange, sweet smell in the air. The soldier trod on something hard. She did not have infrared simple eyes and could not see in the dark. The living light came close and lit up 103,683rd's legs. She had stepped on the corpse of a termite soldier. It was very like an ant except that it was pure white and did not have a detached abdomen.

The ground was strewn with hundreds of white corpses. It was a massacre! Strangest of all, the bodies were still intact. There had not been a fight. The inhabitants were still frozen in the attitudes of everyday work and must have died instantly. Some seemed to have been engaged in conversation or cutting up wood with their mandibles. What could possibly have caused such a catastrophe?

The old warrior examined the grisly statues and found they were drenched in pungent scents. The two ants shivered. It was poison gas, which explained everything: the disappearance of the first expedition launched against the termite hill and the death of the last survivor of the second expedition, who had not been wounded.

If they felt nothing themselves, it was because the toxic gas had had time to disperse, but why had the nymphs survived? The old explorer framed a hypothesis. They had specific immune defenses or had perhaps been saved by their cocoons. They must now be immune to the poison. Insects are notorious for developing resistance to insecticides. Mithridatizing allows them to become immune to gradually increasing doses of poisons by producing mutant generations.

But who could have fed in the lethal gas? It was a real poser. Once again, while searching for the secret weapon, 103,683rd had stumbled on something just as incomprehensible.

The 4,000th warrior wanted to leave and the glowworm flashed its assent. The ants gave the larvae that could be saved a few pieces of cellulose, then left to look for the way out. The glowworm followed. As they went, the corpses of termite soldiers gave way to corpses of workers responsible for looking after the queen. Some were still holding eggs in their mandibles.

The architecture was becoming more and more sophisticated. The corridors, which were triangular in cross-section, were engraved with signs. The glowworm changed color and diffused a bluish light, showing that he had noticed something. A gasping sound was coming from the end of the corridor.

The trio came to a kind of sanctuary protected by five giant guards, who were all dead. The entrance was blocked by the lifeless bodies of twenty or so small workers, and the ants passed them from leg to leg to get them out of the way.

An almost perfectly spherical cave was thus revealed. The noise had been coming from the termite royal chamber.

The glowworm gave off a beautiful white light, which lit up a kind of strange slug in the center of the room. It was the termite queen, who was a caricature of an ant queen. Her small head and scrawny thorax ended in a fantastic abdomen nearly fifty heads long. This hypertrophied appendage was regularly shaken with spasms.

The small head was tossing with pain and screaming in sound and scent. The workers' corpses had stopped up the entrance so thoroughly that the gas had not been able to get in, but the queen was dying of neglect.

Look at her abdomen. The babies are pushing to get out and she can't give birth alone.

The glowworm climbed up to the ceiling and shed an orange light.

Thanks to the combined efforts of the two ants, the eggs began to flow from the enormous procreative pouch. It was a veritable tap of life. The queen had stopped screaming and seemed relieved.

She asked who had saved her in basic universal scent language and was surprised when she identified the ants' scents. She wanted to know if they were masked ants.

Masked ants were a species very gifted in organic chemistry. They were large, black insects who lived in the northeast. They could artificially reproduce any pheromone, whether passport, trail or communication, simply by mixing saps, pollens and salivas judiciously.

Once they had distilled their camouflage, they could make their way undetected into termite cities, for example, and then pillage and kill without any of their victims identifying them.

No, we aren't masked ants.

The termite queen asked them if there were any survivors in her city and the ants answered no. She asked them to kill her and put an end to her suffering but she wanted to tell them something first.

Yes, she knew why her city had been destroyed. The

termites had recently discovered the eastern end of the world. It was a smooth, black country where everything was destroyed.

Strange animals live there that are very fast and ferocious. They're the guardians of the end of the world. They're armed with black slabs that can flatten anything. And they're using poison gases now, too!

It reminded them of Queen Bi-stin-ga's old ambition to reach one of the ends of the world. Could it really be possible, then? The two ants were dumbfounded.

Until then, they had thought that the Earth was so big it was impossible to reach the edge, and now here was this termite queen telling them that the end of the world was close by and that it was guarded by monsters. Could Queen Bi-stin-ga's dream come true?

The whole tale seemed so incredible they did not know where to begin with their questions.

But why have these guardians of the end of the world come this far? Do they want to invade the western cities?

The fat queen did not know anything else and insisted she now wished to die. She had not learned how to stop her heart from beating, so they had to kill her.

The ants therefore decapitated the termite queen after she had told them the way out. Then they ate a few small eggs and left the imposing city, now nothing but a ghost town. At the entrance, they laid down a pheromone telling the story of the tragedy that had taken place there. It was their duty as Federation explorers.

The glowworm now took his leave of them. No doubt he, too, had lost his way in the termite hill when sheltering from the rain. Now that it was clear again he would resume his daily round: eat, give off light to attract females, reproduce, eat, give off light to attract females, reproduce . . . A glowworm's life, in fact!

They turned their eyes and antennae to the east. They could not see much from where they were but they knew all the same that the end of the world was not far off. It lay in that direction.

THE CLASHES OF CIVILIZATIONS: The meeting of two civilizations is always a delicate affair. One of the greatest challenges that has faced mankind was the enslavement of black Africans in the eighteenth century.

Most of the peoples who were enslaved lived inland in the plains and forests and had never seen the sea. A neighboring king suddenly came and declared war on them for no apparent reason and then, instead of killing them all, took them captive, chained them together and made them walk to the coast.

At the end of their journey, they discovered two incomprehensible things: (1) the vast sea; and (2) the white-skinned Europeans. Even if they had never seen the sea with their own eyes, they knew it from tales as the land of the dead, while the white men were like beings from another planet. They smelled peculiar, their skin was a peculiar color and they wore peculiar clothes.

Many died of fright. Others panicked, jumped out of the boats and were eaten by sharks. The survivors had one surprise after another. What did they see? White men drinking wine, for example. And they were sure it was blood, the blood of their own people.

EDMOND WELLS,
ENCYCLOPEDIA OF RELATIVE AND ABSOLUTE KNOWLEDGE

The 56th female was starving. It was not only a body but a whole population that was demanding its ration of calories. How was she to feed the tribe she was sheltering inside her? In the end, she made up her mind to leave her egg-laying hole, dragged herself a few hundred heads and brought back three pine needles, which she licked and chewed greedily.

It was not enough. She would have liked to go hunting but she no longer had the strength. She risked ending up as food for the thousands of predators lurking in the vicinity. She settled down in her hole and waited to die.

Instead, an egg appeared. It was her first Chlipoukanian and she had hardly felt it coming. She had shaken her numb legs and squeezed her bowels as hard as she could. It had to work or it was all over. When the egg rolled onto the ground, it was small and so gray it was almost black.

If she allowed it to hatch, the ant inside would be still-born—and she would not be able to feed her anyway. She therefore ate her first offspring.

This immediately gave her some surplus energy. There was one less egg in her abdomen and one more in her stomach. The sacrifice gave her the strength to lay a second egg, just as small and dark as the first.

She ate it and felt even better. The third egg was a little lighter, but she devoured it anyway.

It was only when she got to the tenth that the queen altered her strategy. Her eggs had turned gray and were as big as her eyeballs. Chli-pou-ni laid three like that, ate one and let the other two live, warming them with her body.

As she continued to lay, the two lucky ones turned into long larvae whose heads remained fixed in a strange grimace. Soon they began to whine for food and the arithmetic got complicated. Out of every three eggs she laid, she now needed one for herself and the other two to feed the larvae.

That is how you can produce something from nothing in a closed circuit. When a larva was big enough, she gave her another larva to eat. It was the only way of supplying her with the protein she needed to turn into a true ant.

But the surviving larva was always famished and writhed about screaming; her sisters made an unsatisfying meal. In the end, Chli-pou-ni ate her first attempt at a child.

I must make it, I must make it, she repeated to herself. She thought of the 327th male and laid five much lighter eggs in one push. She swallowed two of them and let the other three grow.

Between infanticide and childbirth, the torch of life was passed on. It was three steps forward and two back, but the cruel gymnastics finally resulted in the first prototype of a complete ant.

Undernourished, small and frail, she was still the first Chlipoukanian. The cannibal race for the existence of the city was now half won. This degenerate worker could move about and bring back provisions from the outside world: the corpses of insects, seeds, leaves and mushrooms.

Properly nourished at last, Chli-pou-ni gave birth to eggs that were much lighter and firmer, with strong shells that protected the eggs from the cold. The larvae were a reasonable size and the children who hatched from this new generation were big and strong. They would form the basis of the population of Chli-pou-kan.

The first sickly worker, who had brought the egg-layer food, was quickly put to death and devoured by her sisters. After that, all the pain and suffering that had preceded the foundation of the city were forgotten.

Chli-pou-kan had been born.

MOSQUITO: The mosquito is the insect most willing to duel with man. At one time or another, we have all stood on a bed in our pajamas with a slipper in our hand and our eyes fixed on the ceiling.

Yet it is only the disinfectant saliva from its probe that causes the itching. Without this saliva, each bite could become infected. The mosquito even takes the precaution of biting between two pain reception points.

Faced with man, the mosquito's strategy has evolved. It has learned to be quicker, more inconspicuous and livelier on the takeoff. Some bold souls of the latest generation do not hesitate to hide under their victims' pillows. They have discovered the principle of Edgar Allan Poe's Stolen Letter: the best hiding place is the most obvious one, for we always think of looking farther away for something that is very near.

EDMOND WELLS,
ENCYCLOPEDIA OF RELATIVE AND ABSOLUTE KNOWLEDGE

Grandmother Augusta gazed at her cases, which were already packed. She was going to move into the rue des Sybarites the next day. It seemed incredible but Edmond had envisaged Jonathan's disappearance and made provision for it in his will: "If Jonathan dies or disappears, and has not himself left a will, I should like my mother, Augusta Wells, to move into my apartment. If she disappears, or if she refuses this legacy, I should like Daniel Rosenfeld to inherit it, and if he refuses or disappears, Jason Bragel could then come and live . . ."

In the light of recent events, Edmond had certainly not been wrong to allow himself at least four heirs. But Augusta was not superstitious and thought that even if Edmond were antisocial, he had no reason to wish the death of his nephew and mother. As for Jason Bragel, he had been Edmond's best friend.

A strange thought crossed her mind. Edmond seemed to have tried to manage the future as if everything began after his death.

They had been walking in the direction of the rising sun for days. The 4,000th warrior's health was deteriorating all the time but she went on advancing without complaining, her courage and curiosity equal to anything.

Late one afternoon, they were climbing up the trunk of a hazelnut tree when they were suddenly surrounded by red ants, more of the tiny insects from the south who had set out to see the world. Their long bodies ended in a venomous sting and, as everyone knew, the slightest contact with it caused instant death. The two russet ants wished themselves elsewhere.

Apart from a few degenerate mercenaries, 103,683rd had never seen red ants in the Great Outside before. The lands of the east were definitely worth discovering.

There was a flurry of antennae. The red ants could communicate in the same language as the Belokanians.

You haven't got the right passport pheromones. Get out! This is our territory.

The russet ants replied that they were only passing through and wanted to go to the eastern end of the world. The red ants consulted one another.

They had recognized the other two as belonging to the Russet Federation. It might be a long way away but it was powerful (sixty-four cities before the last swarming), and the reputation of its armies had crossed the western river. It was probably better not to go looking for trouble. The red ants were a migrant species and were bound to have to cross the russets' federal territories one day.

The antenna movements gradually calmed down. It was a time for composition. A red ant passed on the group's decision:

You can spend one night here. We are prepared to show you the way to the end of the world and even to take you there. In exchange, you will leave us some of your identification pheromones.

It was a fair deal. The two soldiers knew that in giving away some of their pheromones they were handing the red ants free passage to all the vast Federation territories. But to be able to go to the end of the world and back was worth any price.

Their hosts guided them to the encampment a few branches higher. It was unlike anything they had ever seen. The red ants, who weave and sew, had built their temporary nest by sewing together the edges of three big hazelnut leaves. One served as the floor and the others as the side walls.

The 103,683rd soldier watched a group of weavers busy closing the "roof" before nightfall. They selected the hazelnut leaf that would serve as the ceiling. To join this leaf to the other three, they formed a living ladder from dozens of workers piled one on top of the other until they made a mound that reached the leaf roof.

The pile collapsed several times. It was too high.

The red ants then adopted a different approach. A group of workers hauled themselves up onto the ceiling leaf and formed a chain hanging from its very tip. The chain went down and down to meet up with the living ladder below. When it still did not reach, a bunch of red ants weighed it down at the end.

They were almost there. The stem of the leaf had bent and they were only a few centimeters short on the right. The ants in the chain made it swing to close the gap. At the end of each swing, the chain stretched and seemed to be on the point of breaking, but it held. At last the mandibles of the upper and lower acrobats linked up. *Snap!*

The second maneuver was to shorten the chain. The workers in the middle very carefully left the line and climbed onto their colleagues' shoulders and everyone pulled to draw the two leaves together. The leaf ceiling descended little by little on the village, casting its shadow over the floor.

However, although the box now had a lid, it still had to be sealed. An old red ant rushed inside a house and came back out brandishing a fat larva. It was the weaving instrument.

They made the sides parallel and held them together, then introduced the fresh larva. The poor thing had been building a cocoon in which to moult in peace, but now it would not get the chance. A worker seized a thread from the ball and began to unwind it. She stuck the end of a leaf with a little saliva, then passed the cocoon to her neighbor.

Feeling her thread being removed, the larva produced more to make up for it. The more they stripped her, the colder she got and the more silk she spat out. The workers took advantage of this. They passed the living shuttle from mandible to mandible and did not skimp on the thread. When their child died of exhaustion, they used another. Twelve larvae were thus sacrificed for that piece of work alone.

When they had finished closing the second edge of the leaf ceiling, the village had the appearance of a green box with white edges. On several different occasions, 103,683rd, who was walking about as if she were at home there, noticed black ants in the middle of a crowd of red ants. She could not help asking about it.

Are they mercenaries?
No, they're slaves.

The red ants were not known as slave-makers, but one of them was willing to explain that they had recently met a horde of slave-making ants heading west and had exchanged some black ant eggs for a portable woven nest.

The 103,683rd soldier did not let her off that easily and asked her if the meeting had not afterward turned into a fight. The other ant answered no, the terrible ants were already full up and had too many slaves as it was. Besides, they were afraid of the red ants' deadly stings.

The black ants that had hatched from the swapped eggs had taken on the passport scents of their hosts and served them as if they were their parents. How were they to know that their genetic inheritance made them predators and not slaves? They knew nothing of the world beyond what the red ants were willing to tell them.

Aren't you afraid they'll rebel?

They agreed there had already been hiccoughs, but the red ants generally forestalled incidents by eliminating any isolated recalcitrants. As long as the black ants were unaware that they had been stolen from a nest and belonged to another species, they lacked any real motivation.

Night and cold fell on the hazelnut tree and the two explorers were allocated a corner in which to spend the nocturnal mini-hibernation.

Chli-pou-kan was gradually growing. They had begun by laying out the Forbidden City. It was built, not in a stump, but in a peculiar object they had found buried there: a rusty tin that had once contained three kilos of stewed fruit and was rubbish from a nearby orphanage.

In this new palace, Chli-pou-ni frantically laid her eggs while they stuffed her with sugar, fat and vitamins.

Just below the Forbidden City, her first daughters had

built a nursery heated with rotting humus, the most practical method until work on the dome of twigs and the solarium could be completed.

Chli-pou-ni wanted her city to benefit from all the latest technology: mushroom beds, tanker ants, greenfly herds, supporting ivies, honeydew fermentation rooms, flour manufacturing rooms, mercenaries' quarters, a spy room, an organic chemistry room, etc.

Ants were running about in all directions. The young queen had managed to transmit her hopes and enthusiasm. She did not want Chli-pou-kan to be just another federal city. Her ambition was to make it a center of the avant-garde, the high point of Myrmician civilization, and she was full of suggestions.

For example, they had discovered an underground stream in the region of the twelfth floor of the basement. She felt that water was an element that had been insufficiently studied and that they must be able to find a way of walking on it.

In the first phase, a team was given the job of studying freshwater insects: water beetles, cyclops and daphnia. Were they edible? Could they one day be raised in controlled ponds?

She made her first known speech on the subject of greenflies:

We're moving toward a period of warfare. Weapons are becoming more and more sophisticated and we won't always be able to keep up. One day it may become risky to hunt outside. We have to plan for the worst. Our city must extend as far as possible in depth and we must favor the raising of greenflies above any other source of supply of vital sugars. These cattle will be kept in sheds on the lowest floors.

Thirty of her daughters made a sortie and brought back two greenflies who were about to give birth. A few hours later, they had a hundred or so baby greenflies, whose wings they cut off. They kept this embryonic herd on the twenty-third floor of the basement, where it was quite safe from ladybirds, and they gave it a plentiful supply of fresh leaves and sap-filled stems.

Chli-pou-ni sent explorers in all directions. Some brought back agaric spores, which were then planted in the mushroom beds. The queen was so hungry for discoveries she even decided to realize her mother's dream by planting a row of carnivorous flower seeds on the eastern frontier. She hoped in this way to slow down any attack by the termites and their secret weapon.

For she had not forgotten the mystery of the secret weapon, the assassination of the 327th prince and the food reserves hidden under the granite.

She dispatched a group of ambassadresses to Bel-o-kan. Officially, they were responsible for announcing to the queen mother the building of the sixty-fifth city and its rallying to the Federation. Unofficially, they were to try to carry on with the investigation on the fiftieth floor of the basement of Bel-o-kan.

The doorbell rang while Augusta was pinning her precious sepia photographs up on the gray wall. She checked that the safety chain was on and opened the door a crack.

A middle-aged man was standing there. He was very neatly dressed and did not even have any dandruff on the lapels of his jacket.

"Good morning, Mrs. Wells. I'd like to introduce myself. I'm Professor Leduc, a colleague of your son Edmond. I won't beat about the bush. I know you've already lost your grandson and great-grandson in the cellar and that eight firemen, six policemen and two detectives have also disappeared. However, I'd like to go down there just the same, Mrs. Wells."

Augusta was not sure she had heard right. She turned her hearing aid up to maximum volume.

"Are you Professor Rosenfeld?"

"No. Leduc. Professor Leduc. I see you've heard of Rosenfeld. Rosenfeld, Edmond and I are all entomologists. We share the same specialty, the study of ants, though it would be fair to say that Edmond had a considerable lead on us. It would be a pity if mankind did not get the benefit of it. I'd like to go down into your cellar."

When you are hard of hearing, you study people more closely. She examined Leduc and decided she did not much like the look of him.

"And what are you hoping to find in the cellar?"

"A book, an encyclopedia in which he systematically made a note of all his work. Edmond was secretive. He must have buried everything down there and set traps to kill or scare away the ignorant. But I'm forewarned and a man forewarned—"

"Can just as easily get killed," finished Augusta.

"Let me try."

"Listen, Mr. . . . ?"

"Leduc, Professor Laurent Leduc, of the National Center for Scientific Research, Laboratory 352."

She showed him to the cellar. There was a warning painted in big red letters on the wall built by the police:

NEVER EVER GO DOWN INTO THIS DAMN CELLAR AGAIN!!!!

She nodded her head toward it.

"Do you know what the people in this building are saying, Mr. Leduc? They're saying it's carnivorous and that it eats anyone who irritates its throat. Some of them would even like to fill it up with concrete."

She looked him up and down.

"Aren't you afraid of dying, Mr. Leduc?"

"Yes, I am," he said, smiling sardonically. "I'm afraid of dying in ignorance, without knowing what's at the bottom of the cellar."

It was days since 103,683rd and 4,000th had left the red weaver ants' nest. Two warriors with pointed stings had accompanied them. They had walked a long way together along trails barely scented with trail pheromones and had already covered thousands of heads since leaving the woven nest in the branches of the hazelnut tree. They had met all sorts of exotic animals whose names they did not even know, and had carefully avoided all of them.

When night came, they dug as deep a hole as possible and burrowed inside it, seeking the warmth and safety of their mother planet.

Earlier that day, the two red ants had guided them to the top of a hill.

Is it still far to the end of the world?

It's over there.

From their ridge, the russet ants discovered a world of dark scrubland stretching eastward as far as the eye could see. The red ants informed them that their mission was nearing its end and that they would not be following them any farther. There were places where their scents were not welcome.

The Belokanians needed to carry straight on as far as the fields of the harvester ants. These lived permanently in the vicinity of the edge of the world and would certainly be able to give them directions.

Before leaving their guides, the russet ants handed over the precious identification pheromones of the Federation, the price they had agreed to pay for the journey. Then they hurried down the slope to the fields cultivated by the famous harvesters.

SKELETON: **Is it better to have the skeleton on the inside or the outside of the body?**

When the skeleton is on the outside, it forms a protective shell. The flesh is safe from external dangers but it becomes flabby, almost liquid, and when something sharp manages to pierce the shell, irreparable damage is done.

When the skeleton forms only a fine, rigid rod inside the body, the quivering flesh is exposed to attack from all sides. The injuries are many and permanent, but it is

precisely this apparent weakness that forces the muscle to grow hard and the fiber to resist. The flesh evolves.

I have seen human beings who had forged "intellectual" armor to shield themselves from adversity. They seemed stronger than most. They said, "I couldn't care less," and laughed at everything, but when adversity managed to pierce their armor, it caused terrible damage.

I have seen human beings suffer from the slightest adversity, the slightest annoyance, but still remain open-minded and sensitive to everything, learning something from each attack.

EDMOND WELLS,
ENCYCLOPEDIA OF RELATIVE AND ABSOLUTE KNOWLEDGE

The slave-makers are attacking!

There was panic in Chli-pou-kan. Exhausted scouts were spreading the news throughout the young city.

The slave-makers! The slave-makers!

Their terrible reputation had gone before them. Just as some ants had favored a particular line of development, greenfly rearing, storage, mushroom growing or chemistry, the slave-makers had specialized in warfare alone.

It was the only thing they could do, but they had turned it into an art form. Their whole bodies were adapted to it. Every single one of their joints ended in a curved spine and their chitin was twice as thick as that of the russet ants. Their narrow, triangular heads were able to repel claws and their mandibles, resembling upside-down elephants' tusks, were two curved sabers that they handled with formidable skill.

Their slave-making habits followed naturally from their extreme specialization. The species had come very close to extinction through its own lust for power. They had spent so much time waging war that they no longer knew how to build nests, bring up their young or even feed themselves. Their saber mandibles, so effective in combat, were totally impractical when it came to normal feeding. Yet however bellicose they were, the slave-makers were not stupid. Since they could no longer perform everyday domestic tasks, others would do them in their place.

The slave-makers attacked mostly small and medium-sized nests of black, white and yellow ants, none of which possessed stings or acid glands. First, they surrounded the chosen village. As soon as the beleaguered ants noticed that all the workers outside had been killed, they blocked up the entrances. That was the moment the slave-makers chose to launch their first attack. They easily overran the defenses, opened breaches in the city and spread panic in the corridors.

The terrified workers then tried to make a sortie to get the eggs to safety. It was exactly what the slave-makers had been hoping for. They screened all the exits and forced the workers to abandon their precious loads, killing only those who refused to obey. Ants never killed for the sake of it.

Once the fighting was over, the slave-makers invaded the nest and told the surviving workers to put the eggs back in place and look after them as before. When the nymphs hatched, they were brought up to serve the invaders and, being ignorant of the past, thought that obeying the big ants was the right and proper thing to do.

During the raids, the long-term slaves hid in the grass in the rear until their mistresses had finished mopping up. Once the battle was over, they moved in like good little housewives, put the old eggs in with the new and set to work to train the prisoners and their children. The kidnapped generations were thus superposed on one another wherever their captors went.

It generally took three slaves to serve each of these grabbers: one to feed her (she could eat only regurgitated food and had to be fed a mouthful at a time), one to wash her (her salivary glands had atrophied) and one to remove the excrement that would otherwise have accumulated around her armor and eaten into her.

The worst thing that could happen to these professional soldiers was to be abandoned by their servants. If this happened, they quickly left the stolen nest and went to look for another city to conquer. If they did not find one before nightfall, they might die of hunger and cold, a ridiculous fate for such magnificent warriors.

Chli-pou-ni had heard many legends about the slave-makers. It was said that there had already been slave rebellions and that the slaves, who knew their mistresses well, did not necessarily come off worst. It was also said that certain slave-makers collected ants' eggs, the idea being to have one of every size and species.

She imagined a room full of eggs of every size and color and, inside each of them, a particular ant culture ready to wake up and serve the simpleminded brutes.

She dragged her mind away from such unpleasant thoughts and back to more pressing concerns. How was she to meet the threat of the slave-makers? Their horde had been reported to be coming from the east. The Chli-poukanian scouts and spies maintained that there were between four and five hundred thousand soldiers. They had crossed the river by means of the tunnel at the port of Satei and were apparently quite annoyed because they had had to abandon their traveling nest to get through. They had nowhere to stay and, if they did not take Chli-pou-kan, would have to spend the night outside.

The young queen tried to think as calmly as possible. *If they were so happy with their portable woven nest, why did they feel obliged to cross the river?* She already knew the answer, though.

The slave-makers had an instinctive, if incomprehensible, hatred of cities, which they saw as both a threat and a challenge. It was the age-old rivalry between plains people and city people. They knew that there were hundreds of ant cities on the other side of the river, each wealthier and more refined than the last.

Unfortunately, Chli-pou-kan was not ready to withstand such an assault. Yes, the city had been packed with a good million inhabitants for the past few days, and yes, they had built a wall of carnivorous plants along the eastern frontier, but it would never be enough. Chli-pou-ni knew that her city was too young and untried. Besides, she still had no news of the ambassadresses she had sent to Bel-o-kan to make known their membership in the Federation and therefore could not count on the solidarity of the neighboring cities. Even Guayei-Tyolot was several thousand heads away, and it was impossible to warn the people of the summer nest.

What would Mother have done in such a situation? Chli-pou-ni decided to call together some of her best huntresses (they had not yet had a chance to prove themselves as warriors) for an absolute communication. They urgently needed to work out a strategy.

They were still gathered in the Forbidden City when the watches posted in the shrub overhanging Chli-pou-kan announced that they had picked up the scents of an approaching army.

Everyone got ready. They had not been able to decide on a strategy and would have to improvise. Action stations was sounded and the legions assembled as best they could (they still did not know anything about military formations, experience of which was bought dearly fighting the dwarf ants). Most of the soldiers were pinning their hopes on the wall of carnivorous plants.

THE DOGONS: **The Dogons of Mali believe that when the original marriage of Heaven and Earth took place, the Earth's sex organ was an anthill.**

When the world born of this coupling was complete, the vulva became a mouth. Out of this came speech and its material support, the technique of weaving, which ants transmitted to mankind.

Fertility rites are still linked to ants nowadays. Sterile women go and sit on an anthill to ask the god Amma to make them fertile.

But that is not all that ants did for men. They also showed them how to build their houses and pointed out

the springs, for the Dogons understood that they had to dig under anthills to find water.

EDMOND WELLS,
ENCYCLOPEDIA OF RELATIVE AND ABSOLUTE KNOWLEDGE

Grasshoppers began to jump about all over the place. It was a sign. The ants with the best eyes could already make out a column of dust just beyond them.

It was one thing to hear about the slave-makers and quite another to see them charge. They did not have a cavalry, they were the cavalry. Their whole bodies were supple and strong, their legs thick and muscular, and their fine, pointed heads ended in two mobile horns, which were actually their mandibles.

They were so aerodynamic that their heads made no whistling sound as they clove through the air, swept along by their racing legs.

The grass was flattened as they passed by, the earth trembled and the sand rippled. Their forward-pointing antennae gave off such pungent pheromones that they seemed to be shouting at the tops of their voices.

Should the Chlipoukanians shut themselves in and resist the siege or go out and fight? Chli-pou-ni hesitated, too afraid even to make a suggestion, so the russet soldiers naturally made the mistake of splitting up. Half went out to meet the enemy in the open while the other half stayed holed up in the city to act as reserves and resist in case of a siege.

Chli-pou-ni tried to think back to the Battle of Poppy Hill, the only one she knew, and it seemed to her that it was the artillery that had caused the most damage to the enemy troops. She immediately ordered three rows of gunners to be put in the front line.

The slave-maker legions now charged the wall of carnivorous plants. The predators bent down as they went by, attracted by the smell of warm meat, but they were far too slow, and all the enemy warriors had passed by before a single Venus's flytrap had even managed to nip them.

Mother had been wrong.

Just as they were about to receive the charge, the Chli-poukanian front line let off a loose salvo that took out barely twenty assailants. The second line did not even have time to take up position. The gunners were all seized by the throat and decapitated without having been able to fire a single drop of acid.

The slave-makers' specialty was to attack the head, and they were very good at it. The young Chlipoukani-ans' heads flew but their headless bodies sometimes went on fighting blindly or bolted, frightening the survi-vors.

After twelve minutes, little was left of the russet troops and the second half of the army closed all the entrances. Without its dome, Chli-pou-kan looked on the surface like a dozen little craters surrounded by ground-up gravel.

They were all stunned. To have gone to so much trou-ble to build a modern city and then see it at the mercy of a band of barbarians so primitive they could not even feed themselves!

However many ACs Chli-pou-ni took part in, she could not come up with a way of resisting. The rubble they had used to block up the entrances would hold for a few seconds at best, and the Chlipoukanians were no more prepared to fight in the galleries than out in the open.

Outside, the last russet soldiers were fighting like de-mons. Some had been able to retreat but most had seen the entrances closed just behind them. They were done for but fought all the more effectively for having nothing left to lose. They knew that the more they slowed down the invaders, the more solidly the entrances could be blocked.

When the last Chlipoukanian was decapitated, her body automatically took up position in front of an en-trance and dug in its claws to form a risible shield.

Inside Chli-pou-kan, they waited.

They waited for the slave-makers with grim resignation. In the last resort, brute force was still more effective than technology.

But the slave-makers did not attack. Like Hannibal at the gates of Rome, they hesitated. It all seemed too easy. It must be a trap. If their reputation as killers went before them, the russet ants also enjoyed a certain renown. In the slave-maker camp, they were said to be skilled at inventing subtle traps and were supposed to form alliances with mercenaries who turned up when you were least expecting them. They were also said to be able to tame wild animals and manufacture secret weapons that inflicted unbearable pain. Besides, slave-makers hated being surrounded by walls as much as they enjoyed being out in the open.

So they did not break down the barricades put up in the entrances. They waited. They could afford to take their time. After all, there were still about fifteen hours left before nightfall.

There was surprise in the anthill. Why weren't they attacking? Chli-pou-ni did not like it. She was worried that the enemy was "acting in a way that defied their understanding" when it had no need, being the stronger party. Some of her daughters timidly suggested that the slave-makers might be trying to starve them out. Such an eventuality could be of comfort only to the russet ants: thanks to their greenfly sheds in the basement, their mushroom beds, their granaries full of flour and the reservoir ants brimful of honeydew, they could hold out for a good two months.

But Chli-pou-ni did not think there would be a siege. What the others up there wanted was a nest for the night. She remembered Mother's famous saying: *If the enemy is stronger, do something that defies his understanding.* Yes, the way to beat the brutes was to use the latest technology.

The five hundred thousand Chlipoukanians took part in ACs and an interesting debate finally emerged. It was a little worker who emitted:

The mistake we made was to try to copy the weapons

and strategies used by our elders in Bel-o-kan. We must not copy, we must find our own solutions to our own problems.

As soon as the pheromone was out, they came up with fresh ideas and a decision was quickly taken. Then everyone set to work.

JANISSARY: In the fourteenth century, Sultan Murad I founded a rather special army corps called Janissaries (from the Turkish yeni cheri, meaning "new militia"). The Janissary army had a special characteristic: it was formed only of orphans. When Turkish soldiers pillaged an Armenian or Slav village, they took the very young children and shut them up in a special military school, where they could learn nothing of the outside world. Educated solely in the art of combat, these children turned out to be the best fighters in the entire Ottoman Empire and shamelessly ravaged the villages inhabited by their real families. It never occurred to the Janissaries to fight their kidnappers on the side of their parents. On the other hand, their power grew ceaselessly and ended up worrying Sultan Mahmut II, who massacred them and set fire to their school in 1826.

EDMOND WELLS,
ENCYCLOPEDIA OF RELATIVE AND ABSOLUTE KNOWLEDGE

Professor Leduc had brought along two large trunks. He took an unusual gas-powered pneumatic drill out of one of them and immediately started to drill a circular hole in the wall built by the police big enough to get through.

When the racket had stopped, Grandmother Augusta offered him some herb tea, but Leduc refused, calmly explaining that it might make him want to go to the bathroom. He turned to the other trunk and pulled out a complete spelunking outfit.

"Do you really think it's that deep?"

"To be frank, Mrs. Wells, before coming to see you I did some research on this building. During the Renaissance, it was inhabited by Protestant scholars, who built a secret passage. I'm almost certain the passage comes out in the Forest of Fontainebleau. That's how the Protestants escaped from their persecutors."

"But if the people who went down there came out in the forest, I don't understand why they haven't turned up again. There was my grandson, my great-grandson and my granddaughter-in-law, plus a good dozen firemen and policemen. None of them has any reason to hide. They've got families and friends. They're not Protestants and the Wars of Religion have been over for a long time."

"Are you quite certain of that, Mrs. Wells?"

He gave her a strange look.

"The religions have taken on new names. They call themselves philosophies or sciences but they're every bit as dogmatic."

He went into the next room to put on his spelunking clothes. When he reappeared in a suit that was straining at the seams, his head encased in a bright red helmet sporting a lamp at the front, Augusta almost burst out laughing.

He carried on regardless.

"After the Protestants, the apartment was occupied by sects of all kinds. Some took part in old pagan rites, others worshiped onions or black radishes or goodness knows what."

"Onions and black radishes are very good for you. I can quite see why someone might worship them. Health is everything. Look at me, I'm deaf, I'm getting senile and I die a little more each day."

He tried to reassure her.

"Now, now, don't be pessimistic. You look very well to me."

"Let's see, now, how old do you think I am?"

"I don't know . . . sixty, seventy."

"A hundred. I turned a hundred last week, there's something seriously wrong with every part of my body and it gets harder to go on living every day, especially now I've lost everyone I loved."

"I sympathize, Mrs. Wells. It can't be easy being old."

"You're telling me!"

"I really didn't . . ."

"Do get a move on. If you don't come back up tomorrow, I'll call the police and they'll probably build me a wall so strong no one will ever try to break it down again."

With the ichneumon wasp larvae constantly gnawing away at her, 4,000th could not get to sleep during even the coldest nights.

She waited calmly for death while at the same time engaging in exciting, dangerous activities she would never ordinarily have had the courage to undertake, such as discovering the edge of the world.

They were still on their way to the harvesters' fields and 103,683rd took advantage of the journey to call to mind some of the things her nurses had taught her. They had explained to her that the Earth was a cube bearing life only on its upper surface.

What would she see if she finally reached the end of the world? Its side? Water? Empty space? She and her companion would then know more about it than all the explorers and russet ants who had ever lived.

To 4,000th's surprise, 103,683rd suddenly lengthened her stride.

In the middle of the afternoon, when the slave-makers made up their minds to force their way in, they were surprised not to meet any resistance. They were well aware that they had not destroyed the entire russet army, even taking into account the city's small size, and were therefore on their guard.

They advanced all the more cautiously because they were used to living in the open air and had excellent eyesight in broad daylight but were completely blind underground. The asexual russet ants could not see there either, but at least they were used to finding their way about in the shadowy passageways.

When the slave-makers reached the Forbidden City, it was completely deserted, though there were piles of food lying untouched on the ground and the granaries below were full. People had definitely been there shortly before.

On the fifth floor of the basement, they found recent pheromones. They tried to decode the conversations that had taken place, but the russet ants had left behind a sprig of thyme, which interfered with all the other scents.

The sixth floor of the basement. They did not like being shut up underground. It was pitch-black. How could ants bear to spend all their time in such a deathly dark, confined space?

On the eighth floor of the basement, they detected even fresher pheromones and increased their pace. The russet ants could not be far away now.

On the tenth floor of the basement, they surprised a group of workers brandishing eggs, who ran away when they saw them coming. So that was it! They understood at last. The whole city had gone down to the lowest floors in the hope of saving its precious offspring.

As everything fell into place, the slave-makers threw caution to the wind and ran along the corridors, letting out their famous pheromone war cry. They were already down to the thirteenth floor and the Chlipoukanian workers could not shake them off.

Suddenly, the egg bearers disappeared for no apparent reason and the corridor they were following opened into a vast room. Pools of honeydew were all over the floor, and the slave-makers instinctively rushed to lick up the precious nectar before it soaked into the earth.

Other warriors pressed them from the rear but the room was absolutely enormous and there was enough room and pools of honeydew for everyone. It was deliciously sweet. This was surely one of the reservoir ant rooms a slave-maker had heard about: *It's a so-called modern technique that consists of obliging a poor worker to spend her whole life upside down with her abdomen stretched to the limit.*

While they were indulging in honeydew and making fun of the city dwellers again, one of the slave-makers suddenly noticed something peculiar. The room was surprisingly big to have only one entrance.

She did not have time to think further. The russet ants had finished digging and a torrent of water burst through the ceiling. The slave-makers tried to get away down the corridor but it had been blocked by a big rock and the level of water was rising. Those who had not been stunned by the downpour were struggling with all their might.

The russet worker who had pointed out that they must not copy their elders had come up with the idea. She had asked the question *What's special about our city?* A single pheromone had been the reply: *The underground stream on the twelfth floor of the basement!*

They had then diverted a rivulet from the stream along a channel waterproofed with thick leaves. The rest was loosely based on tanker technique. They had built a big reservoir of water in a chamber and then bored a hole in the middle of it with a branch. The most difficult part of the operation had obviously been to keep the drilling branch suspended above the water. Ants hanging from the ceiling of the tanker chamber had accomplished this feat.

Down below, the slave-makers were thrashing about and waving their legs in the air. Most of them had already drowned, but when all the water had decanted into the lower room, the level of flotation was high enough for some warriors to be able to get out through the hole in the ceiling. The russet ants easily felled them with acid.

An hour later, the slave-maker soup had stopped moving. Queen Chli-pou-ni had won. She then came out with her first historic saying: *The greater the obstacle, the more we must surpass ourselves.*

• • •

A dull, regular knocking drew Augusta to the kitchen just as Professor Leduc struggled out of the hole in the wall. Fancy that, after twenty-four hours! The one man she disliked so much she did not care if she never saw him again and he'd had to come back!

His spelunking suit was ripped to pieces but he was otherwise unharmed. He had also failed completely, it was as plain as the nose on his face.

"Well?"

"Well what?"

"Did you find them?"

"No."

Augusta was all agitated. It was the first time anyone had come back up out of the hole alive and sane. It was possible to survive the adventure!

"What's down there, then? Does it come out in the Forest of Fontainebleau, as you thought?"

He took off his helmet.

"Could I have a drink first, please? I've finished all my rations and I haven't drunk anything since lunchtime yesterday."

She brought him some herb tea she'd been keeping hot in a thermos flask.

"Do you want me to tell you what's down there? There's a spiral staircase that goes straight down for several hundred meters. There's a door and a length of bloodstained corridor crawling with rats, then at the far end there's a wall that must have been built by your grandson, Jonathan. It's a very strong wall. I tried to drill a hole in it but it was impossible. It must actually turn or swing open, because there's a set of coded alphabetical keys on it."

"Coded alphabetical keys?"

"Yes, you probably have to type in the answer to a question."

"What question?"

How do you make four equilateral triangles out of six matches?"

Augusta could not help bursting out laughing, which the scientist found extremely irritating.

"You already know the answer!"

Between two hiccoughs, she managed to reply, "No, no. I don't know the answer. But I'm very familiar with the question."

She couldn't stop laughing. Professor Leduc muttered, "I spent hours trying to find the answer. You can obviously do it with triangles that aren't equilateral."

He put away his equipment.

"If you don't mind, I'll go and ask a friend of mine who's a mathematician and come back again."

"No."

"What do you mean, no?"

"You've had your chance. If you didn't make the most of it, it's just too bad. Kindly take those trunks out of my home. Good-bye, Professor Leduc."

She did not even call him a taxi. Her aversion had gotten the better of her. She couldn't stand the smell of him.

She sat down in the kitchen opposite the smashed wall. The situation had changed now. She made up her mind to telephone Jason Bragel and that Mr. Rosenfeld. She had decided to have a little fun before she died.

HUMAN PHEROMONE: Just as insects communicate by means of smell, man has an olfactory language by means of which he communicates discreetly with others of his kind.

As we do not have antennae with which to emit pheromones, we release them into the air from our armpits, breasts, scalps and genital organs.

Such messages are perceived subconsciously but are none the less effective for all that. Human beings have fifty million olfactory nerve endings, fifty million cells capable of identifying thousands of smells, whereas our tongues can recognize only four different tastes.

What use do we make of this means of communication?

Firstly, sexual attraction. A male human being can perfectly well be attracted by a female human being simply because he likes her natural scents (which are all too often concealed under artificial scents). He may equally well be repulsed by another whose pheromones do not "appeal" to him.

It is a subtle process. The two people concerned will not even suspect that they have taken part in an olfactory dialogue. Those around them will simply say "Love is blind."

The influence of human pheromones may also be manifested in cases of aggression. As with dogs, a man who breathes in the smell of fear emanating from his enemy will naturally want to attack him.

Lastly, one of the most spectacular consequences of the action of human pheromones is no doubt the synchronization of menstrual cycles. It has been observed that when several women live together, they emit odors which adjust their cycles so that their periods all start at the same time.

EDMOND WELLS
ENCYCLOPEDIA OF RELATIVE AND ABSOLUTE KNOWLEDGE

They caught sight of their first harvester ants working in the yellow fields. It would actually be more correct to speak of woodcutters, since their cereals grew very tall and they had to slice through the base of the stems to bring down the nourishing grains.

Apart from harvesting, their main occupation was eradicating all the other plants growing around their crops, using a weed killer of their own making, indoleacetic acid, which they sprayed from their abdominal glands.

When 103,683rd and 4,000th arrived, the harvesters took hardly any notice of them. They had never seen russet ants before and they thought the two insects were at best runaway slaves or ants looking for lomechusa secretion. In short, tramps or drug addicts.

One of the harvesters eventually detected a red ant scent molecule, however. She left her work and came up to them, followed by a friend.

Have you met any red ants? Where are they?

In the course of the conversation, the Belokanians learned that the red ants had attacked the harvesters' nest several weeks previously. They had killed over a hundred workers, both male and female, with their poisonous stings and then stolen all the flour reserves. On its return from a campaign in the south in search of fresh seeds, the harvester army could only inspect the damage.

The russet ants acknowledged that they had come across red ants. They showed them which way to go to find them, and, in reply to the harvesters' questions, told them about their own journey.

Are you looking for the end of the world?

They agreed that they were. The others then let out sparkling pheromones of laughter. Why had they burst out laughing? Did the end of the world not exist?

Yes, it exists and you're there. Apart from harvesting, our main occupation is trying to cross the end of the world.

The harvesters offered to guide the two "tourists" to this mystical place the very next morning. The evening was spent in discussion in the shelter of the little nest the harvesters had dug in the bark of a beech tree.

What about the guardians of the end of the world? asked 103,683rd.

Don't worry, you'll see them soon enough.

Is it true they've got a weapon capable of crushing a whole army at a blow?

The harvesters were surprised the strangers were so well informed.

It's true.

So 103,683rd would at last solve the mystery of the secret weapon.

That night, she had a dream. She saw the Earth stopping at right angles, a vertical wall of water filling the sky and, coming out of this wall of water, blue ants holding highly destructive acacia branches. The ends of these magic branches only had to touch something for it to be completely pulverized.

Augusta spent the whole day playing around with six matches. She had understood that the wall was more psychological than real. There was that famous "you have to think differently" of Edmond's. Her son had discovered something for sure, and he had used his intelligence to hide it.

She recalled his childhood "dens." Perhaps it was because they had destroyed them all that he had tried to make one that was inaccessible, a place where no one would ever disturb him, a kind of inner place, which would project its peace and invisibility outward.

Augusta tried to shake off her torpor. A memory from her own youth surfaced. It was a winter's night, she was very small and she had just understood that numbers below zero could exist. First 3, 2, 1, 0 and then –1, –2, –3. Inside-out numbers, as if the glove of numbers were being turned inside out. So zero was not the beginning and end of everything. Another infinite world lay on the other side. It was as if the wall "zero" had been swept away.

She must have been seven or eight years old, but she had been so overwhelmed by her discovery that she had not slept all night.

Inside-out figures. It opened up a whole new dimension, the third dimension. What a relief.

Good heavens!

Her hands were trembling with emotion and she was crying but she found the strength to pick up the matches. She made three of them into a triangle, then stood a match at each corner so that they met in a point at the top.

They formed a pyramid. A pyramid of four equilateral triangles, one as its base and three as its sides.

The eastern limit of the Earth was a staggering place. There was nothing natural or Earth-like about it. It was not as 103,683rd had imagined. The edge of the world was hard, smooth and warm, and it smelled of mineral oil. And it was black, the blackest thing she had ever seen.

Instead of a vertical ocean, there were incredibly violent air currents.

They spent a long time trying to understand what was happening. From time to time, they felt a vibration. Its intensity increased exponentially, then the ground suddenly trembled, a strong wind lifted their antennae and an infernal din split the eardrums in their tibiae. It was like a violent storm but it had no sooner happened than it was over, leaving only a few whorls of dust to settle behind it.

Many harvester explorers had tried to cross the frontier but the Guardians kept watch. They had caused the noise, wind and vibration as they struck down all who tried to cross the black earth.

Had they already seen the Guardians? Before the russet ants could receive a reply, there was another roar, which gradually died away. One of the six harvesters with them asserted that no one had ever managed to walk on the "accursed land" and come back alive. The Guardians crushed everything.

It must have been they who had attacked La-chola-kan and the expedition of the 327th male. But why had they left the end of the world to move west? Did they want to invade the world?

The harvesters knew no more than the russet ants. Could they at least describe them? All they knew was that anyone who had gone near them had been crushed to death. They did not even know which category of living creatures to place them in. Were they giant insects, birds or plants? All the harvesters knew was that they were very fast and very powerful. It was a force quite beyond them, unlike anything they knew.

At that moment, 4,000th took a sudden, unexpected initiative. She left the group and ventured into the forbidden territory alone, cool as you please. If she were going to die anyway, she might as well try to cross the end of the world first. The others watched, aghast.

She moved slowly forward, alert for the slightest vibration, the slightest scent announcing death in the sensitive ends of her legs. There . . . she had gone fifty heads, a hundred heads, two hundred heads, four hundred, six hundred, eight hundred. Nothing had happened. She was safe and sound.

The ants standing opposite applauded her. From where she was, she could see intermittent white stretches running to the left and right. Everything on the black earth was dead. There were no plants or insects. And the ground was so black it could not be real earth.

She detected plants far ahead. Could there possibly be a world after the edge of the world? She threw a few pheromones to her colleagues waiting on the bank to tell them all about it, but it was difficult to communicate properly at that distance.

She turned around and the colossal noise and trembling began again. The Guardians were returning! She raced back to her companions at top speed.

They watched petrified for the brief fraction of time it

took a stupendous bulk to thunder across their sky. The Guardians had passed by, giving off the smell of mineral oil, and 4,000th had disappeared.

The ants went a little closer to the edge and saw what had happened. She had been squashed so flat her body was now no more than a tenth of a head thick and seemed to be embedded in the black ground.

Nothing was left of the old Belokanian explorer, and her suffering was likewise at an end. One of the ichneumon wasp larvae had just pierced her back and was nothing but a white dot in the middle of the flattened russet body.

So that was how the Guardians of the end of the world struck. You heard a din, felt a rush of wind and everything was instantly destroyed, crushed, pulverized. The 103,683rd soldier was still analyzing what had happened when she heard another roar. Death struck even when no one crossed its threshold, leaving the dust to settle.

She still wanted to try to get across. She thought again of Satei. It was a similar problem. If you could not get over it, you had to go under it. You had to think of the black earth as a river, and the best way to cross rivers was to tunnel beneath them.

She discussed it with the six harvesters, who were immediately enthusiastic about the idea. It was so obvious they could not understand why they had not thought of it earlier. Then everyone started to dig with both mandibles.

Jason Bragel and Professor Rosenfeld had never been mad about herb tea but it was growing on them. Augusta told them everything in detail. She explained to them that her son had designated them to inherit the apartment after her death and that they would probably both be tempted to explore the basement one day, just as she was. She therefore thought it better to combine their efforts for maximum efficiency.

Once Augusta had supplied them with this vital preliminary information, the three of them barely spoke. They had no need of words to understand one another. A look and a smile were enough. None of the three had ever experienced such immediate intellectual osmosis. It went beyond mere intellect, as if they had been born to complete one another and their genetic programs fit together and merged. It was magical. Augusta was very old, yet the others both found her extraordinarily beautiful.

They spoke of Edmond and were surprised at the warmth of their affection for him, in which there was no hint of reservation. Jason Bragel did not talk about his family, Daniel Rosenfeld did not talk about his work and Augusta did not talk about her illness. They decided to go down that very evening. They knew it was the only possible thing to do.

IT WAS LONG THOUGHT: It was long thought that computers in general and artificial intelligence programs in particular would mingle human concepts and present them from a new angle. In short, electronics was expected to deliver a new philosophy. But even when it is presented differently, the raw material remains the same: ideas produced by human imaginations. It is a dead end.

The best way to renew thought is to go outside the human imagination.

EDMOND WELLS,
ENCYCLOPEDIA OF RELATIVE AND ABSOLUTE KNOWLEDGE

Chli-pou-kan was growing in size and intelligence and was now an "adolescent" city. Continuing down the road of aquatic technology, the Chlipoukanians had built a whole network of canals under the twelfth floor of the basement. These waterways allowed food to be transported quickly from one end of the city to the other.

They had had plenty of time to perfect their aquatic transport techniques. The ultimate was a floating cranberry leaf. You could travel several hundred heads on it by water—from the mushroom beds in the east to the greenfly sheds in the west, for example—simply by allowing yourself to be carried along by the current.

The ants hoped to succeed in training water beetles one day. The big subaquatic beetles had air pockets beneath their wing cases and swam very fast. If they could be persuaded to push the cranberry leaves along, the rafts would have a far more reliable means of propulsion at their disposal than the currents.

Chli-pou-ni herself launched another futuristic idea. She remembered the rhinoceros beetle that had freed her from the spider's web. It was the perfect war machine. Not only did the rhinoceroses have big horns on their foreheads and an armor-plated shell, but they could also fly at a terrific pace. Mother imagined a whole legion of the animals, with ten gunners perched on the head of each. She could already see these teams descending, quasi-invulnerable, on the enemy troops and drenching them in acid.

There was only one stumbling block. Like all water beetles, the rhinoceroses were difficult to tame because you could not understand their language. Several dozen workers therefore spent their time deciphering the scents they emitted and trying to get them to understand the ant pheromone language.

The results so far were indifferent, but the Chli-poukanians managed to win their favor all the same by stuffing them with honeydew. In the end, food was the most widely shared insect language.

Despite this collective dynamism, Chli-pou-ni was concerned. Three groups of ambassadresses had been sent to the Federation to get them recognized as the sixty-fifth city and there had still been no reply. Was Belo-kiu-kiuni rejecting the alliance?

The more she thought about it, the more Chli-pou-ni told herself that her spy ambassadresses must have blundered and been intercepted by the rock-scented warriors or allowed themselves to be seduced by the hallucinogenic aroma of the lomechusa on the fiftieth floor of the basement, or some such thing.

She wanted the matter cleared up. She intended neither to give up her recognition by the Federation nor to drop the investigation and decided to send 801st, her best and most trusted warrior. To make sure she held all the trumps, the queen participated in an AC with the young soldier, who then knew as much about the mystery as she did. She had become:

> The eye that sees
> The antenna that smells
> The claw that strikes for Chli-pou-kan.

The old lady had prepared a rucksack full of provisions, including three thermos flasks of hot herb tea. The last thing they wanted was to have to hurry back up because they had neglected to take supplies into account—like that awful man, Leduc. But would he ever have found the code word in any case? Augusta allowed herself to doubt it.

Among other accessories, Jason Bragel had brought along a large canister of tear gas and three gas masks. Daniel Rosenfeld had brought along the latest in cameras with a flash.

Now they were going around and around inside the stone merry-go-round. Like their predecessors, they found the descent brought back memories and buried thoughts—of childhood and parents; their earliest sufferings and mistakes; frustrated love; selfishness; pride and remorse.

Their bodies moved mechanically, tirelessly, as they went deeper into the flesh of the planet and their past lives. How long a life was and how destructive it could be, so much more easily destructive than creative!

Finally, they came to a door with a text written on it.

• • • •

At the moment of death, the soul's impressions are similar to those of initiates in the ways of the Great Mysteries.

First they rush along blindly, twisting and turning, on an endless, anxious journey through the shadows.

Then, just before the end, their fear reaches its height. Bathed in cold sweat, they shiver and tremble, utterly terrified.

This phase is almost immediately followed by a return to the light, a sudden illumination.

They are surrounded by a marvelous glow and move through pure places and meadows ringing with voices and dancing.

Sacred words inspire religious respect. The perfect initiate is free to celebrate the Mysteries.

Daniel took a photo.

"It's certainly a fine piece of writing. I know this text," asserted Jason. "It's from Plutarch."

"Doesn't it frighten you?" asked Augusta.

"Yes, but it's meant to. And anyway, it says that fear comes before enlightenment. Let's take one step at a time. If a little fear is necessary, let's be afraid."

"Speaking of which, the rats . . ."

It was as if they had only had to mention them for them to be there. The three explorers sensed their furtive presence and dreaded feeling them around the tops of their walking boots. Daniel took another photo and the flash revealed the repulsive image of a carpet of gray bodies and black ears. Jason quickly handed out the gas masks before generously spraying his tear gas around. The rats did not wait to be asked to leave twice.

The descent began again.

"Shall we have a picnic?" suggested Augusta at last.

So they had a picnic. The episode of the rats seemed forgotten and all three of them were in high spirits. Because it was rather cold, they ended their snack with a swig of brandy and some scalding-hot coffee. Herb tea was normally served only at tea-time.

They dug for a long time before they were able to come up again in an area of loose earth. A pair of antennae at last emerged, like a periscope, to be flooded with unfamiliar smells.

They were out in the open and on the other side of the end of the world. There was still no wall of water but it was a world quite unlike the one they knew. Although there were still a few trees and grassy patches, the smooth, hard surface of a gray desert stretched immediately beyond and there was not an ant or termite hill in sight.

They took a few steps, but huge black things came crashing down around them, a little like the Guardians, except that these fell at random.

And that was not all. Far ahead of them stood a giant monolith so tall their antennae could not make out the top. It darkened the sky and crushed the earth.

That must be the wall at the end of the world and there's water behind it, thought 103,683rd.

They went a little farther and came nose to nose with a group of cockroaches who had congregated on a bit of . . . something or other. Through their transparent shells, the ants could see all their insides, their organs and even the blood beating in their arteries. Hideous! As they were beating a retreat, three harvesters were crushed by a falling mass.

The 103,683rd soldier and her last three friends decided to carry on in spite of everything. They passed through low, porous walls, still heading for the infinitely big monolith, and suddenly found themselves in a region that was even more disconcerting. The ground was red and grainy like a strawberry. They spotted a sort of well and were thinking of going down inside it to find a little shade when a big white sphere at least ten heads in diameter suddenly fell out of the sky, bounced and chased after them. They threw themselves into the well and just had time to flatten themselves against the sides before the sphere crashed to the bottom.

They climbed out again, panic-stricken, and made off. The ground around them was blue, green or yellow, and the wells and the white spheres that pursued them were everywhere. This time, they had had enough. Courage has its limits, and this world was far too different to be bearable.

They ran until they were out of breath, went back along the tunnel and quickly returned to the normal world.

CIVILIZATION (continued): Another clash of civilizations occurred when East met West.

The annals of the Chinese Empire record the arrival of a boat, probably Roman in origin, in about A.D. 115. It had been battered by a storm and had run aground on the coast after drifting for days.

The passengers were acrobats and jugglers, who had no sooner landed than they decided to win the favor of the inhabitants of the unknown land by performing for them. The Chinese thus watched openmouthed as the long-nosed foreigners breathed fire, tied themselves into knots, changed frogs into snakes, etc.

They had every right to conclude that the West was peopled by clowns and fire-eaters, and several hundred years went by before a chance of undeceiving them presented itself.

EDMOND WELLS,
ENCYCLOPEDIA OF RELATIVE AND ABSOLUTE KNOWLEDGE

They were in front of Jonathan's wall at last. *How do you make four equilateral triangles out of six matches?* Daniel naturally took a photo, Augusta typed the word *pyramid* and the wall swung back smoothly. She was proud of her grandson.

They passed through and soon heard the wall move back into place. Jason lit up the sides of the passage. There was rock everywhere but it was no longer the same rock. Before the wall it had been red, and now it was yellow with veins of sulfur.

The air was still breathable, however, and they even thought they could feel a slight draft. Was Professor Leduc right? Did the tunnel come out in the Forest of Fontainebleau?

Suddenly, they came across another horde of rats, and these rats were far more aggressive than those they had met previously. Jason knew what must be happening but did not have time to explain it to the others. They had to put the masks back on quickly and sling gas at them. Every time the wall swung back, which admittedly was not often, rats from the "red zone" went through into the "yellow zone" to look for food. Those in the red zone still got by more or less, but the migrants found hardly anything to get their teeth into and had to eat one another.

And Jason and his friends were dealing with the survivors—in other words, the most ferocious. The tear gas was totally ineffective against them and they were attacking, leaping up and trying to hang on to their arms.

On the verge of hysteria, Daniel bombarded them with blinding flashes of light but the nightmare creatures weighed kilos and were unafraid of men. Before long, they drew blood. Jason pulled out his jackknife, stabbed two rats and threw them to the others. Augusta fired several shots from a small revolver and they got away just in time.

WHEN I WAS: **When I was small, I used to lie on the ground for hours watching anthills. They seemed more "real" to me than the television. They held many mysteries for me. After I had wreaked havoc, for example, why did the ants bring back some of the wounded and leave the rest to die? They were all the same size. Ac-**

cording to what criteria was one individual judged interesting and another negligible?

EDMOND WELLS,
ENCYCLOPEDIA OF RELATIVE AND ABSOLUTE KNOWLEDGE

They ran along a tunnel streaked with yellow until they arrived at a steel fence.

An opening in the center made the whole thing resemble a fisherman's trap. It formed a cone that narrowed down so that an average-sized human body could get through but not come back because of the spikes around the entrance on the other side.

"Someone put it here recently."

"Hmm, it looks as if whoever made the door and trap doesn't want us to go back."

Once again, Augusta recognized the work of Jonathan, the master of doors and metals.

"Look!"

Daniel lit up an inscription:

> *Consciousness ends here*
> *Do you wish to return to the unconscious?*

They stood there gaping.

"What shall we do?"

The same thought occurred to them all simultaneously.

"It would be a shame to give up after we've come this far. I suggest we go on."

"I'll go first," declared Daniel, tucking his ponytail into his collar to stop it from catching on anything.

They took turns crawling through the steel trap.

"It's funny," said Augusta, "I feel as if I've done this before."

"Have you ever been in a trap that squeezed you and stopped you from going back?"

"Yes. It was a very long time ago."

"What do you mean by a very long time ago?"

"Oh, when I was young. I must have been one or two seconds old."

Back in their city, the harvesters recounted their adventures on the other side of the world, a land of monsters where strange things happened. They told of the cockroaches, the black slabs, the giant monolith, the well and the white balls. It was all too much. There was no possibility of founding a village in such a grotesque world.

The 103,683rd soldier stayed in a corner to recover her strength and think. When her sisters heard her story, they would have to redraw all the maps and reconsider the basic principles of their planetology. She told herself it was time for her to return to the Federation.

They must have gone a dozen kilometers since the trap. It was difficult to know for sure and their fatigue was beginning to tell anyway.

They came to a narrow stream with particularly hot, sulfurous water that crossed the tunnel.

Daniel stopped dead. He thought he had seen some ants floating down the stream on a leaf raft. He got a grip on himself. The smell of the sulfur dust must be making him hallucinate.

A few hundred meters farther on, Jason trod on something that crunched. When he shone a light on it, he saw it was the thoracic cage of a skeleton and let out a loud scream. Daniel and Augusta swept the light from their flashlights all around and discovered two more skeletons, one of which was the size of a child. Could it be Jonathan and his family?

They set off again but soon had to start running when a massive rustling announced the arrival of the rats. The yellow of the walls turned to the white of lime. At last they arrived exhausted at the end of the tunnel and found themselves at the foot of a spiral staircase leading back up.

August fired her last two bullets in the direction of the rats, then they leaped up the stairs. Jason still had enough presence of mind to note that this staircase was the opposite way around to the first and that you turned clockwise whether you went down or up.

The news that a Belokanian had just turned up in the city caused a sensation. Everyone said she must be a Federation ambassadress come to announce Chli-pou-kan's official attachment to the Federation as its sixty-fifth city.

Chli-pou-ni was less optimistic than her daughters. She was suspicious of the new arrival. Supposing she were a rock-scented warrior sent from Bel-o-kan to infiltrate the subversive queen's city?

What's she like?

She's more tired than anything. She must have run all the way from Bel-o-kan to do the journey in a few days.

Shepherdesses had caught sight of her wandering around in the neighborhood, exhausted. She had not emitted anything for the time being and had been taken straight to the tanker ant room to replenish her reserves.

Bring her here. I want to talk to her alone but I want guards to stay at the entrance to the royal chamber, ready to act when I give the signal.

Chli-pou-ni had always longed for news of her native city, but now that one of its representatives had turned up, her first thought had been to consider her a spy and kill her. She would wait until she saw her, but if she detected even one rock-scented molecule, she would have her executed without the slightest hesitation.

The Belokanian was brought to her. As soon as the two ants recognized one another, they fell together with their mandibles wide open and engaged in the smoothest of trophallaxes. At first, they were so moved they could not emit.

Chli-pou-ni let out the first pheromone.

How far have you got with the investigation? Is it the termites?

The 103,683rd soldier told how she had crossed the eastern river and visited the termite city, that it had been destroyed and that there were no survivors.

What's behind all this, then?

According to the warrior, the true culprits for all these incomprehensible events were the Guardians of the eastern edge of the world, animals so strange you could neither see nor smell them. They appeared suddenly out of the sky and everyone died.

Chli-pou-ni listened carefully. However, added the 103,683rd soldier, that still did not explain how the Guardians of the end of the world had been able to use the rock-scented soldiers.

Chli-pou-ni thought she knew. She explained that the rock-scented soldiers were neither spies nor mercenaries but a clandestine force responsible for monitoring the level of stress in the city organism. They stifled any information that might worry the city. She related how the killers had assassinated the 327th male and how they had tried to assassinate her.

What about the food reserves under the rock floor? And the corridor in the granite?

Chli-pou-ni had no answer to that. It was precisely the double mystery she had sent spy ambassadresses to try to solve.

The young queen offered to show her friend around the city. On the way, she explained to her the fantastic possibilities offered by water. The eastern river, for example, had always been considered deadly, but it was only water. The queen had fallen in it without dying. They might one day be able to go down the river on leaf rafts and discover the northern edge of the world. Chli-pou-ni got carried away. There were probably Guardians of the northern edge who could be incited to fight those of the eastern edge.

The 103,683rd soldier had not failed to notice that Chli-pou-ni was full of bold projects. Not all were feasible, but those that had already been put into practice were impressive. The soldier had never before seen such vast mushroom beds or greenfly sheds, or rafts floating on underground canals.

But what surprised her most was the queen's last pheromone.

She asserted that if her ambassadresses were not back within a fortnight, she would declare war on Bel-o-kan. In her opinion, their native city was no longer fit for the world they lived in. The very existence of the rock-scented warriors showed that it was not facing up to reality. It was like a frightened snail. Once it had been revolutionary, now it was outmoded. Someone had to take over. Here in Chli-pou-kan, the ants were making much faster progress. Chli-pou-ni considered that if she took over as head of the Federation, she could develop it quickly. With sixty-five federated cities, her initiatives would be ten times as effective. She was already thinking of conquering the waterways and setting up a flying legion using rhinoceros beetles.

The 103,683rd soldier hesitated. She had intended to return to Bel-o-kan to tell of her journey, but Chli-pou-ni asked her to give up the idea.

Bel-o-kan has set up an army "to avoid knowing."
Don't force it to know something it doesn't want to know.

The steps at the top of the spiral staircase were made of aluminum and did not date from the Renaissance. They ended in front of a white door bearing another inscription:

And I went in till I drew nigh to a wall which is
built of crystals and surrounded by tongues of fire:
and it began to frighten me.
And I went into the tongues of fire and drew
nigh to a large house which was built of crystals.
And the walls of the house were like a tessel-

lated floor made of crystals, and its groundwork was of crystal.

Its ceiling was like the path of the stars and the lightnings.

And between them were fiery cherubim.

And their heaven was clear as water. (I Enoch)

They pushed open the door and went up a very steep corridor. The ground suddenly gave way beneath their feet as the floor pivoted. They fell for so long that they got over being frightened and felt as if they were flying. They *were* flying!

Their fall was broken by a huge, close-meshed net like the ones used by trapeze artists. They felt about in the dark on all fours. Jason Bragel found another door, not with a code this time but with a simple handle. He quietly called his companions, then opened it.

OLD MAN: In Africa, people are sadder about the death of an old man than about that of a newborn baby. The old man represented a wealth of experience that might have benefited the tribe, whereas the newborn baby had not lived and could not even be aware of dying.

In Europe, people are sad about the newborn baby because they think he might well have done wonderful things if he had lived. On the other hand, they pay little attention to the death of the old man, who had already lived his life anyway.

EDMOND WELLS,
ENCYCLOPEDIA OF RELATIVE AND ABSOLUTE KNOWLEDGE

The place was bathed in blue light.

It was a temple without a statue or image.

Augusta remembered Professor Leduc's words. The Protestants must certainly have taken refuge there in former times when the persecution was at its height.

Beneath wide freestone vaults, the room was vast, square and very beautiful. The only decoration was a period organ at the center. In front of it was a lectern bearing a thick folder.

The walls were covered in inscriptions, many of which looked more like black magic than white, even to the uninitiated eye. Leduc was right. Sects must have succeeded one another in the underground refuge, but in olden days there would have been no pivoting wall, no trap and no trapdoor with a safety net.

They could hear the murmur of running water but at first could not see where it was coming from. The bluish light was coming from the right, where there was a sort of laboratory full of computers and test tubes. All the machines were still switched on, and it was the computer screens that were producing the glow lighting up the temple.

"Intriguing, isn't it?"

They looked at one another. None of the three had spoken. A light came on in the ceiling.

They turned around. Jonathan Wells was walking toward them in a white robe. He had entered through a door in the temple on the other side of the laboratory.

"Hello, Gran! Hello, Jason! Hello, Daniel!"

They all gaped at him, speechless. So he was not dead! He was living here! How could anyone live here? They did not know which question to ask first.

"Welcome to our little community."

"Where are we?"

"You're in a Protestant church built early in the seventeenth century by a famous architect. I think this underground church is his masterpiece. There are kilometers of freestone tunnels. And, as you've seen, there's ventilation along the way. He must have put in shafts or made use of air pockets in natural galleries. We don't even understand how he went about it. And that's not all. There isn't only air, there's water, too. You must have noticed the streams crossing the tunnel in places. Look, one of them comes out here."

He showed them the source of the constant murmur, a sculpted fountain behind the organ.

"Throughout the ages, people have come here to find the peace and quiet they needed to do things requiring, let's say, careful attention. Uncle Edmond found out about it from an old book of magic spells and decided to work here."

Jonathan came closer, looking unusually calm and relaxed. Augusta was amazed.

"You must be tired out. Follow me."

He pushed open the door through which he had appeared a little earlier and led them into a room containing several couches arranged in a circle.

"Lucie!" he called. "We've got visitors."

"Lucie? Is she here with you?" exclaimed Augusta happily.

"How many of you are there here?" asked Daniel.

"Until now, there were eighteen of us: Lucie, Nicolas, the eight firemen, the inspector, the five policemen, the superintendent and myself. In short, everyone who has bothered to come down. You'll see them soon. Please forgive us, but it's four o'clock in the morning for our community right now and everyone's fast asleep. I was the only one who got woken by your arrival. You made a bit of a racket in the corridors, you know."

Lucie appeared, also wearing a robe.

"Hello."

She came forward, smiling, and kissed all three of them. Behind her, silhouettes in pajamas stuck their heads around the door to see the "newcomers."

Jonathan brought a big carafe of water from the fountain and some glasses.

"We're going to leave you for a little while to go and get dressed. We always have a small celebration to welcome newcomers, but we didn't know you'd turn up in the middle of the night and we need to get ready for it. We'll be right back."

Augusta, Jason and Daniel did not move. There was so much to take in. Daniel suddenly pinched himself. Augusta and Jason thought it was an excellent idea and did the same. But reality is sometimes stranger than a dream. They looked at each other in bewilderment and smiled.

A few minutes later, they were all sitting on the couches together. Augusta, Jason and Daniel had regained their senses and were eager for information.

"You mentioned shafts just now. Are we very far from the surface?"

"No, three or four meters at the most."

"Can we get out into the open again, then?"

"No, no. The church is built just under a huge, flat rock made of granite. It's the toughest thing going."

"It's got a hole as thick as your arm in it, though," added Lucie. "It used to be a ventilation shaft, too."

"Used to be?"

"Yes, the passage is used for a different purpose now. It doesn't matter, there are other lateral ventilation shafts. We aren't stifling in here, as you can see."

"Can't we get out?"

"No. Not that way, anyway."

Jason seemed deeply concerned.

"But Jonathan, why did you build the pivoting wall, the trap, the floor that gave way and the safety net, then? We're completely trapped."

"That was precisely my intention. It took a lot of time and money but it was necessary. When I first arrived in the church, I came across the lectern. Besides the *Encyclopedia of Relative and Absolute Knowledge* I found a letter from my uncle on it addressed to me personally. Here it is."

They read:

> Dear Jonathan,
> You decided to come down in spite of my warning, which means you are braver than I thought. Good for you. Your mother told me

you were afraid of the dark and I gave you a one-in-five chance of succeeding. It takes will-power to overcome that kind of handicap and willpower is what we are going to need.

In this folder, you will find the *Encyclopedia of Relative and Absolute Knowledge*. As I write these words, it consists of two hundred and eighty-eight chapters about my work. I'd like you to carry on with it. It's worthwhile.

My research is essentially concerned with ant civilization. You'll see what I mean when you read it but first I have a very important request to make of you. When you reached here, I had not yet had time to take measures to protect my secret (if I had, this letter would not have been here in its present form).

I would like you to build them. I have begun to make sketches but I think you will be able to improve on my suggestions since you know so much about it. The purpose of the devices is simple. People must not be able to get to my sanctuary easily, and those who do must never be able to go back to tell others what they have found.

I hope you succeed and that this place brings you as much "wealth" as it has given me.

Edmond.

"Jonathan played the game," explained Lucie. "He built all the traps that had been planned and they work, as you've found out."

"What about the bodies? Are they people who were attacked by rats?"

"No." Jonathan smiled. "I can assure you no one's died in the tunnel since Edmond moved in. The bodies you spotted have been there for at least fifty years. Goodness knows what tragedies took place here then. They must have belonged to some sect or other."

"Aren't we ever going to be able to go back up again, then?" asked Jason anxiously.

"No, never."

"We'd have to reach the hole above the safety net—which is eight meters up—get back through the trap—which is impossible, and we haven't any equipment capable of melting it—and still get through the wall—which can't be opened from this side."

"Not to mention the rats."

"How did you manage to get rats down here?" asked Daniel.

"That was Edmond's idea. He put a pair of big, aggressive *Rattus norvegicus* in a crevice in the rock with a good supply of food. He knew it was a time bomb. Well-fed rats multiply at an exponential rate. They produce six babies a month, which are themselves ready to reproduce after two weeks. To protect himself from them, he used a spray containing a pheromone of aggression that rats can't stand."

"So it was the rats who killed Ouarzazate?" asked Augusta.

"I'm afraid so. Edmond had not foreseen that the ones that passed to the other side of the pyramid wall would become even more ferocious."

"One of our friends had a phobia about rats anyway and really flipped when a big one jumped up at his face and bit a piece of his nose off. He went straight back up before the pyramid wall had even had time to swing back. Did you hear what happened to him after he got back up?" asked a policeman.

"I heard he'd gone mad and been shut up in an asylum," replied Augusta. "But it was only hearsay."

She went to pick up her glass of water but noticed there were lots of ants on the table. She gave a cry and instinctively brushed them off with the back of her hand. Jonathan sprang forward and grabbed hold of her wrist, his hard expression contrasting sharply with the group's previous serenity. His old nervous twitch, which had seemed cured, had come back.

"Don't ever . . . do that . . . again!"

Alone in her chamber, Belo-kiu-kiuni was absentmindedly eating her latest batch of eggs. They had turned out to be her favorite food.

She knew that this so-called 801st was not just an ambassadress of the new city. The 56th female, or rather Queen Chli-pou-ni, since that was what she chose to call herself, had sent her to carry on with the investigation.

She did not need to worry, her rock-scented warriors would deal with her without difficulty. The lame ant in particular was an artist when it came to taking away the burden of life.

However, it was the fourth time Chli-pou-ni had sent her an overinquisitive ambassadress. The first had been killed before even finding the lomechusa's room. The second and third had succumbed to the poisonous beetle's hallucinogenic secretions.

As for this 801st, it appeared that her interview with Mother had been scarcely over before she went down there. They really were in more and more of a hurry to die, but they also got farther and farther into the city each time. Supposing one of them managed to find the passage in spite of everything? Supposing she discovered the secret? Supposing she spread a scent about it?

The Tribe would not understand. The antistress warriors would have little chance to suppress the information in time. How would her daughters react?

A rock-scented warrior rushed in.

The spy has managed to overcome the lomechusa beetle! She's downstairs.

It had only been a question of time.

666 is the name of the beast (the Apocalypse according to St. John). But who will be the beast for whom?
EDMOND WELLS,
ENCYCLOPEDIA OF RELATIVE AND ABSOLUTE KNOWLEDGE

Jonathan let go of his grandmother's wrist and Daniel created a diversion before any awkwardness could set in.

"How about the laboratory on the way in? What's that for?"

"It's the Rosetta stone. Our efforts have only one purpose: to communicate with them."

"Who's them?"

"Them, the ants. Follow me."

They left the lounge for the laboratory. Jonathan, visibly very much at ease in his role as Edmond's successor, picked up a test tube full of ants from the bench and raised it to eye level.

"Look, they're beings, complete beings, not just unimportant little insects. That's something my uncle understood right away. Ants form the second great civilization on Earth. Edmond was a kind of Christopher Columbus, and he discovered a new continent between our toes. He was the first to understand that before looking for extraterrestrials in the depths of space, we ought to begin by contacting the intraterrestrials."

No one spoke. Augusta was remembering. A few days previously, she had been walking in the Forest of Fontainebleau when she had suddenly felt something crunch under her feet. She had trodden on a group of ants. She bent down to look at them. They were all dead, but she was puzzled to see that they were lined up to form an arrow with an inverted head.

Jonathan put the test tube down again and carried on with what he had been saying.

"When he came back from Africa, Edmond found this building, its underground passage and the temple. It was the ideal place for his laboratory. The first stage in his research consisted of deciphering the pheromones the ants used to talk to one another. This machine is a mass spectrometer. As its name suggests, it produces a spectrum that shows the atomic composition of any substance. I've read my uncle's notes. To begin with, he put his experimental ants under a glass bell jar connected by a tube to the mass spectrometer. He put an ant near a piece of apple and when it met another ant, it inevitably told it, 'There's some apple over there.' That was the initial hypothesis, at any rate. He sucked up the pheromones emitted, decoded them and arrived at a chemical formula. For example, 'There's apple to the north,' was expressed as 'four-methyl two-methylpyrrole carboxylate.' The quantities involved were minute, in the order of two or three picograms per sentence. But it was enough. He now knew how to say 'apple' and 'to the north.' He went on experimenting with a multitude of objects, foods and situations. This provided him with a French-Ant dictionary. After he had understood the names of only a hundred or so fruits, thirty flowers and a dozen directions, he learned the pheromones of alarm, pleasure, suggestion and description. He even came across males and females who taught him how to express the abstract emotions of the seventh antenna segment. However, being able to 'listen' to them was not enough for him. He wanted to talk to them and establish a real dialogue."

"Amazing!" murmured Daniel Rosenfeld.

"He began by making each chemical formula correspond to a sound made up of a series of syllables. Four-methyl two-methylpyrrole carboxylate, for example, would be pronounced 'four-M-T-two-M-T-P-C-X,' then 'foremtitoemtipisiex.' Finally he stored in the computer's memory: 'foremtitoemtipi equals apple and siex equals to the north.' The computer translates both ways. When it detects 'siex,' it translates it in writing as 'to the north.' And when 'to the north' is typed, it transforms it into 'siex,' which triggers the emission of carboxylate by the emitting apparatus."

"Emitting apparatus?"

"Yes, this machine here."

He showed him a kind of library made up of thousands of small vials, each ending in a tube connected to an electric pump.

"The atoms in each vial are sucked up by the pump and passed into this apparatus, which sorts them and measures them in the exact quantities indicated by the computer dictionary."

"Extraordinary," Daniel Rosenfeld went on. "Quite extraordinary. Did he really manage to talk to them?"

"Hmm. I think the best thing I can do now is read his notes from the *Encyclopedia*."

EXTRACTS OF CONVERSATIONS: **Extract of the first conversation with a Formica rufa warrior.**

HUMAN BEING: **Are you receiving me?**
ANT: **crrrrrrrr.**
HUMAN BEING: **Are you receiving me?**
ANT: **crrrrrrrrcrrrrrrrrrrrrrr. Help.**

(N.B. Several adjustments were necessary. The signal was far too strong and was suffocating the ant. The microphone must be set at 1 and the receiver turned up to 10 to avoid the loss of a single molecule.)

HUMAN BEING: **Are you receiving me?**
ANT: **Bougu.**
HUMAN BEING: **Are you receiving me?**
ANT: **Zgugnu. Help. I'm shut in.**

Extract of the third conversation.
(N.B. The vocabulary was increased to eighty words this time. The signal was still too strong and again had to be turned down. It has to be set almost at zero.)

ANT: **What?**
HUMAN BEING: **What did you say?**
ANT: **I can't understand a thing. Help!**
HUMAN BEING: **Let's talk more slowly.**

ANT: Your emissions are too strong. My antennae are saturated. Help! I'm shut in.
HUMAN BEING: There, is that better?
ANT: No, can't you talk properly?
HUMAN BEING: Er . . .
ANT: Who are you?
HUMAN BEING: I'm a big animal. My name's ED-MOND. I'm a HU-MAN.
ANT: What did you say? I can't understand a thing. Help! Help! I'm shut in.

(N.B. The ant died five seconds later. Were the signals still too toxic or did it die of fright?)

Jonathan stopped reading.

"As you can see, it isn't easy to talk to them. Accumulating vocabulary isn't enough. Besides, the ant language does not work like ours. It isn't only the conversational signals as such that are perceived but the signals from the eleven other antenna segments as well. They convey the individual's identity, preoccupations and psyche, a sort of global state of mind necessary for good interpersonal understanding. That's why Edmond had to give up. Let me read you his notes."

HOW STUPID OF ME: How stupid of me!
Even if extraterrestrials existed, we would not be able to understand them. We would have different frames of reference. If we arrived with outstretched arms, they might see it as a threatening gesture.
We do not even understand the Japanese with their ritual suicide or the Indians with their castes. We cannot even understand other human beings. How can I have presumed to understand ants!

The 801st warrior had only a stump of an abdomen left. Even if she had been able to kill the lomechusa beetle in time, her fight with the rock-scented warriors in the mushroom beds had shortened her considerably. It could not be helped, or rather it was a big help: she was lighter without an abdomen.

She went down the broad passage in the granite. How had ant mandibles been able to excavate that tunnel?

Down below, she discovered the room full of food that Chli-pou-ni had told her about. She had only gone a few steps into the room when she found another exit. She followed it and soon came to a city, an entire rock-scented city. A city under the city.

"So he failed?"

"He brooded over it for a long time. He thought there was no way out and that he'd been blinded by ethnocentricity. Then a spot of trouble opened his eyes. It was his usual antisocial behavior that sparked it off."

"What happened?"

"If you recall, Professor, you told me before that he'd worked for a company called Sweetmilk Corporation and that he'd had a run-in with his colleagues."

"Yes, that's right."

"One of his bosses had gone through his desk, and that boss was none other than Marc Leduc, the brother of Professor Laurent Leduc."

"The entomologist?"

"In person."

"It's incredible. He came to see me pretending to be a friend of Edmond's. He went down."

"Into the cellar?"

"Yes, but don't worry, he didn't get far. He couldn't get through the pyramid wall, so he came back up again."

"Mmm, he came to see Nicolas, too, to try to get his hands on the *Encyclopedia*. Okay. So Marc Leduc had noticed that Edmond was working hard on some sketches of machines—in actual fact, the first sketches of the Rosetta stone. He managed to open the cupboard in Edmond's office and came across a folder containing the *Encyclopedia of Relative and Absolute Knowledge*. In it, he found all the plans for the first machine for communicating with ants. When he realized what the apparatus was for, and it was sufficiently annotated for him to understand, he talked to his brother about it. Laurent Leduc was obviously very interested and immediately asked him to steal the documents. But Edmond had noticed that someone had been through his things and had let four ichneumon wasps loose in his drawer to protect them from another visit. As soon as Marc Leduc returned to the attack, he got stung by the insects, which have the nasty habit of laying their ravenous larvae in the bodies of those they sting. Edmond spotted the sting marks the next day and publicly unmasked the culprit. The rest you know. He was the one they got rid of."

"What became of the Leduc brothers?"

"Marc Leduc got what he deserved. The ichneumon wasp larvae ate away at him from the inside. It took a very long time, several years, apparently. Because the larvae could not get out of his huge body to turn into wasps, they dug in all directions to find a way out. In the end, the pain became so unbearable he threw himself under a subway train. I read about it by chance in the newspapers."

"How about Laurent Leduc?"

"He did his utmost to find the machine."

"You were saying it made Edmond want to try it again. How was it all connected to his research?"

"Laurent Leduc subsequently contacted Edmond directly. He admitted he knew about his machine for 'talking to ants.' He said he was interested and wanted to work with him. Edmond wasn't necessarily opposed to the idea, he was at a standstill anyway, and he wondered if it wouldn't be a good thing to get some outside help. As the Bible says, there comes a time when you can't go on alone. Edmond was prepared to guide Leduc to his sanctuary but he wanted to know him better first. They talked at length. When Laurent began to speak highly of the ants' order and discipline, emphasizing the fact that talking to them would surely allow man to imitate them, Edmond saw red. He lost his temper and told him never to set foot in his house again."

"I'm not surprised," sighed Daniel. "Leduc belongs to a clique of ethologists, the worst of the German school, who want to change the human race by copying some aspects of animal behavior . . . a sense of territory, the discipline of the anthills. People are always fantasizing about it."

"It gave Edmond a pretext for getting down to work. He was going to talk to ants from a political point of view. He thought they lived in an anarchical system and wanted to ask them to confirm it."

"Of course!" murmured Bilsheim.

"It was becoming a man-sized challenge. My uncle thought a lot longer and decided that the best way to communicate would be to build a 'robot ant.' "

Jonathan waved some sketch-covered sheets.

"Here are the plans for the robot. Edmond christened it 'Dr. Livingstone.' It's made of plastic. You can imagine how difficult it was to make. It's a little masterpiece. All the joints are reproduced and moved by microscopic electric motors connected to a battery in the abdomen and the antennae have eleven segments capable of emitting eleven different pheromones simultaneously. The only difference between Dr. Livingstone and a real ant is that he's connected to eleven pipes, each as thick as a hair, which join up to make a kind of umbilical cord as thick as a piece of string."

"Amazing. Simply amazing," enthused Jason.

"Where is Dr. Livingstone, by the way?" asked Augusta.

She was being followed by rock-scented warriors. As she ran, 801st suddenly spotted a very broad gallery and rushed down it. She thus came to an enormous room at the center of which stood a funny-looking ant of above-average size.

She went up to him cautiously. The scents of the

strange, solitary ant were only half true. His eyes did not shine and his skin seemed to be covered in black dye. The young Chlipoukanian tried to work it out. How was it possible to be so little like an ant?

The soldiers had already flushed her out, though. The ant with the limp came forward, alone, for a duel. She leaped at her antennae and started to bite them, and they both rolled on the ground.

The 801st warrior remembered Mother's advice: *See where your enemy likes to strike you. It's often his own weak point.* When she seized the lame ant's antennae, her attacker writhed furiously. They must have been very sensitive. The 801st warrior sliced them off and managed to get away, but now she had a pack of over fifty killers at her heels.

"If you want to know where Dr. Livingstone is, follow the wires leading from the mass spectrometer."

They could see a kind of transparent tube that ran along the bench as far as the wall, rose to the ceiling and finally disappeared inside a kind of big wooden chest hanging just above the organ in the center of the church. The chest was probably full of earth, and the new arrivals craned their necks to get a better look at it.

"But you said there was solid rock above our heads," remarked Augusta.

"Yes, but I also pointed out there's a ventilation shaft we no longer use."

"And if we no longer use it," went on Inspector Galin, "it isn't because we've blocked it up."

"But if it wasn't you . . ."

"It must have been them."

"The ants?"

"Precisely. A gigantic russet ant city has been built above the slab of rock. You know, the insects that build big domes of twigs in the forests."

"According to Edmond's calculations, there are over ten million of them."

"Ten million? They could kill us all!"

"Don't panic, there's nothing to be afraid of. Firstly, because they talk to us and know us, and also because not all the ants in the city are aware of our existence."

As Jonathan said that, an ant fell out of the chest in the ceiling and landed on Lucie's forehead. She tried to catch it, but 801st panicked and hid in her red hair, slid down her earlobe, tumbled down the back of her neck, dived into her blouse, skirted her breasts and navel, galloped over the fine skin of her thighs, fell down to her ankle and, from there, plunged to the ground. She quickly found her bearings and made straight for one of the lateral air vents.

"What's got into her?"

"How should I know? She was attracted by the draft of cool air from the shaft, in any case. She won't have any trouble getting out."

"But she won't get back to her city that way, will she? She'll come out completely to the east of the Federation."

The spy has managed to get away. If this goes on, we'll have to attack the so-called sixty-fifth city.

Some rock-scented soldiers had made their report with lowered antennae. After they had withdrawn, Belo-kiu-kiuni brooded for a while over the grave failure of her policy of secrecy, then wearily recalled how it had all begun.

When she was very young, she too had been confronted with a terrifying event pointing to the existence of giant beings. It was just after she had swarmed. She had seen a black slab crush several fertile queens without even eating them. Later, after founding her city, she had managed to organize a meeting on the subject, at which most of the queens, both mothers and daughters, were present.

She remembered. It was Zoubi-zoubi-ni who had spoken first. She had related that several of her expeditions had been subjected to showers of pink balls, which had caused over a hundred deaths.

Her other sisters had outdone one another with lists of those killed or maimed by the pink balls or black slabs.

Cholb-gahi-ni, an old mother, remarked that, according to the evidence, the pink balls seemed to move in herds of five.

Another sister, Roubg-fayli-ni, had found a motionless pink ball nearly three hundred heads below the surface. The pink ball was connected to a soft substance that had quite a strong smell. They had burrowed into it with their mandibles and finally come onto hard white stems, as if the animals had shells inside their bodies instead of outside.

By the end of the meeting, the queens had all agreed that such things were beyond their understanding and decided to observe absolute secrecy in order to avoid panic in the anthillo.

Belo-kiu-kiuni, for her part, quickly decided to set up her own "secret police," a work group formed of fifty or so soldiers at that time. Their mission was to eliminate anyone who witnessed the pink balls or black slabs in order to avoid panic in the city.

But one day something incredible had happened.

A worker from an unknown city had been captured by her rock-scented warriors. Mother had spared her because she had told them the strangest thing they had ever heard.

The worker claimed to have been kidnapped by pink balls. They had thrown her into a transparent prison along with several hundred other ants. They had been subjected to all sorts of experiments. More often than not, they were put under a bell jar and received very concentrated scents. It was very painful at first but the scents were gradually diluted and the smells had then turned into words.

In the end, with the aid of the scents and bell jars, the pink balls had talked to them, presenting themselves as giant animals who called themselves "human beings."

They had told her that there was a passage in the granite under the city and said that they wanted to speak to the queen. She could be sure that no harm would be done to her.

It had all happened very quickly after that. Belo-kiu-kiuni had met their ambassador ant, *Doc-tor Li-ving-stone*, a strange ant ending in a transparent intestine, but one you could talk to.

They had had a long conversation. To begin with, they could not understand one another at all but manifestly shared the same exhilaration and seemed to have so much to say to one another.

The human beings had subsequently fitted the earth-filled chest at the end of the shaft and Mother had sown this new city with eggs. In secret, without her other children knowing.

But Bel-o-kan II was more than the city of the rock-scented warriors. It had become the link city between the ant world and the human world. *Doc-tor Li-ving-stone* (a ridiculous name if ever there was one) was always to be found there.

EXTRACTS OF CONVERSATIONS: Extract of the eighteenth conversation with Queen Belo-kiu-kiuni.
ANT: The wheel? It's incredible we've never thought of using the wheel. When I think we've all seen dung beetles pushing along balls of dung and none of us has ever come up with the wheel.
HUMAN BEING: How do you intend to use this information?
ANT: I don't know yet.

Extract of the fifty-sixth conversation with Queen Belo-kiu-kiuni.
ANT: You sound sad.
HUMAN BEING: My scent organ must be badly tuned. Since I added emotive language, the machine seems to be misfiring.
ANT: You sound sad.

HUMAN BEING: . . .
ANT: Aren't you emitting anymore?
HUMAN BEING: I think it's just a coincidence but I really do feel sad.
ANT: What's the matter?
HUMAN BEING: I used to have a female. Male human beings live a long time, so we live in couples, one male and one female. I used to have a female but I lost her a few years ago. I loved her and I can't forget her.
ANT: What does "love" mean?
HUMAN BEING: Possibly that we had the same scents.

Mother remembered the end of the *hu-man Ed-mond.* It had happened during the first war against the dwarves. Edmond had wanted to help them and had left the underground room. But he had manipulated so many pheromones that he was completely drenched in them. Without knowing it, he passed in the forest as a russet ant of the Federation. When the wasps (with whom they were at war at the time) in the fir tree spotted his passport scents, they all pounced on him.

They killed him because they mistook him for a Belokanian. He must have died happy.

Later, Jonathan and his community had resumed contact.

He poured a little more mead into the glasses of the three newcomers, who were asking him endless questions.

"Is Dr. Livingstone capable of retranscribing our words up there, then?"

"Yes, and we can listen to theirs. Their answers appear on this screen. Edmond well and truly succeeded."

"But what did they say to each other? What do you say to each other?"

"Hmm. After his success, Edmond's notes become a little vague, as if he didn't want to keep note of everything. Let's just say that, in the early days, they described themselves and their worlds to one another. That's how we learned that their city is called Bel-o-kan and that it is the hub of a federation of several hundred million ants."

"It's incredible!"

"Both parties subsequently decided it was too early for the information to be circulated among their populations and agreed to keep their contact absolutely secret."

"That's why Edmond was so insistent about Jonathan making everything himself," put in a fireman. "He didn't want people to find out too soon. He couldn't bear to think what the television, radio and newspapers would make of it. Ants would become all the rage. He could already picture the commercials, key rings, T-shirts and rock shows and all the rest of the crap they'd churn out."

"Belo-kiu-kiuni, their queen, for her part, thought her daughters would want to fight the dangerous foreigners immediately," added Lucie.

"No, the two civilizations aren't yet ready to know and understand one another. Ants aren't fascists, anarchists or royalists. They're ants, and everything about their world is different from ours. That's what gives it its richness."

Superintendent Bilsheim was the author of this impassioned declaration. He had certainly changed a great deal since leaving the surface and his boss, Solange Doumeng.

"The German and Italian schools," said Jonathan, "make the mistake of trying to understand them in 'human' terms, which can only lead to a crude analysis. It's as if they were trying to understand our lives by comparing them with theirs, myrmecomorphism, as it were, when the minutest details about them are fascinating. We don't understand the Japanese, Tibetans or Hindus, but we are enthralled by their culture, music and philosophy even when they are deformed by our Western minds. And it's abundantly clear that the future of our Earth lies in hybridization."

"But what can the ants possibly bring us in the way of culture?" wondered Augusta.

Without replying, Jonathan made a sign to Lucie, who disappeared for a few seconds and came back with what looked like a pot of jam.

"Look, this alone is a treasure. Greenfly honeydew. Go on, taste it."

Augusta risked a cautious finger.

"Mmmm, it's very sweet but it's delicious! It doesn't taste a bit like the honey of bees."

"You see! Haven't you ever wondered how we've managed to feed ourselves every day trapped down here?"

"Well, as a matter of fact, I have . . ."

"It's the ants who feed us with their honeydew and flour. They stock supplies of it for us up there. But that's not all. We've copied their agricultural technique for growing agaric mushrooms."

He lifted the lid of a big wooden box. Underneath it, white mushrooms were growing on a bed of fermented leaves.

"Galin is our great mushroom specialist."

Galin smiled modestly. "I still have a lot to learn."

"But mushrooms and honey . . . you must be short of protein?"

"Max deals with protein."

One of the firemen pointed to the ceiling.

"I collect all the insects the ants put in the small box to the right of the chest. We boil them to remove the cuticles. Otherwise, they're like very small shrimps. They look and taste like them, too."

"So long as we're careful," added a policeman, "we've got everything we need here. The electricity is produced by a mini-atomic power station that'll last five hundred years. Edmond installed it a few days after he arrived. Air comes in through the ventilation shafts, food reaches us from the ants, we've got a source of fresh water and something fascinating to do, too. We feel as if we're pioneering something very important."

"We're like astronauts living permanently in a base and sometimes talking to neighboring extraterrestrials."

They laughed and their spines tingled with good humor. Jonathan suggested they return to the lounge.

"You know, I spent a long time trying to find a way to get my friends to coexist around me. I tried communities of various kinds but I never succeeded. I ended up thinking I was an idealist, not to say an idiot. But here . . . things are happening here. We're obliged to live together, to complement one another and think as one. We have no choice. If we don't agree, we'll die. And there's no way out. Now I don't know if it comes from my uncle's discovery or what the ants are teaching us simply by existing above our heads, but for the time being our community is getting along like a house on fire."

"It's working, in spite of us."

"We sometimes get the impression we're generating a common fund of energy we can all draw on freely. It's odd."

"I've heard of it happening in other communities," said Jason. "There's a common spiritual capital, like a bowl they all pour their strength into to make a soup that feeds them all. As a rule, there's always one thief who uses the others' energy for personal ends."

"We don't have that kind of problem here. You can't have personal ambitions when you're living in a little group under the ground."

There was silence.

"And then, we talk less and less. We don't need to anymore to understand one another."

"Yes, things are happening here. But we can't yet understand or control them. We haven't arrived yet, we're only halfway there."

There was silence again.

"Well, then, I hope you'll be happy in our little community."

• • • •

The 801st warrior arrived in her native city exhausted but triumphant. She had done it!

Chli-pou-ni immediately engaged in an AC with her to find out what had happened. What she heard confirmed her worst fears regarding the secret hidden under the granite slab.

She immediately decided to send her forces to attack Bel-o-kan. Her soldiers spent the night equipping themselves. The brand-new rhinoceros flying legion was ready for action.

The 103,683rd soldier suggested a plan. While part of the army made a frontal attack, twelve legions would secretly skirt the city to attempt an assault on the royal stump.

THE UNIVERSE TENDS: The universe tends toward complexity. From hydrogen to helium and from helium to carbon, everything evolves in the direction of ever greater complexity and sophistication.

Of all the known planets, the Earth is the most complex. Its position allows its temperature to vary. It is covered in oceans and mountains. But if it has a practically inexhaustible range of life forms, two of them, ants and men, tower above the rest by their intelligence.

It is as if God had used the planet Earth to carry out an experiment. He set two species, with two quite contradictory philosophies, on a race for consciousness to see which would go faster.

The aim was probably to achieve planetary collective consciousness: the union of all the brains of the species. To my mind, that is the next step in the adventure of consciousness, the next level of complexity.

However, the two leading species have developed along parallel lines:

—To become intelligent, man developed a monstrous brain like a big, pink cauliflower.

—To achieve the same result, ants preferred to use

several thousand small brains united by very subtle communication systems.

In absolute terms, there is as much matter or intelligence in the ants' pile of shredded cabbage as in the human cauliflower. It is a fight with equal weapons.

But what would happen if, instead of running parallel to one another, the two forms of intelligence cooperated?

EDMOND WELLS,
ENCYCLOPEDIA OF RELATIVE AND ABSOLUTE KNOWLEDGE

The only things Jean and Philippe really liked were the television and, in a pinch, pinball machines. They had even lost interest in the brand-new miniature golf course built recently at great expense. As for walks in the forest, if a supervisor made them get some fresh air, they thought it was the pits.

They had certainly had fun killing toads the previous week, but the pleasure had been a bit short-lived.

Today, at any rate, Jean seemed to have found something really worthwhile to do. He dragged his friend away from the group of orphans stupidly picking up dead leaves in order to make silly pictures and showed him a kind of cement cone. A termite hill.

They immediately started to kick it to pieces but nothing came out. The termite hill was empty. Philippe leaned over and sniffed.

"It's been smashed up by the road crews. Look, it stinks of insecticide. They're all dead inside."

Disappointed, they were about to rejoin the others when Jean spotted a pyramid half hidden under a shrub on the other side of the little stream.

That was the one! A really impressive anthill with a dome at least a meter high! Long columns of ants were going in and out, hundreds and thousands of workers, soldiers and explorers. DDT had not yet passed that way.

Jean was hopping with excitement.

"Hey, look at that!"

"Oh no, you don't want to eat ants again, do you? The last lot were disgusting."

"Who said anything about eating them? That's a city you're looking at. That little bit sticking out there is like New York or Mexico all by itself. Remember what they said on television? It's teeming with ants inside. Look at the silly buggers slaving away."

"Yeah, and look how Nick disappeared after he got interested in ants. I bet there were ants in his cellar and he got eaten by them. I don't like being near that thing, I can tell you. It gives me the creeps. I saw some of the filthy things coming out of one of the holes on the miniature golf course yesterday. Maybe they were hoping to build a nest at the bottom of it. Stupid bloody things!"

Jean shook his shoulder.

"You don't like them and neither do I. Let's kill them! Let's pay them back for Nick!"

Philippe thought about it.

"Kill them?"

"Yes, why not? Let's set fire to the city. Can you imagine Mexico in flames just because we feel like it?"

"Okay, we'll set fire to it. Yeah, for Nick."

"Wait. I've got a better idea. We'll stick weed killer inside it. That way, we'll really see some fireworks."

"Great!"

"Listen, it's eleven o'clock. Meet me back here in exactly two hours. That'll keep the supervisor off our backs and everyone will be in the dining hall. I'll go and get the weed killer. You get hold of a box of matches. They're better than a lighter."

"Okay!"

The infantry legions were advancing at a good pace. When the other federal cities asked where they were going, the Chlipoukanians replied that a lizard had been spotted in the western region and that the central city had requested their assistance.

The rhinoceros beetles were buzzing overhead, barely

slowed by the weight of the gunners bobbing about on their heads.

"I've brought some alcohol to make it burn better," announced Philippe.

"Great," said Jean. "And I've bought the weed killer. They wanted twenty francs for it, the lousy creeps."

Mother was playing with her carnivorous plants. Considering how long they had been there, she wondered why she had never used them to make a protective wall, as she had first intended.

Then she thought about the wheel again. How could they use such a brilliant idea? Perhaps they could make a big cement ball and push it along in front of them to crush their enemies. She would have to put the project in hand.

"There, it's all in, the alcohol and the weed killer."

While Jean was speaking, an exploring ant climbed up his leg. She tapped the material of his trousers with the ends of her antennae.

You seem to be a giant living structure. Can you give me your identifications?

He caught her and squashed her between his forefinger and thumb. *Phut!* The yellow-and-black juice ran between his fingers.

"That's one less to worry about," he announced. "Get out of the way now. This is going to make the sparks fly."

"There's going to be one hell of a blaze," giggled Philippe.

"How many of them do you think there are in there?"

"Millions, probably. One of the houses around here is supposed to have been attacked by ants last year."

"We'll pay them back for that, too," said Jean. "Go and take cover behind that tree over there."

Mother was thinking about the human beings. She must remember to ask them more questions next time. How did they use the wheel, for example?

Jean struck a match and threw it at the dome of twigs and pine needles. Then he started to run to avoid being hit by fragments.

At last, the Chlipoukanian army caught sight of the central city. How big it was!

The flying match began its downward curve.

Mother decided to speak to them without delay. She must also tell them she could increase the amount of honeydew on offer without any difficulty. The yield promised to be excellent this year.

The match fell on the twigs of the dome.

The Chlipoukanian army was close enough. It prepared to charge.

Jean dived behind the big pine tree where Philippe was already sheltering.

•   •   •   •

The match fell on part of the dome that had escaped the drenching in alcohol and weed killer and went out.

The boys stood up again.
"Oh, damn!"
"I know what we'll do. We'll light a piece of paper and put that on it. It'll make a big flame that's sure to come in contact with the alcohol."
"Got any paper on you?"
"Er . . . only a subway ticket."
"Give it to me."

One of the sentries on the dome noticed that something odd was happening: not only had several districts just begun to smell of alcohol but a piece of yellow wood had also just appeared on the summit. She immediately contacted a work group to wash the alcohol off the twigs and remove the yellow beam.

Another sentry came running up to door five.
To arms! To arms! An army of russet ants is attacking us!

The cardboard had caught. The boys hid behind the pine tree again.

A third sentry saw a big flame rise from the end of the piece of yellow wood.

The Chlipoukanians charged at the gallop as they had seen the slave-makers do before them.

The whole dome went up in flames at the first explosion.

Sparks crackled and flew.

Jean and Philippe tried to keep their eyes open in spite of the heat. They were not disappointed by what they saw. The dry wood burned quickly. When the flames reached the pools of weed killer, there was an explosion. Detonations and columns of green, yellow, red and mauve flames shot up from the "city of the lost ant."

The Chlipoukanian army came to a halt. The solarium went up in flames first, along with all the eggs and cattle, then the fire spread to the rest of the dome.

The stump of the Forbidden City had been damaged in the first few seconds of the catastrophe. The doorkeepers had exploded. Some warriors dashed in to try to free the single egg-layer, but they were too late; she had been suffocated by the toxic fumes.

The various phases of the alert followed one another thick and fast. In the first phase, the arousal pheromones were released. In the second, there was a sinister drumming in all the corridors. In the third phase, "crazed" ants ran along the galleries, spreading panic, and in the fourth phase, all the valuables (eggs, males and females, cattle and food) disappeared down to the deepest floors while soldiers came back up in the other direction to take a stand.

The ants in the dome were trying to save the city. Artillery legions managed to quench the fire in some areas by spraying it with dilute formic acid. When they saw how effective this was, the acting firemen sprayed the Forbidden City, too. They might be able to save the stump by dampening it.

But the fire spread and trapped citizens were suffocated by the toxic fumes. Incandescent wooden arches fell on the dazed crowds and their shells melted and twisted like plastic in a saucepan.

Nothing could withstand the extreme heat.

EPISODE: I was wrong. We are not equals or competitors. Human beings are only a brief episode in their undivided rule over the Earth. They are infinitely more numerous than we. They possess more cities and occupy far more ecological niches. They live in dry, freezing, hot or wet regions where no man could survive. Wherever we look, there are ants.

They were here a hundred million years before us and, judging by the fact that they were one of the few organisms to survive the atomic bomb, will surely still be here a hundred million years after us. We are just a three-million-year-long accident in their history. Moreover, if extraterrestrials ever landed on our planet, they would be in no doubt about it. They would try to talk to them. Them, the true masters of the Earth.

EDMOND WELLS,
ENCYCLOPEDIA OF RELATIVE AND ABSOLUTE KNOWLEDGE

The next morning, the dome had completely disappeared. All that remained of the city was the naked, black stump.

Five million citizens had died, all the ants who were in the dome and its immediate vicinity.

Those who had had the presence of mind to go down were unharmed.

The human beings living under the city had not noticed anything. The enormous granite slab had prevented them from doing so. And it had all taken place during one of their artificial nights.

Belo-kiu-kiuni's death remained the greatest threat for the future. Deprived of its egg-layer, the Tribe was under threat.

However, the Chlipoukanian army had helped to fight the fire. As soon as the warriors learned of the death of Belo-kiu-kiuni, they despatched messengers to their city. A few hours later, Chli-pou-ni arrived on the back of a rhinoceros beetle to see the damage for herself.

When she reached the Forbidden City, fireman ants were still spraying the ashes. There was nothing left to fight. She asked what had happened and was told about the incomprehensible disaster.

There were no more fertile queens, so she naturally became the new Belo-kiu-kiuni and moved into the royal chamber in the central city.

• • •

Jonathan woke first and was surprised to hear the clatter of the computer printer.

There was one word on the screen.

Why?

They must have emitted it during their night. They wanted to talk. He tapped out the sentence that ritually preceded each conversation.

HUMAN BEING: **Greetings, I'm Jonathan.**
ANT: **I'm the new Belo-kiu-kiuni. Why?**
HUMAN BEING: **The new Belo-kiu-kiuni? Where's the old one?**
ANT: **You've killed her. I'm the new Belo-kiu-kiuni. Why?**
HUMAN BEING: **What happened?**
ANT: **Why?**

Then they were cut off.

Now she knew everything.

It was they, the human beings, who had done it.

Mother knew them.

She had always known them.

She had kept it a secret.

She had ordered the execution of all who could have given the slightest clue.

She had even supported them against her own cells.

The new Belo-kiu-kiuni contemplated her inert mother. When the guards came to get the body to throw it on the rubbish heap, she gave a start.

No, the body must not be thrown away.

She examined the old Belo-kiu-kiuni, who was already beginning to smell of death.

She suggested they stick the smashed limbs back on with resin and empty the body of its soft parts and replace them with sand.

She wanted to keep her in her own chamber.

Chli-pou-ni, the new Belo-kiu-kiuni, gathered together a few warriors. She suggested they rebuild the central city along more modern lines. In her opinion, the dome and stump were too vulnerable. And they would need to apply themselves to finding underground streams and even digging canals linking all the cities of the Federation. For her, the future lay in the mastery of water. They would be able to protect themselves from fire better and also travel quickly and safely.

What about the human beings?

Her reply was evasive.

They're of little interest.

The warrior persisted.

What if they attack us again with their fire?

The stronger the enemy, the more we must surpass ourselves.

What about the ones who live under the big rock?

Belo-kiu-kiuni did not answer. She asked to be left alone, then turned toward the old Belo-kiu-kiuni's body.

The new queen inclined her head delicately and rested her antennae on her mother's forehead. She remained there for some time without moving, as though sunk in an eternal AC.

GLOSSARY

Absolute communication (AC): a total exchange of thoughts by antenna contact.

Age of asexual ants: a russet worker or soldier generally lives three years.

Age of queen: a russet queen lives fifteen years on average.

Air conditioning: the temperature of the big cities is regulated by the solarium, excrement and fresh-air inlets in the dome.

Alcohol: ants know how to ferment greenfly honeydew and cereal juice.

Ant weapons: saber mandibles, poisonous stings, glue sprays, formic-acid–throwing bladders, and claws.

Bat: a flying monster that lives in caves. Dangerous.

Battle of Poppy Hill: took place in the year 100,000,666 and was the first federal war in which bacteriological weapons were pitted against tanks.

Bel-o-kan: the central city of the russet Federation.

Belo-kiu-kiuni: the Queen of Bel-o-kan.

Birds: flying monsters. Dangerous.

Black: city dwellers like to live in the dark.

Bread: small balls of chopped, kneaded cereals.

Carnivorous plants: butterwort, Venus's-flytrap and sundew. Dangerous.

Caste: there are generally three castes: males and females, soldiers, and workers, which are in turn divided into subcastes: agricultural workers, artillery soldiers, etc.

Chitin: the substance of which the ants' armor is made.

Chli-pou-ni: a daughter of Belo-kiu-kiuni.

Chli-pou-kan: an ultramodern city built by Chli-pou-ni.

Cockroach: the ancestor of the termite. The first land insect.

Cold: a universal sedative in the insect world.

Colorado beetle: a beetle with orange outer wings with five longitudinal black stripes. Colorado beetles generally feed on potatoes. Colorado beetle juice is a deadly poison.

Corpse: an empty cuticle.

Degree: a unit of temperature time and chronological time. The hotter it is, the more the degrees-time shrink. The colder it is, the more they expand.

Density: in Europe, there are 80,000 ants per square meter on average (including all species).

Doorkeepers: a subcaste with round, flat heads, responsible for blocking strategic corridors.

Dufour gland: a gland containing the trail pheromones.

Dung beetle: pushes along balls of dung. Edible.

Duodecimal: the numerical system used by ants. They count in twelves because they have twelve claws (two per leg).

Dwarves: the chief enemies of the russet ants.

Dynasty: a succession of daughter queens of the same territory.

Earth: a cubic planet.

Egg: a very young ant.

Excrement: the excrement of ants is 1,000 times lighter than their bodies.

Eyes: a set of facets on the eyeball. Each facet has two

crystalline lenses, a large external lens and a small internal one. Each cell is directly connected to the brain. Ants can perceive only objects that are close to them but can nevertheless spot the slightest movement from a great distance.

Fast: an ant can live for six months in a state of hibernation without eating.

Federation: a grouping of cities of the same species. A federation of russet ants usually comprises ninety nests in six hectares with seven and a half kilometers of beaten tracks and forty kilometers of scent trails.

Festival of Rebirth: the nuptial flight of males and females. It generally takes place on one of the first warm days of the year.

Fire: a taboo weapon.

Flying messengers: a dwarf technique for sending messages by gnat. Edible.

Food: the usual russet diet consists of 43 percent greenfly honeydew, 41 percent insect meat, 7 percent tree sap, 5 percent mushrooms and 4 percent crushed seeds.

Forbidden City: the fortress protecting the nuptial chamber. Forbidden Cities can be made of wood, cement or even hollow rock.

Formic acid: a throwing weapon. A solution of 40 percent formic acid is the most corrosive.

Glowworm: a beetle that produces phosphorescent light. Edible.

Greenflies: cattle. Edible.

Guayei-Tyolot: a small spring nest.

Harvesters: farming ants of the east.

Head: the ant unit of measurement. Equivalent to three millimeters.

Heart: a succession of pear-shaped pockets fitting one inside another. The heart lies in the back.

Height: the higher the nest, the greater the area of sunlight the city is seeking. In hot regions, anthills are entirely buried.

Hibernation: the long sleep from November to March.

Human beings: the giant monsters of some modern legends. Best known are their tame, pink animals, the fingers. Dangerous.

Ichneumon wasp: lays its voracious eggs in your body. Dangerous.

Illnesses: the most common russet ant illnesses are conidium (a parasitic fungus), aegeritella (a kind of rotting of the chitin), cerebral worm (a parasitic worm that lodges in the subesophageal ganglions), hypertrophy of the labial glands (a kind of abnormal swelling of the thorax that manifests itself in the larval stage) and alternaria (deadly spores).

Indoleacetic acid: weed killer.

Infrared simple eyes: three small eyes set in a triangle on the foreheads of males and females that allow them to see in total darkness.

Keep: a secondary tower built on the dome. Keeps are more commonly found on termite hills than anthills.

La-chola-kan: the westernmost city of the Federation.

Ladybird: greenfly predator. Edible.

Lion ant larva: carnivorous sinking sand. Dangerous.

Legion: a mass of soldiers capable of maneuvering simultaneously.

Lizard: the dragon of Myrmician civilization. Dangerous.

Lomechusa: a beetle that supplies a deadly drug. Dangerous.

Males: ants that develop from unfertilized eggs.

Mandible wrestling: an ant sport.

Masked ant: a species with a gift for organic chemistry.

Mayfly: a kind of small dragonfly with a forked tail. The larva lives for three years and hatches into an adult that lives from three to forty-eight hours. Edible.

Mercenaries: solitary ants who fight for nests that are not their native nests in exchange for food and a city identity.

Metamorphosis: a passage to a second form of life, common among insects.

Myrmician civilization: ant civilization.

Mithridatism: the capacity of social species to become so accustomed to deadly poisons that they lay eggs that are genetically immune to them.

Mosquito: the males suck the sap of plants. It is not known what the females feed on. Edible.

Music: sound or ultrasound produced by crickets and cicadas by rubbing their outer wings together. Fungus-growing ants can also make music with their abdominal joints.

Ni: the dynasty of the Belokanian queens.

Nuptial chamber: the place where the queen lays her eggs.

Oleic acid: fumes given off by dead ants.

Orientation of the city: russet ants build their cities with the longest side facing southeast in order to receive the maximum amount of sunlight at the start of the day.

Passport: scent of one's native or, in the case of mercenaries, adopted nest.

Pheromone: liquid word or sentence.

Poison gland: a bladder in which formic acid is stored. Special muscles can shoot the acid at very high pressure.

Poisonous plants: autumn crocus, wisteria, oleander and ivy. Dangerous.

Praying mantis: an insect with an excessive appetite for lovemaking and eating. Dangerous.

Rain: deadly weather.

Rearing: the method devised by some species for taming greenflies and ladybirds and collecting their anal secretions. A greenfly can produce thirty drops of honeydew an hour in the summer.

Red weavers: migrant ants of the east who use their own larvae as weaving shuttles.

Rhinoceros: a beetle with a big horn on its forehead.

Rubbish heap: the mound at the entrance to an anthill on which the ants dump their refuse and dead bodies.

Salamander: dangerous.

Sanitation: a basin that acts as a receptacle for the citizens' excrement.

Seed: russet ants like the elaioplasts of seeds—that is, the parts richest in oil. An average nest harvests 70,000 seeds a season.

Shi-gae-pou: the city of the dwarf ants of the northeast.

Sight: ants see as if through a grid. Males and females have color vision, but all the colors are shifted toward the ultraviolet.

Size: russet ants are two heads long on average.

Slave-makers: a warrior species incapable of surviving without the help of servants.

Smell: asexual ants have 6,500 sensory cells per antenna, males and females 300,000.

Snail: a protein mine. Edible.

Snake: dangerous.

Social crop: the organ of generosity.

Spider: a monster that eats insects a little at a time and puts them to sleep between amputations. Dangerous.

Strawberry Plant War: in the year 99,999,886, the russet ants fought the Strawberry Plant War against the yellow ants.

Strength: a russet ant can pull sixty times its own weight. It therefore develops 3.2×10^{-6} H.P.

Tank: a combat technique in which one large-mandibled worker is carried by six small, mobile workers.

Tanker: a dew reservoir.

Temperature: russet ants can move only at temperatures equal to or higher than 8°C. Males and females sometimes wake a little earlier, at about 6°C.

Temperature of the nest: the temperature of a russet city is regulated to between 20°C and 30°C according to the floor.

Termites: the ants' rival species.

Transport: to transport someone, an ant holds him or her by the mandibles. The ant being carried curls up to create as little friction as possible.

Trophallaxis: the gift of food between two ants.

Venus's flytrap: a predatory plant common in the vicinity of Bel-o-kan. Dangerous.

Walking speed: at 10°C, a russet ant moves at 18 m.p.h. (meters per hour). At 15°C, it goes at 54 m.p.h. At 20°C, it can do up to 125 m.p.h.

Wasps: primitive, venomous cousins of the ants. Dangerous.

Water beetle: a beetle living on and under the water. Edible.

Waves: the smallest common denominator emitted, in one form or another, by all living creatures and moving objects.

Weaving: an operation performed with a larva.

Weed killers: myrmicacin, indoleacetic acid.

Weight: ants vary in weight between one and one hundred and fifty milligrams.

Wind: picks you up off the ground and puts you down goodness knows where.

Zoubi-zoubi-kan: a city in the east, famous for its large herd of greenflies.

56th: Chli-pou-ni's maiden name.

327th: a young Belokanian male.

4,000th: a russet huntress living in Guayei-Tyolot.

103,683rd: a Belokanian soldier.

801st: a daughter of Chli-pou ni, used as a spy.

THE "ACTRESSES"

The real names of the "actresses"
(in alphabetical order) are:

The black shepherdess	*Lasius niger*
The dwarf	*Iridomyrmex humilis*
The federative russet	*Formica rufa*
The harvester	*Pogonomyrmex molefaciens*
The masked ant	*Anergates atratulus*
The mushroom-grower	*Atta sexdens*
The red weaver	*Oecophylla longinoda*
The reservoir ant	*Myrmecocystus melliger*
The seed-crusher	*Messor barbarus*
The silkworm	*Doryline annoma*
The slave-maker	*Polyergus rufescens*

ABOUT THE AUTHOR

BERNARD WERBER is a scientific jour-
nalist who has studied ants for fifteen
years as an avocation. He lives in Paris.